"I have people watc_____ _vels. This protection often exte___ __ __ _____ You want protection? Show me some t_____ship. Wrap up the votes on my legislation. I know you're not speaker yet, but see if you can do it before Sine Die."

"What's Cyanide?"

"*Sign-EEE-dye* . . . the last day of session, when all the shit hits the fan. You don't know that, Mr. Speaker-elect? Well, you'd better learn."

SINE DIE

Welcome to the New Era of Michigan politics. Term limits have ravaged the state's soul, and its Capitol has moldered into a laboratory of reckless ambition, where civility is scarce and motives are bountiful. Centrist pragmatism, the scorn of right-wing purists *and* the indicted Detroit Machine, finds itself further endangered in the wake of a prominent House leader's assassination.

An intricately crafted plot peppered with memorable characters, Sine Die is a novel driven by imagination, raw energy, poetic violence, and unbridled sexuality. An engrossing thriller like no other, Sine Die is intellectual brain candy.

Sine Die: when the shit hits the fan. Soundtrack available on compact disc later this year.

Visit www.matthewjlevin.com

Printed in Victoria, Canada

National Library of Canada Cataloguing in Publication Data

Levin, Matthew J.
        Sine die / Matthew J. Levin ; VAK, cover art ; Shaun Menary, photography.
ISBN 1-55395-536-6
        I. Title.
PS3612.E827S55 2003   813'.6   C2003-900029-X

TRAFFORD

This book was published *on-demand* in cooperation with Trafford Publishing.
On-demand publishing is a unique process and service of making a book available for retail sale to the public taking advantage of on-demand manufacturing and Internet marketing. **On-demand publishing** includes promotions, retail sales, manufacturing, order fulfilment, accounting and collecting royalties on behalf of the author.

Suite 6E, 2333 Government St., Victoria, B.C. V8T 4P4, CANADA

Phone	250-383-6864	Toll-free	1-888-232-4444 (Canada & US)
Fax	250-383-6804	E-mail	sales@trafford.com
Web site	www.trafford.com	TRAFFORD PUBLISHING IS A DIVISION OF TRAFFORD HOLDINGS LTD.	
Trafford Catalogue #02-1261	www.trafford.com/robots/02-1261.html		

10   9   8   7   6   5   4   3   2

Praise for SINE DIE

"The writing is as intoxicating as it is irreverent; the characters as hypnotic as they are real—a great read."
-Steve Birkhauser

". . . a great imagination—I loved the premise . . . the plot and characters were compelling, and the novel polished."
-Jeffrey M. Kleinman, Esq.
 Literary Agent, Graybill & English, L.C.C.

"Charming, romantic, polite, reserved . . . these words cannot be used in a description of Sine Die. Matthew J. Levin takes a raw, honest look at the world of politics, and overlays a warped sense of reality leaving the reader to wonder what is based on fact or fiction. Completely original and innovative, Sine Die will be your best read of the year."
-Chip Reese

"One of the Legislature's brightest minds goes literary, and his imagination is limitless."
-Michigan State Senator Samuel "Buzz" Thomas, III

"Sine Die is the best read I've had in a long, long time. I breezed through it—I could not put it down. This is highly recommended reading."
-Melinda Laine, University of Chicago

"Good story! I really enjoyed it. I'm a Grand Rapids Catholic Central alumni myself!"
-Kira Coplin, Multimedia Product Development, Inc.
 Literary Representatives

"I've seen the future of fiction, and his name is Matthew J. Levin. Throw Stephen King, Emile Zola and Tom Spanbauer into a blender, add a touch of cockiness and a whole lot of insanity—that'll give you an idea of Levin's voice . . . Finally, someone has written a novel that's fun to read. Sine Die is unbelievably fun. When does the sequel come out?"
-Jonny Tesla

SINE DIE

by Matthew J. Levin

This is for my grandmother, Gloria Levin
and my high school English teacher,
Wendy "Sugarfoot" Van Prooyen.

Without their influence, my canvas would be bare.

Our lives are prose begging for edit.

Prologue: Mystic Dream

It's been more than a month since the election as a defeated Josh Brisco hibernates in a makeshift bedroom in the basement of his mother's Grand Rapids, Michigan home. Random scuffling noises pierce his dream state. A soft glow from the digital clock reflects off the wicker nightstand and soaks the dry December air in a haze of red.

3:15 am.

The scuffling grows frantic, stops. Josh floats, his mind downshifts over an image of Slade Pickens running his cracked, middle-aged fingers though black hair as stale coffee spills over a hard marble table.

Helpless.

Josh squirms in his bed. "I let you down, Slade," he says in his sleep. "Please forgive me." A sigh, then silence. The hope of absolution flickers for a moment, then is gone.

Four fucking votes. I lost the election by four fucking votes.

Scratching.

"Silly dog," Josh moans, imagining himself crawling out of bed, his body captured in the corner mirror. Josh, freshly twenty-eight years old, is well preserved in spite of his habits. A new goatee peppered over his chin, he wears nothing but a pair of white Jockeys. The skin on the front of his shoulders is cooked raspberry with brown, peeling, tanning-bed splotches. "You want a yummy, Chez?" he asks.

No response.

Chez?

Mind downshifting: a bronze glare illuminates a set of crooked bookshelves and a rust-colored couch with four sections of torn cushions.

Scott Williams' house!

Scott, completely naked, sits next to Josh on the last section of cushions. Josh is bare from the waist down. Skin of their hips touching, each boy pumps their hands in a frantic race. Josh's eyes roll backwards; in the dream, he cums fast and hard. In reality, his dick is soft and it chafes when he starts to pull on it—incessant attempts to release years of denial, pain, and frustration are rubbing Josh raw.

Scott jumps up from the couch like he's been shot out of a cannon. "You actually liked it, Josh! You must be some kind of pervert."

As a teenager, the urges were easier to handle. Fantasies were of the innocent locker room variety, and his equipment was resilient, fresh, with an unlimited reserve. Now, the three times a day routine (bathroom door locked, blinds drawn, water running just in case) was yet another commitment. Commitments: for years, Pepper had snarfed his money, drained his energy. Even though her round face—gleaming with perfect teeth, bright blue eyes, and a pile of frosted hair—had no effect on him, she was still adept at making him cum. Now that she was gone, his semen-starched sheets and towels were stiffer than Al Gore in debate.

Pristine Pepper, Fiancée Emeritus. Josh suspects that she still tells people that they are engaged.

The room tilts, drifts. Josh floats, more downshifting. He's in the squad car, driving down Cascade Road side-by-side with Hector Paiz in his orange Camaro. Two cars, side-by-side, barreling into the Twilight Zone. Windows down, wind in their hair. Seventy-five miles per hour and Paiz is sucking down swigs from a fifth of Cuervo.

Josh is stern. "You promised to go straight home," he yells.

Hector tilts the bottle to his sandy lips, his eyes bloody, somnolent. "You granted me that discretion last night, off-i-cer," he mumbles. "Straight home. You got it. But today is a different day, man."

A flash.

There's the school bus!

Voices screaming.
Stop!
Brakes screeching.
Too late!

The impact of the collision scatters tiny bodies over glass, pavement, and metal. A little girl, a blond porcelain doll, flies through the hole of a shattered window and onto the grill of Hector's car with a clang. She bounces over the hood and dented side, her neck catching against the steel arm of the oversized side-view mirror. Her corpse, soaked in crimson face paint, dangles gingerly in the wind like a limp clown.

Josh blinks, his brow speckled with sweat. He opens his eyes, looks around: Mom's house again, in the basement. A sigh of relief. His body cools. He crawls under scabby sheets and drifts off when the scuffling returns. *Is this real?* Drugs, booze, and lost sleep blunt his perception.

Guilt infiltrates Josh as his thoughts turn to the *Job.* He hadn't been back since the campaign started. Now that it is over, he finds himself sheltered numb, buried in a self-inflicted leave of absence. Maybe, next week, he would return. Then again, he had been saying that to Mom for six weeks now. Six weeks: forty-one days of chemical abuse, forty-two nights of mangled sleep. *If only I had some focus,* Josh thinks. *If I only had some inspiration.*

The scuffling grows louder, too loud to be coming from Cesare's delicate little paws.

"Pepper?" Josh asks, his tired voice cracking in the dark. Was she back with her book of platitudes? "Can't you just give it a rest?" Josh calls out, his head pounding.

Pepper.

All her prescriptions and all her sorority friends could never put Pepper back together again.

Josh sighs.

More scuffling. A squeak. A sense of twitching. Scurrying, scratching: the bantering of rodents as they hustle over ceiling tiles.

Rats.

Josh is overcome by cold, sweaty dread. "Oh Christ," he mumbles. The noises come again, louder yet, growing incessant. Josh continues to perspire, little beads of salty moisture gathering under his arms and dripping down his back.

Pepper. Van Anders. DutchWay: The room is black with hate.

Josh fiddles for some sort of luminance, but lucidity flashes only briefly.

Radiance. That's what this basement needs, a little radiance.

Mom, from yesterday: *You're not a bad person, you're just in pain.*

Josh stumbles into the bathroom. Raw florescent light floods his eyes with a dry sting. He snorts a spoon of Pepper's abandoned coke and grabs the plunger from behind the toilet, jumps on the bed, and starts poking around the ceiling tiles, probing. This does no good. Bright light fades into a tired, flowered purple. Josh, freaked and cold, clutches a lighter and contemplates burning down the whole ceiling. His toes are numb.

Burn it down and they win.

Josh pauses to pop a Tylenol, three Vicodin, and then snorts a couple more lines of coke before flinging a ceiling tile off its hinges with the plunger butt. His abdominal muscles ripple as he stands tip-toed on the bed, his head poked through the dark, empty rectangle in the ceiling. Sparks of light flicker from his lighter, cascading to the floor like sifted flour.

Nothing.

Josh exits through the sliding glass door, lights a smoke on the patio. The air is balmy, yet full of dancing snowflakes. Dispassionately, Josh watches them drift as he takes several long drags from a Marlboro Red.

A voice calls from the trees: *"Josh Brisco: a cop soft on crime."*

Josh dismisses it with a wave of his hand. "Fuck you," he says, exhaling ribbons of green smoke. "Fuck DutchWay, too."

The voice, louder: *"Josh Brisco: no proponent of Grand Rapids' values."*

"Say all you want. I'm not even listening." Josh gazes blankly into the dead, twisted trees outlining the patio— they are quite a contrast to the immaculate, well-manicured garden that Pepper once kept in the front of their townhouse lawn. Bold flowers, flowing grasses, chirping birds: it was a brilliant façade revolving around a bird feeder decorated tactlessly with plastic crucifixes and other mythical symbols of conformity.

Mom: *"That Pepper. She'd gnaw her own leg off, would it render her more beautiful to strangers."*

Savoring the last taste of tobacco in a tight breath, Josh tosses the butt into the swamp, where it lands with a hiss on a wet, furry carcass. He chuckles with irony as it smolders to a quiet death. The pungent, rotten stench of nightcrawlers sifts into his nose. He gags, peering into the back woods, feeling a sudden urge to piss in them. But the brush is already full of glistening liquid, the hairy beasts in it floating dead and bloated.

Movement: a twisting, leathery coil sends ripples through the water.

Josh reaches over the chicken wire, snagging a six-foot long snake from the water. It writhes slowly as he holds it up in the air with flexed muscles. Josh revels in the creature's pulsing contours, its magnificent thickness, its erect agility. White under the yellow moon, it bends in Josh's grasp with tremendous dark eyes and black striped scales that overlap to convey the impression of diamonds.

Josh is standing on the bed, erect, and his feet are cold with dew. The snake fits perfectly through the open rectangle in the ceiling, so he slides it all the way in and takes a seat on the bed, aroused by ghoulish gurgling and snapping bone noises from above. His head is foggy, the room sickly orange. Josh envisions the snake striking at the rodents, swallowing them whole, sucking them down slowly into burning digestive juices. For a moment, there is blissful silence, and Josh considers keeping the snake for a pet . . . until a large farting noise rips through the air and the snake drops limp from the ceiling to the bed, its belly torn open with dark, emerald green jelly oozing out from its scaly seams, eyes shredded to the point that they're almost totally gnawed out.

A long, spiny tail hangs from above, dangling out from the open tile like a writhing question mark. Josh grabs the plunger and slaps the adjacent tile with such a blow that the beast springboards out of the ceiling, smacks the top of Pepper's headboard, and plops onto the floor with a stunned thud. With an adroit swing of hand, Josh snags its tail, holding the creature at a safe distance as it dangles and twitches. Rushing into the bathroom half-blinded, Josh drops the rat headfirst into the toilet. He flushes five, six, seven times, but the lame swirl can't suck the monster down. Halfway down the pipe, it pops up after each flush, tiny claws swimming, pointed teeth thrashing as it snaps at Josh with desperate, hateful bites. It manages to crawl up the bowl a few times, but Josh smacks it back into the water with the plunger. He remembers a story Mom told him when he was a child about some boy who kept flushing a spider down the toilet, only to watch it re-emerge each time bigger and stronger until it was so big that it finally ate him. Josh pummels the rat as hard as he can, but it won't go down. Reaching under the sink, he grabs Pepper's DutchWay cleanser (America's Best!), her DutchWay super soap (America's Cleanest!), and dumps them into the toilet, shaking each container with voracity. The water turns blue like bubbly soda, and the rat is screaming, rasping in this chemical bubble bath, but it's not dying fast enough, so Josh plugs in his electric razor and drops it into the toilet water, screaming, "Hoo-ahh! Hoo-ahh!" like Al Pacino as sparks fly like the Fourth of July. The rat squeals like a lobster in live boil and now Josh is feeling hungry, thinking of the lobster bisque at Charley's, and the electric razor is gargling up water and spraying electrodes. *Snap, crackle, pop!* The rat implodes, tufts of hair catching fire. Josh is weary of the whole toilet exploding, so he strips off his Jockeys, wraps them around his hand, and pulls the razor plug out of the wall outlet. The rat is burning, blue and almost hairless, looking at Josh shrewdly as blood leaks out the corners of its eyes. Josh flushes the toilet once more so he can see it better in clear water and sticks a pair of long, thin trimming scissors into its abdomen and through its back, finally killing it.

The chimes of a doorbell, voices of a strange and unexpected houseguest, echo through Mother's house as Josh rids himself of the crisped carcass with a series of sustained flushes.

Slade?

Josh glides up the stairs like a happy ghost, flings the door open with little effort and is greeted by a tall, boyish man in long, Carolina-blue shorts. Bare-chested and smooth, he's smiling at Josh, his eyebrows soft and friendly under the drop of thick blond bangs. His large hands palm a basketball, downy flesh rubbing in languid strokes over silken leather.

Josh's heartbeat is skittish. His eyes stare. "Do I know you?" he finally manages.

"Yeah, I think you do," the boy says. His voice is even, masculine, inviting. "What are you going to do?"

Josh is apologetic. "I need to get out of this rut," he explains. The boy nods, his expression both sympathetic and understanding. His round lips move softly, with barely audible sound. Josh strains to hear him as a mist of white noise engulfs the front porch.

"You'll be better once you decide to play," the boy is saying, his sweet voice fading as he slips into a sea of brown and purple fog. "But it's your decision."

"Sorry I'm late," says Nicholas Robert Copacek in a voice brazen and deep, his boyishly slight face flushed pink from the wind outside. Even with cheeks raw, Adam can tell that Nick still feels marvelous, his lips red, full, and soft, just like Jimmy's used to be.

"That's quite okay," says Adam Van Anders, folding the morning edition of the Lansing State Journal over his lap. Adam is almost thirty, and as if that isn't bad enough, he feels so plain, steady, and predictable that it is clear to him that the boredom emanating from his presence is spurring a quiet, smoldering hostility within Nick. Adam rolls the newspaper into his leather cache, sensing Nick's inclination to make up an excuse and cancel the whole lunch.

"Anything interesting in that paper?" Nick asks in a half-sung sigh as a young waiter with a firm, round ass walks by with a large tray in balance between his neck and shoulder.

"More election stuff. They might do a recount in Grand Rapids."

"Wow, that's really gripping."

"Actually, it kinda is. This guy who lost is our age. He lost by only four votes."

"Not our age, Adam. Your age." Nick lets out a small chuckle as he removes his black scarf and topcoat, applying lip balm to his lips just in case they start to wear dry. Glancing at his reflection in a window, he tucks the stick softly back into his two hundred dollar Hugo Boss corduroys and sits down across from Adam in the corner of the booth. The outside light casts a yellow glare over his face, making his hazel-blue eyes seem green. His thick hair, full honey blond, is matted down in wavy tufts, lending itself a light brownish red tint: a fine, conscious match to his lemon custard colored silk shirt. "Maybe you should drive out to

Grand Rapids and ask him out. You could use a date. You know, a real date."

Adam's brow tweaks slightly as his shoulders pull into a shrug. "Maybe so. At least I'd be careful about it if it happened."

"I'm careful," Nick snaps before dipping his voice into a far less surly tone. "I know better than to get myself into bad situations." An old lady wearing a white straw hat with orange flowers on its wide brim is quacking in the next booth. Her laugh, loud and duck-like, disconcerts Nick to the point that he seems to momentarily lose his train of thought. "Like I said," he continues, "I am careful. And picky. Some of these guys are just plain desperate. They'll go home with anything." Nick always drew clear, bold lines between himself and those sorts of boys. "I might have my share of tricks, but I know what I'm doing."

"Still, it's unsettling."

Nick flips open a menu that is as thick and boring to him as a novel. "I'll tell you what's unsettling," he says. "My fucking landlord is rehabbing the apartment below us. Knocked out some walls, and the entire goddamn cable with them. Somehow we weren't paying for it, so there goes our fucking free ride. Cable is like crack, you know, and there's no living without it once you get a taste. We had it free for almost three months, and now all three of us are addicted. My roommates don't have money, so I'm the one that's gonna have to foot the goddamn bill to have it reconnected. Cable. Man, I hate to have to pay for it. Takes away from my thread kitty.

"In addition to that," Nick continues, "I just dumped this guy last night. He really liked me, but what am I supposed to do? A pretty pathetic twink, really. Not my responsibility." Nick cranes his neck, glancing at his reflection in a shiny centerpiece.

"My agency rep says that my skin tone is 'summer,'" he once impressed upon Adam. *"And I know exactly which pastel clothing serves to compliment the summer complexion. Coordinating colors, that is an art. Choosing*

designer brands, well, that's a statement." Nick flips a tiny pocket mirror open from his pocket. "Goddammit," he says, wiping the fog away from its smooth glass surface. "I just cleaned the glass this morning."

Adam James Van Anders sits at a distance from Nick, drinking a Perrier with lime. His lips are also weathered, yet he resists any urge to ask Nick for a swipe of Chapstick. He knows better from prior experience. *"I suppose you'll ask for my toothbrush next,"* Nick would likely chortle. *"Why don't you sleep in my bed and soil my underwear, too? Here, I'll give you the keys to my apartment. Just go straight to my room and romp through anything you can get your hands on."*

The restaurant is shaped like a hollow pear, with cubes of honeydew and bright orange watercolor sprayed over its cavernous walls. The clattering and chattering around Nick and Adam echoes off the tangerine ceiling, escalating as a couple with several young children parades past their table. Hurried waitstaff, mostly Michigan State students, rush in different directions as if in practice for that ever elusive casting call.

"Why am I here?" Nick asks, grabbing a glass of water and pressing it to his menthol-waxed lips. "I remember a personal ad and some e-mail exchanges, maybe a handful of telephone conversations. Then what? We got drunk on the first date and fucked, but it isn't exactly a red-letter memory."

The first date: Adam only remembers fumbling around with Nick's shirt buttons.

"Don't rip my shirt, guy," Nick said. *"You're talking three bills at Nordstrom's. Three big bills."*

"I don't know how much longer I can keep doing these lunches," Nick announces with puckered lips. "I'm trying to remember how this all started in the first place." Nick presses for a reflection, an edge, and something seems to flicker for a moment, but then it is gone. Nick dated so many boys that remembrances were vague, although he just assumed this to be the case with most young people on the rise. "I'm a busy person," he often proclaimed in a tone that implied setting a frantic pace, a step ahead of the rest: with clients and on the treadmill. When he wasn't "working" or at the gym, Nick spent most of his time at home with his door closed, daydreaming about the next boy he would get. They were always smooth and pretty, Nick's boys, and sometimes they all faded into a single, water-colored face that wasn't really a face at all, but an idea . . . a concept . . . a feeling mixed with the incessant pounding of club music.

"Why am I here?" Nick repeats, his bottom lip curling under slightly yellow teeth. "Tell me again." His gaze is harsh, feral, as are the involuntary twitching expressions pulsing through his ruddy face.

Adam feels defensive, introspective, and tries to ignore the vulgar reality spilling out from under Nick's plastic countenance. He is well aware that Nick is seeing at least one other person and fucking many more, but his inner control tells him to mind his own business. Even so, he can't help but feel a sharp sting of jealousy and hurt. He and Nick had been together, occasionally, for almost four months. Yet, the timeline didn't begin to tell the tale of Adam's frustration. Their relationship was physical beginning with that first date, a damnation trap that sucked Adam into its jaws whenever Nick wanted it to. "I want to make love to you," he would say, rendering Adam defenseless.

I want to make love to you.

Except for Jimmy, Nick was the best kisser Adam had ever experienced, knowing how to lead with his lips while engaging the tongue sparingly. He was also formidable in bed; strong and controlling, he would stand over Adam during climax and cum in slow, creamy drips over his chest. Yet, mistaking Nick's skill for passion was a part of the trap holding Adam's mangled, projected feelings hostage. Such was the existence of lonely desperation. On occasion, Adam recognized Nick as a person of shallow existence, yet he was helpless to protect himself from being used. It had been five years already, and he had promised his mentor, state Representative Chuck Hriniak, that he would make an effort to date. He held true to that promise, even as it exposed old wounds and carved open new ones. At every step of his life, thoughts of Jimmy descended over Adam like a warm, heavenly mist—a comfort haze in which he was quietly drowning. Stepping outside of it introduced only colder climes, especially as his misguided affections for Nick rambled wildly to daydreams of mutual dependence and family indoctrinations.

"I'm glad you're dating," Chuck would say, "but I'm not so sure about this Nick character. I don't think he's good for you." Chuck was right. He knew Adam better than anyone else, having served as his adopted father for almost four years.

Nick, to his credit, had been brutally honest from the inception of their one-way courtship. *"I enjoy fucking you, but this is the most you can have from me,"* he once explained. *"The rules for being with me are simple. Fucking involves friendship only, without any commitment. I have no feelings for you, and if you get clingy or tragic, I'm gone. I'm not putting you down, and I'm not a player. See, when I meet Mr. Right, I'll commit. Nothing will be more important to me. But you're Mr. Right Now. I have no qualms about that. If you do, then you should stop calling me.*

"Do you have a clean towel?"

Adam was never able to state personal matters in such plain and simple, almost contractual terms. This was a talent Nick no doubt learned from his parents, whom he described as good, hardworking people. His upbringing was privileged, proper, and he accepted it with all its burdens. He was lucky. He was gay, but not like other gays. He radiated strength and was the well-rounded, All-American boy-next-door sort that fooled people into thinking he was straight—until he opened his mouth and the venom poured out. Nick expected perfection from other people, yet he had little patience for their feelings. *"Why should I be responsible for other people's feelings?"* After all, none of his family or friends back in Ohio knew of his true feelings. *"I don't care about being gay. It doesn't affect me. I'm destined for a successful life because I play by the rules and pay my dues. I'm a perfectionist."* When it came to dealing with other human beings, however, Nick was a perfectionist only in one manner: he always got exactly what he wanted from them.

"Why am I here?" he asks again.

"Well, I wanted to see you, that's all," Adam says blankly, suppressing an unspoken urgency. An image in his head of Jimmy playing guitar, shirtless in his straw hat on his mom's porch, is so clear and vivid that the lyrics play like a spinning record:

> *There's a place not far from this town*
> *Where the lives we have we choose*
> *But right here your friends are enemies*
> *That you never thought you'd lose . . .*

"I wanted to hang out for lunch, you know?" Adam continues. "I mean, why not?" His mind is blinded by blurred frames of Jimmy flashing against his over-romanticized vision of Nick. Adam's mind releases its safety lock and he is rushed by a memory of Nick, standing buck-naked over the bed with a hard-on, fingers wrapped around Adam's knees, pulling him closer, the sheets sliding softly under Adam's back until his calves are resting over Nick's shoulders . . .

I want to make love to you.

Adam takes a sip of Perrier, visualizing Nick's lips through the curved glass, which gives them a sinister twist.

Nick smiles with general narcissism. "No, I meant, 'Why am I *here*?' I hate this place."

Adam resists sighing in frustration. They had gone over this on the phone last night. "I only have an hour for lunch and this is about as far as I can walk without going over my time limit," he reminds Nick.

"Oh yeah. Well, anyway, I hate this place. It's so *college*. And the decor! Christ, it looks like the inside of a vagina. At least it doesn't smell like one."

They both laugh, and Adam resists an impulse to reach under the table and squeeze the warm and soft flesh of Nick's hand. "It *is* a bit Georgia O'Keefe," he says.

"Georgia O'Keefe. Right. Good point. So what should I order? Cheesecake?" Nick laughs at what he thinks is a private joke, but Adam understands that Nick would never order cheesecake. *Too fatty.*

"Actually, the food here is really good. Try one of their pastas—they're excellent and low fat. Trust me."

"Don't worry, I trust you," Nick said wryly. And he seemed to. "You couldn't harm a fly."

A waiter, a slim, waif-like twenty-something with streaked blond hair and various metal hoops stapled up and down his ear, bounces over to the table and asks for their order.

"I guess I'll have the pasta primavera," Nick says, eyeing the kid's nametag. *"Topher."*

Oh shit, another trick, Adam thinks, until he realizes that the boy isn't in on Nick's little game.

"Huh?" the waiter asks.

"I said, 'I'll have the pasta primavera—and a diet Pepsi, *Topher.*"

"What are you calling me?"

Nick explains. "Your name tag says 'Christopher.'" He pauses, wiping his lip with a bony finger. "If it's not *Christopher,* then what is it? What are you called?"

"Yes, *Christopher.* That's my name. *Christopher.* Or *Chris.* Not *Topher.* I don't know anyone named *Topher.*"

Nick waves his hand. "Whatever. What's your last name, then?"

The boy pauses, and Adam can practically see the waves of cognitive dissonance rushing through his temples. "McKenzie," he finally offers.

Nick smiles. "Topher McKenzie, then."

"It's *CHRIS.* Chris McKenzie."

"Oh yeah, I'm sorry," says Nick. Adam just wants to order. Is that too much to ask? Apparently, it is, as Nick continues with his little comedy. "*Chris.* Of course. Christopher Mc*Fadden.*"

"Chris Mc*Kenzie.*" The boy is grinning. "You're getting close."

"Yeah, yeah, yeah. Steve McKenzie. That's what I said."

"I'll have the chicken marsalla," Adam interjects.

"Pasta primavera, chicken marsalla, and a diet *Coke*— we don't have Pepsi." Chris McKenzie scribbles their order on a small pad and walks back to the kitchen giggling.

"That guy clearly plays for our team," Nick says.

"Oh, you think so?"

"Oh, I know so. If he was a little hotter, I'd get his number in, like, ten seconds. I'm so sick of these wispy little fems, though. They're tiny, little, fragile people. Like miniatures."

"Come on, what are you talking about? I don't go for all the hooks and hoops, but that guy was pretty cute."

"You can have him, then." Nick pauses to wink at Chris McKenzie as he brings him his diet soda and skips to a table of boisterous frat boys demanding service near the bar. "People in the gay world—people like him," Nick continues. "They don't know what they want. It makes them *small.* You know it and so do I. It's a problem, probably a result of repressing natural instincts at such a young age, for so many years. That's why there's so much shame, so much baggage. I don't think that many gay men have the intimate relationship skills that straights, with all of their Homecoming Dances and high school dating routines, have. The result is a lot of little, tiny people running around looking for love, not knowing exactly how to find it or what it involves."

Adam is growing weary of Nick's pontificating. "You're kind of making a generalization, don't you think?" he asks. "For crissakes, how would you know what Chris McKenzie wants out of life?"

"*Topher* McKenzie. Trust me, I just know."

For more than half his life, Adam had known *exactly* what he wanted. His name was Jimmy Dillon, and they met on a basketball court after school at East Hills Athletic club. Adam and Jimmy played one-on-one on the hardwood: close, evenly matched games without any predictable script. They'd play best-of-seven. Monday, Adam might clinch the win with a dramatic three-pointer in game six. Tuesday, Jimmy might take it to seven games, claiming victory with a slashing move to the hoop so quick that Adam could do nothing but watch in bent-kneed awe. The games started in seventh grade; Jimmy saw Adam shooting around and asked for a game. They agreed to a match, but didn't finish before it was time to go home. They resumed play the next day, and after that, the routine became a staple. Instantly, they were friends. After a week, they knew each other's last names. After two weeks, they were carpooling home. After three weeks, they were best friends.

Like all the other cool kids, Jimmy went to public school at Forest Hills. Adam's parents, predictably, forced their only son to attend school in the Christian Reformed system across town. They were "strict mother-fuckers," as Jimmy put it.

Getting through each meaningless school day was a chore. Adam, who read his own book selections with vigor each night, ignored the hollow lectures of his provincial teachers during the day, spending all his class time dreaming of Jimmy. It wasn't long before those dreams extended from the basketball court to the bedroom.

Today, Adam has no idea what he wants out of life, and who, if anyone, he wants to share it with. On some level, he might want Nick, but that was confusing. Sometimes, he yearned for Nick's attention: for a note, a call, an e-mail, but that rarely happened. Often, he would drive the Grand River route into work because it traveled past Nick's apartment. The additional stoplights lengthened his travel time by fifteen, sometimes twenty minutes, but Adam didn't care; riding by was a temporary way to ease the longing. Nick wasn't the most genuine person in the world, but Adam wanted a chance with him, an even shot. If it didn't work out, fine. They would part company, both emancipated from the effort. And if it did work out? Five years of futility, loneliness, raised hopes, and spectacular crashes would ride into the sunset and be forgotten.

"I mean, Nick, are you going as far as to say that *you* don't know what you want?" Adam asks.

"No. I'm not talking about *me*. I don't want *anything*, and that's a lot closer to knowing what you want than not knowing. In fact, it's very close to knowing *exactly* what you want."

Chris McKenzie sets their food plates on the table, smiling at Nick before tending to the loud, displeased frat boys.

"Sure you don't want the waiter? He's *something*."

"No. I told you, I don't like these little twink sticks. I'd break that boy in half if I ever tried to fuck him." Nick pauses to fret over his food, twirling a fork into the noodles with slight interest. "Plus, I saw him smoking outside when I first got here. Smoking is a disgusting, filthy habit. I hate the physical results of it. Besides, people who smoke are weak. They're addicts. It's so self-destructive. Unfortunately, sixty to seventy percent of gays smoke, and many of them are very hot boys. I am very sad now, just thinking about it."

"Well, I don't smoke, you can be sure of that," Adam says. He smiles at Nick, but Nick's mind is obviously playing architect to larger conquests. There is an uncomfortable silence, but only Adam seems to notice it, or be affected by it, for that matter. He's thinking about asking Nick out over the weekend but initially holds back for fear of appearing *clingy*. He doesn't want to scare Nick away, and he doesn't want to get hurt. At the same time, he needs Nick's acceptance. As Nick's fork continuously scrapes off his plate, teeth, and back again, Adam gives in to the need for acceptance.

"My cousin and I are going to check out the *Hard Licker* show down at the Rick's on Friday night. You wanna come with us?"

Nick doesn't even finish chewing his food before answering. "Nah, I wasn't too into it last time. And not just the show. I wasn't into the whole thing, actually." Nick is too busy with his plate to see Adam grimace.

I wasn't into the whole thing, actually. What the hell was he trying to say? Was he referring to the sex they had later that night?

I want to make love to you.

He couldn't have meant the sex! *No way!* Adam himself had been driven to a massive orgasm, which was rare, and when Nick pulled out, his condom was saturated with a lake of cum that had bloated the rubber shaft into the shape of a full water balloon. *"Look at this!"* Nick had exclaimed proudly, waving his creamy cock in front of Adam's face.

"Besides, I couldn't go even if I wanted to," Nick adds. "I've got plans with that guy from Grand Ledge. You know, the one that I sometimes see."

"Oh." Adam bristles. *The Guy from Grand Ledge.* He didn't have a name; he was just *The Guy from Grand Ledge,* the high school boy. He was but a phantom, an exaggerated piece of competition that possessed some great trait that Adam didn't have. Adam could only guess and grope at what it was as he hung on, hoping for whatever scraps of Nick the schoolboy left behind. *I know that shit flows downhill*, Adam thinks. *But why am I always the one shoveling the bottom of the valley?"*

Nick continues to look around the restaurant. "Hey, check out that guy over there. Check him *out!*"

"Where?"

"To your left. The one eating by himself."

"I can't see through the pole."

Nick pays Adam's dilemma no attention. "Eating by himself! Pretty sad, especially at a college place like this. Who would come here to eat by himself?"

"Maybe he's just some old and lonely old guy who likes the food?"

"No, he's *my* age. Maybe a little younger. Cute. Blonde, with bangs. A little retro, I know, but it works for this guy. He's really boyish with doe-like blue eyes, Levis, and a gray Nike swoosh tee. He's a hottie."

Adam's heart sinks. He thinks of Jimmy, always wearing the Nike shirts tight around his chest. At Michigan State, when they started working out with weights, he'd cut the sleeves off and his tightly toned muscles would bulge through the fabric with little shags of blond hair sprouting out from under his tanned arms as if airbrushed with fine, smooth strokes. Adam and Jimmy's basketball odyssey continued at college; they'd shower back at the dorm and sometimes fuck for hours in the privacy of their room. No one ever suspected, not even Adam's nosy mom. MSU was their little paradise.

After college, it was hard to be back in Grand Rapids, where tiptoeing around Mom and Dad became a chore. Both boys found support from Jimmy's family, and from a small but close cocktail circle at Diversions Bar and Grill. The pressure on Adam was snowballing, however. Now that college was over, Dad expected him to run the new DutchWay project in Spain while Mother spent her time fretting over the fact that her boy didn't date girls. He was, after all, *of marrying age.* Embarrassing questions began to arise amongst the country club crowd, and it was impossible for Mother to work her connections with such distractions. It was decided, without further adieu, that Adam would be sent to Spain at summer's end. Time for him to forever abandon his boyish ways and explore the family fortune. He'd have to learn how to live away from that damned Jimmy sooner or later, and the sooner the better.

It was a moot point later that year when Jimmy died in hunting accident at the exclusive *Rod & Rifle.* That's when Adam left via his own will, and not for Spain.

It's been five years now, and every day of those five years, Adam thinks of the last time he and Jimmy made love at the cottage; how Jimmy removed his rainbow necklace in the car and hid it in his pocket until Adam's parents finally left. How Jimmy came out of the tiny bathroom wearing only a Nike swoosh shirt and a blue-ribbon blue-veiner already popping with dew. The love they made that day was the kind of love that straight people often wrote about but seldom understood: they both came at the same time, twice in an hour. It was perfect. Jimmy had saved his best for last.

Nick is too self-absorbed to notice that Adam is about to cry, and continues on another segue in his monologue: "Hey, being gay doesn't diminish my ability to be a role model. To my younger cousins—I'm an only child, by the way—I am very much a role model. I've worked hard to get where I am, I respect people in positions of authority, I've stayed clear of crime and drugs—for the most part, and my family encourages my cousins to pattern themselves after me. I feel that being gay doesn't diminish my ability to be a role model, but just the same, I don't tell my family. I'm not sure how they'd feel about it, and it's my business, nobody else's. I would say that most parents would love their kids to be just like me, except for the gay part. The funny thing is, I can't remember having a role model when I was a kid. I work with guys who are making seven figures, but they're not so much role models as indications of where I'll be in a few short years."

Adam is lost somewhere between five years past and the present, caught between heaven and hell, his own demons dancing a chorus line to Nick's self-aggrandizements.

A tap on Adam's door. Jimmy's mom enters near his bed, kneels, takes his hand in hers, and he knows. Oh God, Jimmy. 'He loved you so much,' she whispers in his ear. The air is icy, black; Adam's sighs cast tiny white clouds against the darkness as his heavy tears fall to the floor and splatter with the resonance of something breaking.

Nick continues to editorialize and Adam wants to tell him to fuck off, but, "Hey, Nick, will you excuse me for a second?" is all he manages to say.

"Sure, but don't take too long," Nick says in a borderline mocking tone. "Remember, you have to get back to work soon."

Adam flashes him a pissed look.

"Hey, just looking out for you," Nick explains.

"Yeah, right." Adam hurries to the bathroom and pretends to examine his tired, red face in the mirror. There is only one stall; someone is in it. Adam holds his breath. A flush. The door swings open on quiet hinges. An old man scurries away without washing his hands. Adam slips into the stall and closes the door. The air is heavy with the warm scent of shit, and the aqua-tiled walls are chipped. A short gasp and then Adam holds his breath again, but this time the tears come, squirting over his cheeks in a rapid flow. In a few minutes, it is over: the tears pass. Adam runs cold water over his swollen eyes for about five minutes to regain his composure. By the time he comes back to the table, Nick is immersed in a cell-phone conversation with the Guy From Grand Ledge and lunch is just about over.

To Josh Brisco, Saturdays were like a sack of crap. The deeper you got into them, the more they stunk. Saturday was simply the ultimate crap ending to yet another piece-of-shit week. Double chocolate, so-to-speak.

It hadn't always been like that for Josh. During his grade school days in suburban Chicago, Saturday was, by far, his favorite day of the week. He enjoyed acing Grove Elementary School during the week, and Saturday was his complimentary refuge, a safe day—a day away from his inner-driven competitions with the other kids. Saturday was a quiet day when Josh could relax and do just about whatever he wanted. He might rise early enough to watch *Superfriends*, read a few comic books, take in the early morning movie, then have time to catch about an hour of the Three Stooges before Grandpa would pick him up in the cavernous Mark IV with its vast leather seats and they would go bowling at the ancient *Strike and Spare*. "This place is older than your grandmother, you know that," Grandpa would remark with a sly grin as they pulled into the *S & S* parking lot.

Josh smiled; he actually looked forward to Gramps making this statement each week: it had grown into a tradition shared only between Grandfather and Grandson. On the rare Saturdays when Father or Mother, or, worse yet, one of the semi-retarded cousins would accompany them to *S & S*, Gramps would pull into the parking lot and simply exclaim, "I'll be damned!" and wink at Josh before adding, "The age of this place is simply magnanimous."

Inside, *Strike and Spare* smelled like stale beer, dirty shoes, and Ira, the ruffled clerk behind the counter. Ira was polite enough, but even a ten year-old could tell that he was constantly harboring a nasty hangover. "Ira spends his Friday nights down the way at *Charlie Bee's*," Gramps explained. Josh knew about *Charlie Bee's*. It was a restaurant, but nobody went there to eat. According to local legend, there was a sign behind the bar that said, '*Food is served only at the pleasure of our DRINKING Customers*,' an attitude that Josh would grow to appreciate as he grew older and acquired certain tastes for Budweiser, Old Style, and Jack Daniel's, among other vices.

The old bowling alley was humid and sticky, two conditions that often prompted Josh to complain. "You ever been down South?" Gramps would ask, as if he didn't already know.

"Nope," Josh would humor him.

"Damn good thing," Gramps would respond. "Cuz this is what it smells like down there. They don't call it *Hotlanta* for nothing."

"*Hotlanta?* It's AT-lanta!

"Can we bowl *two* games this time?"

"We'll see."

"How about *three* games?"

"Don't get ahead of yourself, J.B. One game at a time. One game at a time."

Inevitably, they'd bowl two or three games and break for medium-rare steak sandwiches at the Two Doves Restaurant. They'd drink Cokes and Josh would order a crispy wet dinner salad with mint colored creamy garlic dressing. From there, Gramps would take Josh back home, and the rest of the weekend was inconsequential, with Captain America comic books and the old Universal Studios monster movies serving as mere filler until Monday.

Those days seemed like they would last forever, but that was before Father, after a series of embarrassing business defeats, packed up the family and moved it to Michigan, abruptly severing the golden era of Josh's life. For years after, all through adolescence, Josh felt like an abyss had opened under his feet, and, in many ways, he had been continuously falling ever since.

The bowling days are long gone . . . and all that's left is filler.

Michigan Saturdays were lonely without Gramps. Josh was cold and distant in his new school, yet he eventually made friends in the neighborhood and Saturdays became full of sports activities custom made to fit each season, whether it be baseball, football, basketball, or hockey. High school weekends were a blur of drunken parties and half-assed dates with girls. In college, Saturdays served as an outpatient recovery period for often hilarious Friday night drinking binges. Once on the Job, Josh's drinking episodes became random, more frequent, and included the occasional mix of cocaine, Vicodin, and/or pot. Unlike guys like Ira from *Strike and Spare*, Josh was never able to develop a solid drinking schedule, or commit to days sober.

Ira died a year after Josh moved away. They closed *Strike and Spare* and Gramps died four years later.

During his campaign for state representative, Josh's Saturdays were filled with obligations: senior centers, veteran homes, union halls. Those Saturdays were certainly a factor in losing Pepper, who hated every aspect of the campaign, the last days of which served as her breaking point. Once, during a horrible drinking binge, Josh wrote a four-line poem and stuck it in her purse:

> *Never had a breaking point been reached*
> *at such convenience.*
> *Pristine Pepper,*
> *You never really knew my circumstance.*

She was long gone before he even remembered writing it.

Nowadays, Saturday was just like any old day to Josh, blending together with the others in a bland sequence of malaise. Saturday was only distinguishable by the barrage of odd dreams and nightmares that now accompanied its arrival. No work meant no schedule, and besides his workouts, Josh mustered little effort to be productive, instead drinking every night with the sort of vigor that guys like poor, dead Ira saved up all week for Friday and Saturday. That, and Josh's fairly recent penchant for harder prescription and illegal drugs, distinguished him from that crowd loud and clear.

Today is a Saturday distinguished by soft sheets of white snow swirling outside the kitchen window as Josh sits at the breakfast table, sifting a fork through some severely browned pancakes he has cooked up for himself. The fan over the stovetop is buzzing on *high*, but its bawdy inhaling can't swallow the stench lingering from the last burned pancake, although it seems to be sucking the outside snow up from the grass blades to the window. Cesare, Mother's Pomeranian, won't come out of his dog bed, which is more like a cat bed, even as Josh puts a plate of scraps on the floor for good measure. Rather, the dog reverses direction and looks away. "Oh come on," Josh moans, rather flabbergasted by the dog's reaction. Cesare is tiny (only about five pounds), fluffy and fearless. Every night, he'd open the door to Josh's room with a push of his paw and a feisty snort. Then, with a mighty leap, he'd hop into bed with Josh and nestle himself to sleep. They were practically bedmates.

Josh notices something odd about the snow.

Is it snowing on the inside?

His wandering thoughts are interrupted. "Pomeranians are a proud breed," says Hazel Brisco, her voice booming from the family room. Wearing a gold blouse with dangling ties and a pair of snug-fitting black leather pants, she looks barely half of her 52 years. "And you embarrass the hell out of him. What, you expect him to eat that crap? A proud dog like that? Eating that crap? Forget it!" Her heels click against tile as she enters the kitchen area and stands behind Josh. "Look at you, for crissakes! You look like one of those dumb-ass Seattle grunge rockers. I'm afraid to even touch your hair it's so greasy. When was the last time you bathed? You look like a ragamuffin! What are you trying to do, compete with your no-good cousins for the Brisco Family Loser of the Year Award?"

"Oh, thanks Ma," Josh manages with a sigh. He looks through the kitchen window and tiny squirts of sleet are running, spraying, dripping all over the glass in horrible patterns of dread, and Josh is feeling disgusted, a bit on edge, because here is his mother's own dog treating him like he's the dunce of the doggie school. And here comes Mother, all decked out like she's a Solid Gold dancer, and Josh knows damn well that she's gonna push his buttons and try to get him out of the house.

"What, are you eating breakfast?" Mother asks. "Don't even tell me that you're just eating breakfast. Did you just get up?"

Josh scratches his oily scalp. "Why, what time is it?"

"Almost dinner time, for crissakes. Why don't you get cleaned up? You could come out with me and Biz. We're going downtown . . . should be fun."

Josh moans. "What do you mean, '*dinner time*?'" he asks, but gets no answer.

Is it raining or snowing outside? He hopes it is snowing. *Pepper's flowers would die in the snow, unless they proved to be plastic.*

Just . . .

. . . like . . .

. . . her.

"Did you hear about Hudson's today?" Mother keeps talking and Josh has more and more trouble following the conversation. He feels only slightly annoyed, and only a bit dismayed as the confusion in his brain renders him numb towards Mother's quirks. "All the power went out at Hudson's. At *Hudson's*. All day. They couldn't get their computers up, so it was a huge bust. Imagine how much money they lost." *Blah, blah, blah, blah.*

Drizzle continues to slap against the window and dripping sounds echo through the house. "Can't you get those sprinklers fixed?" Josh asks.

"It's raining out, Josh. Get off the drugs. You're wasting away."

If only she knew the reality of it.

Josh blinks his eyes closed for a moment, then opens them. "I'm just kidding," he says. "I know it's raining, supposed to turn to snow later tonight. Was it snowing earlier?"

"Oh, I see," Mother groans, "you're a comedian now. Do you know that you're not very funny?" she asks. "Most of the time you're just sitting at this damn table or sprawled out on the couch like a choked corpse, arms and legs dangling off to the side. It's not healthy. And all that screaming at night? You're driving me and Cesare absolutely crazy. A proud dog like that doesn't need to be startled like that in the middle of the night."

"I can't help it if I have nightmares."

"Yes, you can. All these drugs you're doing, Josh . . . they are a problem."

Oh, she really does know. But how much does she know?

"Admit it, get over it, and clean yourself up or get out of my house. And stop drinking all my Jack Daniel's."

"What, you're pissed cuz I won't go out with you and Biz?"

"No, not with me and Biz. I'm not pissed because you won't go out *with me and Biz*. Believe me, I can think of better times to be had. I'm pissed off because you won't go out, period. You just sit in my house and rot. You won't go to work. You barely make it out of here to play basketball or work-out. Then you come home and lay around. You've been doing it for almost two months now! How in God's name do you keep your figure? And that room downstairs— it smells like an armpit! You just sit down there and decay. Go out. Go out with one of your friends, anyone. Get out of the house for a while. Go *out* and get drunk for once. You know, go to that fundraiser or something. Or is that next week?"

"*Mistletoe to Go*? It's next week. And no, I'm not going. What a great, banner-fucking idea, Mom. I'll just go to *Mistletoe to Go* with no date, and arrive with the stigma of being the biggest huge-ass loser of the entire election. Great practice for the Brisco Family Loser of the Year Award! I could polish up my loser acceptance speech like it was the Golden Globes or something!

"How could you ask me to humiliate myself like that?"

"Slade Pickens was hoping that you would come."

"Well, I'm sorry. Slade is being silly. I'm just a loser, Mother, a big time loser. Slade would be the keynote speaker at this fucking event if I would have done my job and won the election like I should have. Hell, he'd be Speaker of the Fucking House. But no dice. No dice! No victory. No seat. No Democratic majority. No esteem. No friends. No date. It would just be depressing, and I'm depressed enough as it is."

"What about Magdalaine?"

"Pepper? Who cares? You never liked her anyway. No one liked her. I didn't like her. Who was I kidding?"

Josh flinches as a car pulls into the driveway and flashes its brights through the front window.

"It's Biz!" says Mother, gathering her coat and scooping up the dog with a kiss before setting him down on the couch and scurrying out the door. "I won't be too late," she says over her shoulder. "You know, with that twelve o'clock drinking curfew thing."

"Yeah, Republican Prohibition." Josh looks out the window, hoping to catch the transition of rain into snow. But once Mother is gone, the expanding dampness is overwhelming, so he fixes himself a whiskey with a slice of lemon, topped off with a spoon of chopped Vicodin and just ignores the living shit out of it.

CAPITOL BEAT: *News for Capitol Insiders*
REPORT NO. 218 –WEDNESDAY, NOV. 4

ANALYSTS: EMBARASSED DEMS NEED TO RECONNECT WITH MEMBERS, PUBLIC

In order to restore their political fortunes, Michigan Democrats must rally their base *and* reach out to independent voters. This week, Dem leaders took a few days off to regroup and examine their losses from Tuesday's election. "Democratic fortunes won't improve until the public in general again feels some sense of positive ownership with government," explained Frankie DeVine, a polling analyst for Able & Schide. "There's not a great deal of trust amongst the public right now. Republicans in this state have done an excellent job of selling government as a burdensome, unnecessary, and inefficient bureaucracy. Ironically, these same Republicans have expanded government power to regulate certain personal liberties such as sexual behavior (Proposition B) and alcohol consumption (Partial Prohibition). If they want to win over voters, Democrats need to re-establish a belief in government as a vehicle of personal empowerment and opportunity."

Meanwhile, Rep. Slade Pickens (D-Grand Rapids) said that party members should not be too morose, as Democrats did relatively well in pinpointing their leadership problems. "The deck was stacked against us and we almost held on [to the House]," Mr. Pickens said.

"Josh Brisco – that's [sic] one seat where we got screwed," continued Mr. Pickens, referring to his charismatic protégé from the neighboring 75th District. Brisco, the young Grand Rapids police detective, held a six-point lead on Republican Jizzy LeDoux before his campaign was buried in a last-minute barrage of negative ads financed by conservative billionaire Wayne Van Anders, owner of DutchWay Corporation. "Josh's campaign didn't have the kind of money needed to answer all the last minute mud-slinging," said Mr. Pickens. "And still, he only lost by four votes out of twenty thousand. Four votes—I don't know whether to laugh or cry. I do know, however, that DutchWay's soft-money scams should be illegal. We need campaign finance reform, and we need it now."

Thursday night, a standard re-count confirmed Mr. LeDoux's slim victory.

"Any way you look at it, Democrats have their work cut out for them," concluded Mr. DeVine. "Jettisoned to minority status for the first time in a generation—that's going to cause some pain."

Tiny balls of sweat glisten over the brow of State Representative Ira "Slade" Pickens as the temperature of the cabin rises, drops, and then shoots up again in a matter of seconds. "Jesus Christ," he grumbles, beckoning for the stewardess to fill his glass of Dewers. A tall blonde with the kind of long, sharp fingernails that could tear a guy's balls off, she acknowledges him with a *"Service in a Flash"* nod. Satisfied, Slade wipes his face with a nicely woven, white linen napkin with the airline logo embroidered into it and turns his eyes back to the Sports Illustrated in his lap for a few seconds—until Darla Sue bursts through the curtain separating first class from coach and stumbles into an empty aisle seat. "Ah, Christ," Slade groans as his wife's hands grope over the seat as she struggles to balance herself. "What's going on with you here?"

Darla Sue whimpers, Slade feels like a heel. "Sorry. I didn't mean to bark at you," he manages. Shit, it was selfish having upgraded to first class with her fledgling drunk in coach. Yet, he absolutely needed to do it. Time spent with Darla Sue was growing more unbearable by the moment. Coming off a weekend alone with her, who could resist the temptation to upgrade away?

It wasn't the girl's fault. Slade knew that much. He had known what he was getting into, right from the start. Darla Sue was merely the latest in a succession of young wives that he had outwardly chased and conquered following the First Divorce. Ah, the First Divorce: Nancy, his first love. She left him, and their law practice, for a twenty-two year-old physical trainer she met at the club. *"This doesn't work for me anymore, Slade,"* she said that last morning, her voice cold, eyes distant. With a bulging suitcase, thick perfume, and clicking heels, she was gone, and soon after, so was *Pickens and Associates*. It was impossible for Slade to run the practice full-time in conjunction with his responsibilities as a state legislator.

In the nine months following Nancy's departure, Slade quietly numbed himself into a cocoon. This was done with much help from friends like Jack Daniel's and Jose Cuervo, and with rental movies along the lines of *Splendor in the Grass, Some Came Running, Rebecca,* and *A Brief Moment.* The sabbatical almost cost him his job: neglecting his campaign, he barely made it through re-election.

In the tenth month, however, Slade broke out of his solitude with a vengeance. He first seized the reigns of his job, then those of his social life. Met with unprecedented success, his confidence soared out-of-control. Fired by a new, searing desire to prove himself as a formidable chaser of flowery women, he sought, conquered, and regretfully married four young vixens in the span of a decade. Quickly, each relationship transgressed into a ménage of communication breakdowns as Slade grew tired of his prizes. Monica, his second wife, the first *Post-Nancy Edition,* was a buxom, twenty-seven year-old brunette who looked great in white leather skirts and matching boots. That marriage lasted less than a year. *"My trial marriage,"* Slade would joke amongst friends. *"Sure, we were married, but it wasn't serious."* It never hurt to make fun of one's self, Slade thought. A few laughs were always good therapy, as long as they weren't at someone else's expense.

Susan, the second *Post-Nancy Edition,* was similar in appearance to her predecessor, and was exotic in that she experienced orgasm only when wrapped in chamois leather as pet wasps (held captive in a Ragu jar when not in use) stung her extremities. Initially, the sight of Susan writhing in this masochistic ecstasy was a huge turn-on for Slade. During their first couple dalliances, he came to orgasm before managing to disrobe. Not long into their marriage, however (seven weeks to be exact), Slade accepted the crystal realization that Susan didn't, and never would, leave her wasps to seek his sexual offerings. And that meant therapy.

Dr. Fanny Abramowicz, Slade's therapist, was far from sympathetic, however.

"Hey, if somebody likes to dress up in chamois leather and get stung up by bees, then so be it," she said, a large, peach pen dangling from her bright red lips. *"God bless her."*

"Not bees," explained Slade, his voice rising. *"Wasps. Fucking wasps. Literally."*

"Wasps, then," said the doctor, her lips pulled into a sour pucker. *"God bless 'em. God bless her."*

"God bless her? How can you say that? You don't even know her. She won't even set foot in this rattrap." Slade's voice was rising.

"I can't make your wife come to therapy, Slade, you know that." Abramowicz paused, folding her legs. *"Rather than dwell on that, I prefer that you focus on the wasps. Do they sting you?"*

"Of course, they do, dammit. I might be able to roll with this if it involved bees. Wasps, on the other hand, are a whole different story. They're like Detroit politicians. They keep stinging you, stabbing you, needling you for God-knows-what. Then they come back for more."

Slade rolls up his magazine and tucks it away as Darla Sue slumps into the big leather chair, tosses back her hair with both hands, and sneezes violently into the seat ahead. Her face is contorted, bloated, red. "I'm shit-ass bored," she announces as three tiny gin blossoms pop up from under the creamy orange skin of her cheeks. "*Boooor-ed.*"

Jesus Fuck, am I imagining this? Slade wonders, his jaw rigid as he looks past his wife and beckons once again for the stewardess to refill his Dewers.

"What do you want me to do about your boredom?" he asks Darla Sue, slowly enunciating each word so that his voice doesn't break into the kind of ballistic shriek that frightens other passengers. She lets out a sigh, then a belch. Pop, pop, pop! Slade is certain he can see her pores exploding right before his very eyes. "I don't know," she mumbles. Her breath is a mist of whiskey.

"Why don't you go read your book? You know how you love that Sue Grafton." *A is for Asshole. B is for Bitch. C is for Cunt. D is for Drunk . . .*

She belches again. "I can't. I can't concentrate." She pauses, repeats. "I can't *con*-cen-trate."

"I know. You already said that. At least you can read. You should be very thankful for that."

"Ah, crap," Darla Sue groans, catching some wayward spit with her hand as it drips out the corner of her mouth. "God works in mysterious ways, don't He?"

She sighs. "Maybe I could sneak one in the john."

"*Sneak one?* What the Christ are you talking about—a *smoke?*" Slade can't believe it.

"Yeah, a smoke."

This is terrible. She is going to cause an INCIDENT. Slade can't believe it. He can't believe the situation. "Goddamn it, you can't smoke on a fucking plane," he says. "*Period.* They have smoke alarms all over: in the cabins, in bathrooms, behind the toilets, under the sink, even in the overhead compartments in case a midget tries to crawl in there and *sneak one.* It can't be done. You just can't do it. The feds will bust you. Then you'll get sued. The airlines will sue. The other passengers will sue. Everyone will sue and it won't be good at all. It will be a disaster, I swear to Mother-fucking God."

"Sue?"

"Yes. Everybody. They'll all sue you. Then they'll send you away."

"I *need* a smoke. Can't you smoke up here in first class?"

Slade winces as if someone is squirting onion juice in his eye. "This is a better class of people up here. First class. Of course you can't smoke." How did he manage to get himself into these situations? Women! Darla Sue was trouble. Trouble from the start, and he knew it. But she was a prize, the process of winning her was a contest. But now that he had her, he couldn't stand to be around her. It wasn't that she bored him so much as she embarrassed and genuinely *horrified* him. First class? Yeah, first class: Slade considers himself a first class idiot.

The stewardess, making her way to Slade for his Dewer's refill, sees Darla Sue and instead directs her immediate attention to another seat patron.

"You're gonna have to leave," Slade tells Darla Sue. "Go on, go back to your seat. I'll be there in a minute."

Darla Sue grabs onto the leg of his suit pants. "Just get me a smoke. I really need one," she says. Her eyes are full with dancing, blood-shot branches of red willow trees.

Slade looks away from Darla Sue and at once longs to be back home, free from the constraints of this flying sardine can, and free from the fishy breath of his wife. Without doubt, he would rather be with his friends from the Capitol, having a drink at McCoy's. In fact, he can hardly wait for the next Buzz Club, the after-work drinking sessions that made life so much more tolerable.

Slade can hardly wait to get *anywhere*, as long as it is away from this woman, this young thing, this inebriated, large-breasted mistake of a wife.

Harsh thoughts render Slade apologetic. He fears himself degenerating into a grump, a rotten old bastard growing more rancid and vindictive as life's prickly quilt of ironies and disappointments sour him into a constant state of terse reaction. *It's a defense mechanism*, he tells himself. *I am ripe with the fruit of survival, no matter how bitter its juice.* And there is plenty to be sour about. Shitty campaigns. Missed opportunities. Poor voter turn-out. You name it: moments of promise that could never be recaptured. A long list of victims—including himself, including Josh Brisco. *Am I going to lose the caucus election?* Slade wants more than anything to be Democratic leader, and it is his position to lose. He should have every confidence. Yet, the Detroit Africans are stalling the caucus vote; scheming, raising money, tossing out bribes to power-hungry representatives. The Africans. Patsy Kalumba King led their hapless litter, and his mother, Chinita McCloud Clapton King-Hyde, had them riled up like a pack of wolves.

Squeeze my face over the ocean, Slade thinks. *I'm a real lemon.*

He looks out through the clouds and down at the vast blue lake below. In the middle of that lake, he imagines seeing an old man, frail and withered, clinging to a raft amongst the harsh waves of his life.

Ah, the bitter waves.

G.O.P. EXULTS OVER HOUSE CONTROL; DEMS BLAME TERM LIMITS

Elated Michigan House Republicans began preparing for their new majority status yesterday, crediting strong strategy for helping them retake control of the chamber for the first time in 38 years.

Meanwhile, somber House Democrats barely began picking up the pieces before they started sniping at each other, casting doubt over the unusual coalitions they will need to cultivate if they are to stop GOP initiatives from becoming law over the next two years.

Barring any successful recounts, Republicans will have a razor-thin 56-54 majority when the House convenes in January.

"It's certainly fair to say that with a Republican majority, we will begin to see the tax cuts and moral authority which are long overdue," said Rep. Chip Richmond (R-Farmington Hills), who is expected to become the new House speaker. "And we'll get to that in short order."

To better prepare his untested staff for the rigors of majority standing, Mr. Richmond formally announced several new hires today, including former Macomb County President and failed GOP attorney general candidate Carmine Rossi, whom Mr. Richmond befriended in the liquor distribution business some years ago.

Mr. Rossi lost Tuesday's attorney general election to Democrat Leslie Thompson by a whopping 400,000 votes. Ms. Thompson is considered the Michigan Democratic party's rising star.

Pepper juggles a tan and white leather purse over her lap as she sits in Larry Sweeny's office, listening to him ramble on about team strategy in the Democratic workplace. Only, she isn't exactly listening, having absorbed just enough of the day's dissertation to assure herself that yes, indeed, the old boy is stuttering it up again. She pays scant attention to Larry's actual words as the syllables, the constant skipping and re-mixing of repeated sounds, resonate like a retarded medley of broken lyrics.

This would be the last time.

Her given name is Madalaine Robinson, but she has long made a point of having people call her *Pepper*. The name *Pepper* sounded bitchen-ass-cool, like it was the moniker of a movie star or, better yet, one of the Go-Gos. Other than Stuttering Larry, nobody called Pepper "Madalaine." Not even her dead-beat ex-fiance Josh Brisco.

Josh. What a fuck-up.

Pepper supposes that her parents would also call her Madalaine, were they ever to speak, but there wasn't much reason for that to happen. Daddy, when he wasn't driving drunk in his big red Dooley, was busy inventing new and improved methods of torturing animals on the Lowell farm. One day, he drove a rusted nail through a barn cat's ear just to see how long it would take for infection. *"Science,"* he explained. Mother, living on her own in the Detroit suburb of Novi, spent most of her free time hording mascara and spare change from public fountains. *"It's not against the law,"* she insisted. After the divorce, Pepper was quite content to move away from both of them, to East Lansing, where she finished school and landed a job at the nearby Capitol. Almost immediately, she met Josh at a Democratic fundraiser. They dated for a month and then moved in together. What a disaster!

Larry's stuttering continues, and Pepper finds herself drawn to his spitting syllables like a dog to shit. "I'm *tuh, tuh, talking* about *tuh, tuh,* team *stuh-stuh-stuh,* ah, *stra-tuh-gy,*" he coughs. His hacked orations are like Grandma's Friday afternoon oatmeal-raisin cookies: a life constant that was assured, or in this case, incorrigible. Sure, life's big picture was starting to change, bleeding into a mad, twisted burlesque; but no matter what, some of the little things never seemed to fade. Take those cookies for example: even with her Alzheimer's, Grandma continued to churn out quality product with Pareto efficiency, a feat that factored considerably into Mother's selfish family care plan. *"See what I mean?"* Mother asked Pepper last time they met, crumbs falling from her artificially inflated lips. *"Grandma makes these fuckin cookies as good as ever."* This dialogue, to be sure, was as predictable and reliable as the cookies themselves. *"She's as good as ever, maybe even a little bit better than before,"* Mother would continue. A dramatic pause would ensue, followed by her pragmatic, victorious exclamation, *"Rest home? Not for Grandma. Rest home, my ass!"* Unlike Mother, who was over-preoccupied with collagen and liposuction procedures, Pepper did not allow herself the option to ignore the bigger picture for the sake of her own material interests (which admittedly were sometimes grand). Fact was, the Friday cookies were great, but Grandma was shitting her pants, rambling through the neighborhood naked, and didn't know salt from pepper, sugar from salt, and Pepper from Sugar Ray Leonard.

Despite Pepper's protests, Mother was legal custodian; and because the cookies were tasty, Grandma stayed at home in Novi.

Sweat gathers on Larry's brow as the stuttering subsides and he manages to organize words, albeit with the precision of a butcher hacking at a slab of meat with a spoon. "This here Democratic Puh-puh-puh-p-policy Staff, is a staff business founded on the conceptualism of team strategy in a Democratic family business. Thusly, such conceptualism can not be tolerating of your consistent tardiness," he says in a lispy rap, fluorescent office lights reflecting off his pasty, bald scalp like laser strobes.

"I guess disco really is making a comeback," Pepper mutters with a chuckle.

"What?" asks Larry, adjusting a loud paisley tie to the center of his large, olive-stained shirt collar.

"Nothing," Pepper says. She is sick and tired of these foolish lectures. Tardiness. Attitude. Enthusiasm. Work ethic. Larry had a lecture for every office malady. Today, it was tardiness. "P-p-p-puh-punctuality is of the essence," Larry spat, his big lips shaking like pink Jell-o. "Es-s-s-s-specially when you are p—p-p-p-p-p-picking up lunch for Ms. McCloud Clapton King-Hyde."

Ms. McCloud Clapton King-Hyde: that fucking cunt. How Larry coughed out her name without choking on it Pepper would never know. And the way he said it. It was always *Ms. McCloud Clapton King-Hyde*. Not *Chinita*, not *Ms. King* or *Ms. Hyde*. Not even *Ms. King-Hyde*. It was always *Ms. McCloud Clapton King-Hyde*. Always in full.

Pepper had a different name for her: *Super-cunt*.

Jenny referred to her as *Syble the Sun Queen*. On days of clear sky, she would hover in the fifth story window of Morris Hyde's old Roosevelt office, a white mask pulled over her face as she sunned her floppy black breasts in the open air.

"Doesn't she realize that people can see her from down here?" Pepper would ask.

"She doesn't care," Jenny answered. *"She's probably showing off, hoping someone will come up there and suckle her."*

"I'd rather jump out that window and hang myself."

Day after day, Larry would send Pepper out to buy lunch for *Ms. McCloud Clapton King-Hyde*. It seemed like an easy enough task, but each day, Pepper was confronted with a new problem.

"This sandwich is too small," Super-cunt would quip. *"This soda is too big. I ordered a Coke Classic. This is diet."* It was always something. *"Take it back,"* she would

eventually command, her back to Pepper, facing the sunning window in Morris Hyde's large leather chair. Pepper could only see the top of her volcanic black hair. Hell, she might have been topless facing that window.

After two weeks straight of botched orders, Chinita enacted a clause demanding timely, accurate delivery. *"You screw it, you buy it,"* she laughed. It was a cruel thing to do. Pepper, already of modest salary, had just taken a $3,000 pay cut as legislators accepted a $20,000 increase. *"Clerical workers were overemployed and overpaid,"* explained Speaker Morris Hyde. *"Besides, we needed to make cuts somewhere if we wanted to balance the House budget."*

One day last year, Arby's was particularly slow. To complicate matters, Chinita demanded a special order: *"Chicken fillet value meal with a Coke Classic—no mayonnaise on the sandwich, which should be topped off with one slice of ham and half a slice of yellow cheese— warm but not melted, mind you."* By the time the fast-food zombies filled the order, Pepper had only ten minutes to get back to the office. Pressing the accelerator to the floor, she sliced through traffic, sped under closing railroad arms to beat a train, and cut off an old man for a coveted meter space in front of the Roosevelt.

"These are regular fries," hissed the Sun Queen. *"I wanted curly fries."*

Pepper had to make a return trip and pay for the lunch. Worse yet, a sick child in Arby's lobby puked over its teenage mother's shoulder and onto Pepper's shoes, necessitating a quick return home and subsequent wardrobe change.

And then, making a bad situation worse, Larry tore into her about tardiness!

"Yeah, the tardiness of pleasing the Queen!" Pepper snapped.

"Of course, your tardiness means that you will have no break this afternoon," he snapped back.

Pepper's jaw dropped, pulling apart her Rolling Stone lips. She had no respect for Larry, the bald-headed nephew of a UAW boss who never went to college because of his unique, inbred ability to rig an assembly line. Despite having little education, Larry directed policy matters affecting millions of people. He also had the final say on hiring staff, at least after the job-seeking brethren of legislators and big time donors were accommodated. His hires, more often than not, were girls whose tits and torsos were more impressive than their resumes. Known as *Sweeny Girls*, these sorority-pedigreed recruits emerged as the Dallas Cowboy Cheerleaders of the House, hired with glee as the resumes of Michigan's best and brightest applicants were tossed into the recycling heap with a shrug.

Learning the reality of the situation from Jenny, Pepper felt strongly that she was eminently well qualified for such a position.

During the first interview, Pepper used her natural sexuality to enforce a suffocating effect on Larry. The poor boy, sticking to a list of prepared questions, asked Pepper, *"So, Ms. Robinson, what do you know about utility deregulation policy?"* Pepper sighed, licked her teeth and said quite simply, *"Well, you see, when I was in high school, I was a cheerleader and playing on the girls' soccer team. Because of that, I missed government class a lot. Same thing in college, since I was captain of the Alpha Phi volleyball team. So actually, I don't know or have much interest in government or—what was it—regulation?"*

Larry smiled warmly. *"Chuh, chuh, chuh, ch-cheerleader, eh?"* he asked with raised eyebrows. *"And captain of the volleyball team? Those ssss-suh, sss-seem to be positions that require just the sort of leadership we look for here on Democratic staff."*

Pepper was hired on the spot, and the hundreds of resumes from people with Juris Doctorates and Masters of Public Administration were dropped in the shredder.

Only two days passed before Pepper managed to wrestle a foothold in the office politics, recommending her best friend Jenny for a new vacancy. Shortly after, Jenny was called in for an interview. For good luck, they both wore the bluebonnet rings that they had purchased with two hundred dollars gained from a bank teller error. Jenny was hired immediately and soon proved to be a more prolific worker than Pepper, later parlaying her skills and experience into a better-paying position with the GOP.

For Pepper, legislative session was a breeze. She prepared memos and attended committee meetings, sometimes taking notes. The campaign season was another story, however: she hated it.

When Larry and Slade first began the process of recruiting Josh Brisco to run for office, she fell head-over-heals for him, but that was the beginning of the end.

Larry continues bitching, and Pepper's thoughts return to the present-day big picture. This place, *Democratic Policy Staff*, is, in fact, nothing more than a family-owned-and-operated zoo. If the old union boss, Larry's hapless, wheezing uncle, really wanted to keep his nephew busy, he should have torn away all the office partitions long ago, and replaced them with monkey bars for good measure. The building they worked in, *The Roosevelt Building,* was an old and decrepit structure. *"They named Teddy after the building, that's how goddamn old it is,"* Slade would say. An old hotel converted into an office building in 1961, the Roosevelt was convenient in that it was just across the street from the Capitol. Yet, it was potentially hazardous, having been condemned twice since 1986, and was no stranger to varmints, cracks, concave floors, and handicap barriers. At the very least, boss man Uncle Sweeny could come in and clean up the joint, maybe have an exterminator spray for the rats—which were all over the place, bolting through the vents and across the cracked ceiling tiles, from which they would occasionally fall (once, Pepper found one dead and bloated in the women's toilet). Instead, the old kook had relinquished all controlling power to Larry, and the ten-year result was a twelve-seat Democratic majority reduced to what would be a two-seat deficit in January. Larry, along with the soon-to-be defunct Speaker Morris

Hyde, had been big on tax hikes and government spending in an era when tax cuts and downsizing were all the rage with voters. Ignorant with policy, Larry directed his energies toward employee participation and attendance, which, he boasted, were at all-time highs. The big picture demanded a sharp focus, yet the politics of nepotism allowed Larry the luxury of blurring his energies on the smaller pieces of pie, denouncing tax cuts as a passing "fad" and proclaiming higher spending as the "*chuh, chuh,* choice of a more selective audience."

In a foray of varied barnyard animal sounds, Larry clears his throat and startles Pepper back into attention. "There's more than just your tardiness." Dramatic pause. "You know, your pixie gift to Meryle was a bit less than imaginative."

"What?" Pepper asks, her face blushing. For the first time in two years, Larry's words strike her blindside: was he completely mad? "Let me get this right," she asks. "You're browbeating me over a Secret Santa gift?"

Larry leans back in his chair, folding his legs over a large oak desk. "It all adds up to the team strategy quotient of subtraction. It all multiplies together."

Pepper's nails dig into her purse so hard that it almost bursts. "That's it. I can't take this anymore."

"Aw, come on. What do you mean you can't take it anymore? You just need to *sssss-suh,* see things from our point of view, that's all."

"No. That's not all. I mean, yeah, that is all, that's it. I'm out of here. I quit. That's final. That's it, the end. I've fucking had it here. I didn't need Josh's shit, and I don't need YOUR shit."

"Josh?"

"My ex: you know who the fuck he is. You're both fucking morons."

Larry's jaw drops, and his eyes blink involuntarily. He is truly sad, as if, for the first time, he is presented with a brief flash of realization:

Pepper is unhappy here, I'm not the greatest boss to work for, and this isn't a model workplace.

It's all part of a long-lingering perception that women view him as a buffoon, a hard lot to swallow. "Tell me you're kidding," he begs in one last attempt at denial. "Please tell me that you're kidding. You just can't walk out of here like that. You have responsibilities."

Pepper does a double-take; something in Larry's reaction strikes a disconcerting chord within her. The sympathy within his tone is troubling in its allusion toward some kind of bond, a friendship, and a shadow of emotion darkens Pepper's mind. Her head shakes briefly before her defenses summon the ability to remove her from the situation. "Go fuck yourself," she snaps in a sudden, dramatic appeal toward finality. "Tell your washed-up uncle to do the same."

Larry swallows hard and his whole body goes limp. "Oh," he mutters, his gaze falling to the floor.

Had he giggled? Pepper thinks she might have heard him giggle, but she isn't sure.

Denying her emptiness, she skips out of his office with the flair of a newly elected congresswoman. The bouncing of her blonde locks, the twitching of her lips, the swinging of the white and tan purse over her shoulder all produce an independent, momentary euphoria as she steps into a cavernous, vacant elevator. As the Marshall Fields purse bounds upward from her hips, however, Pepper is reminded of her $2,000 credit card obligation. Her keys jingle, reminding her that rent is due in two weeks, car payment in three. A wave of panic engulfs her, effectively flushing away any illusions of long lasting vacations. The reality of lost finances hits her hard—until she slips out of the elevator and into the building lobby, where she is confronted with an incredible sign:

HELP WANTED NOW! APPLY TODAY: GOP RESEARCH STAFF IMMEDIATELY HIRING! CARMINE ROSSI, THE MAN WHO UNDERSTANDS, THE MAN WHO GREETS CONFLICT

WITH A SMILE! COME WORK FOR CARMINE ROSSI, CHIEF OF STAFF FOR SPEAKER-ELECT CHIP RICHMOND. WORKING HERE MIGHT NOT BE FUN, BUT DOING IT WITH CARMINE ROSSI WILL MAKE YOU LOTS OF MONEY!

Pepper never considered herself a turncoat, but now she couldn't care less. What the fuck? Why not switch sides and go work for the Republicans? Jenny was already over there and would certainly put in a good word for her best Alpha Phi sister. It would be a reunion! Besides, the help wanted sign was just about the most honest declaration Pepper had seen since working at the Capitol. And the chance to make more money? That would be golden. And the chance to fuck over Josh, Slade, and Larry? That would be priceless.

Without further debate, Pepper skips down the block to the Olds Building lobby, where she follows a series of yellow arrows leading around a corner to the offices of Carmine Rossi. The progression of events seems natural, and Pepper is at ease with her fate. She is startled, however, by a white-tailed, three-legged rat that burrows down the hallway at her like a crazed shopper. The tiny hairs on her arms prickle, but before she can scream, a thin, greasy man with a waxed mustache scampers after the rat with a large net, astonishing her into silence. The man, dressed in a large fitting plaid suit and bowtie, hustles past her and through the lobby, twisting hurriedly through the revolving door and disappearing after the rat into the late morning sunlight.

Pepper steps into the Rossi office suite and is greeted by a peroxide blonde perched behind a large desk in a wheeled purple fluff chair. She stares at Pepper with one mascara splattered eye, the other side of her face completely concealed by long blond locks which hang down like drapes over her beaked nose and chin. "Hey, Jen," Pepper blurts, her lips spreading into a huge smile. "I'm here for the job!"

Jenny flips her hair. "Oh my God," she shrieks. "That is so off the hook!"

This was bound to work: she'd never have to work for Larry Sweeny or Chinita McCloud Clapton King-Hyde-Sun-Queen-Black-Tits again.

Frustrated by the lack of fluids in her passion-laden marriage, Chinita McCloud Clapton King-Hyde is proud to have wrapped herself in her latest conquest, the office of Democratic leader. Not for herself, but for her wonderful son Kalumba. Fretting for hours on a flowered couch in the King-Hyde Observatory, she's wearing a flowing black dress with a spider broach (Sonny Boy Kalumba's favorite) hanging down her milk chocolate neck. Her mind, sparkling with clarity, explodes with brilliant thoughts as she jots words onto a yellow legal pad. "In a world of changing social, cultural, political, and business climates," she says while scribbling, "a true gentleman of the people is indeed hard to find." Chinita pauses, rubs her chin. "How does that sound, dammit?" She searches her mind for the next line, imagining her son standing at a podium in front of a large group of reputable people. "In the urban community," she continues, "such a gentleman is looked upon to provide the guidance essential to successful civic and capitalistic adventure. This person should be selfless, confident, and without reservation." She pauses, unsatisfied with her choice of words, since a person claiming ownership to all three aforementioned qualities only existed in children's tales and amongst the mad whispers of Sunday worshipers.

Chinita's mind hiccups, and every five minutes or so, an imaginary, bushy-tailed varmint runs past her heels, prompting her to look into the distance, trying to figure out where it had gone. Her taxed mind sputters; rustling sounds dance through her ears. She wanders out the kitchen door and checks the squirrel trap.

Empty.

Larry Sweeny, unlike Chinita, is small, frumpy, and slovenly. Thick, round, wired spectacles barely shadow the rings under his eyes, and do little to hide the many wrinkles spilling out from under, like the sprawling roots of an undying weed.

Larry's head is swollen from his morning squabble with Pepper. His nose is bright red as he enters the observatory; he prays that Chinita doesn't notice. Last time, upon learning of Jenny's departure, Chinita had collapsed into a fit of rage, threatening to chop off the young secretary's hands and string her up over the bathtub by her feet until she bled to death. *"I've always wanted to kill a little vixen,"* she screamed from her fetal position on the hardwood floor. *"And bleed her to death in my tub."*

Larry maintains calm, picking up the conversation right where they had left it in the office a day earlier. "What should we do about Sonny Boy's leadership numbers?" he asks. "Outside of Wayne County, all the Dems think he's a jackass."

Right away, he regrets his choice of words.

A flash of red lightening jolts through the center of Chinita's head and it feels like her eye balls are being pulled inward. A sharp cord cuts through her ears, producing visions of cherry, swirling pools that flash in her brain. She holds her breath for a moment. Closing her eyes in a tight squint, her nerves simmer, and her thoughts return to Sonny Boy. He lacked confidence, held too many reservations, and was not the least bit selfless. Did it matter? Despite his weaknesses, Sonny Boy would be Democratic leader. There would be power. There would be patronage jobs. The family would be pleased. More importantly, the leadership office would serve as Sonny Boy's springboard to the Mayor's office—that's when the real treasures would be reaped.

Chinita smiles. Overall, she is proud of her Kalumba. Even though he is fat, even though he is weak, he looks just like Mom, with his football lineman's build. Sure, his past transgressions had been embarrassing, but now that he is on the right political track, Chinita is more proud than embarrassed.

Chinita is pensive. Something Larry said had angered her, but she can't remember the exact words.

Then it comes to her.

She scribbles something on a sheet of tiny square paper and hands it to Larry. *Call my son a jackass again and I will kill you*, it says.

"My apologies," Larry says, unfazed.

"Write it down," she says.

He does.

"Written apology. Sign it."

He does.

Chinita snatches the paper and quickly swallows it before changing the subject. "Perhaps we should send Sonny to a speech coach," she says. "Both his public speaking and his grammar could use some work."

"What he should do is a giant fundraiser," says Larry. "It could be a magnanimous spectacle—one that would put him on the map as a power player in the party. Do it right away. That would squash most of the rumors and certainly flatten the playing field, give Slade Pickens something to think about."

Chinita lights a cigarette, thinking about Slade Pickens, the ridiculous Jew who was always portraying himself on a mountain top, above the purple clouds, waiting for God to speak to him and answer the eternal political question (*Can I win? Can I win? Can I win?*). She inhales slowly, loud clicks of her stiletto heals against tile echoing about the foyer, reflecting off the cold, curving walls and the twisted wood carvings of gargoyles, trolls, and demons that are affixed to their centers. Each creature appears ubiquitously wooden, fixed into the architecture of the house as if its removal might render it unrecognizable. Chinita's favorite work, a hideous pair of bat-people melted together in a compromising position, sits at the edge of a long and triangular ceiling, an elegant navy blue state flag draped from their adjoined lips. "Pickens is starting to slip," Chinita says. "And no god is going to hold him when he falls."

Chinita is suddenly anxious, waving her arms in discord, muscles pinching under her flesh. "He will never be leader!" she howls. "Slade Pickens will never be leader!" She slides back into the partial shadows created by the early evening calm, bending her large, nylon-skinned legs. Her voice hushes to whisper. "Slade Pickens is expired goods," she says. "Is there anyone else we need to worry about?"

"What about Tonto Rodriguez?" Larry asks, referring to the Latino community activist/slum lord.

"Small potatoes." Chinita taps the drag of her long filter before reinserting it between hungry lips. "He's not leadership material. Too fucking poor and too many drugs. A typical Spanish comedy, that idiot."

"*Mexican.*" Larry shakes his head. "He's Mexican. And he's clean now, having found Jesus."

Chinita is puzzled. "Where'd he find Him?" she asks. "I mean, what happened to the drugs? It seemed like such a fun, innocent addiction."

"He's disavowed them."

"Well, that's a lie. I'm certain of it—because, at that age, coming from *that* neighborhood, if you're not doing drugs, then there's absolutely no reason to be involved in politics and/or Jesus Christ. Drugs, I can handle. The Jesus crap is another story. I have enough to deal with from the Westside Hollanders and their goddamn Christian addictions. Now you're telling me that the Spanish are going that route? Let me tell you, if that goddamn Spaniard doesn't come clean and admit that he's still doing a ton of drugs, I'll be forced to take action."

"What are you talking about?"

"I'll plant drugs on his family of goblins and call the police. Then I'll denounce him in public, ridicule him as a disgrace to Christianity."

"Is there such a thing?"

"Of course not!"

Larry scratches his chin. "I wouldn't waste your time on Tonto," he says. "I think that Slade Pickens presents a much more formidable obstacle, actually."

"Yes, Larry, so much for the competition." Chinita clicks her elongated, raspberry fingernails. Reaching under her black leather boot, she plucks a small tuft of squirrel remains from her heal and tosses it in the wastepaper basket. "Slade Pickens is the competition. We have to watch out for him. And we really need to concern ourselves with Sonny Boy and his *discipline*."

Larry nods. "He hasn't been very attentive to our mentoring program of late," he says, tempted to specifically complain about Kalumba's philandering. He thinks better of it, however. "I wish you were vying for Dem leader," he says instead.

"Oh, dear Larry!" Chinita howls.

"It's true, you should!"

"What would Morris think?"

"Who cares? You've got the looks that kill!"

Chinita's frustrations with Morris are longer and more pointed than her fingernails. Even in the beginning of their marriage, sex with Morris was watery, cumbersome. And contrary to rumor, Chinita never had been receptive to the idea of being fucked in the ass. Almost immediately, maybe a week into the marriage, it was clear to both Morris and Chinita that the rare, brief bursts of sexual pleasure shared between them were not worth the torturous lengths of prerequisite physical intimacy. In a cathartic admission, they acknowledged this openly to each other, rather than leaving it to hang over their marriage in unspoken silence like so many other pathetic, celibate, cheating couples. Morris, his libido emancipated, immediately took to his long-suffering dream of fucking young white girls. Chinita, for her part, found sexual solace in flags, spiked-heels, magazines, prescription drugs, and in *Stomping*—the alterna-college dance craze involving the rhythmic crushing of small, furry prey. As Morris became preoccupied with his trailer trash chicks from the Macomb County breeding grounds, Chinita cavorted with her animals, dancing over them like Ginger Rogers twirling a pirouette. Still, Chinita yearns to graduate to larger and more complicated subjects.

Their sex lives quickly molded into a series of richly cathartic experiences, albeit isolated from one another.

Such was marriage. As the Speaker's wife, it was Chinita's challenge to distract the public from these hidden realities while bombarding them with the abstract and symbolic: an artful, if fraudulent, task once reserved for the countless number of religious leaders, *"So-called Negro preachers,"* as Chinita called them.

Equipped with the resources of the new King-Hyde Mansion, Chinita greeted her responsibility with arms open wide. After all, she is Detroit's First Lady, the rough rider of urban excellence, a true woman of substance in the vein of Carol Mosely-Braun, Elizabeth Bathory, and Diana Ross.

"Who cares about Morris? Fuck him," she says. "He's already served his purpose. I could bludgeon him to death with that fire poker, skin the old bastard, and no one would care!"

"You could even bathe in his blood," Larry says.

Chinita cocks her head back in delight. Her face is almost thin in its partial shadow. "How insipid, Larry," she says, visualizing herself floating naked in a tub of warm, bubbly fluid. "How mother-fucking insipid! I would never bathe in the blood of swine!"

Larry laughs, too, pleased with his skill at managing the conversation. *What fun!* he thinks.

For a second, he's so impressed with himself that he almost forgets the details of his covert deal with Carmine Rossi and the Mexican kids.

Alas, the fun is only just beginning.

Kalumba "Sonny Boy" King waves impatiently as blond, sexy Nick sheepishly tiptoes from the locker area over the coarse brick floor in front of the hot tub. "Get a move on, sweet thang," King yelps, cocaine horses rushing through his blood at a million miles an hour as shocked, blonde highlights dance over the tips of his black curls. The other boy-toys, Keith and Derek, share a line, splashing about the tub buoyantly, their firm, naked bodies glistening with deep blue water as they kiss and giggle, sucking and twisting each other's perfectly ripe nipples under a cloud of rising steam.

Nick shoots King a look so insolate that it almost blows the fat bastard out of the water. "Get a move on? I'm fucking cold!" he rasps. "It's about fifty degrees in here, and I'm standing around in my fucking underwear. This is unprofessional."

"I paid for that underwear, Mr. Copacek," King mutters in his best Ronald Reagan imitation, pausing for another quick snort of powder. "What do you propose to do about that?" His voice, high and loud, cracks in and out like the static frequency of a broken radio. Oh, how Sonny Boy loves his boy orgies! Sure, the boys commanded a pretty penny, but his family had a lot of money, and besides, this was the only thing that kept his mind off of the damned leadership race.

Kalumba feels that his entire future is in the balance—and out of his control. Yes, out of his control, but certainly not *out of control.* Far from it, considering Mother's iron fist micromanagement. She had been calling the shots for some time, casting a tight reign over his each and every move. From the beginning, she was simply manic about the leadership race, leaving Kalumba little wiggling room. Now that the she has Slade Pickens in her sights, there is absolutely no way out—Kalumba is stuck in this fiasco for good.

A friendly child sent to greater Detroit's finest private schools, King is well educated and affable. Yet, is he is also lazy and sheltered, two traits cultivated by years of pampered existence. At the age of twelve, Kalumba fainted while mowing the lawn. Seeing how Mother wasted no time in hiring neighborhood boys to take on the responsibility permanently, Kalumba feigned dizziness whenever chore duty called, whether it involved washing dishes or campaigning door-to-door. For the rest of his life, if there was work to do, Mother simply paid someone else to do it. Remarkably, he won his first House campaign without ever setting foot outside of the King-Hyde family basement. Quite simply, Mother bought him the election with an abundance of billboards, commercials, and professional campaign staffers.

Yet, all of Mother's protectionism couldn't shelter Kalumba from his obesity and homosexuality, two traits that left him open to ridicule as a child and politically vulnerable as an adult. As a state legislator, he is able to keep himself relatively camouflaged, decorating himself in oversized, tailored suits and limiting his sexual liaisons to private frolics with hired whores. Thankfully, the position is innocuous enough to keep Kalumba out of the spotlight. He only makes the trip to Lansing when he feels like it, and for the most part no one notices. It was all under the radar screen: for a while, he was even able to frequent gay bars without any fear of being recognized.

But the leadership race had changed everything. *"I can't buy this one for you,"* Chinita explained, forcing Kalumba to appear at fundraisers, attend floor votes, and even campaign door-to-door. *"So get your fat ass out of bed and start earning your keep."*

"Ah, Ma," he'd whine, raising his hands in protest. *"Can't you just give it a rest?"*

"Don't you sass me," she growled, pulling him up from the bed by an ear. *"You're going to take all the right*

steps to be mayor, and that's that. You certainly don't want to disappoint your mother, do you?" Indeed, Kalumba doesn't want to disappoint Chinita. Furthermore, he does want to be mayor of Detroit, and he understands that, by itself, the position of state rep won't serve as a reliable springboard to that office. Rather, in order to galvanize his aspirations, King desperately needs to win the leadership race. And sadly enough, that meant work.

King looks past Nick and sighs. "Oh, I suppose I could turn up the heat in this room, but I do like the way the cool air makes for a steamy setting." He laughs, his throat hoarse and dry. "Don't worry, though. I've decided to let you come into the water." King pauses for a moment, squeezing his eyelid to help calm the twitching. "You pretty boys are so darling. *'I'm cold.'* That's so precious!"

"Did you mean *come* in the water, or do you want me to *cum* in the water like last time?" Nick asks, cupping his crotch.

King can't help but giggle. He really does love these boys. They're cute, they're smart, and with a stretch of his imagination, he sometimes believes that they like him. Maybe someday they would even like him enough to hang out at the mansion free-of-charge, simply because they enjoyed his friendship and company. "Certainly, you can *come* in the water—join us in the tub, that is. After you do me a couple quick favors. First off, fetch me one of my frosty mugs from the freezer, will you? Yes, that's the one! And that bottle, bring it here." Nick brings King the ice-flaked mug, along with a cold bottle of malt liquor. King rubs the bottle on Keith's nipples before popping the top and pouring it into his glass. "Ah, that's the sweet, sweet stuff," he says, inhaling the beverage in on breath.

"Can I get in now?" asks Nick, his teeth chattering.

"Come on now," moans King. "Does a fireman complain about the weather? I don't think so. Does a policeman refuse to walk his beat when it's cold? No. And what about a football player, for that matter? Did Walter Payton ever refuse to suit up because of the temperature? I mean, not that you pretty little things would know anything about sports, but the fucking analogies are endless."

"I played soccer in high school," Nick says.

"Soccer," laughs King. "Good God!"

Derek and Keith giggle and squirm as King reaches under the water and lets his coarse hands roam between their naked legs.

Nick slides his hand coyly over the small trail of hair leading down from his tight belly button and tucks it under the elastic waistband of his white jockey briefs. "Maybe I could get in the tub and fuck around with the other boys?" he asks, gripping a pulsing erection.

"All of the sudden you're a director now," King grumbles, his face dropping into a frown.

"What do you mean?" asks Nick, his voice growing louder with impatience. King smiles at the way the young man's nipples are starting to perk in the chill.

"*What do you mean?*" King mimics. "How about I shove a twelve inch electric dildo up your ass?" King pauses, his brow raised. Nick shrugs his shoulders. "You wanna get paid or what?" King asks him.

Nick bites his lip in genuine frustration. He is accustomed to putting out for money, letting wrinkled, forlorn men see, touch and suck his naked body for a couple hours a week. Yet, he had always been quick to insist on limits of venue and activity, as not to lose ownership of the situation. For the past couple of weeks, Kalumba King's fetishes had been growing more and more bizarre, pushing Nick to his limit. Yet, because of the money involved with this particular client, Nick makes himself numb to it; as bad as it may be, it sure beats working a real job. "I want to get paid," he says, searching for words that please. "Really, I'll do *whatever*, just let me get into the fucking water! Please, I'm freezing."

Keith moans as King forces one of his stubby fingers up into his anus.

"I really am freezing," Nick shivers, eying the warm, rising steam with envy.

"Good," says King, his forehead mountainous in the blue light. "Then piss your pants."

"What?" The boy is incredulous, and a little bit afraid that the other boys had ratted him out for last week's incident, when he pissed in King's half-full frosty beer, then held his giggles when King returned from the bathroom to drink it.

"I said piss your pants. That's a quick warm-up." Derek and Keith both laugh; King now had each boy perched on a hand and was fingering them like little ass-puppets.

Nick closes his eyes with a dour expression, his bottom lip swallowing the top of his mouth. "Oh, that's it!" King shouts as Nick lets go of his bladder. "That's the sweet, sweet stuff!" A wet yolk forms at the basket of Nick's briefs, expanding rapidly through the cotton as some of the urine spills down the inside of his thigh. Soaked with yellow piss, Nick's underwear grows transparent over his tightly packaged genitals. "Oh, Jesus God Christ!" shouts King. "That *is* the sweet, sweet stuff! Get in the tub, boy!"

Wearing a slight smirk on his cherubic face, Nick prances over to the side of the tub, where he stands over the other boys with his chest protruding. Keith and Derek, giggling like school girls, remove Nick's soiled underpants and pull him into the hot tub, penis first.

"SONNY BOY," a voice shrieks over the house intercom.

"I'm busy, MOM!" says King.

"SONNY BOY, Larry needs to talk to you. NOW!"

"Tonight's my night off from politics!"

"DO YOU WANT TO BE LEADER OR WHAT?"

"Ah, shit." King rises from the tub and grabs a fresh towel. The water level drops by half as he steps out. His swimming suit and cotton shirt cling tightly to his generously flowing skin. He lifts his robe from a hook on the wall and flips open several hundred-dollar bills from its pockets. "Business beckons me, boys," he says, sliding into his slippers.

Flip flop flip flop. He walks over to the side of the tub and kisses each boy.

"One more thing before I go." He rips off his wet shirt and collapses on the floor, shaking like a fat fish. Steam rises from the hot tub and over the bare chests of Nick, Derek, and Keith, who stop molesting each other to take notice of their crumpled sugar-daddy wallowing on the floor.

"Boys, you know what to do," says King, his voice soft, distant, and dreamy. Nick is dry, but Keith and Derek oblige.

King squirms in conflicted ecstasy as they release their bladders over him, consumed with delight, fear, humiliation, and loneliness.

Ah, the pleasure.

Oh, the shame.

Josh's stomach is rejecting a Vicodin & Jack Daniel's cocktail when Slade Pickens bolts through the front door. Cesare, tail wagging, dashes over foyer tiles in a circle, barking relentlessly. Josh is sitting at the kitchen table, coughing. A river of orange vomit runs past the salt and pepper shakers and over the table's edge, gathering in a thick, slow drip on the floor.

"Ah, Christ!" Slade yelps, grabbing a paper towel from the counter. "Look at you. You're making yourself sick." He wipes a blob of barf from Josh's boyish lips. "You're living like a swine."

"You're being a bit judgmental, don't you think?" Josh sighs, his eyes squinting like two royal blue half-moons. He is wearing a Motley Crue T-shirt and Levi's, barefoot on the cold wood floor.

"This is sickening. Where's your mother? What's she doing letting you go to pot like this?"

"Leave my mom out of it."

Slade isn't really sure what to say. "Ugh," he groans. "I mean, look at you. You've gotta snap out of this malaise, or whatever the fuck you call it."

"Slade, it's not that easy." There is torment in the young eyes of Josh Brisco.

"Easy? Of course not. It can't be easy living the way you are living. You have to work hard to get yourself this fucked up."

"After a while it just becomes habit." Josh smiles in pain. He has soft blond eyebrows and thick lashes that make his eyes seem even more sunken.

"Jesus, Josh," Slade says. "So you lost an election and you broke up with your girlfriend." Josh gives him an odd glance. "It happens to everyone. Get over it."

"Slade, do you want anything to drink?" Josh asks.

"No, I had two diet Cokes in the car." The air reeks of vomit. Slade grabs more paper towels from the counter. "Here, let's clean this shit up."

Cesare scampers into the kitchen, prancing on the tile floor with his nose twitching in the air. "What the hell do *you* want?" Slade asks.

"He probably smells the puke," Josh explains. "He'll run out of here in a second."

"I don't blame him," Slade says.

Sure enough, the dog growls, whimpers, sneezes, and runs out of the kitchen.

Slade's cell phone rings; he flips it open, answers.

"This is Slade," he says. "What? Okay." He snaps the latch and sticks the phone back in his pocket. "Josh, turn on the TV, Channel 8."

Josh obliges.

Carmine Rossi is in the center of the picture, walking past a group of kids playing on a park swing set.

"Carmine Rossi wants to thank you," a narrator's voice booms. The camera pans past the children to a black choir, three rows deep and clad in white.

"He wants to thank you," sings the chorus.

A close-up of Rossi.

"That's right, I want to thank you," he says.

"He wants to thank you," sings the chorus.

"When this campaign started, I thought I knew Michigan well."

Shot of Rossi walking over a wooden bridge. Chorus humming in the background.

"Now, I know Michigan even better. In many ways, our campaign was revolutionary. But, if I could do it all over again, I'd make togetherness the focus of my campaign and promise not to leave one single citizen behind."

Rossi approaches the camera in crisp strides. He's wearing a sweatshirt with *Jesus Saves* scrolled across the chest. More humming.

"Togetherness: Protestants breaking bread with Catholics, Jews sharing the wealth with their noble Arab neighbors.

"Ooh, together," sings the chorus.

"Togetherness: Hmong immigrants busing tables at Chinese restaurants.

"Ooh, together," sings the chorus.

"Is this a joke?" Josh asks.

Slade says nothing.

"Togetherness: whites accepting, blacks contributing. Mennonites lending rubber wheels to their Amish brothers."

"Ooh, together," sings the chorus.

That's the Michigan I envision, and I promise to make it a reality for all of you as I stay active in our new Republican House majority.

"He wants to thank you."

"Yes, Michigan, thank you."

"He wants to thank you."

Female voice: "Paid for by the Committee to Elect Carmine Rossi Attorney General." Fade to black.

"The FAILED Committee to Elect Carmine Rossi Attorney General!" Slade yells in exasperation. "Did this guy escape from a nuthouse or what?"

"He lost. What's he running commercials for now?"

"Did you hear him? Jews sharing the wealth with their Arab neighbors? Jesus fucking Christ!"

"Why would he run a commercial after the campaign is over?"

"They've got something up their sleeves, those Republicans. I just know it."

"I wish I had that kind of campaign money when I was running."

"Stop second-guessing yourself, for crissakes. It's over. Time to move on. What's your next move?"

"I haven't really given it much thought."

"Haven't given it much thought? What are you gonna do with your life? Stay inside this house and fart it away?"

"I don't know." Josh looks bewildered, as if he has been squirted out of one world and into another.

"You need to go back to work," Slade says.

"I don't know about that." Josh's voice drops into a whisper. "When I decided to run for office, I did it because I knew I could make a difference. And I did it because it was time for me to move on. I don't want to be a cop anymore, Slade. And besides, I'm not very popular with the Grand Rapids police department right now."

"Why aren't you very popular with the Grand Rapids police department?"

Josh pauses before answering. "Well, for one, I'm a loser."

"That's nothing," Slade snaps. "I know lots of cops who are losers."

"I'll never be a detective again, Slade. That opportunity's lost, so where do I go from here? Nowhere, I'm pretty sure. I mean, I'm pretty sure that I can't get anywhere from here. I have no desire to spend my days writing speeding tickets."

Slade bites his lip, something that he often does while improvising an utterance or action that he will likely later regret. "Listen, Josh, I've got the answer," he says in a rare, gentle voice. "I want you to come work on my staff."

Josh's face brightens. "Huh?" he says, caught completely off-guard. His eyes blink as if they are tingling.

"It's simple," Slade explains. "I have two years left in office. Two years and out. This is my last term. You come work for me and I'll groom you as my successor. Then you'll run for my seat next election. Clean slate, second chance."

"How could I do that? I don't live in the 76th."

"You don't have to. Switch your legal address to my house."

Josh scratches his head. "Can you really hire me, though? I mean, Dems lost the majority. You'll have to *cut* staff, not expand it."

Slade smiles. "Let me tell you something," he says.

Josh shakes his head. "No, Slade. I won't take someone else's job. Not after all the hours your staff gave to my campaign. I could never do that to them.

"Let me tell you something," Slade repeats.

"No, Slade—"

"Let me finish!" Slade's adrenaline is flowing, his eyes wide with passion. "We're not firing people, Josh—at least not the people who work hard. The patronage hires? Yes, they're good as gone. Larry Sweeny, for example. Sweeny is a big-time union drip, and worse yet, he was Morris Hyde's old point man during the corrupt years. Now, he's Kalumba King's $65,000 personal adviser, scheming up ways to bump me out of leadership. Consider his ass gone, and it has nothing to do with us having to pare the payroll." Slade wrings his hands together. "Besides, who says we're going into the minority anyway? I wouldn't be just so sure yet."

"What are you talking about?" For the first time in a month, Josh has a pulse.

"You'll see. Do you think I'd just give up like that?" Slade snaps his fingers. "I've got a trump card of sorts, my friend. And I'm gonna play it next week."

"How reliable is this trump card?"

"Very reliable."

"Are you serious?"

"Yes," Slade smiles. "But that's all I can tell you right now. Keep this hush-hush."

"But I have a lot of questions."

"Keep them to yourself.

"Here's what I want you to do: go down to Lansing tomorrow and meet with Willie Medville, deputy director of staff. Medville's part crackpot, but he's one of my guys. Have him give you the tour and explain the ropes, but don't say much. After all this shakes down, I want you to be my policy guy. I'll pay you Sweeny's salary. Do we have a deal?"

Josh laughs for the first time in a long time. "$65,000? Holy shit, yes!" he says, laughing some more. Then his face grows pensive, and his lips harden with concern. "But what if I fuck up? I mean, I'm not sure that I've hit rock bottom yet. Maybe I need to crash and burn before I start over. Otherwise I might not get this shit out of my system. Maybe I have some issues I need to take care of?"

Slade sits at the table, resting his elbows where the puke had been flowing a few minutes earlier. "That question is irrelevant and hypocritical," he says, eye-level with Josh, "because you already accepted the job. Now, what I want to see, more than anything else, is Josh be Josh again, back to your smart-ass self, working out, playing basketball, even reading."

Josh shakes his head, smiles. "Reading? Aren't you asking just a bit much, Slade?"

"So you'll go down there and meet with Medville tomorrow?"

"Okay. What time?"

"Anytime before lunch." Slade was excited to have the kid coming onto staff and wondered why he hadn't thought of it before. "Remember, Josh: in this business, we justify our actions by appearances."

Slade leaves; Josh pours the glass of whiskey into the sink, deciding against numbing himself on the couch again. He likewise dumps Cesare's water bowl, replacing it with a fresh reserve. "G'nite, little monster," he says, retiring downstairs to his bed.

Josh's breathing slows, and with each hefty breath, with each slow, sucking intake of cold air into his lungs, his mind fills with cloudy images that kick into motion and disappear with each exhale. Nightmares from his past: Jizzy LeDoux and Van Anders dancing under a mistletoe; Pepper, Jenny, and all their sorority friends, laughing with long, bent faces and bright red lips; Hector Paiz, driving drunk on the wrong side of Cascade Road; Kurt Schrek, his purple penis thrusting into the swollen vagina of a sixth grader; Helen Voorhees, lighting her twin sister Francesca on fire with a can of gasoline and a book of soggy matches.

The images fade. A shirtless boy, tall and smooth in Carolina blue shorts, bounces a basketball on a smooth wooden floor. His eyebrows are soft and friendly under the drop of thick blond bangs. Josh lunges forward, tries to whisper a question, but the momentum takes him away into a different dream . . .

Josh is in the back seat of Uncle Gerald's Blazer. His younger cousins, Marcus-Paul and Marlo, are kicking and scratching at each other, knocking his can of diet Coke from the arm holder. Milo, twelve, the oldest and fattest of the three, is somehow sleeping through this onslaught of fists and feet, drool sliding down his chin and over the pale, corpulent fingers on which it is perched.

A green Volkswagen Bug passes them to the left and swings itself ahead into their lane.

"Slug Bug!" yells Marlo, eight, punching Marcus-Paul's bony little arm. Marcus-Paul is ten.

"Green!" screams Marcus-Paul, answering Marlo with a hard left to her chest.

"That's not fair," cries Marlo, gripping her flat breast, forcing a cough, holding back tears. "I saw it first. I called it."

"You didn't say the COLOR, dumb-lick," says Marcus-Paul.

"Colors don't count."

"Yes they do. One punch for the Bug, one for the color. You only got one, dumb-ass. Deal with it."

Uncle Gerald, middle-aged and tired, takes his eyes off the road and glares over his shoulder. "Maaaaarcus-PAUL! Watch your language or I'll turn this car around!" he threatens.

"I wouldn't care if you did," Marcus-Paul says, thumbing through a stack of comics.

"We never play Slug Bug with colors," continues Marlo.

"Yes, we do. Always," Marcus-Paul corrects her. "Ask Fatty."

Marlo reaches over Marcus-Paul and Josh to pinch an inch of fat in Milo's leg. Milo stirs, but doesn't wake. "He's always sleeping," shrugs Marlo.

Josh picks up his diet Coke can from the floor as fizz foams out its top, leaving what's left inside flat and tasteless. Worse yet, some of Milo's drool spills on his sleeve.

Uncle Gerald glances at Josh through the rear-view mirror as a ray of sunshine flashes through the window and reflects off his bald head like a disco ball.

"Jesus, Josh," he says. "Can't you be a little more careful? I've got this on a Smart-Lease, for crissakes."

Felicity, Gerald's second wife, looks at Josh from the passenger seat and shakes her head. "No drinks . . . allowed . . . in this car . . . from now on," she says slowly, dramatically, running her crimson fingernails over the sharp crease in her shiny satin pants. Felicity is Uncle Gerald's junior by a hostile twelve years.

"Yeah, no drinks from now on," mimics Marlo, pursing her lips with a giggle. Her little white dress is decked with tiny hearts and little smudges of chocolate from a Snickers bar she stole from the check-out counter at the Jewel-Osco. A matching umbrella, minus the chocolate smudges, rests on the floor at her knees. It surprises Josh that she hasn't attempted to open the umbrella in the car; he figures that she must have forgotten about it.

"NO DRINKS . . . unless I say," continues Felicity.

"Unless Mom says," adds Marlo, waving a tiny finger. Marcus-Paul is reaching over Josh, twirling his pinky finger up Milo's left nostril until Josh slaps his hand away. Milo continues to drool, so badly that the front of his oversized, leopard-patterned silk shirt is dark and wet with saliva. Just looking at him makes Josh uncomfortable, especially since his leg is touching Josh's leg and it's making Josh feel hot and sweaty. Marcus-Paul is crammed into his other thigh. Felicity, perched in the front passenger seat, keeps telling Gerald to turn the air conditioning down. "I'm frigid," she says. Josh has no diet Coke—which really pissing him off since he could really use something to drink as the Vicodin and whiskey are dehydrating his system.

"Mom?"

"Yes Marlo, honey?"

"Do we really have to go see Grampa?"

Felicity looks at Gerald with a pained look. "Yes, honey, I suppose we do," she says as Gerald stares blankly out into the expressway. Josh, startled, attempts to say something, but his voice is but a wisp of choked air.

Marlo, sensing the reluctance in her mother's voice, begins to whine. "Why?" she asks.

"Don't worry, this will be the last time, honey, I promise," says the young mother, who herself had been complaining all morning long about this one-hour trip. "You're not the only one inconvenienced by your grandfather's demands. Momma had to miss a beauty parlor appointment again," she says, throwing a nasty glance at Gerald. "God only knows how many opportunities I missed to work on my connections."

"Wait a second," Josh finally manages. "You mean to tell me that Grandpa is alive?"

"What kind of shit are they feeding your brain over at that Michigan State?" asks Felicity as everyone but Milo laughs. "Of course he's alive, that old—"

"Felicity!" protests Uncle Gerald.

"Don't interrupt me again, Gerald. I'll say what I want."

Marlo begins fiddling with her umbrella, getting it caught between the seat and door. "Grampa's gross," she says.

"And mean," adds Marcus-Paul.

"And mean." mimics Marlo. "Mom, can we say 'shit'?"

"No."

"Fine. I still say Grandpa is MEAN, MEAN, MEAN!"

"How would you know?" Josh asks. "He died before you were even born!"

"I told you, he's still alive," says Felicity. "Even if he wasn't, it doesn't really matter." She points to her children. "They're the trust fund babies, not you."

Josh slips away from the vehicle for a while, back to the time when Gramps offered the explanation about the lawyers. "You've been a son and a grandson to me, Josh, but the money goes directly to my kids to split up, not my grand kids," he says slowly, as if a big lump of coke is lodged somewhere in his sinuses. He didn't have to say any more, for Josh fully understood the hostility between his father and grandfather.

That was the last time Josh saw Gramps, and it was dismal. He could barely talk, his lips white, eyes cracked open, fixed, glassy, a lighter shade of blue, like faded paper. When Mom got the call from Carlos a few days later, Josh expected the worst.

Marcus-Paul and Marlo settle on a comic book featuring overly muscular characters beating and torturing each other with leather straps. There is a topless woman illustrated on page three, and the children are giggling, laughing at this and at a depiction of a severed head chewing on a naked, hacked torso. Josh is looking past them, out the tinted window towards a train running down the center of the highway. The train is spinning by too fast for him to make out any details from a vast sea of gray passengers inside, but he imagines them tumbling, somersaulting up and down the aisles. Outside, at the wait stations, there are people of mixed races lingering, and Josh is thinking about how the city is such a great melting pot and at the same time feels excited about the prospect of Gramps being alive, even though he knows deep inside that it is too good to be true. Yet, it had to be true! Otherwise, how could this be happening? Josh is deep in thought when Marcus-Paul looks up from his book and says, " WOW! Mom, look at all the Nigras out there!"

"I bet they have no teeth!" says Marlo. "Toothless Nigras!"

At this, Milo awakens from his slumber with a quiet hack, adding, "We had one in our class last year. His name was Cadillac Johnson and he smelled like landfill."

"Most Nigras do," explained Marlo.

"You're stupid," says Milo, wiping sleep from his puffy eyelids. "It's not Nigra, it's Negro. NEE-GROW. Got it?"

Felicity is laughing but Uncle Gerald tells the kids that enough is enough, which doesn't stop Milo, who's well-rested and eager to participate in discussion. "He DID smell like landfill. Even ask Ms. Barnhart."

"Ms. Barnhart is a she-pig and has a huge mole on her cheek," says Marcus-Paul. "I'll kill myself with a harpoon if I get her next year. I hate her."

"Be nice, Marcus Paul," Felicity says half-heartedly as she represses as giggle.

"They're very different than us," says Marlo.

"Who's they?" Josh asks angrily. "You mean people?"

"No. Them—the Nigras. They're different."

"Yes, they are," Milo assures Marlo, grabbing her wrist with both hands and twisting.

They arrive at Gramps' estate a half hour late, right behind Aunt Faylene, Uncle Randy and their Red truck with the two "Jesus Saves" stickers affixed to each side of the bumper. Faylene is wearing a flat, thin black dress that looks like an expensive nightgown, and a heavy red blouse with patterns of blue parrots and pink flowers pulled over it. She gallivants up to the van and starts in on Gerald with nervous hysterics before he can even open the door. "What on earth does he want? What does he want from us? Why do we have to come here? I thought he was dead!" She's talking in some bizarre, forced accent that isn't real, and Randy is wearing these blue overalls that make him look somewhat retarded.

"Who knows, maybe he is risen?" Randy slurs. Faylene frowns in strong disapproval. "Well, I just thank the Lord *that we all made it here in one piece," he offers in a poor attempt to placate his wife. Josh senses that Randy has been drinking, an observation that makes him extremely jealous as Randy excuses himself, goes over to the garden, and pisses on the brick side of the house leading to the courtyard. Josh wonders if Randy has a hole cut in the crotch of the overalls since they own no visible zipper. Josh is thinking about how Faylene and Randy never leave tips for waitresses when Randy lets out a huge belch and says, "Man, for all the taxes we send up here from Downstate, you'd think they could fix up them roads a little better, you know." He licks his thumb and runs it over the door of the Blazer. "Thought you were a Ford man, Jerry," he says.*

"Gerald. My name is GERALD," snaps Uncle Gerald, his face long and white. "And I never had a loyalty either way." He pauses, trying to remember something, then says, "And actually, Randy, the Tri-State is a toll road. It pays for itself with user fees, not Downstate taxes."

Faylene bats her eyes at Josh. She has a quick, nervous habit of squinting her eyes whenever she finishes a sentence. "What does the old ghoul want?" She asks. Squint, squint. "What can he possibly want?" Squint, squint. "You must know, Josh." Squint, squint. "After all, you're the only one of us who speaks his language."

"Lingo!" Lingo!" says Marlo. "We call it Lingo, and anyone with half a brain would know that!"

Leo, Gramps' Pomeranian, sticks his head out through a trap door, barking with voracious vigor, then scurries back into the house as soon as he sees the children spring out of the Blazer and run toward him. Marlo has her matching umbrella and is twirling it, pounding it against the grass, slapping it against the side of the house, sticking it in the trap door, hoping to frighten the dog.

"He looks a lot like Cesare," Josh comments.

"Who's that?" asks Milo.

"Nevermind," Josh says, not wanting to explain the generational connection between the two dogs.

"I hope the estate ain't screwed up," Randy mutters. This frightens Felicity; her eyes grow bulbous and moist.

"You mean the trust," says Gerald. "It can't be screwed up. It's a permanent trust. He can't change it."

"I don't care what you call it," says Randy. "I just hope it ain't screwed. My job at the county ain't good for much more than gas and cigarette money."

Carlos, Grandfather's modest assistant, opens the gate and greets everyone at the steps. "Mr. Brisco awaits you upstairs," he says with folded arms.

By the time they make it upstairs, the paintings in the foyer are blinking with impatient eyes and the kids have wandered all over the house, touching and smearing everything in their reach. Chasing after Leo, they break a glass table as he scoots out of their reach.

"I still can't figure out why he wants us here," says Faylene. She is wearing so much mascara that Josh wonders how it doesn't cake and fall off in dry biscuits. "We're family," she says. "We have rights."

"And he's already been on his last rites," jokes Felicity, nervously.

"I HEARD THAT!" Gramps' voice is hoarse and strong, permeating the hallway like a heavy mist as the portraits smile with glee.

"Please, go in," offers Carlos. The adults are tentative, and the children go scampering in ahead of them. "Here, pooch pooch," shrieks Marlo, who stops in her tracks at the sight of her grandfather.

"Dogs are naturally clever," he says, sitting up, erect, his eyes sharp and colored, hair full and dark. "And Leo has a special knack for recognizing impending evil, even when it's masqueraded as a charm school aspirant like yourself, Marlo."

Felicity steps in front of her husband. "In fact," she announces proudly, "Marlo recently graduated from the Baird School first grade. You should have seen the ceremony."

Gramps grins, lights a smoke, takes two long drags off of it. "I didn't realize that first grade graduations were all the rage in today's private school circles. Surely, I would have made an arrangement to attend, were I not so busy being dead."

Felicity is unfazed. "Well, perhaps a congratulatory present, you know, money or something, is in order?" she says.

Gramps smiles with thin, elongated lips, puts out his Marlboro. "Oh Felicity, dear Felicity," he says. "Who could ever say that you sold the family out?"

Felicity's face turns cranberry red. "Surely you care about the education of your grandchildren?" she snaps, her voice cracking.

"Perhaps, yes, at least for the sake of society," Gramps says, turning to Josh with a wink. "But I think it's too late already."

Marcus-Paul grabs his mother's leg, complaining that he wants to go home. "Mommy, this place sucks," he whines. "And look at the spots on the old man's head!"

"I wouldn't be caught dead looking like that," says Marlo, tapping her umbrella up and down the wall. "He must smell like a Nigra."

"I bet his handwriting is horrible," adds Marcus-Paul, peering from behind his mother's round hip.

The pink plastic tip of Marlo's umbrella smacks a hidden switch and the wall starts to move, then opens, revealing a glistening glass cabinet of sodas, fine bottled waters, and trendy fruit drinks. "Mom, I want soft drink!" the three children whine. "PLEASE PLEASE PLEASE!!!"

"Ah, the manners of banshees," bemuses Gramps.

"Father, these are your grandchildren!" Gerald squeaks.

"Yes, as are James and Paul," Gramps points out, referring Uncle Gerald's two sons from the first marriage. "Where are THEY?"

"Uh, with their mother."

"With Edith, I see. Kind Edith. Well, this is a family get-together and those boys should be here too, and I don't care what your current wife says about it."

Felicity's right eye is twitching uncontrollably.

"Felicity would never do anything to hurt those kids," says Gerald.

"No, she'd just drive away with the bodies, that's all," Gramps growls. "Don't dance around the bush with me. I know how you North Shore assholes operate."

Randy, his skin blue as an orangutan's ass, grumbles that he needs to find "the john" and Carlos accommodates him accordingly. Faylene is quiet, still, and her face looks like it's made of tiny pieces of tile that are starting to break and chip at the edges. Gramps lights a joint and starts to suck on it as all the adults freak out. As if in triumph, he lifts it up into the air, holding it loosely between finger and thumb.

"Jesus-God!" cries Gerald. "What the Christ are you doing?"

"Not in front of the innocent children!" begs Felicity.

"Oh, what is he doing? What is he doing?" Faylene asks over and over again. Squint, squint.

"Not in front of the children," Felicity repeats. "Gerald, do something! We have rights!"

Faylene clutches her rosary beads, quietly murmuring to herself.

Randy traipses back into the room, stiff like a mummy. "Randy! How did you enjoy our facility?" Gramps asks. "A step up from throwing one against the house, I imagine, huh?"

"Huh?" Larry is eying the huge wet bar that is sticking out of the wall adjacent to the soda cabinet. Next to it, a cappuccino machine is hissing and chortling on a smooth vanilla counter.

Faylene snaps out of prayer. "Father, what are we here for?" she asks.

"Well it's the day before Easter," Gramps explains. "People from all over town are getting ready to rise from the dead—and this time, they're pissed."

"Father!"

"Well, Pious Faylene, truth is, I've been dead for a while now, and let me be the first to tell you that there ain't no fucking Jesus, and there ain't no fucking god. At least not like you think there is. I hate to burst your bubble and point out all your wasted efforts, but I have to say that He's nothing like your people have Him all chalked up to be. They made that shit up, dummies."

"Blasphemy-ous!" says Randy.

There is a short, quiet pause, and Josh wondering, not as intensely as the rest of them, what else Gramps has up his sleeve. Carlos slips into the room and Gramps announces that he has "shocking news."

"Seriously, I have shocking news," he says. "And here it is: aside from Josh, I hate all of your fucking guts and I want you to return my inheritance."

"Father!" cries Gerald. Felicity is gasping, holding his arm, saying "I knew it, I knew it," over and over. Marcus-Paul is holding her leg.

"Goddamn it all!" says Randy, who turns to Gerald. "You said he can't do nothing about it. Can he?"

"We have rights!" Faylene shouts. "You're not even alive anymore!"

"Besides," adds Felicity, "That money is already spent."

Nobody says anything for what seems like a long time. Josh is calm, maybe even buzzing, astounded by Gramps' energy abound. The pure atmosphere is overwhelming, and never has a modern dead man put on such a performance. The room smells of bottled perfumes and fresh fruits that have replaced the stale, medical scents that had lingered here earlier. Moderate light pushes away the looming shadows as the children eye the soda cabinet. Randy stares at the wet bar. Gerald, Felicity, and Faylene are lust after the cappuccino machine. Josh goes to the soda cabinet and pops the top off a diet Coke. Gramps is reaching over to his nightstand for the phone and Josh can see the blue veins twisting under the skin of his arm. He places a quick call, mutters his address, and hangs up.

"Okay, you're right," he announces. "I can't change my trust since I'm dead and nobody believes anything that the dead say or do unless it was written about in Christian folktales. So be it." He pauses, pulling a small mirror and vial from a cabinet above the bed. "However, since I am dead, I am fairly certain that in the great state of Illinois, I don't need your legal or religious consent to do a little blow with my grandson. This isn't Michigan, after all." He shakes some powder out of the vial and uses a razor blade to cut it into three lines on the mirror, one of which he snorts up with a plastic straw. "All of your lawyers and all of your priests can't fuckin stop me." A thin line of blood trickles out of Gramps' nose and drips off his lips. Before Felicity, or Faylene, or even Randy or Gerald can say anything, Gramps instructs them to grab a beverage of their choice from the far wall. "A final toast before I go back. At the very least, you will indulge me in such a wish, for it's required in the small print of my will. That's really why you are here. Carlos, a Certified Notary Public, is our impartial witness. You must join me for one last toast."

"Notary Republic?" asks Randy. "What, does he think he's his own country or something?"

They choose their pleasures, and Gramps beckons for Josh to stand bedside and do a line of coke with him. "Put that diet drink down and have a real coke and a smile," he says. The others are too busy choosing their drinks to protest. "Carlos, come over here and cut us some better lines, won't you?" Gramps asks. "My hands are weak as rotten leaves."

Carlos skillfully cuts up a couple piles and hands Josh his on a separate mirror. Gramps offers a surprisingly lame toast, and they all drink up while he and Josh opt to snort.

Josh's thoughts are loud and warm, but it's quiet in the room as the relatives all stare at each other when Gramps' eyes glass over, then close. Felicity mutters that she once took some nursing classes and that she thinks Gramps has finally passed—probably for good. But then he starts convulsing, coughing, spitting a mist of blood backwards over his head where it speckles against the wall.

"Grody!" shouts Milo.

"Oh, yeah, that's a total gross-out," agrees Marlo.

"We justify our actions by appearances," Gramps says blankly, coughing up what looks like a fist-size chunk of bleu cheese. Josh's head is spinning, everyone is screaming words in black and red and other colors that don't make any sense and all he wants is to tell them to fuck off as their voices get louder as Grandpa's fades away.

"We justify our actions by appearances." The words spin in circles as Josh wakes up all cold and sweaty, his dry eyes bright red and skin a dehydrated alabaster white.

This place is fucking odd, Nick thinks as he approaches the torn façade of McCoy's. No matter how hard he tries to knock it out of his mind, the specter of the Kalumba King appointment lingers, poisoning his mood. Even after cleaning himself up and changing clothes, Nick still feels dirty. *That sick fat ass.* Nick decides that next time, he'll shake him down for an extra hundred bucks, bringing his fee up to a gaudy $400. If Kalumba balked, it would be sayonara, fat boy. *Find someone else to piss themselves, you sick fuck,* he imagines telling him.

It doesn't take much, however, for Nick to horn himself up for some *real* fucking. Casper, his latest conquest, is cursed with a stupid name, yet blessed with fashion-plate good looks. On top of that, his languid, smooth voice is intoxicating. And those bangs! Wow! Who cares if he was wearing Levis at lunch? The Nike shirt was also a tad bit proletarian, but at least it wasn't white trash Adidas or nigger FUBU. The clothes didn't matter to Nick, since they'd be coming off anyway. Fully expecting an excellent lay, Nick wasted no time in phoning Casper, calling him right after lunch to make plans for tonight.

"Meet me on the Southside at ten," Casper whispered. *"At a place called the 'McCoy's.'"*

Even as Nick walks from the bus stop to the bar, he is consumed with thoughts of orgasm, wondering about Casper's disposition, daydreaming about his naked body. *God, just give me a nice, smooth chest, and a firm, bubble-butt ass to fuck,* he prays. *Not some soft, faggy fairy with a strong personality.*

As Nick enters McCoy's, all his senses seem exaggerated, outrageously acute. Scents of garbage, decay, pot and old gin—they rush his nostrils as if someone is blowing bad breath into them through a straw. An old broad, with the wingspan of a bat, is behind a horseshoe counter that is cluttered with stragglers and bums on tall

80

stools. To Nick, the rustic decor and limited perimeters prove cozy, almost inviting. *McCoy's* isn't an unpleasant place, so to speak, but beneath all the layers of stench, there exists an air of foreboding. He descends a narrow, steel stairway and passes the bar, the smell fades and music from the jukebox strikes him with a twinge of nostalgia; he feels a subtle urge to sit at the bar and have the old bat behind it slide him a gin and tonic. He sees three handsome sailors, blooming with youth and drunkenness, sitting at the corner table, tipping beers as they take turns pinching and slapping the overtly round buttocks of a female companion. The girl, blushed from drink, giggles coyly as she dances around the table, intermittently kissing each boy on the lips. Her movements simulate intercourse; scissoring legs and vibrating hips slide in time with the jukebox song *Copacabana*. This disgusts Nick, all but destroying his prior illusion of wistful yearning.

He turns his attention back to the bar, where a twisted little man is crouched under an antique chandelier of Budweiser Kleidsdales that hangs limp from the ceiling. He's wearing a green knit sweater with JESUS SAVES embroidered across his chest in red and white satin, along with thick, foggy glasses and a neatly waxed moustache that rises from his lip in a single line, curling into the air in front of his ears like a bent pipe cleaner. Fake hair, a shiny black wig, floats on his head like a piece of sod tossed in the ocean. "Well, I don't care how fucking hot it is outside," the Jesus man says to the old bat tending bar. His large, exaggerated enunciations startle Nick. "I *said*, honey," he continues, "that I don't care how fucking hot it is, I will wear *this* sweater any damn time I please." He pauses and looks around as if to allow for acclamation, taking a tiny sip from his martini. "After all, it is my favorite sweater. I wore it on the campaign trail, wore it on TV."

"That's probably why you lost, jackass," yells a voice from across the counter.

"Ah, fuck you. Like I said, the bourgeoisie can *lick* my asshole. I love this sweater. Why, I even wear it in *August*, when the late summer heat just makes it stick to my *clammy* skin!"

The image makes Nick's stomach turn. He looks at his watch: 10:00 p.m. Was Casper a punctual person? He hoped so. Nick is very timely for a homosexual, and he expects the same from his dates.

"Damn it," continues the little man. "I'd even lay out in the hundred degree sun wearing this sweater!"

Nick winces, and an involuntary twitch of his muscles sends his wrist banging off the hollow bar with a bang.

The old bat behind the bar looks up with a pursed grimace, her eyes narrow and wrinkled. Her hair is long and white with a bold streak of black down the middle, pulled back into a ponytail so heinous that strands of hair are floating in the air around her head in static bolts. "Oh, look," she announces to the bar in a loud bark. "It's our friendly neighborhood seal-boy!" Most of McCoy's patrons only offer token glances toward Nick, yet the little man in the Jesus sweater turns around with huge, deep socketed eyes and laughs violently.

"Ahhhh!" he shrieks in a scolding, joyless banter.

"What are you trying to do over there?" the Old Bat asks Nick, much to his bewilderment. "Run me dry?" Her thin lips are serious now, pulled downward in a tight frown. "I gotta pay the rent, ya know." Nick is naked as her eyes run up and down his body, searching for a revelation with which to judge him.

"You should make him pay the bills!" snorts the Jesus Man, as if reciting a great, hilarious punch line. He downs his martini and burps with fishy cheeks, his magnified pupils drawn to the tight curves of Nick's chest.

Nick, exposed in their attention, swallows nervously. "I . . . uh, don't understand." His words are short, uneven, coughed out as if he was struggling to grasp English. "Is there a cover charge?"

"Ahhhhh!" screams the Jesus Man, clapping his fruity hands in approval. "*Is there a cover charge?*" he imitates with pleasure, a horrific mockery.

The Old Bat stands listless, speaking through the contempt of her gaze.

"What do you say to that?" Jesus Man asks Nick, pointing at the Old Bat, laughing like the devil. "What do you—"

He interrupts himself with laughter. "What do . . . what do you say to that?" he finally manages to squeak out.

The laughing is relentless, and Nick is unable to offer an immediate response. Dew stains the seat of his jockeys as sweat drips down the middle of his back and gathers just above the crack in his buttocks. Words gather at a sluggish pace, but he is able to push them out in necessity. "What," he asks, "is the goddamn problem?"

The Old Bat breaks her silence, spitting words with venom. "I'll tell ya what the problem is. I got rent to pay and you come in to listen to the music like a freeloader. Either you keep that box running by putting some coins in it, or I'll just turn it off. Completely. How about them apples?"

"How about *them* apples!" mimics the Jesus Man, standing up from his stool and pointing at Nick. Nick is embarrassed, a little frightened, and burns with hate for having been made to feel this way by these feckless people. Sweat rolls down his back in beads. He considers leaving, then remembers Casper's hot, sexy bangs.

"Well, what about it?" the Old Bat snaps.

"Are you talking about the jukebox?" he blurts, his face blushing pink. "I know nothing about it. I just walked in here."

"Oh, I don't think so," boasts the Old Bat, much to the delight of Jesus Man, who claps his monkey hands in amusement. "You crossed that line. And once you do, you can't escape it."

The outside lights flicker on, and through the narrow twin windows adjacent to the marble vestibule, Nick sees Casper pull open the heavy black door and enter through the dim hallway, swinging the door shut with such a bang that it startles even the sailor boys and their dancing whore.

"Welcome to the Southside," Casper says, swinging over to the jukebox and flicking a switch that makes the seven Kleidsdales spin into a tight dirge above the bar. Nick looks over at the Jesus Man, now slumped in his stool . . . calm, small and pale, as if the yellow light illuminating from the horses has rendered him weak and shrunken. His wrinkled lip is still, and Nick notices how his brittle fake hair is sprayed wet and greasy. McCoy's is very still and no one makes any gesture of greeting Casper, as if the horses have fixed all the patrons into stone. The Old Bat is similarly calm, lighting a new cigarette between her lips with a long match while watching the horses. The instant, however, that Casper's shoes click over the dark tiles in front of the counter, she moves impulsively forward and kisses his cheek, smiling for the first time. Nick feels at ease, as all the tension is sucked out of the place in a vacuum. Casper orders them each a gin and tonic as he shakes Nick's hand. "Nice to meet you, Nick," he says, the feel of his skin clammy cold. "Officially, that is."

"Gin and tonic . . . how did you know?" Nick asks.

"I just had a feeling that gin was your only weakness."

"I don't have any weaknesses."

Casper laughs. Nick does too.

They talk about a few things, and Nick brags about his general resume and credentials—not out of insecurity, but to give Casper an honest assessment of what kind of level he's playing at.

"So, you're in the big leagues, huh?" asks Casper, his lips smooth and full.

"Yeah, and I followed all the right rules to get there. I've earned it."

"The right rules? What do you mean?" Casper asks in a slow whisper. "Doesn't everybody follow the same rules?"

"No. Most people stray . . . they're too weak. I followed a certain path to get to where I am today." Nick looks around. "Much different than these sad souls hanging around here." He nods towards the Jesus Man. "Especially him."

"Ah, I see. Well, he follows rules, too."

"Yeah, but not—"

"Everybody makes up their own rules. There are very few rules that aren't challenged, like the rain falling to the earth, for instance. It isn't too often that you see it falling upward to the sky."

Nick laughs uneasily. "I don't know anything that falls upward," he says, the initial rush of warm gin dancing through his blood. He and Casper both finish their drinks, order another round, and finish that one, too.

"Yeah, see what I mean? Your belief in rules is overrated, limited only to what you know and understand, which isn't as much as you think." Casper's eyes cut into Nick. "Overrated, I say, just like this conversation. Let's just cut to the chase. Your place or mine?"

Nick doesn't hesitate. "I have roommates, so we can't go to mine. Besides, you live right around here, don't you?"

"See that door? Right up those stairs. Fall up the stairs to my place."

Casper's place is coated in cherry light from a neon sign just outside the lone window. The wood floors creak under their feet as Casper pulls Nick through a dark, narrow hallway of fallow walls partially coated with burlap wallpaper to an oblong room naked but for a queen-sized bed and a red lava lamp resting on top of a chintz covered chest.

Their lips lock as Nick's feet traipse over the wood floor to Casper's bed. The sheets are downy, redolent of floral, earthy smells. Casper falls on top of him. They make out, petting with soft, gentle strokes. Casper's lips are strong, commanding. They pull off each other's clothes and tumble around naked amongst the whirl of red lava bubbles that swim across the walls, melting into little demons and fishes and mocking spectators that slip away into the shadows before reappearing for another peak. Casper grabs Nick's cock with his left hand, casually slipping his right index finger behind Nick's balls and into his sweaty asshole. Nick, a proud top, jumps like he's been electrocuted.

"Ouch!" he screams.

Casper moves away, off the bed, his arms wide open, almost mocking. "I'm sorry, did I hurt you?" he asks.

"I'm not a bottom," Nick explains. "I don't like it in *my* ass."

Casper stands above the bed, naked amongst the cherry bubbles. His body is smooth, firm. "I want to make love to you," he says, looking deep into Nick's eyes. Nick is startled, confused by the suddenness, the unpredictability of it all. He struggles to put it in context, but can't. It makes him weak. Vulnerable.

"What did you say?" he asks.

"I said that I want to make love to you."

Nick is dying to get Casper back in bed. "Okay," he says.

"Okay?"

"Okay."

Casper descends on the bed, flips Nick over on his side, and sticks a finger back in his ass. Nick gasps as Casper wriggles in a second finger, but after some prodding, it feels good. Nick moans. "Stick it in," he says. "Give me your dick. I'll bottom for you. I'll do it. I want you inside of me."

"You want my cock?" Nick's hips are grinding.

"Oh yeah!" he sighs. "Do you have a condom?" To Nick's surprise, this actually feels good.

"Yes, I have two." Casper snaps a rubber over his perfectly shaped penis and squirts it with gel before guiding it through Nick's virgin cheeks. Completely inside, he reaches around Nick's hips and squeezes Nick's dick, which is only semi-hard because of the intense throbbing in his ass. "Here let me put this one on you."

Nick is puzzled. "Why do I have do wear one?"

"I don't want you dripping your little lemon drops all over the bedspread while I'm fucking you." These words chip at the cornices of Nick's edifice, for he always considered his own orgasms to be warm and smooth trophy material, not clotted globs of coagulated mess that most guys would shoot.

Casper's gyrations are perfect, and before long, Nick's tract muscles relax and his erection is rock hard as he begins to lose control of his quietness. He moans in heavenly bliss, panting, growling. Finally, he screams with a wicked, primal pleasure and cums hard, filling up the condom from its bubble all the way back up his shaft. He continues to moan after finishing, an unusual experience for someone who prides himself in being a quiet cummer.

Casper peels the condom off Nick's dick, careful not to spill a drop. "Here, I'll take care of that," he says.

"Are you sure?"

"A little semen never hurt anybody." Casper milks the excess dew off Nick's bare cock, licking it off his fingers like peanut butter. His lips seem to glow as he rises from the bed and drops the dirty condom in a ring box near the lamp. Nick feels cold, frigid. His ass is sore and he feels empty. Did Casper cum, too? A wave of apprehension sweeps over Nick and he longs for the comfort of his own bed and doesn't want to stay over. He feels used, discarded. Casper is leaning over him as the cherries speckle and burst into the darkness. Must be the gin, he concludes just before passing out.

Must be the gin.

Josh is wired, unable to sleep. For the first time since the middle stages of the campaign, hope and excitement generate a wild energy inside him. "Your eyes look like they're ready to whirl out of your skull," says Danny Embry, who agrees to let Josh stay at the gym past close without protest. "Just make sure you lock up this time."

Headphones blasting, Josh works his leg, pectoral, arm, and back muscles until they just won't contract anymore. Then he shoots baskets for a few hours, working on his jump shot and post moves. At first, his arms are limp; airball after airball drops in front of the rim and bounces dead over the floor. Josh takes a break, stretches his arms, then legs, imagining the lactic acid draining out of his tissue and into the air in sour vapors. It works: after about twenty minutes, the shots are falling. He moves over the three-point line, jukes, fires.

Swish.

He imagines them coming at him from all directions: little green and black monsters, swiping at the ball, hacking his arms on each shot. One of them is Wayne Van Anders. Josh slides past him, elevates over the free throw line, tosses the ball toward the hoop with a crisp flick of the wrist.

Swish.

Jizzy LeDoux sneaks up from behind, tries to steal the ball. Josh bursts through him, fires.

Swish.

Pepper Robinson blocks the lane.

Swish.

Hector Paiz, Kurt Schrek, Helen Voorhees.

Swish. Swish. Swish.

The boy in Carolina blue shorts: Josh sees him clear as day. *Where is he from?* Palms up, his thick, nearly hairless legs are bent at the knees in a defensive stance as if he's challenging not only Josh's basketball skills, but also his memory. Somewhere between the age of twenty and twenty-five, he has smooth, slightly toned arms that bulge through a Nike tee with cutoff sleeves. He is absolutely gorgeous: the best-looking boy Josh has ever seen.

The boy from the hunting accident at Rod & Rifle, that's who he is!

Josh stutters, stops, and loses control of the ball, which dribbles off his foot and rolls out of bounds.

Much to Pepper's chagrin, Carmine Rossi is the odd little man she had witnessed dashing down the hallway on her way in. Stale dental scents emanate through his long and pale office, which is comprised of adjoining suites. Rossi, withered and frail from apparent exhaustion, nestles himself in a brown leather chair. His eyes, round and wide, are on Pepper with cocked brows and she imagines that he might like to eat her if he had the chance. Liquid, either sweat or snot, drips from his bony nose and moustache onto the oak desk beneath his elbows. His oversized hands, cropped with random spurts of thick black hair, rest together over a brown paper sack.

"I am Politics, the resonance of life," he says, his gaze over Pepper spreading even wider. When she doesn't react, he breaks into laughter, cackling like an old woman. "I run a political house here, sweetie. Politics is all around us. Politics is knocking outside the door." He snaps his fingers to an imaginary beat, singing out of key. "You know, it's true with everyone in every occupation, every walk of life, from the White House to the outhouse: Politics will find away. Politics is my business, and business is good. Life is temporary, honey. Politics lasts forever. This job, these jobs, all these jobs here at the Capitol . . . they are our life. Our death? Term limits."

"That doesn't bother me in the least," Pepper manages, reaching into her purse for a piece of gum. "I know what it's like to work here. I worked on Dem Policy Staff for nearly two years. And my old job was full of corpses, so to speak." She unwraps a long stick and stuffs it over her tongue. Rossi leans back, his lips pursed in amusement. A drop of liquid falls from his nose onto the paper sack with a soft plop.

"You're one of those *clever* girls, I see," he says, his voice dropping. *"Whaddaya hear, whaddaya say, kid?"* he mutters quickly.

"Excuse me?"

"You know. Anyway, Jenny told me all about your work for the Democrats. That's fine and dandy, your experience with them. But don't you come over here thinking that you're some kind of *expert* on politics. Those people, they represent the lawyers, baby killers and welfare Negroes. We have little sympathy for those types over here, so if you got some kind of allegiance to them, you better leave it at the door on your first day. Got it?"

"Yes," Pepper says, tempted to walk out with a triumphant "fuck off."

Carmine Rossi stares at Pepper, his face tightening as if he is squinting at something unrecognizable. "Have you ever considered your place in the world's moral dichotomy?" he asks.

"I never much thought of it," says Pepper, spitting her gum back into its wrapper.

"Well, think about it.

"You've got the job—you can start Monday. Be sure to wear a bra when you come into the office. I've seen enough of you broads fall from the cross, you know. On your own time, do what you want." Rossi pauses and Pepper thinks of Larry Sweeny's startled look as she walked out on him. "And you might want to spend less time reading and more time getting to know your church," Rossi suggests, pausing again in a failed attempt to suppress a sneeze. "Damn it," he says, letting out a tiny squeal. As if in response, the paper sack on his desk begins to crumple and writhe from within. "Ah, ha! The snitch lives," Rossi shrieks with abandon, his temples swelling with rage. Rummaging through his desk drawers, he pulls out a large black bullwhip, hunches into a stance and cracks it on the tile floor with a curdling snap. Pepper jumps out of her seat and is ready to run for the door when the tan and white purse falls to her feet as if a reminder from the credit bureau.

Rossi sits back into his chair and the sack is still. "As I was going to say," he says in a calm whisper, "You wouldn't believe the amount of money the Wayne Van Anders pours into this party. Really, truly, he runs the show here. And although he might not be very book smart, he is a good Christian. One of the best, as a matter of fact. That's why I suggest you familiarize yourself with the church—and the Bible. Because folks at DutchWay might not know the classics, but one book those gentlemen sure do know is the Bible." He raises a finger. "Don't try to escape it."

Pepper is still from shock and amazement.

"Stay away from your former Democratic colleagues," Rossi adds, emphasizing the *tic* in Democratic. "They are the enemy, plain and simple."

"What about social events?" Pepper asks, thinking of free drinks at McCoys.

"What about them?" Rossi asks, his eyes wider yet.

"I mean, I might bump into some of the old Dems over at McCoys every now and then. I'd still like to go there once in a while."

Carmine sighs, spit bubbling at the sides of his mouth. "That Patrick McCoy is a good man," he says. "But you best be careful in that establishment of his. Lots of spirits poured, lots of demons exorcised. Lots of demons. And like I said, those demons are our enemy. You know who's Public Enemy Number One?"

"Who?"

"Leslie Thompson. Dirty bitch. Woman wins attorney general, thinks she's Queen of the World. We have to take her down at any cost."

Pepper nods in a gesture of understanding, and after quick negotiations, they settle a generous salary. "I want you to call me Carmine," Rossi says with a wink, offering her a ride home so she might "avoid the rats and vermin on the bus."

"How did you know that I don't drive?" she asks him.

"Jesus told me," the little man says, grinning like a nervous coyote. "Did I ever tell you about the time Wayne

Van Anders let me ride in his convertible with the top down?"

Not the least bit tired from an all-nighter at the gym, Josh makes it to the range less than ten minutes after it opens. He is working up a sweat firing out rounds, wondering about the boy from the dream.

The hunting accident at *Rod and Rifle*: it was his first case, roughly five years ago.

The boy had died.

It was deemed an accident by Norm Washington, Josh's partner. The hapless Washington, at the urging of Lieutenant Tesanovich, closed the case without further adieu.

Josh would have preferred to investigate further.

I wasn't aggressive enough, he thinks. *I didn't have enough confidence to follow my instincts.*

Josh's thoughts are interrupted by Tom Miller, the High Priest of the shooting range. Miller approaches, barking some shit about using earphones. "Headphones aren't earphones!" he yells in Josh's face. Calmly, without raising his voice, Josh tells Tom Miller to go fuck himself. Miller shakes his head, walks away. Josh turns up his Motley Crue, continues unabated. He has his whole case of guns, not just the standard issue .38, and he works them all.

Hunting accident. Something about it is fishy, even after all these years.

I don't doubt myself now.

Josh assembles his favorite weapon: a 1911-A Government Model Colt .45 Automatic. Its large heavy grained bullet and a slow muzzle velocity meant stopping power. It would be accurate up to 25 feet, and on good days, Josh could stretch it to 30. Sometimes, when he was feeling really drunk and twisted, Josh would fantasize about assassinating Wayne Van Anders: he'd imagine waiting for the bastard in the DutchWay parking lot, hiding behind the topiary bushes. Using a hollow point bullet for icing on the cake, Josh would give Van Anders a neck shot at ten feet and blow his fucking head off.

Grandpa's voice in his head: *"Why would you waste your energy thinking like that?"*

Slade's voice follows: *"Wayne Van Anders isn't even remotely worth it."*

Josh is barely nervous when he walks up to the security desk inside the Capitol. A pale, spectacled woman with stringy hair and a long, tube-like nose points him to the door. "Democratic offices are across the street in the Roosevelt Building," she says in monotone. "Republicans are across the other street in the Romney. Dems north, Republicans east."

The lobby of the Roosevelt smells of cheap melted cheese and fried foods cooked up by a man in black-rimmed spectacles thicker than bullet-proof glass. He works behind a disheveled newsstand, tossing blackened, oil-soaked French fries from a wire basket onto a shelf layered with paper towels. A *Rosie the Riveter* poster stares out from behind a glass trophy case as Josh passes the security desk, where a couple of elderly sergeants engage in a slow shuffle of cards. They pay absolutely no attention to Josh as he enters the elevator.

Deputy Director Willie Medville's office is full of smoke, dirty coffee cups, and cluttered stacks of papers.

Medville glances up and adjusts his wire rim glasses. "You won't bust me, will ya?" he asks, tapping his drag over a crowded tray of ashes. He holds his hands out, palms up, in a mock willingness to be cuffed.

Josh doesn't find this funny. "Only if those cigarettes were paid for with taxpayer dollars," he says.

Medville laughs uncomfortably and stabs out his cigarette. Large brown eyes protrude from his pale, round face, magnified by his spectacles. With a sigh, he slips a tweed suit coat over his arms and offers his hand in a *let's get down to business* manner. "Willie Medville."

"Josh Brisco. We met at the Democratic Gala last year."

"Sure, Josh, I remember." Medville' voice is high, squeaky. His large pink lips bounce up and down like a fleshy beak as he talks. "*Brisco the Kid.* How are ya? Jeez. Sorry about your race, man. I really thought we had that one in the bank there."

"Yeah, I know."

"Well, things tend to have a way of working out for the best." He motions with his arm. "Here, close the door behind you, will you? Provided you can breathe, that is."

Josh kicks away the doorstop and clicks the door shut. "Yeah, my dad was a smoker. Smoked up our house all the time."

Assured, Medville slips a new pack of cigarettes out of his tweed coat, smacks it against his palm, twists off the protective plastic, and lights himself a fresh Camel. "Listen," he says, exhaling. "It'll be nice to have you around here, provided things work out. We could use a real go-getter here."

"What do you mean, *provided things work out?*"

"Well, provided Slade Pickens holds on to everything. And believe me, I'm doing all I can to help make that happen." He pauses to convey the importance of his role. "But there are a lot of agitated folks around here. So until that caucus vote is final, I suggest you keep a low profile."

"Do you want me to leave?"

"Not at all." Medville licks his palm, using it to flatten down three wayward hairs on the top of his bushy head. "Don't get me wrong, kid. I want you on staff. God knows we could use some competence around here. You just need to keep a low profile for now. A lot of people would be pretty riled up if they knew the nature of today's visit." Medville is sucking down his cigarette between words like it's on a shot clock. "Got it?"

"Got it."

"Beautiful." He crushes what's left of his Camel into the sea of cigarette corpses and adjusts the black elbow patches on his coat with two sharp tugs. "About half our kids are pretty good workers," he whispers. "The other half are usually here behind closed doors, getting drunk in their offices, when they bother to come in at all."

"You've gotta be kidding me. You put up with that?"

"Patronage hires. I have no choice. I have no control over most of the hiring here—it's all controlled by the Hydes, the unions, and Larry Sweeny. What can I do? Nothing. I just keep holding out for change. I mean, I've seen us go from a twelve-seat majority to where we're positioned to be in January: two seats in the hole. Was it inevitable? Absolutely not."

"Do you think that Slade's chances are pretty good?"

Medville sighs. "Well, let me put it to you this way: session-to-session, nothing around here is guaranteed, except that the speaker's office will remain in the Capitol. And sometimes I'm not even so sure about that. Slade's chances? Fuck if I know. Slade's really been blasting Morris Hyde in the press this week and that has the blacks all riled up."

"They don't still support Hyde, do they?"

"The blacks? Of course they do. He's black, isn't he? Look at the voting patterns in every American precinct. Blacks support blacks. Period. And they're all Democrats." Medville' lips sag. "So why is Slade going out of his way to antagonize them?" Suddenly, Medville looks directly at Josh, waiting for an answer.

"Um, I don't know."

"I'll tell you why! Slade desperately wants to distance the rest of the party from Hyde and all his indictments. He should wait, though, until after the caucus vote. Why create another black/white riff now?" Again, Medville looks at Josh for an answer.

"I don't know. I'm not Slade confidant in this matter."

"Well, I guess Slade felt like he had no choice, especially after Hyde's involvement in that abortion on the lawn."

"What?"

"Yep, a real live abortion. Hyde and his wife Chinita staged it in public, right across the street on the Capitol lawn. Some poor girl from their district—I doubt if she knew what she was getting into."

"Jesus."

"Yeah, the Right to Life people were not amused. And there are a lot of those people in Slade's district."

"Don't get me wrong, I'm pro-choice," Josh says. "But a public abortion? That's pretty outrageous."

Medville sighs. "Yeah, to say the least. They threw the spoiled fetus into the street. It landed on my daughter's school bus."

"Oh my God."

"Yep. Let's hope that Slade pulls this off. Even without all the scandals, this place is pretty divided."

"How so?"

"The connected people on staff, the people with relatives in office, pull huge salaries and do nothing. Meanwhile, my hard working proletariat kids do all the work for very little pay. And we're supposed to be the party of the working people." Medville' words have the ring of a talk show host. "This place is divided into poor people who work their asses off—and pigs at the trough who do nothing. I'll tell ya, if Slade doesn't pull this thing off, this whole place is likely to blow up right in our faces."

The thought of it is enough to make Josh want to drink.

It is beneath Wayne Van Anders to pander to any rogue politician, regardless of leadership standing. Chip Richmond is an exception, however, for two reasons: term limits have resulted in Quixotic, unpredictable officeholders; and, Richmond is a loose cannon devoid of couth and expertise, the sort of person who doesn't read books, magazines, or newspapers.

The sort of person ripe for guidance.

So, Van Anders makes the exception, paying visit to Animal House, the decrepit rental dwelling of Richmond and three other freshman representatives: Jizzy LeDoux (R-Grand Rapids), Ken Green (R-Midland), and Marvin Williamson (R-Traverse City). As usual, Van Anders' reliable assistant Cobb is at his side. Cobb is a brooding figure, his square head and hard jaw betraying soft skin that might otherwise hint at a once-innocent past. Decorated by a thick helmet of rusty hair cascading into thick bangs above his brow, Cobb's black, piercing eyes dart back and forth nervously. His stubby fingers are tucked under a floppy black coat, pressed against a leather belt. They tingle with intensity, ready to free and fire a concealed .38 should the situation command it. With his boss next to him, Cobb enters Animal House like a dog kicked too many times, ready to pre-empt a perceived attack with one of his own.

Animal House it is. Walking over a family room floor scattered with newspapers and candy wrappers to the back den, Van Anders nearly covers his eyes to shield them from the sin in their midst. Ken Green, the self-described Christian conservative, is snoring drunk in a torn chair, a bottle of Captain Morgan dripping over his bare belly and unzipped pants. Jizzy LeDoux, newly elected and not even sworn-in, contorts to musical rumblings with a topless woman, his lips lunging for the sepia nipples of her over-sized breasts. Stepping over warped wooden floors and up rickety stairs in shiny black leather shoes, Van Anders coughs away the stench of sweaty beer as Cobb opens the door to Chip Richmond's resident den.

"Quite a handsome abode you have here, Representative Richmond," Van Anders says, looking around before taking a seat in a stiff wooden chair. A converted bedroom, the office is the size of large closet with a ceiling that slants down toward the far wall. Chairs, none of them matching, are set around Richmond's desk, which is empty but for his resting feet. The walls are cluttered with various posters with curled corners. *Trojan: Because I Care*, reads one. *Can't Get Enough*, reads another. Both feature scantily clad models in stages of sexual intercourse.

Cobb finds a place in front of the hallway door, plants himself, folds his arms, and observes. Enthusiastic shrieks and pounding music vibrate off the wall behind him.

"This place smells like a movie theatre that hasn't been cleaned in months," Van Anders snaps. Yes indeed, quite a handsome abode."

"I detect a little sarcasm, *Wayne*." Richmond's eyebrows are cocked, his hair short and prickly. On closer inspection, his desk is but a wobbly aluminum card table. Van Anders bristles at the informality of being called by his first name. "Elected officials should conduct themselves with more respect," he says.

Richmond's forehead wrinkles and his lips pucker slightly. He lights a cigarette. "I'm sorry if tonight's celebration isn't more to your liking. I didn't have time to line up your usual posse of caterers, holy men, and blue-blooded debutants. Rather, I was more focused on creating a situation that would allow me and my colleagues to free ourselves."

"Free yourselves?" Van Anders's eyes dart from the door to Richmond's face. "Yes, I couldn't help but notice Representative-elect LeDoux freeing himself all over the house harlot on my way in. I enjoy your rationalizations, Representative, I really do. If you tear the exterior off this place, however, all you'll find behind the drywall is a sty.

Men acting like pigs. Grown men, elected officials. Men whose campaigns have been financed with my money! I expect better!"

"Oh come on, Wayne. What are they doing that's so God-awful bad?"

"Are you serious?" Van Anders cannot believe the young representative's cavalier attitude. "Green is passed out, drunk. And Jizzy LeDoux, a married man, is dancing around downstairs with a topless woman." Van Anders, hands folded over a sticky television tray, is impeccable in his gray Brooks Brothers suit. "I financed his election. It was a great moral victory."

Richmond snickers. "Ah, yes. We barely squeaked that one out, as I recall. That Brisco kid was pretty damn tough!"

"It was all in hand," Van Anders assures him. "My precinct people had a plan to throw away the absentee ballots just in case Brisco pulled ahead," he says. "There was no way the wunderkind detective was going to pull out a victory under my watch."

Richmond turns his chin up slightly, then back down. Smoke flares from his nostrils. "Let's cut to the chase, Wayne. I don't want to waste any more of my free time than I have to . . . let's talk about Partial Prohibition."

"What about it?"

"Although it's your baby. It's bad public policy and it's got to go."

Van Anders puckers his lips, feigns surprise. "Why? Partial Prohibition only affects Grand Rapids. Why, that's a *local* issue that should elicit little, if any concern from Lansing." Van Anders props his eyebrows and waits for a response. Richmond, heir to the largest liquor distribution company in the Midwest, is silent. Van Anders is fully aware that Partial Prohibition is costing the Richmond family millions of dollars a month. He had done his research. His face is calm and set. "Indeed, Partial Prohibition is simply a matter of local control."

Richmond stabs out his cigarette, smearing charcoal streaks across aluminum. "Local control my ass. First of all, it may only affect Grand Rapids, but it was the Legislature that passed the fucking law. Secondly, if you want local control, why don't you go out and buy all the fucking bars and clubs across the state and close them yourself. This isn't about local control. To you, it's about inflicting your intolerant religious views onto others. To me, it's about my family. It's about money. We're in the liquor business, and this fucking law is costing us millions of dollars. It's killing everyone, from the distributors all the way down to the small pub owners. You don't give a fuck, though, because you already have all your millions and don't have to worry about it. You're just holding other entrepreneurs down, exercising that chip on your shoulder. But trust me, Chip Richmond is one chip you don't want on your shoulder."

Van Anders sighs. Richmond notices his perfectly parted white hair, so thoroughly groomed it seems airbrushed. Richmond likes Van Anders' appearance; he is genuinely impressed with the manner in which the old man presents himself. Calm, classy, Wayne Van Anders conveys the image of a better sort of person. A better *breed*.

"Some things are of a higher calling than dollars," Van Anders says.

Richmond raises his voice. "That's easy for you to say. Like I said, you already have all your fucking money."

Cobb, yellow circles under his eyes, steps forward. Richmond flinches.

Van Anders raises his hand. "It's okay, Cobb."

"Watch your tone," he says to Richmond. Guided by a strong will and character infused in him from a proper upbringing, Van Anders isn't one to listen to that sort of banter. "Even if you had my blessing to remove Partial Prohibition, you could never muster the legislative votes to override it."

"Yes, I could. I have the votes, even without you whipping up the right wing. Step one, I'm gonna move

Chuck Hriniak from Appropriations, maybe stick him on Commerce."

Van Anders lets a brief chuckle slip.

Richmond licks his lips, proposes a deal. "I know that Partial Prohibition is your puppy. But let me put something on the table here. I also know about your Diamondlife Dialysis. You have a quite a successful little monopoly with it, but it ain't gonna last."

Van Anders's bright blue eyes narrow. Chip Richmond, rogue politician, has his full attention.

"The new attorney general is gonna tear you up," Richmond continues. "As soon as she's sworn in, she's coming right after you. It's no secret."

"I'm not afraid of Leslie Thompson," Van Anders says.

"Well, you should be. She's gonna bust up your monopoly, re-open the market. That non-profit group, Health Alliance, is picking up clout. They're totally behind her, and she has the constitutional power to rip you apart."

Cobb stirs: Richmond has his attention as well.

Van Anders brushes thin fingers through his perfect hair.

Richmond continues. "You need an exemption passed so that Thompson, the Democrats' savior, doesn't come in riding in on her shining horse and run you out of town. If we put a carefully worded exemption into law, she can't touch you."

Van Anders holds his hand close to his vest. Enacting Partial prohibition was a great moral victory; however, it really wasn't practical when applied. It was hurting the West Michigan economy and a few bars already had closed their doors for good. Secretly, he had approached the legislature to repeal it last session. He had the votes—until Chuck Hriniak, originally a staunch opponent of Partial Prohibition, withdrew his support just to stick the screws to Van Anders. *"I told you this law stunk to high heaven," Hriniak lectured in private caucus. "But you went ahead and pushed it though anyway. Well, now you're stuck with it. Enjoy."* The caucus took place last March, just after the Green fundraiser, where Hriniak had instructed Van Anders to *"back off of Adam."* Back off? Van Anders had attempted to reach out, save the kid. Had a $20,000 deposit wired to a clinic in Salt Lake. *Second Chance,* it was called. Specialized in cleansing homosexuality from the system. Could have been a win-win for everyone, but the kid didn't know what was best for him. And Chuck Hriniak was giving him support, feeding his non-sense lifestyle with misdirected approval.

"You want to abrogate the attorney general's oversight powers?" Van Anders asks.

"I want to strip it away in exchange for your support on abrogating Partial Prohibition."

"Thompson does present quite a quagmire, but garnishing a 2/3 majority of both houses is a challenge in itself. Repealing Partial Prohibition only takes a simple majority, but amending the state Constitution is another matter."

"We need a two-thirds majority for that?" Richmond shifts in his seat. "I had no idea."

"And to think, you are the nascent speaker." *A fine reflection of term limits.*

"Okay, look at it this way: you have the votes in the senate, since it's two-thirds Republican anyway. That's small potatoes. The House will be tough, but I can get you the votes. Two-thirds? Yes. Even two-thirds. What is that, sixty, sixty-five or something?"

"Seventy-three."

"Seventy-three. Fine. I can get it."

"How?"

"The blacks. They're dying for a deal."

"How so? Is that middling crook Morris Hyde involved?"

"Indirectly. The blacks'll do anything to keep power within the Democratic party. That means raising a lot of money to thwart Slade Pickens' leadership bid."

"I don't like Pickens, but I don't want any association with Detroit. Pickens is a pest, Detroit is an anathema. Let them fight it out in the Democratic caucus room.

"Hear me out, please. It's all under the table: you cut my charitable foundation a check, my foundation cuts a check to Kalumba King's foundation, and he worries about laundering the money into his campaign coffers. He buys his caucus votes, gets leadership of the Dems, and we, in return for our investment, get the twenty or so crossover votes we need to take out the A.G."

"I don't trust them to deliver the votes."

"Wayne, it's a done deal. Leslie Thompson is pals with Slade. King's mom hates her. Believe me, she'll deliver the votes even if her son can't."

"How much money are you talking about?"

"They need a couple grand to kick off a winter fundraiser."

"A couple grand? What kind of fundraiser is this?"

"A charity circus."

"Charity circus? Good Lord. Let the clowns bring in the clowns. The money—is it traceable in any way?"

"No. No way at all."

Van Anders thinks about it for a while. How sweet would it be to take Chuck Hriniak and Slade Pickens down in one swing?

"Just a few more things," Van Anders says.

"Tell me."

"You said that you're taking Hriniak off Appropriations. Keep him off. And keep him off Commerce. He's unpredictable, hard telling the trouble he'd stir up on Commerce. Last thing we need is him screwing with the bankers and the insurance industry. They're our bread and butter."

"I have to give him *some* committee, don't I? There's no precedent for stripping a member of all their assignments, except as disciplinary action."

"Consider this a disciplinary action, then. Besides, you don't have to keep him off of all the committees. Just keep him off Appropriations and Commerce. Give him something remedial, like Ethics."

"Ethics?" Richmond smiles like a growling wolf. "That works for me. Anything else?"

"Yes, without a major committee assignment, Representative Hriniak won't be needing a full staff. I want you to cut his staff allocation."

"By how much?"

"Cut it all together."

Richmond waves his hand in tacit approval.

"Cobb, bring me the committee checkbook."

Van Anders writes the check. "And one more minor thing, Representative. *Mistletoe to Go* is next week. I want you there to voice your support for the Diamond and Lifeco dialysis merger. I want you to voice the *legislature's* support for it, lay the groundwork necessary to quell the inevitable murmurs of public concern."

"Consider it done. You know how Grand Rapids is. Get out the good spin. The press is already behind you, so are the churches. Inspire a few proactive editorial pieces, homilies, and sermons and you're good to go."

"People can't discern the difference between reality and metaphor," Van Anders says. "So work up something good." He hands Richmond the check. "Go ahead and reach out to the Africans. I'll have all my soldiers marching in place. If the Africans renig, then it's your head on a platter. I won't protect you."

Richmond beams. "I can handle myself with those people," he says.

They close the deal.

"I almost admire that kid's moxie," Van Anders says to Cobb as they walk back to the car.

Adam sits in a lump at the Red Lobster bar, straightening himself out every seven minutes or so to check the time on his Woody Woodpecker watch. The watch, an eighth-grade birthday gift from Jimmy, sparkles in its new black band. *What a waste of a Friday night.* Adam sighs, finishes his diet Coke, looks at his watch again. Nick is forty-five minutes late. *Fuck him.*

A cell phone call later, Adam is out the door and on his way to the Michigan Athletic Club. *Yes, sir, we are open 'til eleven.* That's all he needed to hear.

The gym is empty; Adam slips into his baggy white and blue Tar Heel shorts, checks out a ball and stages his own shoot-around. He spends hours driving through the paint, slicing to the hole, and launching NBA-range three pointers. His Air Jordans squeak with determination against the smooth, polished wood floor. *Spin move at the top of the key.* A memory of Jimmy. *Spinning.* Adam floats over the blocks and lays a shot off the glass with a soft finger-roll.

Jimmy: *"One thing you could do was the finger-roll."*

Adam laughs at the remembrance as the ball slides down through the strings of the net with a mellifluous snap. *That was one of your moves, Jimmy.* Jimmy could float, he could dance. He could glide through the lane like a bird taking flight. Adam was more of an outside player, a three-point specialist.

Jimmy: *"The way you play—grinding it out, playing solid defense, working for the open shot to win—could make a straight man cum."* Adam lets one rip from 25 feet.

Swish.

"Too bad we never got to play on the same high school team."

Yeah, buddy. We could have gone all the way.

Adam scoops up the ball and rests it between his feet. He is standing under the basket, bent over, hands grasping the legs of his shorts just above the knees. Sweat drips from his bangs onto the inflated leather, where it spatters with tiny pings. *Good workout.*

Chuck Hriniak calls as Adam is undressing in the locker room. "Hey boss, what's up?" Adam asks, flinging his sweaty underwear into a clear plastic bag.

Heavy breathing on the other side of the phone. Not the sex kind of heavy breathing, but the kind of heavy breathing that comes from someone who is constantly agitated and exhausted. Typical Chuck Hriniak.

"Chuck, you there?"

"Ah, Christ, Adam. I'm pissed. Pissed to the hilt."

"What's wrong?"

"Listen to me. Where are you? You in Grand Rapids?"

"No, I'm in Lansing. East Lansing. At the club."

"Fuck."

"Why? What's going on?"

"Ah, shit."

"Tell me."

"I just got word that Richmond is taking me off Appropriations."

"What?" Adam drops his towel.

"You heard what I said."

"Oh, shit, Chuck. I thought you were gonna be the next chair."

"So did I."

Think of something to say. "Why is Richmond doling out committee assignments now? I mean, it's not like he's speaker *yet.*"

"It's only a matter of formality, Adam. He can do whatever the fuck he wants."

"Shit. You supported him for leadership, so why is he going out of his way to screw you?"

"I have an idea why, but at this point is doesn't matter. What matters is that I am not gonna be chair of Approps, I'm not gonna have a larger staff allocation, and I'm not gonna be able to give you a raise."

"Chuck, don't worry about me." Adam's voice cracks. "This isn't about me, it's about you."

"Well, I'm worried. It's time to burn some more bridges. What are you doing on Sunday?"

"I don't know. I'll probably watch the Lions lose again."

"Well, listen. If you can swing it, I'd like to have a priority one meeting here in Grand Rapids. Priority *one*. We are going to burn some bridges. Big ones, starting as soon as possible. Can you miss the game? "

"Just tell me when and where."

"Two o'clock, my house."

"I'll be there."

"Good. We're not gonna take this shit sitting down."

"Chuck, are we switching parties?"

"Son, you can read into this all you want to. All I'm gonna say right now is that we're not gonna take this shit sitting down."

Adam showers, dresses, figures that he needs a drink. *Chuck Hriniak, screwed again by his Republican brethren.*

Father was behind this one, no doubt.

Mother decides not to sit in on the meeting and that is fine with Kalumba. Surprisingly, it is Larry Sweeny behind the request. *Stuttering Larry.* Thing is, Larry seldom stutters around Kalumba and never stutters around Chinita. When around them, he feels a rare confidence, he feels in control.

What does Larry want? Kalumba pounds his head for ideas. *Education? Safety? Public works?* Was it even a policy idea? If so, none of it would be workable with this current group of shit-head House members. Skimming through a wad of day-old telephone messages, he notices that one of the notes, scribbled quickly in Mother's green ink, says that Nick called, will be late for tomorrow's appointment. *Nick.* Kalumba drifts into a sea of dreamy climes, of penises and buttocks: a pool of smooth, naughty, firm-nippled boys, hundreds of them. Shifting the heaviness between his legs, he focuses on Nick, the Fairest of All Boys. Nick . . . touching Nick, feeling Nick, sliding inside of Nick. Showing his love to Nick.

Sliding open his top desk drawer, Kalumba rummages through old paperclips and coins for a spare vial of cocaine. Nothing. Slamming it shut, he pulls open the bottom drawer and pulls out a bottle of scotch.

The heir of Detroit's political dynasty remains deep in thought until the den's door swings open and slaps against the wall. Larry Sweeny, vibrant, riled, and totally out of character, pops into the room as if shot out of a cannon. "Where there's Sonny, there's sodomy," Larry announces, a joker's grin on his face.

"The boys are gone, you asshole," sighs Kalumba, trying to hide his glass of Dewer's.

"Ah! I saw that!"

"Who are you, the cops?" Kalumba dips deeper into the bottle. "So I like scotch—it's my only weakness. Sue me."

"Really?" Larry is mockingly pensive. "What about all the boys, and all the drugs?"

Boys and drugs. Boys and drugs. Drugs and boys.

"This is bad timing. What do you want?" Kalumba wishes that his step-father, Morris Hyde, would have fired Larry's ass long ago, but the piece of crap has too much dirt on the family. Plus, he had jockeyed himself into position as the sole confident of Mother as she continued to slip farther into a sublime existence. Nope, there is no getting rid of Larry Sweeny. If Kalumba is to ascend to the position of Democratic leader, he'd even have to give the rat-bastard a healthy raise. "I don't have all night, Larry. Tell me what's on your mind."

Larry is pacing. "I wanted to talk to you last night," he says. "But Ms. Chinita McCloud Clapton King-Hyde said that you were out with the boys."

"Yeah, Tuesday night is boys night."

"Well, We've got trouble."

"Whaddaya mean, trouble?"

"On a couple fronts. Are you hungry?"

"I'm always hungry. Mother has me on this ridiculous diet of lemons and cottage cheese."

This is Larry's opportunity to get Sonny Boy out of the house. He knew he'd be hungry; Sonny Boy is immense, and therefore predictable when it comes to food. Larry needed to get out of Sonny's office for two reasons: one, nights of drinking and sex had taken a toll, leaving a stale booze/cum stench. Two, he couldn't risk the chance of Ms. Chinita McCloud Clapton King-Hyde listening in on the conversation. Slade Pickens, the fuck, had made it personal, and now it was time to pull out all the stops, make all the right alliances and moves. It was something part of him had been waiting for a long time. The real Larry Sweeny was about to stand up.

The tiny diner is empty except for a lonely trucker sitting at the bar just in front of the kitchen. Kalumba and Larry sit at a corner booth, their table situated under a framed photo of Jimmy Hoffa smiling in a gray satin union jacket.

Kalumba is stuffed between the booth and table, which is affixed to the ground. His belly hangs in folds over his silverware. "Pickens tried to fire you?" he asks, his eyes wide with child-like amusement.

"He has no right. He has no fucking right. He's already assuming that he's the next leader. It's not carved in stone."

Kalumba wishes they would have gone to a bar. He is thinking about Nick and eating out his ass. *Those smooth, hairless legs!*

"Are you paying attention to me?" Larry asks. "Jesus Christ, your worse than some of the broads that've worked for me."

"You mean the *Sweeny Girls?*" Kalumba laughs.

"Fuck you."

A waitress tiny but for a pair of generously full breasts brings them water, carefully placing their glasses upon the table like they were full of gold.

Kalumba's elbows are stuck; he maneuvers to free them, jerking up the table and nearly spilling both waters. Really, though. Do you think that Pickens has it wrapped up?"

"Fuck no. But you have to get your act together." Kalumba winces, looks away. "Listen to me."

"I am listening."

"Make eye contact when I'm talking to you. I'm not here to shit you. I'm not here to babysit you. And I'm not going to bullshit you and tell you some wonderful fairly tale about your family's political dynasty and how you're the insurmountable heir and all that fucking bullshit. Right now, your family is in a political shit hole. Your step-father is a felon. Your mother is a political vampire, and they're both the state champions of unbridled abortion. People can't handle that shit. And other Democrats don't want to be associated with it. That's an uphill battle for you to overcome. On the plus side, Slade Pickens' vanity makes him weak. He has a blind side. Josh Brisco lost the highest profile race in the state, and he was Pickens' baby. That cost us the house and lots of people are bitter about it. We need to drive that point home. Also, I have people in Grand Rapids looking to dig up some dirt on Slade. Talking with his ex-wives, looking for something, anything negative to feed to the press and bring him down."

"What can I do?"

"Good question. For one, you have to clean up your fucking bullshit. No more boys, booze, and drugs. None. You've got to spend all your time raising money, dishing out favors, and building alliances."

Kalumba gives him a hopeless, exhausted look.

"What?" Larry barks. "It's too hard for you to act like a real elected official for a couple of weeks? Is that asking too fucking much?"

"Whose side are you on? The other Dems hate me. Who are we kidding? I could never beat Slade Pickens. There's nothing wrong with him. The other reps only know my weaknesses. If they knew me, if they saw how I feel, or what I've tried to do, my vision of this state, maybe they'd understand better."

Larry lifts his hands in the air and wraps his fingers into tight fists. "Who cares what they think?" he says, clapping his fists together like a boxer preparing to spar. "You should only care about how they vote. Believe me, they all want to be in leadership, all of them. Each representative not in leadership is on the outside looking in. And they resent it to the point of always scheming to revolt. But as long as they have a leader who is willing to give them money, make them look good, and do them favors, they'll stay in line."

Kalumba claps his hands. "I can reinvent myself," he explains. "Hell, Harry Truman did it. So did Jerry Brown. I can reinvent myself. I can earn the faith of the people in my party. They're not that stupid. All it might take is for someone like me to restore their reason."

Larry laughs. "Reason is a dangerous thing, Sonny Boy. Especially in this state."

"I'm not worried about that, Kalumba says. "I am worried about raising money, though. I've already had both my standard fundraisers, and I don't want to have to pander to the lobbyists. You know how they've fucked me in the past."

Larry's eyes are bright, alive. "That's why I propose a little fantasy, a little escapism if you will. One big event to raise all the capital your leadership drive needs."

"Huh? What kind of escapism?" Kalumba feels like escaping, and he starts to think about little Nick, naked, in bed, sweaty and quiet. If only the world would stop and Kalumba could just be naked with Nick.

Larry is still talking. "A little fun for ladies and gentlemen, children of all ages," he says. "We throw a little charity circus: Representative Kalumba King's Charity Circus. Great publicity. Great fun. Raise lots of money!"

Kalumba is calm. For once, he doesn't feel the need to argue with Larry. His thoughts grow pleasantly pink and sugary, like cotton candy. "Yes! What a great way to get back on track!" he says. "We can hold the event in Lansing and generate monies for my charitable foundation. Then we can divert the monies from the foundation into my leadership fund!"

"See how easy it is? I knew you'd love it." Larry seems genuinely pleased. "Great. We have a press conference scheduled for today at 2:30."

"Today?" Kalumba's jaw drops.

"Don't worry about it," Larry reasons. "I've got your speech already written. Plus, this thing could raise about two hundred grand, easy, and the law provides us with a money laundering loophole bigger than Liz Taylor."

"I'll need every cent for the new vote. Wouldn't it be something if I could outmuscle Slade Pickens?"

"It's very doable. We just have to get it organized and scheduled for the week between Christmas and New Years."

"That's not a lot of time. What about up-front costs?"

Larry nods slowly. "It's taken care of," he says.

"What did you mean, It's taken care of?" Kalumba asks.

"I said that it's taken care of. What's the problem?"

Kalumba sighs and Larry can smell the remnants of a cottage cheese and lemon dinner whistling between his teeth. "The up-front costs have got to be steep. How can it possibly be taken care of?"

"I arranged it. We have allies. Everything is all lined up: up-front funding, a venue, performers, clowns, elephants, you name it. All you have to do is get on the phones and sell tickets! We'll get everyone on policy and communications staff working the phones, too. All on the taxpayers' dole."

"Elephants?" Kalumba asks. His skin is pale.

"Yes, we have one." Larry flags down the waitress with a wave of his hand. "We decided to go with Delhi, the elephant from New Delhi." Larry observes Kalumba for a quiet moment as the waitress returns to their table. "Take these waters away," Larry tells her. "We need coffees. Black, both of them."

"Yes, sir," says the waitress as she hurriedly takes the waters away.

"I would have consumed that water," Kalumba says, scratching the top of his head. "Now she has no choice but to dump those glasses down the sink. What a waste." Kalumba's voice cracks a bit, and he sighs again. He cracks his knuckles like snapped walnuts. Larry can't believe how one man's breath can smell like an entire fucking sewer. "Wait a second," Kalumba finally says, his eyes narrow and turned upward, as if he is thinking out loud. "You're telling me that you went with the elephant Delhi? Is this correct?"

"That's correct," Larry admits as the little waitress comes with their coffees.

"Do you need menus, gentlemen?" she asks.

"No, that's okay. I know what I want," Larry tells her.

"I do need a menu, thanks," Kalumba mutters, almost in protest, and she departs the table to fetch him one.

Larry looks at his watch hard and long, as if critiquing it. "What's your problem with elephants?" he asks.

Kalumba stares at him, expressionless, as if his twitchy nose and sullen eyes are frozen into a large, weaseled caricature. "Del-hi from New Del-hi?" he asks, carefully enunciating each syllable. His face is still except for the lips, which move with subtle efficiency, as if they are superimposed onto a cardboard dummy. "Don't you watch Animal Planet?"

"No, but I'm sure you'll enlighten me." There was no avoiding it, even though at this point in the conversation, Larry certainly isn't interested in an inordinately long and morbid fable based upon the life story of a stupid fucking circus elephant from India.

"Delhi is an angry elephant," Kalumba explains, his lips quivering. "An-gry." The waitress is back with his menu and she takes their order. Sonny Boy, true to form, can't settle on anything and simply decides to order the exact same thing as Larry, that being the French toast.

"Would you like that cut into six or eight pieces?" asks the waitress, tussling her long curly hair with a pen.

"Better make it eight," Kalumba says. "I'm very hungry."

Larry rolls his eyes. "Six is fine for me, thanks."

Much to Larry's chagrin, Sonny Boy continues on the elephant subject. "Hiring this an-gry elephant to perform at my circus is like hiring the Manson family to perform the knife tricks."

"Manson? What's she got to do with this?"

"No, not Gloria. *Charles* Manson, as in *the* Manson family. As in, '*Oooops! Don't get too close to the clowns, children!*' Hell, I'm sure my mom would volunteer to go out there and juggle human fetuses while you're at it. What fun."

"Oh, come on!" Larry protests. He had listened to about enough of this ridiculous banter. "How can you possibly know this elephant? Is this a joke? I mean, give me a break! An angry elephant? What can it do? It's got no tusks for crissakes."

"Elephants are big, Larry. We're not talking about a de-clawed house pet here." Kalumba pauses, sucking a swig of coffee through his puckered mouth. Something in the hot liquid swishes around his gums and jars loose a whole new conglomerate of barnyard smells, sending it in an invisible mist across the table. Larry winces. Kalumba swallows hard. "About two years ago, Delhi ran amok after Indian settlers infiltrated and occupied her grazing area of over 35 years. I mean, really, she just went fucking crazy, plundering crops, destroying villages, and trampling to death at least twelve settlers. I saw the story several times. It was horrific."

Larry takes a sip of his coffee and imagines the retarded beast stomping over a screaming, fleeing sect of towel-headed natives, their bones splintering under her grassy paws like broken tooth picks. "You need to stay away from the animal rights fanatics," he says.

Kalumba nods, waves his hand. "No, it was on TV, and there's more: the Indian game warden finally managed to have Delhi trapped and subsequently transferred to a wildlife preserve, where she was held and later sold to American interests. Upon her arrival in Florida, she trampled, stomped, mauled, and killed two veterinarians. You see, once an elephant goes on a rampage, it never stops."

Larry nods. "An elephant never forgets," he says.

"Exactly. That's why I strongly recommend that we go with a more happy elephant, maybe one from Barnum & Bailey. It might cost a little more to lease, but the safety factor makes it way worth the extra cost. I'd be more than willing to put that recommendation in writing. After all, it is in the best interests of the Michigan taxpayers."

Larry shakes his head. "No, it's not in the best interests of the Michigan taxpayers," he says in his best attempt to explain rather than argue. "The taxpayers have nothing to do with it. This is a fundraiser. Fuck the taxpayers. The up-front costs of this fucking circus are being paid for by Wayne Van Anders, not the taxpayers."

The world stops.

"Wayne Van Anders? Wayne Fucking Van Anders? What kind of shit-fucking deal—"

"Let me finish." Larry's voice is rising. "I got Van Anders to pick up this tab, and nobody knows it, but somebody has to pick it up, because you sure as hell can't afford to."

"What kind of deal did you cut?"

"This is secret, Sonny Boy." The waitress emerges with two plates of carefully cut French toast with fried potatoes and places them in front of Larry and Kalumba.

"Why Van Anders? Something with DutchWay?"

Larry stares down at his toast and shrugs. "It was an easy deal. I promised them that we'd deliver our caucus on legislation legalizing his dialysis monopoly. In return, he promised to give us lots of money for the circus."

"Monopoly?" Kalumba is genuinely incredulous. "Isn't that a federal issue?"

"Yes and no. Van Anders already has the feds bought off. He's worried about Michigan's new attorney general, Leslie Thompson. He thinks she'll go after his company unless the legislature changes the law."

"What about the Senate?" Kalumba asks.

"He's already bought it."

"Jesus."

"Yeah, he's more powerful than you think. And he hates Slade Pickens. Even more than your mom does."

Kalumba's concerns revert back to Delhi the elephant. "Even so, he says, "you can't run a circus with this elephant you have. Believe me, money won't be saved in the long run. You figure, even if she commits minor damage to a few props and surroundings—"

"Kalumba, it's not all about the money here. Van Anders has some pretty deep pockets." Larry pauses, reaches for the salt and pepper, shakes them both liberally over his potatoes, and quickly concocts a little white lie. "I tried Barnum & Bailey, believe me, I did. Problem is, some crazy old biddy shot the hell out of their star elephant in Cincinnati. Mistook it for the devil in disguise—you know how people are in that town. Anyway, it's still alive, just not well enough to perform, and Barnum &Bailey have been misers with their elephants ever since."

Kalumba buys the story hook, line, and sinker. "What is it with old people today?" he asks, chewing on a piece of his breakfast.

Larry swallows his first bite before answering. "It has a lot to do with technological innovations in the health care industry. Quite simply, God didn't mean for people to live as long they do. They're outliving their natural life spans, and their brains are the first thing to go."

"Interesting." Kalumba is still talking with his mouth open; yellow globs of soggy bread flake the sparse hairs over his chin. "Hopefully, you're bringing on a good crew of expert trainers for this Delhi, then."

"I'll leave that to Van Anders," Larry snaps. His food is fantastic and he wants to gobble it up before the plate turns cold. "He'll contract it out."

"Contract out? The unions are gonna be pissed."

"Fuck em. Look what those cunts did to my uncle. Ran him out of the UAW like he was Jack Kemp." It is Larry who is now chewing and talking simultaneously.

"People are not going to be happy!" Kalumba says, his voice rising with excitement.

Larry drops his fork in disgust. "People are not going to know the difference," he says. "People are stupid. So is the name Delhi. I want a new stage name for the beast, something trendy, something people can relate to. A name like *Chewbacca*."

Kalumba seems amused. "Chewbacca?" he asks. "That's from Star Wars!"

"Yes, I know. A marketing bonanza."

"You can't steal a name like that. There are trademarks, copyrights. How about something similar, but different, like, uh, Carmello?"

Larry laughs. "Too faggy," he says.

"How about Hans?" Kalumba is really groping.

"No way. Too foreign: scares away nice, middle class families. We're going with Chewbacca. That's a winner."

"We're gonna get sued," Kalumba laments.

"No, we aren't."

"Somebody's gonna get hurt, then. Maybe even financially."

Larry picks up his fork again and stabs at his toast. "It's always fun until somebody gets hurt," he says. "Then it's fucking hysterical."

They both laugh, and as Larry starts working his food, Kalumba's thoughts change channels and float back into bed with sweet, sexy Nick and his little round ass.

Nick's ass is killing him. He lifts his head, a slight tinge of groggy discomfort throbbing through his nerve endings. It seems like morning, but the apartment is dark except for the orange glow of sunlight flickering through a crack in the shades and spilling across the splintered floor. Even in its limited form, the sunlight is a sustained flash against Nick's vision, stinging his red-veined eyes. He blinks, rolling on his side, finding himself naked and exhausted on Casper's clean bed. Sheets, blankets, bedspread, and pillows are tossed and folded perfectly. No condoms, no wrappers, no puddles. Spotless. *Where is Casper?* Gently tapping weak, pappy fingers against a clammy forehead, Nick squints in an attempt to focus his thoughts. The tapping has a circulating effect; it soothes him as sounds from the bathroom leak slowly through cracked walls like lazy, rising steam. Running water whistles; a razor clicks against a ceramic sink. *Where are my clothes?* He lifts his slick leather jacket from the floor boards; his money wad is still tucked under the inner breast pocket.

The bathroom door opens. "Oh, you're awake, I see." Casper is fresh, glowing in khaki Polo cargo pants and a black Hugo Boss shirt. "I like these clothes," he says.

"Glad to hear it." Nick swallows, coughs, clears his throat: something anyone, not just a frightened person would do first thing in the morning. His lungs seem to wither. "What am I supposed to wear?" He rolls over on his side, using his left hand to cover his cock.

"What? Why are you in such a hurry?" Casper smiles softly, clearing the chintz covered chest. "I was hoping to get a little more of that little ass-pussy of yours this morning," he says, pulling some clothes from the top drawer. "Why are you acting so shy?"

Nick removes his hand. His anus is burning, his insides gassy. "I can't. I'm sore. *Really* sore," he says. As if on cue, an extended, involuntary fart rips from his ass. "Oh my God, I am so embarrassed." A small glob of liquid shit drips between his legs and onto Casper's white bedspread. "Oh jeez." *This is about as low as it gets.*

Casper chuckles, tosses Nick a towel and some clothes. "Here, get yourself cleaned up."

"I'm so sorry."

"What? Forget about it. Sometimes you strike oil. I drilled you pretty hard last night. Tonight, I'll give you the pleasure. If you want to come back, that is."

Fear and embarrassment fades; Nick is overwhelmed by a lusty desire to fuck Casper up the ass. Serving as Casper's bottom had opened him to the stigma of a less masculine existence, a feeling he could shatter with a good night of topping. If he worked his dick long and hard enough, maybe he could even the stakes by causing Casper to fart shit, too. It was a challenge he would look forward to all day long: another wonderful conquest. "What time?"

"Same as last night. Meet me at McCoy's."

"I hate that place, but fine."

"I'll give your clothes back tonight, then. Oh, one favor?"

"What?"

"Can you bring a fuck buddy with you?"

"Huh?"

"Bring a fuck buddy." Casper digs into his wallet and pulls out a wad of cash. "You can fuck me, but I want some ass, too—and yours is gonna be too sore to fuck. So here's $500. See if you can convince one of your buddies to join us."

Nick smiles. "Sure, no problem." Derek or Keith would fuck for $200, and he could keep the rest without them even knowing about it.

"Discretion assured?"

"Discretion assured," Nick promises. "I'm not out, either."

"Out?"

"Yeah. *Not* out. You know, I'm still in the closet."

"Super." Casper wipes his hands on the black Hugo Boss, grinning. He has the little fucker exactly where he wants him.

Josh pulls out of the Capitol, ventures ten minutes down Michigan Avenue, just past the sloping campus of Michigan State University, where at some points the trees seem to climb into the clouds.

Like dreams.

Josh stops at the Peanut Barrel, his old college watering hole and washes down a tuna melt with a couple Budweisers. His plate empty, he peels damp labels from brown glass, folding them into a neat pile. *Willie Medville: what a talker.* Josh imagines him with his own show on some cable news channel. Willie Medville, wearing his tweed coat and just plain talking—about anything. *Tweed Talk with Willie Medville.* Josh would be perfect as the inaugural guest, offering insight about Capitol. *"Sure,"* he'd say, microphone clipped to the collar of his green Eddie Bauer sweater. *"I'm totally overwhelmed by the Capitol. Democrats one block to the north, Republicans one block to the east. I'm overwhelmed."*

Medville with pursed lips: *"Overwhelmed? Please explain."*

"Well, I've got a great job opportunity waiting, possibly. A possibly great opportunity, you see."

Medville with raised eyebrows: *"A possibly great opportunity, or a great opportunity that is just a possibility?"*

Josh crosses his legs. *"The second one, yeah. But it looks like it might be snatched from me before I even start it."*

Willie Medville sits back, adjusts his tweed coat, looks directly into the camera. *"I bet there are many people out there tonight who can empathize,"* he says.

Applause from the audience.

"I don't think so." Josh spreads his hands, palms up, and gestures. *"I just ran for office, you know. And lost.*

"I was so close I could taste it."

The audience claps, Medville nods in appreciation. *"But it turned into a tease,"* he says.

"Yes, it turned into a tease."

"And you're afraid of a repeat here on Democratic staff. A job. A new start.

"A tease."

"Yes, another tease."

Indeed, life is full of teases. The good things, they are just temptations, ephemeral manifestations. Josh knows this from experience. The love of a grandfather, the camaraderie of a best friend, the rapture of a passionate kiss: they were but preludes to loneliness, antecedents to pain.

I am alone.

Malaise grips Josh; a rush of paranoia rips through his stomach like a steak knife through the soft flesh of a tomato. Thrusting both hands into khaki trousers, he fingers his pockets for pills.

None.

The cozy restaurant is loud. Couples sit together, laughing, sharing. A group of friends mucks it up at the window table. Three drunks argue about football at the bar.

They have each other, even the drunks.

Josh sits alone in a smog of personal quiet, reaches for his beer. Tired fingers slip over sweaty glass; the bottle tumbles to the floor in a spray of crystal shards. Splinters and suds glister over discarded peanut shells.

"Glass over garbage," Josh says to himself. A waiter wearing long black curls and a wayward beard scrapes up the spill and produces another Bud. "I see," Josh says. "A replica."

"On the house," says the waiter.

"Thank you, that's very nice of you." Josh stares at the new bottle. *Exactly like the other one,* he thinks.

Meet the new bottle.

Same as the old bottle.

Maybe it was the old bottle, the broken one, it's pieces put back together with diligence.

Just like the Schrek case.

At 26 years-old, Josh was a bold detective, fresh with ideas and full of ambition. It was a drizzly March afternoon when Lieutenant Tesanovich sent him and Norm Washington out on their second case together, a case that would soon be known as the Middle School Murder. Norm, having conspired with Dewey Long on patrol for almost a decade, was a fat a cat on the dole. Didn't want to do anything, Norm Washington. Yet, the man was promoted to detective. Funny how things worked out for certain people and didn't for others.

Norm unpacked his flask, fedora, and attitude on the school grounds, returning to the car after delivering a few perfunctory stock questions to bewildered parents. Josh made the best of it. He pushed the interviews, combed the area for evidence. The girl's body was left in the service dock, greasy rainbows of truck oil blending into a sanguine puddle of water and blood. A black janitor had found her stripped, raped, and bludgeoned to the point that half her face and most of her brains were missing. *The sky is sweating and the people are crying* was all Josh could think as he tried to piece the events together. Everything was amplified: voices, smells, wetness. *Pain.* There was so much pain. The mother struggled, twirling wet blond hair in her fingers as her husband held her.

A pig-tailed little girl with doe-like brown eyes, Heidi Russell was a seventh-grade student who had missed her car pool ride. The star of the drama club, she stayed after school to rehearse her part as Emily Webb in Thornton Wilder's *Our Town.* She went to her locker after rehearsal and never came back. *"They didn't wait for her!"* the mother cried. *"They just didn't wait!"* Between sobs, she labored to explain that Heidi had just experienced her first menstrual period and was likely taking some time to deal with it. *"How could they not wait?"* she asked. Josh didn't know what to say.

The prior week, *Our Town* played a Friday afternoon show for the whole school. The cast toured area retirement homes on the weekends, their youth seducing the old folks attention like an elusive promise.

Stripped, raped, bludgeoned in the service alley: Heidi Russell was dead, the show cancelled.

Promise over.

The community immediately suspected Nelly Peeps, the school janitor. Coincidentally, Nelly was the only black person living in Forest Hills at the time, unless you counted his wife Loretta, who was actually mulatto. *You gotta wonder about those people* was the prevailing bias. The local, semi-professional digest, (aptly titled *Forest Exposure*) ran two features on Maury Peeps, Nelly's incarcerated brother, and one on Poppy Peeps, Maury's illegitimate son.

The community frothed, smelled blood. *Forest Hills, Shining City on Top of the Mountain.* Forest Hills, tragically shocked into reality, longing for explanation, demanding justice.

Josh worked hastily. The glass splinters in Heidi Russell's scalp were a tacit implication that she had been bludgeoned repeatedly with a bottle, yet, Crimescene couldn't locate the weapon. After a few false leads, Josh returned to the school for one last survey of the grounds. It was a sunny day; kids in green shorts and white shirts ran in motley pairs down pavement as a masculine woman timed them with the click of a black stopwatch. Puffing smoke out its rear, a white milk truck pulled out of the service alley as Josh approached. That's when he saw it: a reflection, a glimmer—not from the truck, but from the ground behind it.

To the side of the alley, below ground: a sewer gutter hiding the shiny glimmer of glass over garbage.

Enlisting the help of Nelly Peeps and some heavy tools, Josh pulled out the steel grating and gathered the remnants of glass, shattered and stashed. Hands wrapped in yellow plastic gloves, he picked out the shards and brushed them into a clear bag, transporting it to Crime Lab. He and Gordon Tyler, the forensic wizard, worked all night fitting pieces together until their puzzle strongly resembled three-quarters of three wine bottles, one of which served as a sample large enough for Gordo to lift a print from. Working clandestine over the weekend, Josh returned to the middle school and lifted fingerprints from the desk of every teacher, administrator, assistant, and janitor. There was no *Our Town* performance that weekend, but Josh found his leading man: Kurt Schrek, Heidi's long-toothed math teacher. Schrek matched the print and was taken into custody that Monday morning. Within the hour, he broke down and confessed that Heidi was about to tell her parents about their six-week affair. He panicked and silenced her, breaking several bottles over her head after one last fuck in the loading dock.

Fourteen: she had just experienced her first period.

A bottle: Josh had put the pieces together, but that didn't give Heidi Russell her life back. Her parents, more embarrassed than relieved, never bothered to thank him. Josh, at times, wondered if he was being egotistical for expecting as much.

The case made Josh sick to his stomach, but it earned him hero status in Forest Hills. Even his old high school masturbating buddy Scott Williams called to voice his pride, see if Josh wanted to come over for a drink sometime. Nelly Peeps was vindicated; the Superintendent of Schools promoted him to *Assistant Custodian in Charge.* Similarly, Tesanovich awarded Josh with several ribbons of precinct recognition. Things were looking up, and all the pieces seemed to be in place.

Today is an antithesis of yesterday. Josh knows that somewhere along the line, he lost his way, just not sure when. The election loss stood out as a watershed, but the slide had actually begun, in small doses, long before then.

I really want to put the pieces back together, he thinks, envisioning partially reconstructed wine bottles, cracks and crevices of dried glues running up their sides.

It is a puzzle, this lost soul: Josh doesn't know parts of himself, hadn't in a long time. Some of the pieces were missing; it was like the Voorhees case, a case with strong potential for an unhappy ending. Maybe that's not the sort of case he wants to solve. Staying numb is easier. There were some clues, gone. There are other clues, still there, thoughts and feelings kept hidden away in a lock box mind. Should he open it, or is it too much, too soon, too fast?

Fuck it, just deal with it.

Josh orders a fifth beer, peels its label and folds it between damp fingers, letting it slip to the peanut shell-cluttered floor. Then he finally musters up the balls.

Time to check out *Paradise.*

Paradise. It seemed innocuous enough, the dank brick building looming purple in the middle of downtown Lansing. Nameless, faceless, *anonymous*—it hovered quietly in the midst of Washington Plaza, an intermittent series of pretty faces, circuit boys and fems slipping behind dark glass doors to invade its premises. Six beers in him, Josh is tingling, sweating, his heart racing. His groin tingles, a frightened numbness shaking his ankles as he approaches the black glass door. It looks dark inside. *Maybe it's not open,* he wonders, giving himself the chance to bail out and turn around. A boy and girl holding hands walk by, giggling. Josh doesn't want to be seen standing outside the premises. What if Medville drove by, or worse, one of the Republicans? Gossip and innuendo would ensue, no doubt. Josh would be ridiculed behind his back, hassled to his face, be all-around humiliated.

A tall waif with spiked hair steps in front of Josh and pushes open the door. Josh follows, slips inside. His eyes are flooded with strobes as the door swings shut behind him. Thumping club music bullies his ears. "Five dollar cover, honey," shouts a kid at the door. He has both ears and a nostril pierced, a blue tattoo crawling up his neck. He licks his lips like a hungry cat. "Need ta see your ID, too," he adds.

The place is long and cavernous on the inside. Light and music bounce off mirrored walls. Two counter tops run end-to-end down both sides of the perimeter, the bar on one side, bathrooms and poolroom on the other. People, mostly males Josh's age and younger, mingle with drink in hand. Boy-toy dancers shake their bare asses on the counters for the clientele, who reciprocate by shuffling dollars into their g-strings. Straight ahead is the dance floor, a magnanimous stage with cages on either side, and more mirrors. Hands waving, bodies shaking with sweat: the room is pulsing. A rainbow-colored flag hangs in the corner. Mirrors, rainbows, and plants dance all over the place.

Josh approaches the bar and ducks away, afraid someone might touch him. "Do you want something, honey?" asks a shirtless waiter.

"Um, sure," Josh manages to say. He can't help but stare at the candy kiss nipples protruding from the boy's smooth chest. "I'll have a Bud. Please."

The waiter smiles. "How proletariat," he says. Josh pops a boner.

Josh pays and tips, choking the neck of the bottle as he wanders sheepishly past the bathrooms into the poolroom. All eyes are on him, or at least that's how he feels. He wants to take a piss, but is afraid that someone might grab his crotch at the urinal. *Most of these guys are gay*, he thinks. *Not like me.* Under the wildest consideration, Josh would label himself bi-curious, if not straight. *Curious, not gay.* Definitely not gay. Bi-curious: that's what it was. He'd check *Paradise* out, see that it isn't anything he is missing, then go back to a regular life dating girls and such.

The poolroom is mostly empty; the pool table is open. Josh adopts a *Don't Even Think About Touching Me* defensive stance, sips his beer, and worries about his appearance. Does he look good in khakis and the tan sweater with a black tee under it? Maybe he should have worn jeans. Does he look too formal? Office Casual is Club Formal. He glances at himself in the mirrored wall, internally admitting that the black tee is a nice touch underneath the sweater. But the sweater is too loose. Most of the guys in the bar are wearing tight clothes, showing off their body contours. A pale guy with a shaved head is wearing a pair of shiny faux leather pants, candy apple red. *Hideous.*

Josh wonders what it is like kissing a guy, sucking a cock. *This is happening so fast.* He wonders if Scott Williams ever felt bi-curious. The idea of him meeting someone normal here, someone like Scott, who is now married with kids, strikes him as outrageous.

Josh figures he'll play some pool, puts his money down on the table.

Sitting at the bar, Adam nearly slaps himself for biting his nails again. Oh, the suspense is driving him nuts!

"Son, you can read into this all you want to." That's all Chuck would say. That, and, *"We're not gonna take this shit sitting down."* The suspense is good. *Very good,* Adam keeps telling himself. Suspense actually suspends him from the melancholy. Chuck knows that, too—it is probably part of his scheme, not telling Adam the story over the phone. Adam's juices are flowing, his boyish nature standing over the edge, looking down, speculating on the life below.

Which is pretty mundane if you don't count Chuck Hriniak's role. Chuck is actually thinking about switching parties—wow! What balls! Adam imagines the stir such a deal would create in Grand Rapids! Father'd be frothing so much he'd likely choke on his own spit. Adam can't help but laugh out loud. Thank God for Chuck Hriniak—life at the Capitol would be dull without him. More specifically, Adam's life would be unbearable. For the past several years, Chuck has been like a father to Adam, taking him under his wing at the House. As a result, work evolved into the one pillar in Adam's otherwise fragile world.

To Adam Van Anders, Chuck Hriniak is good people and good company. Throw Chuck into any situation, he'll manage to make it better. Give him dire straits, he'll straighten them out. *"Chuck can take two pieces of cement and tie a knot out of them,"* Adam once explained to Nick, who seemed genuinely confused and annoyed by the analogous statement. Chuck Hriniak is a fighter, a producer of results. Highly skilled in discourse, he once delivered a floor speech on term limits that inspired Slade Pickens to call it, *"The best goddamn extemporaneous speech I have ever heard."* When legislators cut staff salaries while approving their own pay raises, Chuck donated half his increase to charity, the other half to boost Adam's paltry salary. Unlike his peers, Chuck is actually in command of the issues facing the Legislature. He knows what he is talking about when he talks about it. Unlike people Adam's age, Chuck immerses himself in groups without having to be the center of conversation. Chuck is more interested in listening to other people's problems that he is in discussing his own. From Partial Prohibition to health care policy, Chuck always does what feels right, no matter the political stakes. That's why his re-elections are so tight in a district that should provide a Republican landslide. That's one reason why Republicans are so uneasy with him—he isn't a yes man.

That's why Father hates him so.

Father and all his museums and buildings and money, his fingerprints all over Grand Rapids, but no longer over Adam's life. Adam doesn't have much use for the old man, or the old city. His old friends back in G.R., the old high school and family acquaintances, they are all straight and married to their spouses and their conservative views, constantly making one-sided conversations about their beautiful kids and cavernous houses. The gay friends aren't much better. After Jimmy, the few homosexual men Adam met all seemed shallow, any potential depth loaded with baggage from family estrangement. Adam accepts the reality of that perception, yet the realization of causation burns at his moral fiber: when society labels you "Piece-of-Shit" at a very young age, you grow up believing it. In Lansing, Nick was no different, and at this point, Adam is pretty much ready to give up on guys and people of his generation in general. *Shallow.* He made a promise to Chuck; however: *I will try dating again.* He did try, and scars from the effort made him more miserable than ever.

Kevin, the 130-pound bouncer, scoots by in a pair of bright orange pants. "Hiya sexy," he says. Adam nods, offers a hello. Ed and John from Grand Ledge follow in matching blue jeans and tight white t-shirts, slipping Adam soft-cheeked kisses as they pass. Despite its warehouse grandeur, *Paradise* is familiar, comfortable. Yet, Adam is restless, his mind spinning in rabid analysis of his upcoming meeting with Chuck. *Sunday can't come soon enough,* he thinks, feeling a need to distract himself from heavy thought.

He decides to take in some pool.

Adam puts his money on the table, noticing the new guy right away: his sturdy frame almost concealed by a tan sweater and baggy khakis, he is running the pool table, cleaning out flamboyant Michael Blackman. Michael, the house shark, isn't accustomed to losing; no doubt he would much rather have the new boy cleaning his cock at home instead of his clock here.

Smack! The boy rifles a royal blue four into the corner pocket before tapping the eight ball softly into the side to finish the game. Michael is grinning in defeat, his lusty stare encircling the new boy as they shake hands in a ritual of sportsmanship. Adam walks over to Michael, kisses him.

"Nice try, champ" he says.

Michael corrects him: "Former champ."

The new boy flashes them a startled *"I don't believe you just kissed in public"* glance.

He's definitely new to the scene, Adam thinks. *Probably still considers himself a bisexual.* The boy pulls the tan sweater over his head and ties it in a knot around his waist, tight muscles bulging out from under his black t-shirt as he does so.

"Nice couple of shots you had there," Adam says.

"Thanks," says the boy. "Are you up next?"

Adam bobs his head, smiles. "Reckon I am," he says. He feels confident, saucy. *Wow, I haven't felt like this in a long time. What a difference a few minutes can make.*

"Loser buys shots?" the boy asks.

"Shots of what?" *Is he trying to get me drunk?* Adam figures him too naïve to be playing that game. In fact, it looks to him like Josh is just hitting his stride after a few drinks.

"Loser's choice, I guess."

"Sure, why not? I'll play for shots." Adam feeds the table his coins and begins to rack the balls.

"Uh, sorry, buddy," the boy says, shaking his head. "Money breaks." His dark blond hair is perfectly moused over his forehead in cut spikes.

"Oh, I'm sorry." Adam's face blushes slightly.

The boy loads the balls, his biceps rippling under smooth pink skin as he moves the racked triangle back and forth over green felt.

Adam takes Michael's stick, lines the cue ball against the triangle mass in a power-angle. Feeling all eyes on him, he quickly ropes a shot, scattering balls in a broken stream of marble. The nine-ball plunks off the rail and buries itself into a corner hole. "Guess I'm stripes," Adam says. "And by-the-way, my name is Adam."

"Hi, nice to meet you." The boy takes a swig of his beer.

"Well, what's yours?" Adam asks.

The boy pauses. "Oh, um, Josh." Adam, not sure if the boy is being honest or not, fires up a Marlboro light.

"Josh indeed," he says, just like Chuck would say it.

"Don't plan on making it to thirty, do you?" Josh asks, smirking. He takes another swig of beer.

"Don't plan on driving home tonight, do you?" Adam snaps. Josh's face drops, then he smiles again.

Adam lines up the three, banks it into the corner.

"Are you one of those angry-bitch chain smokers?" Josh asks, smirking again. Adam busts out laughing and misses his next shot.

Josh rubs chalk on the end of his stick, lines up a shot on the four.

"Are you an alcoholic?" Adam asks, hoping to interrupt his shot.

The four ball shoots into the pocket with a snap.

"No, I'm more of a binge drinker. I get into these binges and just keep going. It's hard to stop sometimes."

"Don't you worry about drunk driving?"

"Yes, of course I do. I usually drink at home, though. Oops, I probably shouldn't have said that."

"It does kind of make you look like a loser."

Slung over the table like a hungry spider, Josh knocks in a trifecta of balls with strong, short, sharp strokes before missing on the two. Adam is just as quick on the draw, closing out the five, one, and thirteen with a crisp series of clicks and thuds. Josh embarks on a final run, clearing his balls from the table in what looks like an effortless victory.

Adam and Josh swallow shots of schnapps as Michael puts money on the table, asks to play doubles. Michael and Homo Hank versus Adam and Bi-curious Josh: a couple dozen spinning shots later, Michael and Homo Hank emerge victorious.

Drink is flowing, especially for the new boy. Adam looks at his watch: one-thirty. Usually, Adam is out the door before last call: that was one of his own personal rules. He wants to get Josh's phone number before he leaves, however, which could prove to be a challenge. *Will he give me his number? If so, will it be his real number? Is "Josh" even his real name?*

Josh walks away from the table, buys them each another beer. "Thank you," says Adam, who has no intention of drinking his.

Josh sighs, covers his mouth and turns away to belch. The booze is hitting him. He leans over to Adam like he wants to ask a question, pauses, scratches his head. "Do you think I could post you up?"

Adam laughs. "Is that a come-on?"

"No . . . I meant," he burps, hand-to-mouth. "Basketball, you know." He waves his hand. His checks are flushed pink, still cute. "We're, like, the same size. It's hard to tell who would be tougher in the paint. In basketball, you know."

"I know what you're talking about. I play hoops. I wouldn't have minded, though, if it *was* a come-on." He smiles.

Josh's eyes widen like those of a surprised child. Then he just chuckles. "You call it hoops? That's funny."

"Everyone calls it hoops. You're not from around here, are you?"

"Where do you think I'm from, *Afghanistan*?"

They both laugh.

"So, you play?" Josh asks.

"Yes. I love hoops. I love sports." Adam looks Josh up and down. "And I doubt if you could post me up."

"How tall are you?"

"Five-eleven, one-hundred and seventy pounds."

"I see. I'm–"

"Five-eight, one hundred and fifty-five pounds."

"How did you know that?"

"I can just tell. Guys' bodies are easy to read. Women? Forget it. Tits and hips are much harder to figure."

"Do think I'm hot at five-eight, one hundred and fifty-five pounds?"

Adam laughs, nods. "Sure. Hot and wild."

"Wild?"

"Yeah, when you finally start to let loose. Wilder than Brooke Shields, as a matter-of-fact. Brooke Shields without underwear."

"Really. Hmmn. Well, I *am* wearing underwear. These clothes, though, what do you think? Do you think I look okay in these clothes? They're not very gay."

Gay. He said it. "You look fine."

"Sexy, even?"

"Sure. Sexy. In a third-world kind of way, you know."

Josh giggles. "You're cracking me up."

"You're the one who's funny. I'm usually not that humorous."

Josh purses his lips, makes to lean against the bar and almost falls over.

"Can I give you a ride home?" Adam asks. "Please?"

"That depends . . . what kind of car do you drive?"

"A Blazer."

"Is that romantic?"

"Sure it is."

"Gay romantic?"

"Definitely . . . whatever that is."

"Umm. Okay. What about my car, though?"

"Leave it here . . . what kind of car is it?"

"A Malibu."

"A Malibu? Definitely leave it here. Nobody's gonna touch that."

"Hey!"

Adam is shaking with laughter. "No, you misunderstood me," he lies. "I drive a Chevy, too, you know . . . I simply meant that the Malibu is a tough car—a tough car to break into. Leave it here. It'll be fine until the morning. The parking meters go in effect at 9am."

"Where am I taking you?" Adam asks. Josh fiddles with the tuner on the stereo, finds Motley Crue's *Wild Side.*

"You tell me," Josh says.

"Well, where do you live? I told you, I'll take you home."

"Grand Rapids."

"What?"

"I live in Grand Rapids."

"Oh jeez."

"That's okay." Josh reaches for the door. "I can drive home, really, just let me out. There, that's my car, right there. I don't wanna leave it here tonight anyway."

"No, I'm not going to let you do that."

"You can't drive me all the way back to Grand Rapids, even if I wanted you to. I'll pass out and you'll get lost."

"I doubt it. I'm from G.R."

"You're shitting me?"

"Nope." Adam pulls into the street, heads home. "But tonight, I'm taking you to my place in East Lansing," he says. "I've got a nice couch."

Josh sits quietly for a while; Adam isn't sure if he is immersed in the music, nervous at the thought of staying at a stranger's place, or just plain drunk. *We are strangers,* Adam thinks, *strangers with potential.* If he thought of Josh as just a trick, Adam would take him home and fuck him right now, end his bi-curiosity once and for all. But there is something about Josh, something that makes all the coldness within Adam warm again.

Adam cracks the window and lights a cigarette.

"I'm tellin ya, that habit is gonna kill you sooner than later," says Josh.

"Stop editorializing," Adam warns. "People don't take kindly to critical boozers."

"It used to be much worse," Josh explains. I've been cutting down the last couple days."

"Jesus," Adam mutters in a cloud of smoke, not sure if Josh is serious or not. "So, what do you do for a living?" he asks him.

"Huh?"

"Your job. What do you do?"

A long pause, then: "Um, sales."

Um: that meant that he was probably lying. Adam decides not to press the issue. "Sales," he says. "Very competitive." He cracks the window, ashes.

"Why do you do that?" Josh asks, visibly agitated. "Doesn't your car have an ashtray?"

"No, it doesn't."

"What do mean *it doesn't?* You know, it's fucking freezing outside. And you're cracking a window. What if someone was sitting in the backseat?"

"Well, I don't see anybody sitting in the backseat. If you're cold, Josh, I can turn up the heat."

"No, it just reminds me of my old man. I'd always be sitting in the backseat on family trips and he'd constantly crack that window to ash and I'd freeze my fucking ass off, cold air spraying all over me."

"Is he still living, your dad?" Adam asks.

"I guess you could say that."

"Not a good man?"

"Asshole. Haven't spoken to him in years. What about yours?"

Adam pauses. "Asshole." They laugh. "I don't even know who he really is anymore."

"What about yourself? Do you know who *you* are?"

"Now you're sounding drunk."

"No, really. Most people don't know who they are, they don't know their real selves. And if they do, if they get a glimpse of it, it scares the shit out of them and they make up some story, some image of who they want to be."

"Interesting." Adam thinks about Nick:

I want to make love to you.

"You think that all people are like that?" he asks.

Josh shrugs. "Most people," he says. "When confronted with themselves, they go plumb crazy. My grandfather was different. He knew himself. He just *was*. You know, he was one of the few people I've known that was totally comfortable in his own skin. My mom is kind of like that, but she's been hurt pretty bad in the past and that takes a toll on your confidence. Do you know anyone comfortable in their own skin?"

"Yeah. I did. Once." *Jimmy.*

They exit the freeway and come to an intersection near Frandor Mall. "Don't *you* worry about drunk driving?" Josh asks.

"No. I'm not drunk. Besides, cops are stupid."

Josh bristles, is about to strike back, but remembers that he decided to be in sales tonight.

They park, climb some stairs to Adam's apartment. Josh stumbles, scrapes his knee. Adam pulls him through the door to the couch, turns on the TV. A few blankets and a brand-new toothbrush later, Josh is already in dreamstate.

Sales. I wish I hadn't lied to him like that. For the first time in a long time, pieces had felt like they were in place—that's the way he felt around Adam: comfortable, at ease. Yet, he had blown it, he had lied.

Josh wonders if he will ever feel that safe again.

Drifting, Josh wanders into dreamland, thinks he is back at Mom's house.

Josh is burned out and empty. He's motionless on the couch, confused, retarded, taking it all in as his hands grow cold, numb, and his hair turns white, brittle, flaking off his head like snow. Josh's cheeks are hot, racing, and the voices on TV are barking at him like wild jackals. For some reason unknown, his knee is bleeding and this disturbs him. He cowers, in the corner, clothes wet and sticky, as Pepper, old a decrepit like her grandmother, is on television, interviewed by Willie Medville in his tweed coat with the black elbows. During the interview, Pepper speaks rapidly as she jumps about a black and white country house setting. She's wearing a girlish, checkered outfit that reminds Josh of the dress worn by Dorothy in The Wizard of Oz—except for the long, black, Nazi-issued storm-trooper boots pulled up to her purple, knobby knees. "Found ya," she squeals, looking right through the picture tube and into the family room. Her voice is sharp, gruff, sounds just like Jimmy Cagney. Her hair is an electric waterfall: long, gray, frazzled with static. Josh is hiding behind a chest in the corner of the family room, but he is consumed by the dreaded sense of knowing that she can see him. She points at him with long, twisted fingernails and her eyes are glistening with fury. Josh scrambles to his feet and darts into the kitchen. "Don't try to escape it," she yells. He runs into the bathroom and slams the door, but her screams are omnipresent over the house, echoing through every door, wall, vent, and pipe. She's clawing at the glass screen, trying to get out—Josh can hear the scratching escalate, and the thought of this mad, murdering woman running through his mother's house and destroying all her belongings unsettles him to the point that he flings open the door and runs back to the family room. "Top o' the world, Joshy Josh," the old Pepper is screaming. One of her black leather boots sticks out from the set, dripping tiny pools of thick, colorless moisture onto the carpet. Josh grabs the TV, shaking it as hard as he can, until the muscles in his tired arms ache, their veins bulge blue, and the old broad falls back into her TV-land kitchen with a flat thud. Her head smacks against the side of a porcelain counter as she hits the floor, black blood spraying out from above her ear in a quiet mist. "Ain't that a honey?" she asks, groping the wound with her gnarled, thin fingers. She sits there quietly with heavy eyes for a few minutes, blood mellifluously misting from her head, until one of the floor-level cabinets pops open and a fat, buck-toothed rat busts out from the pots and pans and scampers over her legs, across the tile floor, and into the bathroom. Pepper, screaming, neighing like a wild horse, jumps to her feet and tears after the creature, knocking over a table and some chairs.

Pan to the bathroom. The old girl is very agitated, and who wouldn't be, with blood spraying from her head and all. She has the rat cornered between the toilet and shower. The rat is cowering, shaking; a spiral, corpulent tail tucked between its legs. She's reaching down to swipe the creature, capture it into her hands, when a cheap, opaque plastic curtain flings open from the shower and Josh's father steps out from the tub wearing a long, black coat and matching fedora. "What is done cannot be undone," Father says, swiftly swinging a hanger-sized ax down over the Pepper's neck once, twice, finally decapitating her with a poetic third swing as fluids swell out of her mouth and throat stump. Her face is twitching on the floor as Father picks up the severed head and sticks his left hand through the hollow neck and up inside it. He pops out her eyeballs with two fingers and moves her face about like a puppet toy as the spray of blood from the wound subsides to a trickle. The eyeballs fall against the toilet rim and softly cascade into the yellowish water, where the rat gnaws on them like white chocolate eggs until Father grabs the eyeballs in a fist, stuffs them into his mouth with a gurgle, and swallows. "Now that's a spicy eyeball!" he screams, flushing the rat down the toilet with a flick of his wrist. "That's a fuck of a doozey there!" he coughs, pulling a .38 from his coat pocket, *firing it at random, again and again, as if his ammunition knows no limits. He's still chewing, swallowing, and when he's done, Josh hears him scream, "You like boys? That's wonderful, Joshy-Josh." He's yelling this over and over again, repeatedly firing the gun like a madman, and Josh is running all over the house for safety, but the noise is everywhere, so he runs outside into the yard, into the brutal cold, and the wind is nipping at his cheeks, at his eyes, and through his shirt, pants, and underwear. He's screaming, crying with bare feet, and the neighbors react by turning off their lights and locking their doors. Josh runs across town, across Grand Rapids, in a matter of seconds—over to Tesanovich's house, and Tesanovich lets Josh inside, albeit reluctantly.*

Josh is sitting in Tesanovich's kitchen, warming his feet in hot water as a caricature of Tesanovich stands by the stove, stirring soup with muscular, tattooed arms. Josh feels content and safe, and he doesn't care how many hairs cascade from Tesanovich's beard into the kettle. Yet, he forgets to object when Tesanovich goes for the TV—and it's too late—the set is on, blasting that horrible campaign commercial:

> *"Josh Brisco . . . Democrats want you to think that he's tough on crime. But Grand Rapids Republicans know better . . ."*

"Fucking turn it OFF!" Josh is screaming like an asylum inmate as a full-color kaleidoscope, featuring Mattie Josephs and Hector Paiz, floods over the screen and overflows into the kitchen.

"Shut up already," commands Tesanovich. He sets down his spoon and slaps Josh firmly. Josh's face stings. "Just shut the fuck up, you know."

He slaps Josh again and there's a snapping, a certain kind of . . .

(flash)

"So can I go Dad, or what?" The boy, about fifteen, thick blond bangs falling together in perfect sync just above his eyebrows, is asking Josh. The boy, as always, looks familiar, and just the sight of him fills Josh with warm comfort. Yet, there's a different intimacy this time, and Josh feels white, pale, and he's sweating, dressed in a tight-fitting navy wool suit with a white cotton shirt and silk paisley tie with raspberry speckles. He's frightened, unsettled—even though the boy doesn't seem overtly threatening, there's something even more familiar about him this time, as if a secret riddle is about to be revealed. His eyes are soft, blue, and he's looking at Josh, waiting for an answer from him, like Josh is his father. At first, Josh is incredulous, but soon it all soaks in and starts to make sense.

"Well, for goodness sakes, honey, answer him," chimes a long, tall blonde version of Pepper as she strides into the kitchen from who-cares-where. She winks at Josh, her eyes also ocean-blue, and Josh thinks, by condition, that if she's his, then he should want to fuck her brains out after the boy goes wherever he's supposed to go.

But Josh doesn't want the boy to go anywhere.

"I really wish YOU would go away once and for all," he says to Pepper.

She tilts her head back, laughs.

"So can I, dad?" the boy asks.

"Of course, son," Josh says in a succinct manner, with just enough moxy to cover up the fact that he has no clue to the boy's name.

"Oh, geez, Dad, thanks so much," the kid says, springing to his feet with vigor, throwing Josh a high five as the wife tilts her head in loving approval. Then he's gone and Josh just sits at the table, looking at this blonde, this long, tall, gorgeous dame, and she's looking back at Josh, waiting for him to say something.

"You know, honey," Josh finally says, "I think I'll just skip work today, give us some time to rediscover each other."

"Rediscover each other?" she asks, confused, looking over her shoulder at something behind her. A bad, awkward feeling builds in Josh's throat. He's flushed, embarrassed. "Jesus Christ," she says in a different, deeper voice, rolling her eyes. "Do you think this is fucking improv?" she asks, throwing her arms up in disgust. "And you think that piece of ass is really your son? You're the same fucking age, for crissakes!"

Josh starts to say something, but it's too late and all he feels is this . . .

(flash)

"Looks like your running on the wrong cylinders there," says the blonde, maybe eighteen, as Josh stands behind him in a dank, greasy garage. He's bent over the front of a black Ferarri, shirtless, and the muscles in his shoulders are flexing as he turns a large, rusted wrench over some knobs under the hood.

"You're the basketball player, the Carolina Blue Boy. Where do I know you from?"

He smiles at Josh over his right shoulder as he switches the wrench into his left hand and continues to turn, twist. His Levi's, a size or two too large, drop below the bronze tan line around his waist as he reaches deeper under the hood and as his arm stretches Josh can see a faint trickle of moisture nesting in the soft, brown hair fluffed under his arm. He's resting a knee on the front bumper, digging in further, and his jeans drop to the point where Josh can see his smooth, white ass in its entirety. Although Josh fights himself from visualizing it, he knows if the jeans drop any further, he'll get to see . . .

"Maybe you should drive it home?" the boy suggests, and Josh is at a loss for any response. His head is jumping, tingling.

"What?" Josh manages to say.

"You know, like a test drive," the boy says, pinching a piece of dried grease from his nipple. "How will you know if you like it unless you try it?" He turns around to face Josh and his hairless chest is pulsing.

"The car?" Josh asks.

"Yes the car." There's a faint line of light brown hair starting under his belly button.

"Wanna see for yourself?"

"Huh?"

"Wanna see what's under the hood?" The boy shrugs toward the car, working his fingers over his fly, popping it open with a 'bang!' Josh hopes that the boy won't pop his dick out because not only will that bang be much louder, but Josh fears that he won't be able to resist, control hiself, and everything he knows says that he shouldn't want to see this boy's penis, but he does want to see it . . . to touch it, rub it, put it in his mouth and suck it until he . . .

(flash, squirt).

Josh wakes up on Adam's couch, his creamed underwear wet and sticky. The light from the television shines over his puffy, dehydrated face. *What time is it?* Looking for a clock, Josh rolls over and is greeted by a small, framed photo standing by itself on an empty bookshelf: a shirtless boy in Carolina blue shorts, blond bangs, holding a basketball at his hip, illuminating a faint, reassuring smile.

"This habitation is in some kind of discord, let me tell you," moans Lady Patricia, sitting in a corner chair behind the kitchen table, motionless as a wax statue.

Leslie Thompson is biting her tongue. Adequately efficient, Leslie would be the first to admit her housekeeping shortcomings. Even if she had been classified as meticulous, there was little doubt that Lady Patricia, her robotic mother-in-law with the bottomless glass of scotch, would find some fault in her cooking, in the layout of the family room furniture, or even in the abstract selection of colors that decorated the kitchen interior. The criticisms were constantly forthcoming and occasionally grating. Lady Patricia, a self-described *Lady of Privilege*, knew nothing about the demands of working full time *and* raising three pre-adolescent children. While balancing conflicting responsibilities was one of Leslie's strengths as a mother *and* an elected official, Lady Patricia had little appreciation for such a skill. She did know a sloppy house when she saw one, however.

"I find it incomprehensible, this house," Lady Patricia says in a sonorous tone, although her lips don't seem to be moving. After her first husband's death, Patricia Thompson of Belmont, Michigan, had briefly married an impoverished British Lord who was as attracted to her late husband's millions from resort holdings as to her questionable charms. With that second marriage now far behind her, Lady Patricia chose criticizing her daughter-in-law as her new association in life. Even though Leslie, a scholarship student at Brown, was very much aware that Lady Patricia was putting on airs, some of her criticisms still managed to sting, bringing back memories of her own efforts to break free from her lower middle class background. "And this political business—what nonsense!" continues the Lady. "Who runs for a job that pays less than it costs to obtain?"

Lady Patricia had a point. The campaign for attorney general had cost the Democrats over $6 million, $150,000 of which came out of Leslie and Germaine's rainy day account. Unfortunately, Lady Patricia had come across that information last night while watching a Fox news story on campaign finance laws. *"That money was for the children!"* she gasped. *"My son should be ashamed of you. Instead, he traipses around the house with an attitude so cavalier that I find it horrifying."*

Lady Patricia sighs loudly. "Well, I do find it quite a shame that we sit here for dinner at such an early hour," she says, a napkin tucked under her green turtle neck like a bib. Her voice slices through the comfy kitchen air like a fighter jet through the clouds. "It's only slightly less than ridiculous, this *Something and Mistletoe* fiasco. What a fracas!"

Again, the old bat had a point. Leslie did not want to go off to the west side of the state for anything tonight, especially the phony-baloney *Mistletoe to Go* 'fiasco,' but there was no way she could get out of it now. Even if she could, she wouldn't leave Slade Pickens kicking for his life like a cow in a sea saturated with piranhas. No, she would not do that, no matter how much it yanked the chain of the good Lady Patricia, who keeps muttering, "Utterly ridiculous!"

"I don't find it ridiculous at all, Grandma," says Spencer, Leslie's blond-haired, blue-eyed eight-year old. He is attending to a Batman coloring book, sitting at the window seat of the table, across from his eleven-year-old twin sisters Jane and Alphie.

"Dear me," Lady Patricia grumbles. Her leathery lips stretch into a frown, the corners of her mouth are red ditches of wayward saliva and blotched lipstick. "I don't know how many times I must say it, really I don't." She looks at Leslie, then at Spencer. "Dear child, please do not refer to me as *'Grandma.'* I shall be recognized as *'Lady*

Patricia,' and nothing less. It's a matter of proper courtesy. Much more decent that this political monkey business."

Alphie and Jane chirp in as Germaine enters the kitchen with a plastic bag of oven mitts. "I like the political business," boasts Alphie. "I'm gonna run for governor some day."

"And I'm gonna run as her Lieutenant Governor," says Jane.

"What about me?" asks Spencer. "Where do I fit in?"

"You can run for the state Senate," says Jane.

Spencer throws his fork on the floor as his brow curls. "They're all Republicans!" he yells. "I'm not gonna be no damn Republican."

"Spencer!" Leslie raises her voice in an authoritative, controlled manner. "You watch your mouth, young man!"

"Oh, my," sighs Lady Patricia. "The cursing in this household! Children cursing! And so casually endorsing the local labor party! I have not experienced such discord since my thyroid operation back in January!"

"Did you say *thyroid operation?*" asks Spencer. "Mrs. Martinez's dog, Sasha, had a thyroid operation last year. And then all his hair fell out!" The girls howl in laughter.

Leslie bends over the counter to prevent herself from laughing. "Spencer, we don't talk like that in this house," she says carefully.

"Mrs. Martinez?" asks Lady Patricia. "A Spanish teacher, no less."

"There are *some* Democrats in this state Senate," Alphie informs her brother. "Just not a lot. But if you're a good candidate, you can win, even for the state Senate."

"Perhaps you could try your fortune at running the state prison," adds Lady Patricia.

Spencer frowns as Germaine bends over the oven, pulling out the roast. "Mom," Spencer says, "when does *Lady Patricia* go back home?"

"That's enough, Spencer," Leslie warns, suppressing a smile. "Kids, be nice and help your mother set the table so I can get out of here on time."

"How disrespectful," says Lady Patricia, a strong air of austerity in her voice. Her eyes, tired and drawn from too much afternoon whiskey, dance about in worn, drooping pockets. Despite her drunken condition, the Lady possesses a certain witchy beauty unique to the spirit of the very rich . . . it is as if her command of privilege is a protective barrier to a set of values that were wrangled and self-questioning, and therefore vulnerable in the face of progressive thought. "A woman should keep a house, and that would seem to include all the cooking," she snaps. "Beef roasts over political roasts would be preferred."

"Now, Lady Patricia, that's quite enough fussing already," says Germaine, the roast steaming on the counter, its peppery scent filling up the house. Germaine has never been allowed to call the Lady *mother* or *mom*, not even as a little boy. "You know, you're having dinner with the Attorney General-elect of the Great State of Michigan."

"I don't see what's so great about it," snaps the Lady. Leslie barely manages a crude smile as Lady Patricia projects another deep, audible sigh, adding, "And dear me. A girl like that in office? A rattling good situation indeed! Imagine."

Slade is tired and still a bit drunk, even after a brisk walk. Somewhat disoriented by the bright city lights, Slade worries he is late and rushes into the Sierra Room, crashing his nose on the glass door separating the lobby from the cozy inside of the establishment. "Ah, Christ," he mumbles, careful to catch the blood drops in his hands so that they don't stain the front of his crisp white Polo button-down.

"Did anyone fucking see that?" Slade asks in a muttering grumble.

"Probably not," laughs Leslie Thompson. Her wavy blond hair hangs in teased curls over her forehead, cropped short over each ear and back to her neck. She's wearing a purple blouse under a black blazer pulled snugly over both shoulders. In his injured condition, Slade can't see her matching skirt and purple high heals, but with a quick look, he is reminded that Leslie Thompson has the best tits of any broad ever elected to public office. He makes a mental note of it, tilting his chin upward to help plug the bleeding. Blood runs down into his throat and he starts coughing like a madman.

"Leslie and I were just talking about legislative priorities for next session," says State Representative Charles Hriniak as he pats his good friend Slade on the back. "You'll have to chime in once you settle down. That's a real storm you got cookin in them sinuses of yours."

Slade gathers his breath, "Hello Chuck," he finally manages.

Hriniak looks at Slade and laughs in his creepy but harmless Boris Karloff cackle. "Jesus, Slade, you gotta be careful with them doors," he says, scuffling in his brown Hush Puppies. Chuck Hriniak is never one for standing still.

"*Them* sinuses? *Them* doors? Nice command of the English language there, Chuck." Slade notices that, for once,

Hriniak's toupee is screwed on straight. "Definitely a Grand Rapids Westsider if I ever heard one."

"Only in dialect, Slade," Hriniak says. His fake hair is combed straight down, dangling in bangs that rest just over his eyebrows. "Only in dialect," he repeats. The wig is a Thomas Jefferson model, dark brown, and matches poorly with the unkempt, wiry gray locks that sprout over and behind Hriniak's ears. "I'm not otherwise easily catagorized. Your nose done bleeding? Go get me a drink, will you?"

Slade laughs. "You Republicans are all horribly bossy people, you know that, don't you?"

The twitchy corners of Hriniak's mouth break into a wide grin as he shakes his head. "That's not *exactly* true, Slade," he says, his head rocking back and forth like a bobble-head doll. "All horribly bossy people are Republicans, but not all Republicans are horribly bossy." Leslie laughs, which only encourages Hriniak's head to bobble faster, in the kind of harsh motion that might cause the toupee to slide off his head and onto the ground. Slade had seen it happen before—twice as a matter of fact— during heated debate on the House floor. Each occasion had amused and delighted a majority of the representatives, yet the wayward rug provided no comic relief for Slade, who was no stranger to the pain of public embarrassment. True to the memory of his late mother, Slade Pickens never reveled in laughter derived from someone else's humiliation.

"How quickly you forget, my friend, that I've supported your appropriation recommendations time and time again!" continues Hriniak, his hair still in place. "In fact, I think that's gonna cost me my seat!"

"Yes, Slade, and he supported me," says Leslie, her smile intoxicating. "Let's not forget that."

"*Unofficially*," Hriniak says, shooting a quick glance over each shoulder. "And that's hush-hush around here. I'm already an endangered species, you know. If word gets out that I supported you, that just might be enough ammunition for Richmond to make me extinct."

"Has he stripped you of your committee assignments?" Slade asks.

"We'll talk on Sunday," says Hriniak, his tone serious.

Slade gingerly touches his nose. "The bleeding's stopped," he says. "Why don't I run us up some drinks?"

"Now who's talking like a Westsider?" Hriniak asks. "You know, Slade, you should consider growing a moustache. You'd be Old School Westside, and besides, it would help cover up that large schnoz of yours."

Slade grimaces, shakes his head. "I'll get those drinks," he says. "What'll it be?"

"Jack on the rocks," says Hriniak as Slade checks his khaki Polo slacks. *No blood.* "Slice of lime."

"Cosmopolitan," says Leslie, her smile slightly crooked: a genetic trait she inherited from her father.

As Slade tiptoes through a cluster of schmoozing GOP debutantes, a microphone squeaks, the room hushes, and DutchWay co-founder Wayne Van Anders takes the stage amid a bit of dissipating chatter. "I'd like to offer a prayer to Christ," he says, spinning into a long-winded sermon giving thanks to God for allowing the rich to reach their political and business fortunes. His voice, loud, baritone, and piously sincere, drones on through Slade's five-deep wait at the bar. "We are DutchWay, we are God's people."

Enthusiastic applause ensues.

Hriniak's face turns candy-apple red. "Do you believe the banality of this?" he asks Leslie. "These are God's people? When? On Sunday, when they're taking a break from tearing people apart? These bastards, I've seen them *ruin* people. I've seen Van Anders almost ruin *his own son.*"

Leslie's sly smile fades into a flat grimace. She is well aware of Van Anders' billions and his standing in Fortune 500. She is vaguely familiar with DutchWay, his multi-billion dollar pyramid-marketing scheme. However, she knows only bits and pieces about his personal life. "Well, Chuck, at least we were invited here," she says.

"That's Slade's doing, and I'll tell you, that in itself is a surprise. The Chamber of Commerce usually doesn't listen to him . . . I mean, the horny bastard is a genius and they don't even give him the time of day. It's not about ideas to them. It's about money."

"I agree, Chuck, but it's about money to a lot of folks."

"Especially now, with term limits setting in. Those damn term limits are gonna ruin this Legislature."

"Why do you say that?"

"Because, term limits allow people like Van Anders here to control who runs for office, who wins elections, and how they serve in the Capitol."

"I don't know, Chuck. It was about money back when I served in the House, and that was before they came up with term limits."

"Yeah, but it's worse now. Buying politicians off is a big time business. Look at these guys from DutchWay. I'm telling you, they own every Republican in the state."

"They don't own you, Chuck."

"Great. I'm the only one who doesn't march in line. The freshman legislators–you should see them. They don't even *think* about thinking for themselves. It's dangerous. And you know what scares me the most? They think they're on a mission from God. Van Anders and his little army are like Nazis!"

"Nazis? Isn't that a little strong, Chuck?"

"Let me tell you something, Leslie," Hriniak snaps. "When tonight's party is over, you get to go back home to your nice, little, enlightened Oakland County suburb: secular, educated, serene. I have to stay here, with these conservative Christian soldier yahoos, in this culture of repression. There's no escaping it."

Slade comes back with the drinks, shaking his head. "Cash bar, can you believe it?" He passes a Cosmopolitan to Leslie and a Jack Daniel's to Hriniak, holding onto an olive-less Manhattan for himself.

"You deliver, as always, Slade," Leslie chuckles as all three of them touch glasses in toast.

Wayne Van Anders continues, finishing his introductory prayer. "Thank you, everyone," he says. "Thank you for coming. And thank the Lord God for making this all possible."

"Amen," mumbles a majority of the crowd.

"I want to take this opportunity to talk to you all about something very important," continues Van Anders. "More than a few people here tonight are familiar with the achievements of the People About Christ Political Action Committee—"

Thunderous applause.

"Yes, People About Christ: the PAC PAC. For those of you who aren't familiar with its legacy, let me explain." He pauses, looks up from his notes, smiles, and continues. "What's the PAC PAC all about? Well, let me tell you. PAC PAC is about taking a stand. It's about standing up against bad people and evil ideas. It's about standing up to godlessness, the *Right to Die* movement, for example. A membership to the *Right to Die* movement is a passport to hell. At no time did the Lord give man His consent to kill the weak. Not in cold blood, not in what they call 'humane' circumstances. Euthanasia is simply a euphemism for *murder*. You all know that Christ Our Lord would not support the convenient slaughter of our elderly. Euthanasia is murder, and it too often is at the expense of society's weakest individuals, individuals that we should be moved by spirit to protect: the sick, the elderly, and of course, the unborn. Oh, the unborn. How can we as a nation continue to oversee their Holocaust with but a shrug? Abortion is the legalized slaughter of our beautiful and precious unborn children. And like abortion, the liberals are fighting to legalize euthanasia. In fact, they're gathering signatures for another ballot drive as I speak. Together, we need to stop this. PAC PAC brings people together against abortion and euthanasia. This year, PAC PAC raised over $950,000 to help defeat Proposal A—assuring that no one but God will determine when a patient shall die. That was statewide. Locally, we drafted and passed the SSI: the *Safe Streets Initiative*, calling for all Grand Rapids retailers, restaurants, and bars to cease serving and selling alcohol at midnight. At first, we met stiff opposition from some retailers. They were being selfish. Personally, after giving so many millions of my own dollars to philanthropic causes, I found myself disgusted with business leaders who don't give anything back to the community. And I'm still disgusted. But in the end, we showed them." Van Anders pauses to acknowledge more rising applause before continuing. "PAC PAC has been proud to combat the liberals of this state. The liberals may mean well in practice, but their lack of moral balance deems them inappropriate for West Michigan. Although some folks in this room may not be as partisan inclined, it was very pleasing for community activists and morally conscious businessmen to see Republicans gain four seats in the state house, giving us a 56-54 majority."

Slade winces, spits angrily into his napkin as more murmurs of approval circulate through the crowd. Leslie, sensing an eruption, grabs his wrist. Her grip is calming.

Van Anders continues. "Now, the Grand Old Party has control of the House *and* the Senate, and with our very own Jack Bungle entrenched in the Governor's mansion, we have all the pieces in place for a real powerhouse of a law-making machine—and a *Christian* machine at that. We are creating history. That's what PAC PAC is . . . we're all about the American dream, apple pie, and promoting the Lord's Will."

Thunderous applause. Hriniak feels like puking.

"Thank you, thank you," says Van Anders. "Please, really, thank you. Thank you, West Michigan."

The applause simmers, Van Anders continues.

"There's more. Although we have build great momentum to ride into the future, we need to build upon it by reaching out to Michigan's youth. In my role as founding father of PAC PAC, I feel that as a society, we need to become more balanced. We need to be better listeners." Van Anders purses his lips and pauses, blinking his eyes. "Sure, we're all good talkers, but sometimes we talk a little too much. We need to listen. I could love somebody just by listening and so can you. Talkers just don't want to listen." His eyebrows arch into half circles as he smiles and tilts his head, looking at the microphone as if it is talking to him. "Young people in general don't want to listen. They are talkers. Young people don't want to follow rules. They lack respect for law and order. And their bad behavior cannot be excused by saying 'my heart is right.' We have to stop excusing people and start holding them accountable. We have to change their wayward ways. Only then will we be successful in providing the balance that our society so desperately needs.

"Before I introduce our next guest, I would just like to say that I'm sure that the Good Lord is proud of what we are doing here in Grand Rapids, and I do hope that He sees fit to have us continue to prosper. In Grand Rapids, we are truly blessed as the Lord Our God continues to shine His special light on us." Van Anders pauses and grins. "Oh, and the Lions, too: may the Lord see fit to help them out against Tampa Bay this Sunday. May it be the Lord's will that the Lions win!"

Applause and laughter emanates from the crowd.

"This is something else," mutters Slade as Leslie just shakes her head. "It's pretty damn easy to rail about respect for law and order when it's your money that's shaping the goddamn laws."

"On that note," continues Van Anders, "I'd like to cut to the chase and present Dr. Dick Feenstra, President of GRADE A: the Grand Rapids Alliance for Dialysis Enhancement. For those of you unfamiliar with GRADE A and Dr. Feenstra, let me just preface by saying that this man and his Alliance have done more for the quality of Grand Rapids area dialysis than any man or organization in our fine city's rich history."

"Alliance?" asks Leslie. "What alliance? GRADE A is no alliance!" Her eyes are incredulous, almost wild. "We covered this in the campaign . . . I mean, this is one of the issues that I beat Carmine Rossi over the head with . . . GRADE A is nothing but a monopoly! How can they spin this Feenstra as a hero? Do you know this guy?"

"I know a little bit about the dialysis scam, yeah," says Hriniak. "Governor Bungle was involved in that one, too, wasn't he?"

Slade, a virtual historian of Grand Rapids' political developments, nods his head. "Yeah. His organization practically blackmailed St. Mary's into giving up their outpatient treatment center. Then Feenstra and Van Anders bought off all the doctors, bought all the equipment, and began charging patients $800 a treatment session—versus the $140 a session it cost at St. Mary's."

"Is this how Grand Rapids works?" Leslie asks.

"It's the DutchWay conspiracy, honey," says Slade. "Van Anders and his buddies have been milking this town for decades. There's a lot of shit going on under the radar that people just don't know about."

Hriniak slurps his Jack and nods his head. "That's right. Van Anders gives all kinds of money to the community, but it comes with strings attached. For every dollar he gives, he reaps five or six from taxpayers. His bought-off politicos virtually guarantee it."

"It's the DutchWay conspiracy," repeats Slade. "Van Anders has a little contest with himself to see just how many publicly financed buildings he can get his name on."

"Don't give me that, Slade," Leslie says. "I'm Dutch on my mom's side and we never went around fucking people over in the name of Christ and capitalist cupidity."

Slade smiles. "I said '*DutchWay.*' One word. Not 'Dutch *way.*' That's two words," he explains. "Van Anders is a billionaire. He has a grip over the city, and to some extent, the state. His is the typical conservative philosophy: *Hooray for me, fuck everybody else.*"

"Van Anders has his hands in everything," says Hriniak. "And I'm at the end of the road with it."

"And you *choose* to play ball with these people," says Slade.

A rare frown flashes across Hriniak's face. He thinks back to his brief tenure as a Democratic staffer during the Watergate Era. That was a lifetime ago. "I had no choice but to run as a Republican in '84. Times were different back then."

"Back then? What, there's been a revolution since?" asks Slade. "How can you go to bed with these people? It was wrong for you to do it then, and it's growing more and more wrong each day, Chuck. I mean, just look at the shit going on in this town. I'm the only elected Democrat and I can't do anything about it by myself."

"I told you that I'm at the end of the road with it. We'll talk more on Sunday."

"Fine. I was thinking about naming a task force to investigate this price gouging. But I need more clout than a task force to really make a difference. If I was speaker, I could appoint a sub-committee. Now *that* would turn some heads."

"You've got Leslie. This is something the attorney general should look into, anyway, not the Legislature."

"He's right, Slade," adds Leslie. "I already warned Feenstra that I was going to look into this as soon as I take office in January. I had no idea how much muscle was behind him, though. I'm totally outraged that he is represented here tonight as if part of some philanthropic organization."

"Somebody has got to do something," says Slade.

The three of them take a table in the back as Van Anders, Feenstra and company stop talking and an orchestra prepares to play on the stage.

"I think I'm ready for another drink," says Slade.

"Better hurry up and order a couple of rounds, we're approaching midnight," sasses Hriniak with a grin.

"Very fucking funny," says Slade as Leslie stares out the window into the teeth of swirling winds.

"Is that the little *social* club you and Slade run?" she asks.

"That's the one," says Hriniak.

"Well, it sounds like a good old boys club to me."

"Far from it," explains Hriniak, his face animated. "We have a few female members, as matter-of-fact. Representative Gloria Manson, a few staffers, Adam."

"Who's Adam?" she asks.

"My legislative assistant," Hriniak says with obvious pride. "I'm surprised you haven't met him." Hriniak neglects to mention that Adam is *Adam Van Anders,* son of their *Mistletoe to Go* host.

As a freshman legislator, Chuck had met Adam on the House floor, where the Michigan State sophomore was working as a college page under the guise of *Adam Anderson.* Hriniak instantly took a liking to the kid, who used to bring sodas and coffees to his desk without prompting. He'd have Adam sit in the folding guest chair and they would talk about basketball and rock music between votes. Hriniak had no idea the kid was a Van Anders until a year later, when he brought him into his office as an intern, where he was a natural fit.

Chuck Hriniak, a second-generation American, began his career in banking, working his way through college as a bank teller. Decades later, after sweating his way up to vice president of operations, he took an early retirement spurred by rapid mergers and a desire to run for public office.

Chuck Hriniak was familiar with the sacrifices involved in putting one's self through school, and he appreciated Adam's work ethic and determination.

But Wayne Van Anders didn't see it that way. From the House lobby, he phoned Hriniak, screaming into his cell phone like a madman. *"How dare you hire my son behind my back?"* he demanded. Hriniak, on his cell, watched Van Anders covertly from the staff lounge. *"I'll sue!"* Van Anders threatened, stomping his feet near the marble stairs.

"Who? For what?" Hriniak laughed.

"DO YOU KNOW WHO YOU'RE TALKING TO?" screamed Van Anders, his cheeks bulging like ripe tomatoes.

"I'm sorry, sir, I think you have the wrong number!"

Van Anders slammed down his cell so hard that the receiver fractured, scattering tiny pieces all over the stairs and lobby.

Van Anders continued to call, but his extended haranguing only galvanized Hriniak's steadfast desire to defy him.

That a Republican was thwarting his every move drove Van Anders nuts, especially when Hriniak was able to temporarily derail the Partial Prohibition legislation as it made its way through Commerce Committee.

"DO YOU KNOW WHO YOU'RE FUCKING WITH?" Van Anders screamed at him right after the committee meeting ended.

"Quid pro quo," explained Hriniak, shrugging his shoulders. *"Quid pro quo."*

Hriniak is distracted by commotion at the front door as Chip Richmond marauds into the Sierra Room flanked by assistants. Richmond, youthful and brash, is obviously basking in his ascension to Speaker-elect. "Big Daddy is in the house!" yells Richmond, handing his wool overcoat to an auxiliary. Heads turn, some smile.

Detached, alienated, and perturbed by his impending exclusion from Appropriations, Hriniak can't help but express disgust at the display. Only four years earlier, Chip Richmond leapfrogged past Tonto Rodriguez, a politically inept incumbent, to snag one of Kalamazoo's Republican seats. In no time, Richmond made a name for himself at the Capitol, usually by posing as the poster boy for the spoils system. Hailing from a family of liquor distributors, his first mission as Commerce Committee vice-chair was to cut a "bipartisan" legislative deal with Speaker Morris Hyde that forever handcuffed retailers to contracts with the Richmond family. It was the kind of price-gauging that made the thieves like Dick Feestra jealous. Prices immediately shot up, manufacturers had no leverage whatsoever, and consumers were hit with what was essentially an illegal monopoly tax. When the conflict of interest was called into question by the press, Richmond simply ducked it, hiding behind a smoke screen of local church leaders who denounced drinking altogether and hailed *any* liquor tax as "The Lord's Tax." That's not to say that the monopoly legislation benefited everyone in the Richmond family. In fact, it didn't. But Chip, with help from his friend Speaker Hyde, took care of unaffected family members, too, appointing sixty-eight of them to state positions, despite the fact that many of them actually lived in Indiana and Ohio, not in Michigan. Hyde, who took a twelve percent kick-back from the sixty-eight salaries, enthusiastically approved the appointments. It took three years, but the *Lansing State Journal* finally exploited the controversy in a front-page feature article, eventually earning Hyde the first of his five indictments. Richmond, who escaped on technicalities, was almost re-called by the voters in his district. The lobbyists, lead by bizarre alliance of Carmine Rossi and the National Rifle Association (NRA), came to Richmond's rescue by dumping millions of dollars into his special election campaign so that he might survive the recall. On Election Day, a revitalized Richmond emerged victorious with the words, *"Left-wing communist sympathizers, this is your reckoning day."* Touting issues like Guns (*"An armed society is a safe society."*), Religion (*"If God didn't want the Ten Commandments displayed in our classrooms, then he wouldn't have created walls."*), and more Guns (*"Guns don't kill people—minorities kill people."*), Richmond cultivated a vocal, angry, and loyal constituency not only in his district, but across the entire state.

In the Capitol, Richmond was the kind of discipline problem usually reserved for the worst of prison classrooms. Once, during a debate on gun control, he whipped out a concealed weapon and shot it at the hallowed roof of the House chamber. When Rep. Barney Johnson recommended that House colleagues vote to suspend Richmond, the Capitol was engulfed by a violent protest organized by arduous Richmond supporters from the

Michigan Militia, a quasi-Nazi group of drunken conspiracy theorists. Although there were no fatalities, three men were shot, one stabbed, and an elderly woman was hit in the face with a rubber brick. During the chaos, Richmond himself vacated his floor seat to join his followers outside. Armed with a loud megaphone, he denounced Johnson as "Representative *Dick-less Johnson*" and urinated into a sewer duct. The crowd of rabid Richmond supporters grew, swelling from street corner to corner, and police were reluctant to act. This went on for hours, until the crowd finally exhausted its supply of whiskey and hooch.

The speaker-elect walks up to Slade Pickens, accompanied on each side by two enormous bodyguards clad in ill-fitting tuxedos. *Tweedle Dee and Tweedle Dumb,* thinks Hriniak.

"Well, what do we have here?" asks Richmond, his spiked hair pricked forward like little brown blades of grass. "I know these two bums," he says, chuckling, motioning to Slade and Hriniak. "However, I don't think that we have had the pleasure, Madame Attorney General-Elect." His eyes take a walk all over her figure.

"Leslie Thompson," Leslie offers, extending her hand. To her dismay, Richmond takes the hand and kisses it. Slade is red like Bob Hope in a marathon. "Actually," Leslie says, "We *have* met. I was the Chair of Commerce Committee when you were an assistant for Representative Ford."

"Oh, sure, sure. That dirty old bastard. I almost forgot about him." Chip seems embarrassed, a reaction which confounds Leslie. "Anyway, as I'm sure you know, I've come a long way from those days."

"Sure, those shoes are some pretty big ones to fill."

Slade mutters something about a shoe stepping in shit.

"What did you say, old man?" Chip asks, an air of challenge in his voice. "Sounds like you've already lost your majority *mind-set*."

Slade's hands clench into fists.

Hriniak steps in. "Hey, fellas, let's cool down here, huh?" he says.

"You always were the level-headed sort, Chuck," says Richmond.

Hriniak looks Richmond in the eye. Their noses nearly touch. "Yeah, they used to say that I brought tremendous balance to Appropriations," he says.

Richmond is silent.

"No comment? Well, I heard through the grapevine that as far as the Party goes, I'm low man on the totem pole."

Slade: "That's too bad. If you came over to my side of the aisle, I'd make you a general."

Richmond squirms on his heels, only to be saved from the awkward moment by Jizzy LeDoux, who saunters over to join the crowd. Richmond promptly introduces Jizzy to Leslie, but to Hriniak and Pickens, the mousy LeDoux needs no introduction. "This guy's a real fighter," Richmond boasts. "Did you see how he took down Josh Brisco? I mean, what a hard-fought campaign it was." There is no sense of irony in his voice. "Listen, I'll be right back. Another round?" Everyone nods. "You heard them, another round," he says to Tweedle Dee. "I'll be right back."

Hriniak and Pickens say nothing. Leslie, who doesn't want to come across as rude, is trapped. She searches for something to say to Jizzy LeDoux. "The amount of money involved in your victory was amazing," she finally manages.

"Oh, yes, yes," says LeDoux. His eyes, round and wide, are on Leslie with cocked brows. "I'm already building up my war chest for re-election. My goal is to have so much money in my campaign by the filing deadline that your fellow Democrats won't bother to challenge me with a top-tier candidate. Right now, I'm selling autographed photos for twenty bucks."

"What?" Hriniak laughs. He thinks LeDoux is joking.

"Yeah, twenty bucks." LeDoux shows them a photo of him standing under a tree outside the Capitol. He proudly smiles with teeth brown as wood.

"Ah, Christ," mutters Slade, "You're actually serious."

"Sure, why not?"

The Speaker-Elect's henchmen descend upon them with a fresh round of drinks. "A Manhattan, no olives for you, Slade," Richmond sings, his men handing out the cocktails. "A Jack Daniel's for Chuck—how proletarian! And for Leslie, of course, a Cosmopolitan."

LeDoux mentions that his Uncle Earnest introduced him to Manhattans at the age of eighteen. "Yes, he made me my first Manhattan, but by that time he was borderline senile. He cut his finger while slicing a lime, his blood swirling all over the glass and into the drink. He didn't feel a thing and I didn't want to embarrass him, so I just drank it without complaining."

"That's a charming anecdote," says Slade.

Richmond offers a cheer and they toast in half-hearted ceremony, tipping glasses and bottles. Slade's face turns sour. "Jesus Fuck. *Olives.*"

Richmond leans over, examines the drink. "Slade, there aren't any olives in your glass."

"Bullshit. There aren't now, but someone dropped some in there and then pulled them out, thinking I wouldn't notice. I can taste an olive anywhere."

Both Tweedles shrug their shoulders.

"This thing tastes like landfill." He sets it down.

The orchestra kicks into their first number; the Richmond posse scatters.

"Bodyguards, autographed photos . . . what the hell is this state coming to?" Slade asks as the three of them leave *Mistletoe to Go.* "*Jizzy LeDoux.* Sounds like a porn star. You'd think maybe, just maybe, he'd have a little charisma to make up for a name like that, but you saw the guy!"

"He thinks he's a movie star with those photos, Slade," says Hriniak.

"Movie star? I'm not sure if the House is turning into Hollywood or a damn circus. These new representatives are fucking freaks!"

"Fuck Chip Richmond," Hriniak says with exasperation as he, Slade and Leslie step outside the Sierra Room and are engulfed by the cold.

"Absolutely," adds Leslie.

The three of them are laughing; Hriniak grabs a couple cigars from his coat pocket; he and Slade try in vain to convince Leslie to smoke.

"Watch this," says Hriniak, who lights a cigar, inserts in his nostril and inhales, coughing a cloud of smoke out through his mouth.

"You guys are nuts," laughs Leslie.

"Where are you two parked?" asks Hriniak.

"I took a cab," says Slade.

"Me too," says Leslie. "Why don't we share this one? Is my hotel on the way to your house?"

"Nah, you don't wanna cab," says Hriniak. "Let me take you guys home. Heading south to the Westside, Slade?"

"You got it!" Smoke pours out Slade's stern lips.

"Over there." Hriniak points to his car. "I'm parked on the street south of here by the river, just under the bridge."

"You mean to tell me that you don't have your own driver?" Slade is sarcastic. "Or your own fat-ass bodyguards? I don't believe it!"

They all laugh and Slade doesn't recognize Norm Washington on security duty as they walk past him.

"That Richmond," continues Slade. "He thinks he's really something, don't he?"

Hriniak chuckles. "Well, the last laugh is gonna be on him, let me tell you, Slade. What's gonna be his claim to fame now? That he was *almost* speaker for a week? What a loser."

"He'll still be speaker," cautions Slade. We'll be co-speakers. The House will be deadlocked at 55 each side."

"What pushed you over, Chuck?" Leslie asks. "It seems to me that you took a lot of crap for a long time before you finally broke."

Hriniak is pensive as smoke dances from his lips. "I don't want to loose my seat on Approps," Hriniak explains, his eyes glistening. "And I don't want to lose my staff. My staff works hard. And Slade, just so you know, a clear-cut majority isn't out of reach. I know that Gloria Manson is very unhappy."

"And for good reason!" Slade shakes his head. "I'd rather have shared power than have to baby-sit Gloria Manson—she's like a poison." Slade pulls back his coat sleeve, takes a look at his watch. "It's only 10:30," he says. The prospects of going home and dealing with Darla Sue don't seem very attractive. He wants another drink instead. "I know of a fairly decent pub not too far from my house. What do you say we go for another couple?"

"I could go for that," Hriniak says. "I wanna know about my new committee assignments, Mr. Speaker."

"How about Appropriations?" asks Slade. "I'll make you the fucking chair if you can handle it. I told you I'd make you a general."

"I like what I hear. Let's talk more over some drinks without olives. Leslie, what do you think?"

"Approps sounds good, Chuck, but I might push for a staff raise, too. It'll be good to have you on our team—officially, that is." She pauses before continuing. "I'm gonna pass on the drinks, though. I'm tired and getting crabby. You guys go ahead. I'll get my own ride."

"Are you sure?"

"Yes. Look, there's a cab. Let me grab it."

Slade waves his arm to flag the taxi and kisses Leslie goodnight.

55-55. Shared power wouldn't be so bad, Slade thinks. Speaker of the House is so close he can taste it. His loins itch and his mind is abuzz. *There is a God, after all!* he reasons.

It would be his very last thought.

"You ever been to Detroit?" Pedro asks Tommy, his nose and feet a little numb, stinging from the cold even after the four malt liquors.

"What, you trying to make conversation so we don't freeze to death?" Tommy takes a swig of his malt and shifts his weight over one cheek, pushing a blast of air out from his ass.

"Oh, that's nice." Pedro's annoyance is accentuated by thinly-guised fear. Tommy was his favorite cousin, a darling of the family, and he hates mixing the kid up in monkey business. The idea of it, the idea of the smooth-skinned, good-looking eighteen year-old with the good grades, flowing hair and coffee-with-cream complexion getting involved in this deal is upsetting.

"You're having second thoughts, aren't you?"

"Nope. No way," Pedro lies. He stiffens, pulling his shoulders back and pursing his chapped lips. "Not having second thoughts at all." He tries to change the subject: "You never answered me. Have you or haven't you been to Detroit?"

"Nope." They finish their bottles and pop open a new round. The storefronts and bars past the bridge glisten under the pale gray moon. Orange street lights hover like spaceships floating in the chilled air. "This is good shit. Where'd you get it?"

Pedro decides to talk tough. "My guy in Detroit bought it for us. This ain't no pussy shit from the Grand Rapids suburbs."

"Fuck. I should go down there with you sometime. It'd be fun."

"No. You wouldn't like it one bit."

"Why not?"

"It's full of niggers."

Tommy shakes his head. "So what? We got 'em here."

"Niggers like you've never seen here in Grand Rapids, man."

Tommy makes a face as if questioning Pedro's credibility.

"I'm talking about *coon-ass niggers*," Pedro continues. "The kind that ain't been in Grand Rapids since way before we were born. They own Detroit. Run it like they're getting even or something."

"What the fuck are you talking about, man?"

"*Coon-ass niggers* is what I'm talking about. There haven't been any of them here or in Canada since the cops ran them out of Kent County during the riots in the sixties."

"*Canada*? *Riots*? What the fuck are you talking about?"

Pedro looks at Tommy and knows that he needs to say something wise. Nothing is coming to mind, however, so he just blurts out, "You know, the sixties. Free-love, Vietnam, protests, riots. It's a chicken and egg type thing."

Tommy rolls his eyes. "Whatever," he says as the door to the Sierra Room swings open in the distance and a group of suits stumbles out. "Hey! Is it one of them?"

Pedro springs up in the driver's seat, only to be disappointed. "No," he grumbles. "Not even close. Besides, it's only 10:30. The stuttering guy said that nothing would probably happen until close."

"Let me see the picture again."

"It's in the glove box."

Tommy pops open the glove box and studies the glossy 8"x10" as Pedro cracks his door and takes a leak into the street.

"You got it all figured out?" Tommy asks, sort of stupidly, considering that they had gone over the plan at least a hundred times since Pedro got back from Detroit.

"Yep. You know it, baby." Pedro sighs as he finishes his piss, zips up his pants.

Tommy takes out his gun and rubs it on this inside of his thigh. "Well, buddy," he says, "consider the job dead on payday. In fact, I'm gonna blow this bitch away and then go with you to Detroit and collect the rest of our money."

Pedro is relieved to have the company. "You're sure you want to do that?" he asks.

"Definitely." Tommy is smiling with a distant, dream-like expression on his face. "I'm gonna get that money tonight, take it directly to the registrar's office and sign up for classes first thing tomorrow. That way I can start school next semester, right after the Christmas break. It's all about getting a good education, you know. I don't want to get stuck cleaning toilets for the rest of my life."

"Outstanding, man," burps Pedro as Tommy lifts his leg and blurts out another fart. "That's the way to go about things. I respect that. Me? Well, you know me. I'm gonna spend my *allocation* on the usual: booze, whores, drugs, bitches, etcetera!" They both laugh.

"I know that's right!" says Tommy.

What neither of them knows is that their car trunk is loaded with enough chemical explosives to blow up an entire office building: a mixture of ethylene glycol dinitrate, a version of nitroglycerin, small amounts of RDX and HMTD, and 118 pounds of urea fertilizer—fused up to a circuit board with a timing device made from cheap Casio watches that is set for detonation at 1:15 A.M. Eastern Standard Time.

Norm Washington is slumped comfortably against a light post outside the Sierra Room, thinking that shit, this is one posh, mother-fucking place. He'd never been inside, of course, but what cop in his right mind would frequent a joint that charged $7 for a bottle of Budweiser? Christ, who needed *that*? Especially on a Grand Rapids beat cop salary.

Demotion sucked.

The night is pale, cool, but not especially frigid for the early winter. There is a constant breeze, the kind that offers less of a gust and more of a soft, quiet blow; and in it, wind driven-snow drops from the sky and cascades into an angled canopy of white against the blanched, worn, smitten city streets.

Norm: tall, sturdy, mysteriously black in his long, leather trench coat. Norm is known for carrying his own flask, but not tonight. Too much on his mind. He doesn't mind working the extra, off-the-job security gigs. They usually paid well, and besides, there was no one at home: Sheila walked out on him after the second fat lip.

The Sierra Room. The people inside have no idea what it is like to work two jobs. For them, counting investment returns and inheritances is a second job. Fuck, this place has the stench of money. They need this extra security so that their political patrons/donors can feel safe at the end of the show, when all the bars will dump their drunks out on the street at midnight. *Partial Prohibition: The Safe Streets Initiative*. Shit. What a prince of an idea. *Let's close the bars at midnight*. Did that make the streets any safer? Probably not. It just meant that more people, more drunks, would be out on streets for longer durations and more frequent occasions. Norm had already seen it. People were boozing in a frenzy, swallowing in one hour what they would normally consume in 2-3 hours. Safe streets? People were spilling out of the bars so drunk that they weren't just fighting with each other, they were walking into moving cars, running into light posts, driving into you-name-it. Goons and drug dealers polluted the streets, descending on vulnerable prey. The police force couldn't keep up. Manpower was short. Local Republicans, in an attempt to expose flaws in President Clinton's community policing program, cut department funding in half. *Clinton's fucked,* whispered the conservatives. *Spread the word.* They drugged the cat, cut off its legs, and threw it in the water. *See, I told you. The cat can't swim.* In the last month alone, three rapes, two murders, and one O.D. rattled the bar district. And this was a "Christian" town. Jesus Christ. Partial Prohibition did for safer streets what *Just Say No* did for drug prevention.

Tiny flecks of snow gather in clumps over Norm's fedora, glistening for a moment in the mellow streetlight before they melt and drip off the brim of his hat, gently streaming over his left shoulder. Tonight, he might have chosen a heavier, polyester-padded winter coat, but the leather trench is his *signature.* Being that this gig was happening downtown, signature won over practicality. To counter the nippy cold, Norm sensibly padded himself under the leather with two sweatshirts, a tee, double socks, and a pair of long underwear.

The brisk cavalry of beautiful people arrived early; most of the invited elites are already inside basking in the buffet of riches. Norm is relaxed, bored. As the light from the street posts vacillates, so does his mind. He reminisces about the good old days, when he and partner Dewey Long window shopped for free liquor, shaking down immigrant store owners and the underage booze hawks that frequented them.

Norm watches with interest as a hooded vagabond wanders around, shuffling over a drain and crossing the street before finally sitting at a small bench near the Sierra Room. Norm straightens up, moves closer to the restaurant's window, making his presence felt. The light post he abandons at the corner casts a yellow glow onto the street, and its ray begins to twitch, growing orange and thick before it crackles violently and goes out completely.

Darla Sue Pickens, the former Darla Sue Whitenheimer, tried reading books. She tried staying fit, living a healthy lifestyle, and she had tried desperately to get pregnant. None of it had worked for her and the longer she was married to Slade Pickens, the more she wanted and the less she got. Some might say that she suffers for her vanity, but that is silly. People suffer from being ugly, not beautiful, and that's what Darla Sue is: beautiful. Momma had told her that from day one, or at least as far back as she could remember.

Now in her early thirties, Darla Sue isn't a woman given to recollections. Sure, Momma's words still echo, having been ingrained in her head since birth, but that is about it as far as voices from the past are concerned. Darla Sue isn't one given to memories: she devotes little thought to the beer drinking first husband who slapped her around like a donkey. Nor does she speak in anecdotes of her high school days, which were climaxed senior year with her crowning as Miss Kent County. Thirty-three years old (on the cusp of mid-thirties, a frightening thought), Darla Sue is a woman given to fear: fear of the growing flabbiness of her porcelain white arms, fear of the crow's feat beginning to gravel around her eyes, fear of the extra five pounds gathering in her hips, fear of the strange brown splotches bursting out from under her skin, fear of the purple veins swelling under the parchment skin of her legs.

Then there is the matter of Slade: other than fear, no other diversion consumes her time. The exact time and occasion eludes her, but Darla Sue vaguely recalls having liked Slade immediately upon their first meeting. She was enormously amused by his witty observations and astute command of profane language. He knew the names and likes of every politician who had ever lived, and maybe every president and king, too. While he was considerably older than the boys she was accustomed to dating, the nimble Slade had swept her off her feet with a youthful vigor that was much more vibrant than that of her generation, which was starting to slow down and grow fat and slovenly as it passed the marker of its third decade. Slade was unique, special. Darla Sue married him without reservation after a quick courtship. Momma, the cancer chewing up her insides like termites, barely lived to see the wedding and had never been more proud. She was dead by the time the honeymooners returned from Hawaii. Darla Sue, devastated and lonely, returned from the Pacific Islands to her own isolated island. She turned to Slade for support, but after a brief effort to console her, he lost his patience. Once he had her, he completely lost interest, like a child tiring of a new toy.

Darla Sue's head aches, her back throbs. Too much drink and too much pot is feeling like it's not enough. Her brain is soggy dull and her pain is boldly sharp. She misses Momma. A wave of paranoia settles in. Nobody loves her. Slade is likely cheating on her, philandering all over Grand Rapids. She has a good sense for these things, or so she thinks.

In a last gasp measure to save their struggling marriage, Slade had taken her back to Maui. It was a big mistake. They thought it was going to be a celebration, which it was far from. He was miserable from the unexpected election losses within the party. His misery spread like Mad Cow Disease. He yelled at her for raiding the mini-bar in their hotel room. *"A three hundred dollar room now costs me six hundred, thanks to your boozing,"* he grumbled at checkout. She had seen the bill, though. Slade had racked up over a hundred dollars in long distance calls.

Presumably to his mistress.

She sits in the Chrysler, her toes and tiny hands numb from the cold and alcohol. *That's fine*, she thinks. The recoil from the revolver will have less of an impact. If her hand is numb, she won't feel the pain. Gloria Manson

Slade Pickens and his two musketeers swish by without a hello. Norm flicks his cigarette in disgust and it lands into a puddle of hardening slush with a hiccup. He begins to say to himself, "Fucking ass—" when he is startled by the old vagabond shuffling forward a few yards behind him.

"Hey, Mr. Copper," the toothless woman coughs in a heavy drawl. Her left coat sleeve, filthy and tattered, is sheared at the elbow to show that there is only half an arm in it. Her right arm, full in length, but small and frail, clutches to a battered old picnic basket, its flaps bent and molested to the point that they don't shut properly. Her face is browned, weathered from advanced age and too much sun. Her fatty cheeks hold wide, cucumber eyes and a carrot-like nose. Strands of coarse white hair twist out from under her tightly fixed red bandana and dance in a stiff breeze as her gaunt figure lists slightly to the side like a thin, brittle tree. "There's some real suspicious care-o-chures sittin in one of them cars over there," she says, her voice quiet and grave.

Norm looks past her to the long line of cars parallel-parked on the bridge. "What do you mean *suspicious*?" he asks.

"Spanish boys, I sees," she says. "They jus waitin to jump somebody with switchblades or worse, but I ain't got nothin they want. Young peoples today, they hide themselves in cars and behind bushes and then jump you before you know it. It's a teen problem, these young people is, an it requires an adult soloochin."

Norm strains his vision, thinks he sees some movement inside of one of the parked cars, but that was nothing unusual. An '88 or '89 Ford Escort rocks back in its space before pulling forward as Slade and his friends cross the street.

"There's our target!" says Tommy, a little too loud for Pedro's comfort.

"Keep it down, man, you're gonna rouse the chickens!"

"Look. There we go! Absolutely no doubt."

Pedro isn't so sure. "It's an hour and a half early. Gimme that picture," he says.

Tommy hands Pedro the photo.

"Okay, bingo," Pedro agrees. "That's definitely our game. You ready?"

Tommy pulls back the hammer of his .38 with a click. "Born ready. Warm it up, man."

Pedro turns the ignition, but before Tommy fires, a gold Sebring whirls past them and cuts off their view. "Shit," Pedro yells, stepping on the gas. "What the hell is this?"

The Sebring pulls up to the curb, right in front of their target. A blonde woman lunges out the driver's side window, slowly extending her arms toward one of the men on the sidewalk.

"She's got a gun!" Tommy yells. He fires three times in the direction of their target, his view partially obstructed by the Sebring.

Confusion. More gunshots.

"Fuck! My ears are killing me." Pedro straddles the curb as long as he can before swerving around the Sebring.

"Wait!" Tommy yells.

Pedro steps on it towards the highway. "Fuck!" he screams.

"Go back, man!" Tommy is yelling. "Can you hear me?"

"Did you drop the target or not?" Pedro asks.

"I don't know! Let's go back."

Sirens in the background.

"We can't fucking go back."

"What about the money?"

"Let's just hope you dropped the target."

They hide in an alley for over an hour before Pedro crawls the Escort along hidden back streets to the highway. He and Tommy argue for about ninety minutes, until the bomb in their trunk explodes, blowing them to bits along an otherwise quiet stretch of I-96.

"For Christ's sake!" Hazel Brisco moans, her heals clicking over hollow steps. "I can't believe you dragged my ass here . . . again."

Cathy squeaks out a mousy laugh as they climb to the top floor of the tired, three-story mall of bars known as the "BOB," an acronym for "Big Old Building."

"Building of Bimbos, is more like it," says Hazel, now surrounded by big hair, plastic faces, and the stale smoke of young people. The ubiquitous sounds of the Dave Matthews Band blast from the dance floor like a gust of bad breath.

"Oh, they don't bother me, these little dancing bitches with the porcupine hair," Cathy says.

"I hate everything about this damn bar," Hazel adds. "It's so tired. Really, it is."

"C'mon, there are some cute guys here. Can't we stay?" Cathy begs. She is a diminutive, fair-skinned woman with sculpted hair and a mellifluous voice that entices men to make passes. A penchant for wearing leather mini-skirts, Cathy is blessed with tiny feet that fit nicely into virtually any pair of heels, and smooth hands with long fingers. Her nails, perfectly manicured, match her burgundy coiffure. She is a man-killer with a certain charm and mystery; a femme fatale at age fifty.

Men enjoy the company of Hazel and Cathy because they're fun, because they're pretty, and because they're confident. This is lost on Hazel, who couldn't care less what men liked these days. There had been time when she bothered herself with such pursuits, but not anymore. Years ago, she had THE epiphany:

Enjoy the pursuit and savior the catch, but throw him back in the water before he stops breathing on his own.

"Just where the hell are all these 'cute' guys?" Hazel asks.

"In the pizza shop. You can't go wrong with guys in the pizza shop. How about you get a table while I go to the bar and find you a cute guy and a glass of wine?"

Hazel isn't too fond of pizza, but a cute guy and a glass of wine sounds pretty good. "Pino Grigio" she says. "If they don't have that, I'll take a Merlot. No White Zin, okay? And no guys under 30."

"Fine. You got it."

Cathy saunters up to the bar, greeting patrons as Hazel approaches the restaurant host, a flat-faced youth in a white chef's apron and bow tie. "Brisco, table for two," she says. "Non-smoking, please."

The host fidgets with his pencil as the skin on his long forehead wrinkles in tiny waves of rose petal pink. "I can't seat you unless the whole, *entire* party is here, ma'am," he says with a very sour expression on his lips.

"The whole, *entire* party?"

"That's the policy. I can't put your name down on this list unless your whole, *entire* party is ready to be seated."

Hazel laughs. "The other half of my whole, *entire* party is right there, getting us a drink," she says, pointing to Cathy at the bar. "Does that comfort you?"

"Sorry, ma'am, you'll have to wait until your whole, *entire* party is standing *here,* ready to be seated."

Cathy pays for, and picks up their drinks.

"Come on now," Hazel begins to explain. "Let's be reasonable. Look, here she comes now. Could you please–"
A dozen college boys, cloned in spiked hair, baggy jeans, and Abercrombie shirts, step in front of Hazel. "Henry, party of twelve," says one of them, "and we're all *here.*"

The host grins with thin lips and seats them as Cathy hands Hazel her drink.

"Ma'am, you dropped somethin," sasses one of the boys as he and his friends walk past. His voice is raspy and effeminate, holding the tonality of a big black woman.

Hazel looks down at the floor. *Dropped what?*

"Ha! She looked," he teases. "Share the *LOVE*, lady!"

His friends break into laughter.

"I'd bet you'd like that, wouldn't you, you little asshole," Cathy growls.

"We're both here now," Hazel snaps to the host as he returns to his station.

"What was the name?" he asks.

"Brisco. B-R-I-S-C-O. Please make a note of it."

He scribbles on a plastic coated blotter with a crayon. "Okay, I have you on the list. We'll call you when a table is available."

"Isn't there a table available?" asks Cathy.

The host's expression remains sour. "Obviously not," he hisses. "You can expect a twenty-five minute wait."

"Fuckin A," Hazel moans as they find seats at the bar. See why I hate this place?"

"Well, at least the host was kinda sexy," teases Cathy.

"Who, Lurch?"

"Yes, but I think that is his father you're thinking of," laughs Cathy. "He's Son of Lurch."

"Really, he was a prick." Hazel feels that he had acted against them for no good reason. As a waitress in college, she had never treated patrons with such disdain. In fact, she went out of her way to be pleasant and make people happy. Hazel enjoyed her stint as a waitress, never much minding the long hours. She earned decent tips, paid her own bills, and met lots of new people. That's how she had met Daniel, who made her quit work *and* school once they eloped.

"Oh God, will you look at this, Hazel?" Cathy's voice is tickled with amusement, hoisted by the brimming effect of the beer. A stout man with twelve wiry strands of hair combed from one ear to the other walks through the bar and winks, offering a meek wave at Hazel as he passes the bar.

"Oh God," Hazel sighs. She takes a sip of her wine, wishing for something harder, like Jack Daniel's. *Good old Jack, on the rocks with a twist of lime.*

"Ain't he a honey!" Cathy squeals, and they both have a good laugh at the poor sucker's expense. "You always had a special magic attracting comb-overs, Hazel. You should ask him out on a date!"

Dating. Hazel isn't much for it anymore. She much prefers going out with Cathy and avoiding disasters of the Grand Rapids singles' scene like this one. *Why did I let her drag me here?* she wonders.

Except for her optimism on dating, Cathy's ideas, acceptances, and beliefs run parallel to those of Hazel. Their life experiences are also similar: Like Hazel, Cathy has a son in his late twenties, the product of marriage that had ended over eighteen years ago.

Chronology is the only similarity in their divorces. Whereas Cathy's divorce from Buck had been amicable, the split between Hazel and Daniel had been downright ugly. During the last stages, Hazel focused her energies on sheltering Josh, sending the ten-year-old away to summer camp amidst his wild protests. At summer's end, Josh came home with a new best friend, a boy from the neighborhood named Scott Williams. The boys remained inseparable through high school. Years later, they left together for their freshman year at the University of Michigan, where Scott worked the fraternity scene for more substantial connections, leaving Josh behind. Today, the boys seldom speak, despite the fact that Scott lives less than a mile away.

Different paths.

Josh is floundering from the election and Scott is married with kids, working for his father-in-law and living in an expansive, wedding-gift house.

Tough life, Hazel thinks.

Once, Hazel's life had been like that: fast and rich, without effort. The young bride of a successful lawyer/politico, she developed an appetite for material aspects. Daniel had money, lots of it. He was also strong and handsome, with thick, wavy black locks and wide, blue eyes that radiated with confidence. Hazel was his love, and she bathed in his confidence, dying her hair a beautiful cherry red so that it would appear coy and lustrous during the cold months, flowing over her long mink and coyote furs. Grand cars, shiny rings, and crystal Waterford glasses: the medallions of status were her hobbies, her items to collect.

Until Daniel got caught. After that, she didn't want the material items anymore. She didn't care. It all went sour.

Daniel avoided jail by cutting a deal: his cronies in the prosecution arranged for him to rat on his friends in exchange for immunity. "I'm home free, baby!" he screamed at the press gathered on the lawn. "I'll show you sons-of-a-bitches!" His hair was Clark Kent perfect.

But before he could show them anything, Daniel was stripped of his certification from the Bar Association.

Disbarred! Hazel could hardly believe it.

"Those goddamn meddling Democrats!" Daniel spewed over and over again as he moped around the house. "Your parents are Democrats, aren't they?" He looked at Hazel with contempt. "Well, fuck them, those white trash bastards."

Hazel glared at him. "My parents own a grocery store," she snapped back. "*White trash* they are not!"

That's when Daniel retorted with a hard fist to her chin. She thought for sure that her jaw had snapped.

The last months of their marriage passed in a slow drip. Daniel ran up several credit cards to feed his incessant golfing, gambling, and coke habits. He spent most of his days coked and/or drunk in his home office den, haggling his connections for a reinstatement. There were lines on the mirror and the debt was rising. Hazel wanted to help with the finances. She landed work as a waitress and later as a paralegal, but Daniel made her quit both jobs. He wanted her to stay at home, not embarrass him. "I'm the breadwinner in this house, goddamn it," he'd say, his eyes glassy red. When he was passed out, which was often, she'd study for her real estate certification test. When she earned her license, she told him. He was yellow and livid, his skin dry, crisp, with rings under his eyes. There was little he could do to argue, or *make a case*, as he would put it, because they had already lost two of the three cars, and the house was soon to follow.

"Fuck it," he finally said. "I'm gonna file a Chapter 13."

Hazel lost it. "You have too much chauvinist hubris to let me work, but not enough pride to avoid bankrupcy? What the fuck is wrong with you? *Chapter 13?* Jesus Fucking Christ, Daniel! What are you thinking? *Please* don't do this. What about our family? What about Josh? You know how this town thinks! He'll be humiliated at school."

"I'm sure he already is."

Hazel let out a sigh.

The bartender places a fresh, tall glass of wine in front of Hazel. "For you ma'am," she says. "Compliments of the gentleman at the other side of the bar. His name is Mr. Auggie."

Cathy's eyes are wide with amusement. "Mr. Auggie?" Hazel asks. "Sounds like one of the Muppets." She glances around. "The guy with the comb-over?"

"That's the one."

"Horny little fucker, ain't he?" says Cathy.

Mr. Auggie saunters over to them with a wide grin. "Good evening," he says, taking Hazel's hand and pressing it to his lips. "You are such a beautiful creature. Are you from these parts?"

"I'm originally from Chicago," Hazel says.

"The Windy City. How nice." He smiles with angled teeth, dips into his martini for an olive. "Would you care to go downstairs and dance with me?" he asks, his tongue swatting bits of chewed pimento from his fatty lips.

Hazel attempts to be polite. "Oh, no thank you," she says. "My girlfriend and I are waiting for a table."

Mr. Auggie's face blushes and the lines under his eyes fold into a glower. "Oh," he growls, staring Hazel right in the eye. "So, what is it? Are you two dykes, or what? Or is it just that you think you're better than everyone else?"

"Oh, for crissakes," Hazel moans. She doesn't notice as Cathy slides a tiny pair of scissors out from her purse.

Two deft snips later, Mr. Auggie is left bald and screaming, his bristly fleece wafting past his knees as Hazel and Cathy bolt the premises. They make it down the steps and out the door before his hair even hits the hardwood.

"Oh my God, I can't believe you did that!" Hazel shouts between shrieks of laughter. They laugh their way past the bouncer outside and ignore him when he asks if they want their hands stamped.

"You don't want us back!" Cathy yells over her shoulder, waving her hand as tears trickle down her cheeks.

Bright lights reflect off the sable in their eyes as high heels click against pavement. Misted breath rises as they continue to laugh and giggle, carrying on until Hazel stops at the corner. "Hey," she says, pointing across the street. "That's Slade Pickens with Chuck Hriniak and Leslie Thompson."

"The new attorney general?" Cathy asks. "I voted for her!"

A Chrysler Sebring pulls up to the curb, cutting off Slade and his friends. Slade's expression is hard, then his face falls amidst slow movements from the blonde behind the wheel. "Oh, it's Darla Sue," Hazel exclaims.

A gesture from Slade. Leslie Thompson yells something.

Gunshots.

Slade falls to the ground clutching his neck. Chuck Hriniak stumbles forward and falls into a bush. Darla Sue's neck goes limp, her heavy head diving into the steering wheel pillow. A second car peels out around the corner and disappears. The horn of the Sebring blares under Darla Sue's chin. The vehicle is still moving. It picks up speed and rumbles over the curb, where it hits Leslie Thompson head-on, dragging her under its front wheels before finally kicking her under both sets of tires and crashing into the side of a brick building.

Norm Washington comes running from across the street. Hazel recognizes him right away. Cathy is screaming, her laughter turned to horror. "Norm!" Hazel yells as she and Cathy run across the street. She calls Josh on his cell. No answer. Sirens approaching.

Oh my God.

Part Two

Josh wishes he had some cocaine wrapped in his pocket, or tucked away in the glove box. He tilts his pounding head, running a coarse hand through crispy, unwashed hair while clutching the steering wheel with the other. Bright, morning sun floods his eyes as the Malibu travels eighty miles an hour down I-96 west, windows slightly cracked, heater blaring. Aerosmith's *Toys in the Attic* hums in the player. Josh reeks of bar smoke. His lips are chapped dry, torn. White jockey briefs stick to his ass like wet rubber. *Cocaine.* It had been awhile—he can't remember exactly how long, though. There hadn't been dust in the wind since Corey Crespo, his self-proclaimed crafty dealer, was stabbed in the head with a screwdriver. *Not so crafty,* Josh thinks.

Cocaine: God's Breath.

Emotions whirl through Josh like the changing colors of a kaleidoscope. *I do want to put the pieces back together,* he thinks, once again envisioning partially reconstructed wine bottles. *But it's more complicated than I thought.* The puzzle had many more pieces than he anticipated, perhaps too many to sort through. Emotions, like rats, scurry out of him in combinations. Without drugs to blunt them, Josh is no longer able to keep them dormant in the crawlspace of his mind.

The drive from East Lansing to the southeast side of Grand Rapids is only an hour, but the hangover is brutal. At 28, Josh feels like 100 years old. His red forehead drips sweat. 82 miles an hour feels like 55. Stereo turned up to the tilt. The CD player clicks out Aerosmith, clicks in Matty J. *Unconditionally* pounds out of the speakers, lifting his pain back into its crib of dormancy.

The dreams. The boy. What was the deal with that fucking photo? *North Carolina shorts.* He was the boy in the dreams, no doubt about it. And he was the boy who died at *Rod & Rifle*, no doubt about it. Where did he fit in? How did it all fit together? It's there, Josh knows it is there. He just can't put his fucking finger on it. Then again, maybe he doesn't want to. A shadow, a sense of pervasive dread, follows him. At first, Josh linked it to his constant hangover. Today, he knows better. Solving the puzzle of Josh Brisco involves connecting the dots, opening the Pandora box.

Adam. Feeling awkward and hung-over, Josh had been in a hurry to leave this morning. When Adam lunged forward to hug him, Josh had recoiled. He wishes he had that moment back. He imagines an embrace, then a kiss— on the cheek. Then he lets himself imagine a kiss on the lips. Soft lips: he is sure Adam has soft lips. And a nice tongue . . .

Josh adjusts his penis as blood rushes it hard. He turns up the stereo again, wipes his brow.

The music is loud. *"So just be yourself . . ."*

The boy in the shorts: who was he? Was he Adam's boyfriend? His brother? Josh glances at his reflection in the rear view mirror. His face is choleric, pasty. *Fuck.* He tilts the mirror away so he doesn't have to look at himself.

"And gel your hair up pretty . . ."

Feelings for Adam simmer. There is an excitement, a tingling that had never been there with Pepper, no matter how hard he tried. Oh, the futility of that relationship.

"Tonight we'll go out . . . on the Windy City."

Josh hadn't felt such tingling since . . . *Scott Williams.* Feelings for Scott had always been so forbidden, so secret, so unattainable . . . so easy to ignore.

Josh pulls over twice to avoid falling asleep at the wheel. After floating across highway lanes twice, he makes a desperate stop at McDonald's, throws a piss, buys a diet Coke for the duration. His cracked lips are a tired contrast to the smooth red and white striped straw through which he sucks his caffeine.

Finally, after what seems like an entire day, Josh makes it home. He drags himself through Mom's front door and turns on the television. He drops on the couch, face buried in soft cushions. Cesare follows him, light paws tapping over muscled flesh as the Pomeranian snuggles himself into the small of Josh's back just before they both fall asleep.

The hug had been awkward. Adam wishes that he could take it back, offer a handshake instead. To Adam, a hug was nothing, but he knows that Josh isn't likely ready for such male affection. Too much, too soon for someone too new to the boy thing: Josh had stiffened like cooling steel before leaving in haste. The sudden departure left Adam a bit cold, a little empty, longing for Josh's warm, male glow. As brief as their touch was, it managed to sear the feel of Josh's neck into Adam's longing. Downy soft, Josh's nape was silky smooth.

Earlier in the morning, Adam slipped in and out of a gentle slumber, dreaming of Josh. They would do breakfast together; it would be his treat. He'd clean Josh up, give him some fresh clothes to borrow. *Don't worry about it,* he'd say. *Just bring them back next time.* Josh is so cute—and gone.

No breakfast.

At least Adam managed to give him his phone number, written on a banana colored sticky note in bold, legible blue digits. Adam flirted with giving Josh one of his House business cards, but then thought better of it. Too personal, too soon. It was too much information to share, especially since Josh hadn't been honest with him.

Sales. Yeah, right.

Adam wonders what Josh *really* does for a living.

Teacher, maybe?

No. Josh is too neat, too good a dresser—male teachers were sloppy, even the gay ones.

No, it felt different, this aura from Josh that he was picking up on.

Adam sits down at the end of the couch, sniffs the pillow Josh slept on. It smells mostly of bar smoke, with a faint hint of coconut-scented beeswax. Adam leans over the couch and picks up the photo frame of Jimmy. "Even his hair crème is like yours," he whispers to the photo.

Following another freaky appointment with Kalumba King, Nick takes a moisturizing bath and then walks four blocks to Ian's apartment. Despite a half hour in the tub, his cock is still tingling from Kalumba King's bubble gum lips. *What an afternoon,* Nick thinks. The 'water sports' were tiresome, and now Kalumba wants to be called "Big Daddy." *But hey, four hundred bucks is four hundred bucks.* That aside, all Nick can think about is how much he wants to fuck Casper. *Fuck him up the ass. Yum.* And just as promised, he would bring Ian along for the ride. It was a win-win for everyone: Nick would get man-pussy from Casper, Casper would get it from Ian, Ian would get fifty bucks for his trouble, and Nick would make out with the lion's share of the $500 payout. What a scenario: money and fun and fucking!

Nick thinks of Casper's smooth, torqued chest with its pink, ripe nipples, and that round, silken ass. Nick's appetite for conquering strikes a fever pitch. His dick is hard, he can't wait to stick it in.

A block away from Ian's, Nick walks by a fancy furniture shop with trendy, bright patterned models in the display window. Predicting himself wealthy in a few short years, he imagines living in an elaborate house with a swimming pool and video games. *I'll buy a couch, table and chairs like these,* he thinks, gazing into the shop. *I'll set them up in my estate for a month, then dump it all on the street. Then I'll buy some new stuff: real classy stuff. Just because I can!*

A freckled boy on the corner, no older than twelve, calls out, "Hey pops, you got a smoke?" Nick ignores him, continues on his way. The boy catches up to him. "Hey, I asked you if you got a cigarette."

"I don't smoke," Nick says.

The boy smirks, parting lips revealing an unnatural gap in his teeth. "Yeah, right," he says.

Whiplash: Ian drives them to McCoy's in his rusted blue Barreta. "You even drive like a fag," Nick grumbles as they saunter into the bar. The place is empty but for the Old Bat, Jesus Man and the sailors, all of them fixed into the bar like characters left to dwell in a forgotten story. Jesus Man is hooting, offering informed discourse on the use of rattraps. "Who wants severed tails and rodent fluids squirting all over the place?" he asks. "Someone tell me that, okay?" The jukebox kicks on. Weird, thumping music that Nick doesn't recognize pulses in the background like a frantic, amplified heartbeat.

"And forget poison," chirps Jesus Man. "It gets them drinking tons of water. Then they either puke it up or explode all over the place!" He slumps against the bar like a deflated balloon, legs crossed as if to suppress a bowel movement. There is a girl sitting next to him, beautiful but for the emptiness of her gaze. She is new to Nick; he is immediately drawn to the fancy splendor of her bluebonnet ring.

The Old Bat sweats as she rinses the inside of a beer mug with a damp washrag. She curls her lips at Nick and Ian. "You boys want something?" she asks.

"Give us a minute," Nick answers, determined to stall the goofy bastard and avoid paying for a drink.

Jesus Man continues his banter as the girl with the bluebonnet stares into space. "You ever find few dead rats in your kitchen cupboards?" he asks the Old Bat. "Or one floating in your toilet, all puffy and bloated? Christ."

The Old Bat shrugs. Striking a match over the bar, she squeezes a bent Marlboro between her lips and lights it. "Fuck it, Carmine," she says. "Rats are here to stay and you can't escape them."

"Ahhhhh," he screams, straightening up awkwardly with a clap of his big-knuckled hands.

Nick rubs a moist palm against Ian's crotch, throwing a glance at the sailor boys, who are once again doing business with their dancing whore. "I wouldn't mind fucking a couple of *them*," he grunts under his breath as Ian giggles. He points with the thumb of his free fist and pauses, as if to say more. Instead, he rubs Ian's cock like he owns it. Ian moves closer, his dick up like a shot to the sky. Nick imagines that it's Casper's cock in his hand. The bar smoke grows heavy; he squints in anticipation. The song in the jukebox ends. In the new quiet, boots click like hollow sticks against the wooden steps leading from the upstairs apartment to the bar's front door. Casper descends the stairwell and props open the door, smiling at Nick through a three-inch crack. "Oh! I see that you brought your friend," he says without even entering. "Why don't we just go upstairs?"

They go upstairs, chop up some coke. Casper puts on some really cool Dave Mathews Band music. Then he shows them how to chop up the coke real good.

"I know how do it," Ian says.

Casper instructs Nick, slipping a gold razor blade into his hand.

"Wow," Nick says. "Is this real gold?"

"You bet. Ain't it a honey?" Casper is so handsome. So boyish. So ripe.

A few more chops, then they snort it. Nick feels like Superman. "Is this what they call *a line?*" he asks. Casper taps the gold blade against the mirror, scrapes some powder into a thin white median strip. "*That's* a line," he explains. "Give it a snort."

Nick is bursting with fun; he lays his chin on the plate and sucks the coke into his right nostril.

Blood: first in tiny specs, then in cascading falls.

"Need to settle down a little." Casper: reassuring. He has Kleenex and a vial of clear liquid. Ian's eyes are bulging—he looks totally stupid. Nick laughs at how stupid Ian looks, even though the blood spraying out of his nose is making him queasy.

"Here, drink this." Casper pours the clear liquid from the vial into a half-empty glass of water. "Go ahead. It'll take the edge off."

"What about the bleeding?"

"Oh, it'll definitely help with that."

Nick drinks the concoction in three large gulps. His motor skills are instantly slowed, his brain numb and tingling. The apartment swings.

Up, down.

In, out.

Darkness, bright light.

Flashes.

They fall into the midst of sex without discussion or provocation. Nick is flying, his body radiates fire. "Loosening up, huh?" Casper asks him, working his fingers into Nick's asshole. Ian is upside down, milking Casper's cock from behind like it's a cow spigot.

"Oh, there he is," Nick says, laughing, or maybe just smiling. It's hard to tell what is inside and what is outside. Everything is blurred.

Casper's fingers tickle inside him. "I thought *you* were going to bottom for *me*?" Nick slurs. The drugs are dulling. He floats. The scene starts moving rapidly, very fast. Then it stops, goes blank.

New screen: Casper is inside him again—that's all he can make out, comprehend. The thrusting is chaotic, hurtful. The bed is bouncing back and forth, scraping against the floor like a car without shocks. Everything is black and red. *Ian is milking the cow and I'm getting fucked,* he thinks, winking the sweat out of his eyes. Time and sex compress, crystallizing in a flash of heat and . . . (pain). Nick worries about shit and blood leaking out of his ass and nose because it's all out of control. Ian is slumped over. Nick finally cums like gangbusters. Casper wipes the cum into a plastic baggie and places it into a jewel box. "What the fuck?" Nick mumbles as he loses consciousness.

Josh wakes up to his mother's serious face, spinning, turning. She looks so young: her face is soft, curious, and the expression on it reminds him of when he was a little boy and she used to take him shopping and to Grandma's store.

He falls back asleep for a brief moment, floating back to a better time . . .

Three years old, his hand tucked into hers, tiny and soft with trust. His feet, fastened neatly into saddle shoes, aren't more than a few inches long; they click as he shuffles to stay pace with Mom. Walking, running, scuffling, the whole time looking up at Mom, who is so tall and beautiful in her red hair and blue summer dress. Without relinquishing his grip on her hand, Josh jumps over a concrete bench sticking out from the plaza storefront. "You're floating, Josh," Mom says, boosting him over the plain. They go to the plaza and watch Grandma change the mannequins in the store window. Josh watches, breathlessly: Grandma and her red hair, pulling off step-throughs, pull-offs, gloves, dresses, pants, bras, wigs, hair . . . pulling off arms and legs—yes, the arms and legs come off, too! Wow! Mom is explaining something to him, about sleeping over at Grandma and Grandpa's and how he was going to be a big boy and could watch Bela Lugosi on the Creature Feature without getting scared because he was a big boy and big boys didn't get scared of monsters or the dark. "Big boys don't cry, big boys don't cry," she whispers, like the song on the radio. And he isn't scared: it's fun watching the Creature Feature, fun sleeping over at Grandma and Grandpa's, just like it's fun watching Grandma pull the arms and legs off the people-sized dolls.

A sudden kick in the wind distracts Josh, and he looks across the street at the park. Behind the Village Green, the sky is so blue, speckled with white puffy clouds and streaks of silver that in adult retrospect remind him of Dali. And through it, piercing through the clouds are sandals, floating up, over the clouds, then back down again, in and out of the sky: a little boy's sandals—a little boy on the swing set, Josh's age, his blond hair flowing into the Carolina blue and white sky like crazy foam dissolving into bath water. His shorts are like the sky: they shimmer bright. Mother's hair, red like Grandma's, swaying in the wind. "Mommy, isn't it a beautiful day?" Josh asks her.

"Yes honey, it is." she lifts him up to her face and kisses him, soft but firm: the way a mom's kiss should be. "And don't you forget it!" She tickles his tummy.

Josh giggles and laughs, his mother tickling as the blonde on the swing set is swinging. It is a great day, a snapshot from a better time.

"Josh, wake up!" Mother's face is dour, serious. "Josh?"

The house is warm, Josh's face is sweaty. Cesare is digging gently at the nape of his neck. *It's not morning yet, is it?* Josh wonders, wishing he was back in the dream.

"There's been some trouble, honey," Mother says. "Oh boy, there's been some big trouble."

"I'll deal with it later." Josh falls back asleep. He can't help it.

Nick wakes up smothered in warm silence, his skin clammy in sticky, sweat-soaked sheets. There is no light, and the darkness is blinding. He dawdles in and out of sleep, losing track of time and place. Sweat, semen . . . the bed under him is so wet—Nick hopes it's not blood or liquid shit from his ass. He dozes off, at sea, floating in the beach water, the sun tanning his young, wet, glistening skin. He drifts, peacefully, until a sharp, bitter smell rips through the air like the stroke of steel against glass. His nostrils flare. Startled, he straightens up, the cool dampness lining his skin. He feels around: the whole bed is soaked. His hand stings, wet. He rubs his eyes. Wet. A sliver of light cracks through the window, illuminating fierce splashes of blood on mauve walls, scattered everywhere, like a kindergarten watercolor. Ian's body, limp as a torn sack, lays crumpled at his feet.

It's amazing what tragedy and a fifth of Jack can do to quell a hangover.

It was during a teary-eyed soliloquy, Mother's relay of the wrenching news, when Josh went numb, his body too dry for tears. An hour later, Mother still sits on the couch, hands folded, Cesare's tiny head propped over her thigh. She thinks Josh is in the bathroom, staring at the mirror, losing time.

Josh slips downstairs with the Jack and a two liter of diet Coke, pours himself a series of rapid-fire tall ones. Mother doesn't hear him go out through the garage. Neither does Cesare, who doesn't utter a peep as Josh fires up the engine of his car with a twist of the ignition.

> *Holdin' on to alliances*
> *I took a shot on the chin*
> *I'm gonna put back my pieces*
> *And come right at you again*

More Matty J. blasting as Josh straddles the highway downtown, parks in a free lot. The cold is bitter against his parched face; his coatless arms prickle with goose bumps. *What the fuck am I doing?* he asks himself, wandering the darkening streets. There is a gay bar somewhere in the district, but Josh isn't sure of the exact location. He walks down Monroe, Ionia and Fountain streets. Nothing. He walks back up Fountain, spots a canopied barfront airbrushed with rainbow colors. His dizzy head tingles, wild rushes of drunken energy drive through his body like tiny racecars.

He trips over the stairs as he enters the bar, falling on his hands.

"Sorry, buddy," says the bouncer, a masculine woman with heavy cheeks and round spectacles. "I can't let you in."

"Why?"

"Looks like you've already met your quota for the evening."

"What are you talking about?"

"You're drunk. I can't let you in."

Josh groans. "Is this a bar or a fucking church?"

"Come back some other night, bud."

Josh stands listless, eventually leaves. *Fuck, it's cold.* He leans against the corner of the building, hands in pockets, dumbstruck.

A dark figure approaches. Josh is deep into the bag; he can't even make out the features on the guy's face, which looks like a big nose with brows. "Hey, what's going on?" the nose asks, mist rising as his breath folds into the cold night. "Why you slumped against the wall like that?"

"Fucking dyke won't let me into the bar," Josh grumbles in an angry slur. "And I'm not drunk. I tripped on the stairs, that's all."

"I can see that," says the nose. "She must have made a mistake. Who was working the door? A manly girl type?"

"Yeah." Josh's eyes are heavy.

"Oh, that's Sue. I know Sue. I could go talk to her, talk to her about you. I'm sure it was some kind of misunderstanding."

"Really?"

"Sure. I'll talk to her, talk to Sue, and work it all out for you."

"Oh, that would be great. I'm not drunk. That would be great."

"No problem, but it might take me a while. Sue's real stubborn, you see. I'll go talk to her, but you'll need to keep your buzz going in the meantime. Do any drugs?"

"Huh?"

"Pot, mescaline, E, coke—"

"You have coke?"

"You like that stuff, huh?"

"Yeah. You have it?"

"Sure. Come here, let's go around the corner for a little privacy."

Josh follows him into the alley, where the nose unwraps a little triad of paper, holds it open. "Go ahead," he says. Josh leans over, snorts it. "Good stuff, huh?"

Little stars rush Josh's brain, a stroke of clarity rips through his drunken fog.

"That little pop is forty bucks," says the nose. "Well worth it, huh?"

"Oh yeah, oh yeah." Josh is grateful. He dips into his pocket for money.

"I usually don't do this, but for $60, I'll throw in another hit: it's not coke, but some real good material I got from Peru. If you like coke, you'll *love* this stuff."

Josh hands over $60.

"Great." The nose hands him a tiny wad of paper. "Don't open this here. Let me go talk to the bouncer. You know, Sue. Let me go talk to her. Wait right here."

"Okay."

The nose disappears for a while, comes back. "Yeah. You came in there about ten minutes ago, right? She thought you were drunk 'cause you stumbled when you were coming up the stairs."

"Yeah."

"It's cool. I put in the good word for you. She'll let you in." He reaches out, opens his palm, revealing a tiny baggie of white powder. "A little extra for a rainy day?"

Josh pulls a wad of fives, tens and ones from his jeans. "This is all I have left."

"That's fine," says the nose, taking the wad, peeling a five from it. "In fact, keep this for the cover."

"Huh?"

"Cover charge—at the bar. Use this to pay it. You can open a tab with your credit card once you're inside."

"Oh, yeah." Josh re-pockets bill. "Thanks."

Snow falls like scattered dust. Flakes speckle the black toes of Josh's Doc Martens. "Enjoy yourself, cowboy," says the nose, his departing words. A soft rustling and he disappears into the night.

"I will," Josh murmurs. The night is quiet.

He walks back to the bar, gliding over snow-slicked pavement like a stainless steel blade on ice. His strides are crisp, any caution smothered by narcotic induced boldness. There is a line at the door as the lesbian checks ID's. Cocaine horses run through Josh. The line moves slowly, music pulsing in his veins as the door approaches.

One boy ahead of him now: a fat twenty-something wearing a pink Mohawk and black leather jacket. The bouncer checks the kid's ID, looks up, makes eye contact. Drooping lips, soft round eyes: she's the same dyke that wouldn't let him in before. But Josh is confident. The nose is his ticket. He remembers what the nose said: *Oh, that's Sue. I know Sue.*

Josh gets close enough to read her nametag: *Sidney.* Josh realizes he's been duped.

Duped by the nose.

"You're not going to let me in, are you?" Josh asks.

Sidney smiles. "No, honey," she says with a sad smile. "I'd be happy to call you a cab, though."

"Is there a Sue that works here?"

"No, honey, I'm afraid not."

"They ever call you *Sue?*"

She laughs. "My name's Sidney, just like the tag says."

"Ah Christ. What time is it, anyway?"

"It's almost eleven-fifteen."

Josh is lucid, boiling with confidence. *I can get into any place but this one,* he thinks. But it's too late for another bar. Partial prohibition meant that first last call was in fifteen minutes, final last call in a half hour. By the time he skated around the corner to the next venue, they'd be putting the stools upside down over the tables. *There's no point to it,* he decides. *No point at all.*

He drives home five miles over the speed limit, coming to a complete stop at every stop sign. He pisses in the toilet, flushes, and falls down the basement stairs, Levi's wrapped around his ankles. Tonight's take-home purchases, which turn out to be an expensive baggie of flour and an empty piece of notebook paper, are wrapped into a ball inside his pockets.

Josh wakes up the next morning when Chuck Hriniak calls.

Cobb Nelson has no idea about the Slade Pickens assassination. In flight to Puerto Rico, he sips a plastic cup of iced pineapple juice and concentrates on settling an old score. Cobb never had a thing for alcohol; a can of pineapple brought him all the drinking pleasure he could handle. He's flying first class, but doesn't care for it much. First class? Big fucking deal. More room: great. The rest of the so-called perks? Fuck them, with a capital F: the stewardesses are still cunt-rag bitches and the flights are still choppy exercises in risk-taking. The food? Who cares? And fuck the free booze: that was for the corporate hacks and their frat boy sons.

Even in first class, Cobb found himself hassled.

"We're gonna run out of pineapple juice for our mixed drinks," complains a plastic-lipped attendant. "That would be very bad for our drinking customers. Very bad."

Cobb offers no response. Rather, he just sits expressionless, contemplating the torturous methods and techniques under which he might kill the girl most viciously—if he chose to do so. The glow in his eyes must have spooked her; she reaches into the cart and puts two cans on his tray without further comment.

Seven juices later, Cobb finds himself in San Juan. He's inside the second floor of the local hospital, which is a mess of dying patients and crying relatives. Doctors and nurses scurry about, squealing in quick Spanish lisps.

Here I am again, between the walls of this shithole. Cobb tries to estimate the number of lives having expired here under Dr. Ricardo Cruz's blurred watch. *Thousands, at least tens of thousands,* he thinks.

Twelve years have passed since Cruz inexplicably botched Cobb's vasectomy. Jagged, chaffing cuts from the knife of the drunkard surgeon resulted in complications that left Cobb in the hospital for months, until he ultimately underwent a medical castration to survive.

Indeed, Cobb had survived. And he hadn't forgotten.

Donning a blue doctor's coat and matching gear, Cobb quietly blends into the environment surrounding him. His task well choreographed. In his breast pocket rests a plastic baggie with a cloth in it. Back at the hotel, the knives are shined and the video camera is mounted and ready to go. Everything is set . . . except for Doctor Cruz, who is sure to arrive soon.

The deal with Richmond had been perfectly executed, and Cobb's boss, Wayne Van Anders, seemed pleased.

Van Anders had been surprised at Cobb's request for time off, but that was expected—Cobb hadn't asked for one day off in nine years. This week, he had requested two. It wasn't much time off for most working people, but for Cobb, it was a full vacation holiday. Van Anders obliged without further question. Cobb appreciated that.

Poetic, broad strokes of a blade: Cobb relishes the opportunity to slice up Cruz. It would be easy, fun. Cobb has visions of carving the doctor into fancy filets. The *urge* is back: a haunting, tribal taste for blood that once intoxicated Cobb. For the first time in years, he feels a *need* to kill. It makes him feel young again. Medical scents dance through Cobb's nostrils like the sweet smell of cotton candy. Childhood memories from the little brick house across from Metropolitan Hospital come rushing back . . .

Cobb was a solemn, quiet child, the sort of boy who didn't like to celebrate his own birthday. "I don't care for the kids in my class," he explained to his mother, who had aspirations of throwing a party to celebrate her only son's thirteenth birthday. "And I don't much care about birthdays. They're nothing special. It's not like I did anything special by being born. It's just like any other day."

And it was, until a sweaty, tatter-kneed Cobb came home from baseball practice to find his twin sister in tears. "What's the problem?" Cobb asked.

She choked out the story amongst coughing sobs: Mickey Wilson and a couple of his neighborhood thugs broke into the backyard and stole Sampson, her toy poodle. "Mickey said they'd cut off his ears unless I blew them," explained Madeleine.

"Blew them?" Cobb asked. He was puzzled by the wording.

"As in giving blow-jobs."

Everything around Cobb turned white as he flew into a quiet rage. His body remained still as his contorted soul shot across the room in a blind stampede. He gathered himself, said nothing, went into his room and put away his bat and glove. Coarse hands shuffled through masses of white cotton as he pulled out a stolen tin of Savage Tribe Chewing Tobacco from his underwear drawer. He popped the tin open, deposited a pinch of mossy grounds between his cheek and gum. The buzz was instant, jolting. As the nicotine shot to his brain, Cobb imagined conversations with the red Indian silhouetted on the tin's cover. They spoke of loneliness, of isolation. They shared observations and experiences. The noble savage called out to him. The noble savage was Cobb's hero, his brother . . .

. . . through him, all things were possible.

Cobb slid his bowie knife into its leather case and packed it into the inside pocket of his jean jacket before heading over to Mickey Wilson's. Everything around him had a whiteness to it, as if set against a bright backdrop.

As expected, Mickey and two loser buddies were hanging out in the garage of his mother's quasi-ghetto bungalow. They were smoking Camels, beer bottles scattered at their boots.

"Hey look, it's one of the twins—the one with the dick!" laughed Mickey. His eyes were half-shut and bloodshot, his lips cracked and dry. He held himself like a 250 pound linebacker, yet, like his two buddies, he was rail-thin in jeans and a tight tee.

"Where's the dog?" Cobb asked, expressionless.

Mickey flicked his cigarette to the floor with defiance. "Your dog's dead, man. Dead. Fed it to my Rottweiler." He looked over at his deadbeat friends, who laughed.

"That was my sister's dog," Cobb said plainly.

"Well, you shoulda seen how Biff Daddy tore it apart. Like it was dropped in a paper shredder or somethin."

More laughter. One of the boys rose from the stack of papers he was sitting on, disappeared out the side door and returned, holding up what had been Sampson's collar: chewed, ravaged, dripping with blood.

Much brightness; however, Cobb never lost control. It was one against three, but the Spirit of Noble Savage was with him, not to mention the bowie knife, which he thrust into Mickey Wilson's neck with a force that nearly decapitated the poor sucker. The other two boys tried to runaway, but they were slow, drunken stoners, whereas Cobb was a swift and agile athlete. He had their organs split into several pieces before they even reached the door. One of them lost a couple fingers when he tried to grab Cobb's knife, but other than that, it wasn't much of a struggle. It was easy.

Cobb thought about going out back and killing the Rottweiler, too, but something in the Noble Savage told him to move on, that revenge was complete.

As Cobb walked home through the back woods, the Wilson's garage was quiet but for the misting of blood from Mickey Wilson's trachea.

There were no witnesses.

Cobb scratches his nose, pulls out a wayward hair. A couple of nurses swish by him in soft-soled shoes.

Oh, how he hates the idea of a surviving witness!

He had killed many times since the days of his childhood, never once leaving a witness to history. He had killed most often for revenge (it was remarkable how people would go out of their way to screw one another), sometimes for profit. A few jobs were commissioned by Wayne Van Anders, who Cobb respected as a fine boss and efficient task manager.

Cobb paces the hallway. His pulse is frenetic. Then, as if on cue, the highly recognizable Puerto Rican surgeon saunters past in a distinguished, purposeful gait and disappears into the unoccupied men's room.

Perfect, thinks Cobb, unzipping the chloroform cloth from its plastic bag. He follows Cruz into the john and locks the door behind him.

Dressed in a black raincoat, Norm Washington squeezes through Hazel Brisco's front door like a wet balloon, raindrops cascading from the brim of his fedora. Tucked under his left arm is a box of Duncan Donuts.

"Been out window shopping again?" Josh asks with a snide curl of the lip. His meeting with Chuck Hriniak is in less than an hour; otherwise, he would have been sleeping when the door rang.

Norm sighs, slumps his head, visibly upset that Josh still associates him with corrupt on the Job behavior. "I bought these," he says quietly, shuffling his wet feet over the doormat. "May I come in?"

Josh senses trouble, drops his sarcasm. "I'm sorry," he says. He reaches out, touches Norm's shoulder. "I was just kidding."

"No, you weren't. That's what sucks."

Norm sits at the kitchen table. His hands are pale, almost white. Josh sits across from him. The box of donuts hangs open and untouched, a potpourri of glazed, chocolate, and assorted sprinkles. Cesare lies in a bed on the floor, gnawing on a stick of rawhide.

Josh wipes his brow. "What the fuck are you telling me, Norm?" he asks.

Norm speaks in tired, staccato sentences. "The Slade Pickens case. City Hall has ordered it closed. Tesanovich isn't pursuing anything. The DA's office can't bring up any charges."

Josh is puzzled. "Well, Darla Sue is dead, correct? Who are they gonna bring charges against?"

Norm is silent.

"It was Darla Sue, right? She killed him, then shot herself. Every report, every witness said so."

Norm blows through soft lips, shakes his head.

Josh's heart drops. "What the fuck's going on, Norm?"

"I saw the police report."

"And?"

"It says that Darla Sue fired three shots. Missed twice before hitting Slade in the face. One of her misses glanced off Chuck Hriniak."

"Then she turned the gun on herself and blew her brains out with the car still in drive."

"Yes," Norm nods, "according to the report."

"You disagree?"

"Four bullets total, all recovered from the scene. All were shot from a .38. A .45 was found on the floor of Darla Sue's car when her body was recovered."

"Yeah?"

"Josh, do you know what a .45 would do to a woman's head if fired at point blank range?"

"It would blow it right off her neck."

"Her head would have sprayed all over that car like an exploding watermelon. I was there, Josh. I saw them remove the body. She was intact. Her head was bleeding, but believe me, it was intact."

Josh shakes his head, says nothing.

"I've got a source in forensics—a reliable source. That slug in Darla Sue's head was from a Saturday Night Special, not a .45. And it sure as hell wasn't fired at point blank range. I could have told you that from my first hand observation. There's no wat Darla Sue shot herself, and I'm not so sure she shot Slade, either. Your mom was there; she and her friend are on record saying that there was another car present—one that they said fled the scene after the shots were fired."

Cesare stops chewing his rawhide, balancing it between his paws with a sigh. He tilts his head slightly, studies Josh as if waiting to hear his response.

"Does Lieutenant Tesanovich know about this?" Josh asks.

"He couldn't care less. The case is shut—boxed and locked. Heard a rumor that City Hall gave the order to close it before questions started springing up."

"Fucking A, Norm."

"I knew that you'd wanna know about this. I felt you needed to know, that I needed to tell you. Maybe you'll be able to figure it all out, make some sense of it. I don't know. I don't have any ideas. Maybe you can do something. I'm out of it."

Josh stares at his hands, rubbing them together anxiously. He has Norm go over the details again and again, like a little boy devouring his first morbid tale. "Be more precise," he says.

"I am being precise. I've told you all I know."

"Will you work with me on this?"

Norm's expression fades. "I told you, I'm out of this."

"You're the only guy that can lend credibility to this theory. I mean, it's your theory, after all."

"I'm out of it."

"Why?"

"I have my reasons."

"You always do." Josh scratches his head. "Tell me something," he adds, "what do you remember about that kid who was killed at *Rod & Rifle* five years ago?"

"*Rod & Rifle?*"

"Yeah, it was the first case I worked with you. Caucasian male, my age. He died, shot to death. You and Tesanovich dismissed it as an accident, closed the case."

Norm's eyes shift from the donut box to the floor. "I don't remember anything about it," he says.

"This is over the top, cowboy!" Chip Richmond is screaming, red-faced, neck bulging with thick purple veins. "Way over the top!"

Wayne Van Anders, despite his exasperation, is still strong. He slaps Richmond with a swing of his large hand, nearly knocking the speaker-elect off his bar stool and onto the floor. "You damn child," he growls. "You small little man. Keep your voice down. This is a public venue."

McCoy's is quiet, empty in the mid-day except for Carmine Rossi, Richmond's wayward chief of staff. Van Anders knows Rossi from his miserable run against Leslie Thompson for attorney general. If Rossi hadn't screwed up that campaign, Van Anders never would have been in this predicament, having to form an alliance with Chip Richmond and sell his soul to the Africans.

Rossi is seated on the other side of the bar in a presumably well-intended *Jesus Saves* sweater. "What's this all about? What's it all about?" he asks in a panic that seems fake.

Keep quiet over there," Van Anders snaps. "Jesus is on my side."

A rotund, middle-aged bartender works the counter. Van Anders finds her extremely attractive. At first, she approaches to take Van Anders' order, but when she realizes who he is and sees his aggravated state, she backs off and continues to rinse glasses, wringing them with a blue rag in a large trough bucket sink.

Richmond is panicked. "Did you do it? Did you do it?" he asks.

"I told you to keep your voice down!" Van Anders warns. "The smitten temerity of it all. Last thing I need is for the eyes and ears of the Capitol to wedge themselves into this."

Richmond grimaces like he's in pain as he loosens his tie. "There's nobody here, Wayne."

"I don't care. You keep it down. What are you all worked up about, anyway?"

"Assassinating a state representative," Richmond whispers, "is *Biblical.* Slade Pickens was a seventy-five-thousand-dollar-a-year man—one hundred-thousand if you count his supplemental leadership salary!"

Van Anders moans. "I don't believe you. What's wrong with you? Our hands are clean. We had nothing to do with it. Just keep your damn mouth shut." Although his words come out bold, Van Anders is nervous. *Where the hell is Cobb? When is he coming back? Tonight, that's right. Tonight. Calm yourself. Cobb never would have taken this situation into his own hands . . .*

"Wayne, we both know how this plays out for you. If Thompson dies, you don't need that alliance with the Negros."

Van Anders bristles. "I'm a man of my word, Mr. Richmond. And I'm telling you that I had absolutely nothing to do with what went down in Grand Rapids over the weekend. Furthermore, I have no intention on reneging on my deal with you and the Africans. Even if I wanted to, what would that say about my culpability?"

"Yeah, but what about Hriniak? It's kind of a mute point what Hriniak does now, isn't it? He's a martyr. I can't strip him of *any* committee assignments now. The press would be at my throat—and the voters would be right behind them. In their eyes, Hriniak is a survivor, a hero. It's useless now. We have to leave him alone. And now that Slade is gone, there's no guarantee that the Negroes will uphold their part of the deal—"

"Bullshit!" Van Anders slams his fist on the counter. "They WILL uphold their end of the deal. Plain and simple!"

"Wayne, I think it would be best if we dropped this alliance with *them*. What if the cops found out that we were working with them to thwart Slade? Wouldn't that make us seem like suspects?"

The cops. Tesanovich had called right away, warned Van Anders about the mismatch in bullet slugs. *That jackass—he just assumed I was involved.* At least now Wayne knew the inside story: Slade and Hriniak had both been hit with bullets from a .38, Slade fatally. Van Anders doesn't remember the exact make, but he knows damn well that the gun in Darla Sue's possession was not a .38. *Cobb had a .38 snub nose. Good God.*

"This alliance will remain intact," says Van Anders. "You will see to it. And I want Hriniak removed from those committees ASAP."

"Jesus Christ, Wayne. My political career is on the line here!"

"Nonsense. We had a deal."

"My ass is on the line. Why do you have such a hard-on for Hriniak, anyway? It's because of your kid, right? Hriniak supports your little son as he's out there flaunting his lifestyle in your face."

Van Anders lets the reference to Adam slide, tries to change the tone of the conversation. "Buoyant spirits, Chip!" he says. "You need to focus on the new session. The legislature is yours. You'll be speaker during a time of great change. This will be the last of the great sessions, the last before all the veteran legislators are term limited out. After that, rapid decline. What a shame, the disgrace that awaits us. This is the session to end all sessions. A noble age is dying, so go for broke. The House, the Senate, the governor's mansion: we have complete control. It's time to celebrate the past, consolidate the present, and make the laws we need to keep our business influence in the future."

"That's great. Maybe you should be speaker." He pauses as Van Anders bristles. "I need to protect myself. I don't wanna go to jail for something I didn't do."

Van Anders scratches his chin. "No one is going to jail, dammit," he says. "Stop worrying about protecting yourself. You sound like an old woman. I want you to focus on your career, think about what lies ahead. What will happen to you after the House? An election to the Senate? Doubtful. Perhaps a lobbying career? Maybe. You have the looks for it, if not the brains. Indeed, your whole future might be determined by how you handle this situation. Play it cool, portray yourself as being above the fray. Voters love it when their elected officials are a source a calm during times of crisis. In the meantime, stick to the plan. I want Hriniak disposed of—politically, that is."

Richmond itches with impatience; he hates Van Anders' perseverance. His mind shuffles through possible ways out of the deal. He's tempted to have Rossi call on his bodyguards, but fears that Van Anders has Cobb dwelling nearby, hiding in the shadows, quietly awaiting conflict. "Pickens is dead," he says, "which renders Hriniak nothing more than a political eunuch. So why do you still give a fuck what he does?"

"You need to relax. This will all calm itself over the next couple of weeks."

"Couple of weeks? Calm itself? Me relax? This isn't about me. It's about *you*. It's about you getting to your kid through Hriniak. What's up with that?"

Van Anders' lip curls at the second mention of his son. "You let me worry about my own business," he growls. "I can take care of things." The wrath in his eyes is unbridled, with a ringing, whirling force behind it. Chip Richmond sees it loud and clear: Van Anders is wound into his own agenda and there is no getting out.

"Fine," he says to Van Anders. "You take care of things. If you don't, I will."

Van Anders turns his head at a sharp angle, glaring at Richmond from the sides of his eye sockets. "I'll take care of things," he growls. "I *always* take care of things. If I wanted Pickens, Thompson and Hriniak dead, I would have done it myself, and you can be rest assured that there wouldn't have been any survivors. That having been said, nobody is going to jail. Not me, not you, not anyone. Darla

Sue, the lone gunman, is dead. Case closed. You still want me to protect you? Fine. You will need my protection sooner or later, and I sense that you're finally beginning to realize that. I have people watching out for me at all levels. This protection often extends to my friends. You want protection? Show me some friendship. Wrap up the votes on my dialysis legislation. I know you're not speaker yet, but see if you can do it before Sine Die."

"What's Cyanide?"

"*Sign-EEE-dye* . . . the last day of session, when all the shit hits the fan. You don't know that, Mr. Speaker-elect? Well, you'd better learn."

Chip gulps, nods.

The WBCG's studios are small and decrepit, with egg yolk paint peeling from the walls. The tight quarters never bothered Albert Dawson when he was working as *Dr. Sex*, the locally renowned host of *Motor City Sex Talk*. But now that he is relegated to a button-pushing back-up boy, the confined nature of the workplace only reinforces the restricted nature of his continuing employment.

Motor City Sex Talk was yanked off the air three weeks ago by Clarence Clancy, the prudish station manager. *"I don't care about your ratings,"* Clancy cried. *"The show is a clear violation of my banned word policy."*

"Banned word policy?" Dawson was incredulous. *"What about the bottom line?"*

"The banned word policy is my bottom line. The Christian Coalition is barking up a storm about your show's content. I have sponsors pulling out left and right."

"What, those people don't have sex issues?"

"Of course they do. They just don't want people talking about it. They can't stand any talk about bodily fluids, especially cum."

"Cum? What's so bad about cum?"

"They just don't like it."

A middle-aged father of three, Dawson had no other choice but to retire *Dr. Sex* and accept a reduction to co-hosting Gloria Manson's call-in show. Long, frizzed hair framing her perfectly round face, Manson is a mercurial state Representative with a distinct appearance and dominating personality. Possessing enough misguided energy to power a locomotive, the wooden-legged Macomb County native is adored by her loyal constituents. Known as *"The Darling of the Doublewides,"* she is effortlessly entertaining, a natural for radio. Dawson describes her as "belligerent by accident, acidic on purpose."

Today's show is a typical pain-in-the-ass. Thirty seconds into it, Dawson already has a headache, his heavy mustache twitching as he lines up callers while the bug-eyed Manson concludes an awkward poetic tribute to slain colleague Slade Pickens.

"That's what they call a soliloquy," she boasts upon its conclusion.

"I think you mean *sonnet*," says Dawson, slipping a finger under an undersized headset for a quick scratch of his itchy scalp. The headset, ill-fitting and cheap, barely fits over his thick mass of curly brown hair.

"I don't think so," snaps Manson. "If anyone knows the difference between a sonnet and a soliloquy, it's me."

"Okay, okay." Dawson doesn't feel like arguing with her. "How about if we take our first caller? Donna from Royal Oak, you're on with Gloria Manson."

"Hi. Representative Manson?"

"Yes, dear."

"I was wondering if you find yourself at a disadvantage on the campaign trail, you know, with the wooden leg and all?"

Manson laughs. "Not at all. I'm proud of my wooden leg," she says. "In fact, it's an advantage. I have an ashtray carved into it, as you may already know. It comes in handy on the campaign trail, let me tell you. Like many of my constituents, I do enjoy a good smoke every now and then. Thanks for calling. Next caller."

"Gary from Southfield, you're on with Gloria Manson."

"Yes, I was wondering if you were good friends with Slade Pickens before he died."

"Indeed, Tony, I was."

"That would be *Gary* from Southfield," Dawson corrects her. "*Gary.*"

"I *said* Gary. Anyway, as I was saying, *Gary*, yes, I was very good friends with Slade Pickens. We may have had our philosophical differences from time to time, but we were friends. Slade was a great man and his loss with be mourned in Lansing for quite some time. Thanks for the call, Gary."

Dawson: "Okay, we are going to take a quick break and will be right back with more Gloria Manson." The studio light goes off and a commercial runs.

"Don't *ever* sass me when we're on the air," Manson screams, teeth exposed from behind curled lips.

"I wasn't sassing you." Dawson's head is ringing in pain. *I wonder if it's too late to get that writing gig with Capitol Beat,* he wonders.

Manson continues in on him. "You did it twice. Don't do it again."

The light comes back on.

"We're back with Gloria Manson," Dawson announces.

"I'd just like to say something before we take another caller, Albert."

"Go right ahead."

"Okay, well, never mind. Let's take that next caller."

"Leon from downtown, you're on with Gloria Manson."

"Yeah, Manson, if you're so great, how come you've never sponsored a bill into law since you've been at the Capitol?"

Manson blushes. "I've had my problems, yes. Political obstacles, I guess you could say."

"You have an excuse for everything, lady. It's pathetic. You've been in office for eight years. Eight years and not one of your bills has made it to law."

"It's not that simple, sir."

"My name is Leon. And yes, it IS that simple. Kalumba King has only been in office for two years, and he already has six bills signed into law. What do you think about that?"

Gloria's voice begins to rise. "Sir—"

"Leon."

"Leo—"

"Actually, Gloria, the caller's name is Leon."

"Oh, shut up, Albert. Listen, caller, whatever your name is, that's just fine that you show such support for

Kalumba King. You think he's such a skilled politician? Well, let me tell you something. It's not that tough to pass bills into law when your mommy and daddy are running the Capitol with their slick little machine of corruption."

"Kalumba King is a great man!"

"Great, yes—as in *enormous*. But that big black buck certainly isn't great on account of any notable merit."

"You're just saying that 'cuz you're a racist! Kalumba King is a great man!"

"My friend, you are just saying that because you are black. Black and stupid."

Dawson tries to cut her off, to no avail. Where is a censor button when you need it?

"You weren't no friend to Slade Pickens, either!"

"How dare you say that?"

"I'll tell you how! My cousin knows the Grand Rapids Police. They say that you gave his crazy wife that gun and taught her how to shoot it!"

Gloria pounds the counter, jarring Dawson's microphone. "Not true!" she screams. "I took her shooting once, that was it. We were friends. Slade and I were friends, too."

"You keep talking yourself into a hole, baby. Keep digging your grave . . ."

"At least I can afford a grave!"

"I should come down there and bitch-slap you one, lady!"

"Bitch-slap? Me? I'd like to see that, hotshot!"

Dawson can hear Clancy complaining into his headset. *"Dissuade her from saying that,"* he says. *"'Bitch-slap' and 'bitch' are on the station's list of banned words."*

"I bet you would," continues Leon from downtown. *"In fact, a lot of folk would like to see it."*

"You low class niggra . . ." Manson blurts.

"Is that on the list?" Dawson whispers into his headset.

"Niggra? What's that?" asks Clancy. *"If she means 'Negro,' then I think that's acceptable."*

Gloria is screaming, her words dissolve into an incoherent rant. She utters *"niggra"* few more times, but by the time she is on her third *"fuck you,"* Clancy has already ordered the studio under management shutdown.

"Well, that's the end of the Gloria Manson Show," he mutters. *"Looks like Dr. Sex will cum again after all."*

It is an unseasonably warm December day in Lansing, the kind that inspires city kids near the Capitol to play outside in floppy spring wind breakers, jumping about, throwing rocks at windows and carving graffiti into trees with tiny pocket knives. Carmine shouts violently at several of them along the way home. "Out of the road, *bastardos!*" he screams, leaning his torso out the window, cutting off several drivers in the process. "*Que chingandos!*"

Pepper sits in amusement, cluttered papers and old cups scattered at her feet as she marvels at Carmine's ability to weave in and out of traffic without watching the road.

"Do you mind if we stop here for a second?" he asks her, tilting his head at the *7-11* nestled into a corner strip mall, right next to a laundry mat. Pepper remarks that she couldn't care less, which seems to please Carmine as he swings his chipped white and tan Monte Carlo into the lot. Pepper is content to have pleased her new boss, but her remark is a lie. Truthfully, she can't wait to get home to have a drink.

"I'll be right back," Carmine says, stepping out of the car.

As Pepper waits, a rusted Lincoln pulls into the neighboring space with its windows down and stereo roaring to a proletarian country-western anthem. Three little girls ragged like savaged dog toys, sit in the Lincoln as their top heavy mother lumbers into the laundry mat with a basket of rumpled clothes. Celebrating the absence of authority, the girls jump about, squealing, shaking the car. The oldest girl, maybe seven, tumbles over the front seat, pulls out a bottle of Windex and squirts it around like a gun. "Shoot her, shoot her," yell her sisters from the back seat. The girl points the bottle directly at Pepper, the soiled sleeve of a yellow turtleneck bent loosely over her wrist.

"Hey lady," she yells, much to Pepper's chagrin. "Hey lady," she repeats, flexing the Windex. "Bang, bang, you're dead." At that moment, Carmine, a crate of plastic diet Pepsi bottles saddled in his arms, makes his way out from the store. "Ooh, look, here comes her *boyfriend*," yelps one of the sisters, a chocolate stain smeared across her cheek. "I wonder if she's gonna kiss him," chirps another.

"You *know* she is," the oldest giggles. "If he's her boyfriend, then she's his girlfriend. And she has to kiss him. That's how it works."

"Look at the way he's dressed!" exclaims the smallest girl. "I bet they do the nasty," says the mid-sized. Pepper blushes, ashamed, as this comment causes her to unwillingly visualize an image of Carmine bent over her, thrusting his hips, his small and furry body naked but for tiger striped underwear pulled over his bulging genitals, sweat cascading off his nose and down over the twisted, hairy flesh of his belly-button. As much as the thought repulses her, Pepper cannot block it from her mind.

"You *know* they do the nasty."

Pepper's head buzzes with alarm as she imagines her hands sliding down Carmine's prickly back and under the tiger skin as he drives himself inside her. She shifts uncomfortably, realizing that this macabre, addicting thought has resonated inside of her body, spurring a hot, sprinkling wetness between her legs.

Carmine, red-faced, sets the case of soda in the back seat before getting into the car and starting the ignition. "Ugly man, *ugly man*," the girls chant, presuming they are out of Carmine's hearing proximity. "Slut girl, slut girl," the largest child screams at Pepper, her arms hanging out the driver's side front window. "*Sluuuut girl!*

"Ancient damnation!" Carmine screams. He hits the break, throws the Monte Carlo into reverse, and punches his foot over its gas pedal. His eyes are wild with anger as the Monte barrels backward and into the Lincoln. There is a loud snapping noise, an unpleasant splintering, like breaking bone, and the girl disappears into the Lincoln as her Windex bottle drops to the pavement with a crack. "Ancient damnation!" Carmine screams again, staring at the sisters with an unbridled intensity, a rage Pepper has never seen. The girls scream bloody murder, jumping about the car like slaughterhouse chickens. Their swollen mother, Camel drag dangling from her lips, stumbles out of the cleaners, unaware of what has just happened. "Shut the *fuck* up," she yells to her children. She opens the driver's side door and a river of blood squirts out of the car and into the parking lot, spraying over the glistening river of Windex. Pepper is white, nauseous, her forehead cold and numb. Carmine, laughing like mad, drops the car into drive and runs his front tire dead-center over the Windex bottle. "Watch *this*," he says to Pepper. Shifting into reverse, he backs over the broken plastic again, throws forward and drives over it once more for good measure. Laughing, blood-shot eyes bulging, he points to the girls in the Lincoln and gestures to them with his thumbs up. "Friends in Low Places, girls," he says, driving off.

Pepper's eyes sting and her stomach feels heavy. The ride home is quiet but for the ringing in her shell-shocked ears.

"Guess there are rats and vermin everywhere," Carmine says. "But don't you worry. You just come to work on time everyday, and don't try to escape it. Things are bound to change eventually."

"Did you break her arm?" Pepper asks. "I mean, you know, that girl's hurt. Seriously hurt."

"Aw, you don't know that for sure. And the fuck if I know," he answers curtly. "If people are going to act like animals, well, then that's how I'm gonna treat them."

Weaving the Monte through sparse traffic like a serpentine through sand, Carmine hops a curb, cutting the corner at Washington and Kalamazoo. "Kalama-ZAM!" he shouts.

"What the fuck are you doing?" Pepper screams.

"I'm not waiting for that fucking bus to move its slow ass!" Carmine yells as the transmission drops from his car like a piece of dung from a cow's ass. "What's that?" he asks, color fading down his neck.

"That was a piece of your car—probably the motor!"

Carmine's face crumples. "You don't know anything about cars," he says. "I'll take care of this, just like I take care of *everything!*"

They sit motionless in the middle of the road as Pepper strains her neck looking in all directions for cops.

The coast is clear. "What are you going to do?" she asks.

"I said I'll take care of it!" Carmine snaps.

They walk across the street a few blocks to *McCoy's*, where one of the dozen Ameritech lobbyists is running a tab. When they emerge five hours later, the car is gone.

"Told you I'd take care of it," Carmine boasts. "I was gonna dump that car sooner or later. It's not registered in my name anyway."

The WBCG snub is the last straw: Gloria Manson is mad as hell and she ain't gonna take it anymore. Years of African House leadership had stifled her every effort, and now the Suits were sure to treat her no different. All the Lansing cocks think of politics as a man's game. Chip Richmond and Jizzie LeDoux are no different: they are establishment boys to the core. Who is worse, the Democratic Africans or the Republican Suits? Gloria can't differentiate, she doesn't discriminate: she hates them both with equal opportunity.

Eight years—for eight years, Morris Hyde and his posse succeeded in denying Gloria committee hearing after committee hearing. When, on one generous occasion, Slade Pickens threw enough bi-partisan clout to release her gender equity bill from committee, Hyde made sure that it was dead on arrival at the House floor. *"That bouffant bitch Manson gets nothin,"* Hyde boasted. *"This is my fuckin House, baby. My fuckin House."*

Gloria danced on the House floor three weeks later, the day it started raining indictments on Hyde.

"This is my fuckin House, baby," she mocked.

The Africans never gave two shits about gender politics. All they cared about was the race factor, and they were willing to set women back twenty years if it meant they could jockey themselves into some handouts.

Fuck the Africans, Gloria thinks. She imagines herself squatting over a toilet, pissing on Hyde, Chinita and her beloved Kalumba as their lips gasped through splashing urine for air.

Maybe the Suits will help me.

Chip Richmond's office is quiet, stale. The air is dry. Gloria squints at a peroxide blonde perched behind a large wooden desk. The sparrow-faced secretary stares at Gloria through blonde locks that are like curtains over her face. "Speaker Richmond will return momentarily," she sputters in a monotone drone, twisting her lips into an insecure half-frown.

"Gotta time estimate?" Gloria asks.

"No." The secretary snaps her tongue impatiently and drops her pencil over a white blotter. "Just have a seat in the meantime, you know."

Careful not to show any visible signs of intimidation, Gloria finds a chair near a coffee table and glances through the adjacent magazine rack. The secretary observes her closely, chuckling dryly. "You won't find any gun magazines in there," she says. "This ain't no rest home, you know."

Something in the secretary's voice rings familiar, sparking Gloria's curiosity. She looks her over. The secretary, sensing this realization, hisses, "What, didn't your mother tell you not to stare?"

"Oh, I'm on to you, sister," Gloria states matter-of-factly. "You're Josh Brisco's ex. Maybe you put some of your old Democratic Party reading in that rack?" The girl's face drops as Gloria's serrated words cut her down quickly. "When the going gets tough, the sorority girls bail out," she continues.

The secretary bristles, shakes her head. "I never dated Josh Brisco," she protests. "You're thinking of Pepper, and she's not here. I'm *so* sure!"

Richmond's head pops out from behind his office door.

"Come on in, Gloria," he says.

Gloria takes a brief look around Chip Richmond's office, which is filled with mahogany shelves supporting various books and hunting trophies. She isn't the kind to waste time, however. "I want a committee hearing on my gender equity bill," she says with confidence.

Richmond's reaction is smooth; he offers no response, kicking his heels up over his desk, leaning back deep in a leather chair. He is handsome, cocksure, no doubt a good fuck. In days gone by, Gloria would have seduced him with her large bosom, big hair, muscled legs, and calculating wit. Racy, bold, and imperious, the younger Gloria fueled her ambitions with unbridled sexual exploits. Her first week in office, she uttered, *"Can't anyone here get laid?"* in exasperation at all the old, married bastards that occupied legislative office. In the years since, the utterance had grown legendary.

Throughout the years, she enjoyed playing the role of legislative vamp, relished in it.

Except when Morris Hyde tried to fuck her up the ass in Escanaba.

Gloria is no longer brazen and spontaneous. The lines in her face bear testimony to all the packs of cigarettes, the long nights of bottomless bottles of cheap wine, and tireless weeks of sun, sex, and parties. Gloria is well aware of her softening jaw line. With every new wrinkle around her eyes, she loses a little confidence. With each degree of sagginess in her mouth, she loses a bit of spell. Although her natural sexuality is no longer having a suffocating effect on men, she is still resolute as ever about her grandiose passions and petty jealousies. And she had consciously adjusted her behavior away from sexual exploits towards more tangible awards. God was taking away her looks, but Gloria Manson was determined that the Motherfucker wasn't going to take away her brain, too.

Fuck Him, she thinks. *Jesus is a Cunt.*

Chip Richmond snaps up straight from his relaxed position. "What do you know about state regulation policies for health care?" he asks. "Kidney dialysis, to be specific."

"What the hell does that have to do with the price of tea in China?" she snaps. "I'm talking about gender equity. Equal pay for equal work." Her words are razor sharp.

Richmond is unfazed. "Don't you mean the price of *labor* in China? That's *your* puppy," he laughs, "and I have my own dogs to feed . . . I'm talking about a possible deal with you here. You know, *quid pro quo* . . . a little *tit* for tat."

Gloria shakes off a memory of Morris Hyde panting over her breasts. "I don't find that amusing," she says. "There's nothing worse than a stiff in a suit who laughs at his own jokes." She looks at her watch, a stunt she learned from a high-priced lobbyist. "I don't have time for jokes, Mr. Speaker. I came her to get a hearing on my bill."

"I'm not Mr. Speaker . . . yet," Richmond cautions with a sexy wiggle of his finger. "Couple more weeks, sure. But let's not get ahead of ourselves."

"Don't fuck with me," Gloria warns. "I know you're already setting an agenda. Are you going to give me a fair shake or not?"

"I told you that I might be looking to deal." Richmond sighs. "But you're too impatient. Who can deal with you? Nobody. I'm being more than fair just by meeting with you, Gloria. It's not like you're in a leadership position. What have you been doing over the past eight years? Jack shit, that's what. Don't point the finger at me. If anything, you should be pointing the finger at yourself."

Gloria is exasperated. "Ah, Christ," she moans. "You know what I went through with the Africans."

Richmond grins like Kurt Douglas Craven, the fast-talking purloiner of Gloria's fourteen-year-old virginity. Kurt sucked her, fucked her, and ate out her pussy, only to come out of the closet two years later.

"Well," Richmond says. "It seems that Kalumba King and his mother are putting together a solid leadership coalition. You should talk to them about your frustrations. I mean, your bill is more likely to generate enthusiasm on the other side of the aisle, anyway. Too bad old Slade isn't here to lend you a bipartisan hand."

"Fuck that." Gloria's angry lips tremble. An image of Slade flashes and fades, replaced by a distracting vision of her and Richmond entangled in baroque decadence.

Richmond leans back in his chair again. "Or, you could take it up with Rep. LeDoux," he says. "After all, he will be chairman of the House Committee on Labor."

"That weaseling little pussy boy . . . he won't give me a hearing without your approval." As much as she tries not to, Gloria can't help but whine. "You goddamn know that!"

In a foray of cacophonous hacks, Richmond clears his throat with startling volume. "Maybe you should put your request in writing."

"I will."

"Well, then there you have it."

"You're not gonna support me at all?"

"I'm not too fond of artificial wage buttresses." He shrugs. "That's just me, though. Too bad you're not a Democrat. Or perhaps elected to office in some place like New York or California. I'm sure their speakers might be quite a bit more receptive to that kind of liberal scheme."

Gloria bristles. "You owe me a hearing, Chip. You owe me, dammit!"

"Come on now, Gloria. Don't threaten me."

"*Quid pro quo*, Mr. Speaker." Gloria bites her lip so hard that she draws blood. "*Tit for tat.* I closed up my leadership race and supported you."

"That was *your* decision. You did that on your own."

"Bullshit! Wayne Van Anders approached me and specifically asked me to step aside."

Richmond laughs. "Well, Wayne doesn't work well with women. Most important men don't."

"Fuck you!"

Richmond looks at his watch with grossly exaggerated, animated eyes. "Oh, my! It's after ten. I'm afraid that I'm going to be late for my ten o'clock over at *McCoys!* Thanks so much for stopping by."

"You're gonna regret this," Gloria barks over her shoulder as she storms out of the Speaker's office.

Pepper is shocked when Carmine brings an extra desk into the office, along with a surreptitiously hired new girl who begins work instantly. "Jenny and Pepper," Carmine smiles, "I want you to meet Lonna."

Jenny bends her headphones back slightly and looks at large Lonna with raised brows. "*Momma?*" she asks sarcastically. "As in *Momma Cass*? What a fitting name."

Carmine's angry laugh bears chipped yellow teeth. "It's *Lonna*," he says. "Even though the clouds are gray for you, pretty girl. And, for your information, Lonna *is* one hell of a singer!"

"She ought to be, with all those rolls and all," Jenny shoots back. Pepper restrains a nervous giggle. Lonna stands limp in the doorway, her eyes sullen and lips pulled down at the corners of her mouth into a tight grimace. Her dress, long, black, and with a large purple flower blooming from the collar, conveys the appearance of a wayward circus clown. *Perfect for Kalumba King's charity event*, thinks Pepper.

Carmine's lips draw into a flat grin, his eyes reflecting red intensity. "We've got a lot to do here," he says. "So get to work."

The sudden addition of the new girl is a direct violation of Pepper's comfort zone. It is a numbing process, dealing with Carmine's complexities, and Pepper tries her best to be hip with it. She sees the situation as similar to those encountered by people who have to work with crazy retards or old Grandmas who shit their pants—you just adapt to it.

Pepper shows up to work everyday, on time. She is sick over the death of Slade Pickens, but manages to focus her energies on getting to know and somewhat appreciate Speaker-elect Chip Richmond, who has Hollywood looks and acts like he knows it. Richmond is rarely in the office, but Carmine almost always is, losing his patience with both Pepper and Jenny on a daily basis while praising Lonna at every opportunity.

In no time, Pepper loses her patience with the big girl.

In the refrigerator, Lonna leaves behind a troubling assortment of mossy foods. In the break room, she falls asleep hunched over the lunch table. Worst of all—most deplorable of all—she carries a menstrual stench capable of obliterating the bathroom for days at a time. Sometimes, the sour odor trickles into the main office. *You never smelled anything like that*, Jenny tells their friends at McCoy's. *Unless you'd been at Auschwitz*. Pepper isn't exactly sure just what '*Auschwitz*' is, but it sounds about right.

Lonna arrives to work early, works late, and spends much of her day improving the administrative structure of the office. Pepper sees this as a direct affront. Just as annoying, Lonna is always using silly expressions like *Golly Gee Willikers!, Goldarn!, Jimeny Christmas!, Shazam!, Fiddlesticks!* and *Sweet Humble Pie!* in place of the classics *goddamn, fuck,* and *shit*. This kind of baby talk grates on Pepper's nerves even more than Lonna's self-righteous filing methods.

On an especially freezing day a week before Christmas, the Capitol furnace is going berserk, pumping out heat until the red on the thermometer is approaching triple digits. The Capitol offices are in unworkable condition; most of them close early, sending sweaty and befuddled employees home for the day.

By noon, all the Capitol offices are closed—except for the office of Chip Richmond. Carmine allows Lonna, who is hacking and coughing all morning, to go home. Pepper and Jenny have to stay and work.

Pepper's pants, shirt, and underwear are sticking to her clammy skin as Jenny complains about the heat.

Carmine is listening. "It's a *dry* heat," he yells from behind his slightly ajar door. "Deal with it!"

"Fucking Christ," Jenny moans. "This is fucking painful."

"I heard that, goddamn it!" Soaked with perspiration, Carmine is hunched over his desk, crafting his new House Rules to perfection. He wears gloves to protect the documents from his hand secretions. *"My hands have more sweat glands than most people's armpits,"* he often found himself explaining.

"I don't care what you hear," Jenny snaps, and, suddenly, the heavy door leading to Carmine's office is sent flying off its hinges and into the wall as Carmine rushes through.

"Who the fuck has been drinking my diet Pepsi?" he demands.

Pepper shakes her head. "I wouldn't touch that crap with a pole," she says, lifting up her can of diet Coke, which, unbeknownst to Carmine or Jenny, is spiked with rum. "I only drink D.C."

"What about *you?*" Carmine asks Jenny. From her angle, Pepper can see Jenny's hands covertly tuck a Styrofoam cup into her desk. *"'What about you?'* I said," Carmine repeats. Jenny shrugs her shoulders and Carmine runs to her side, propping her mouth open with his crusty, yellow-gloved fingers. *"God-man-damn* it!" he squeals, sniffing her breath. "Diet Pepsi! I smell it—I can smell that shit anywhere!" He rips off his gloves, slaps them in Jenny's puckish face, and bolts from the room in a loud shuffle.

"I don't have to take this," Jenny yells after him. "I don't have to take this!"

Carmine pounces back into the doorway in mid-stance, cracking a bullwhip over the floor with a thunderous clap. "Your politics are thin and rotting, Jenny," he huffs, chest bold and expanded, eyes savage. "Because you are nothing more than a stuck-up sorority cunt." He cocks the whip again, and on its backlash, it strikes the fluorescent light panel, shedding its glass about in a tiny electrical storm. "DIME A DOZEN, DIME A DOZEN!" Carmine screams repeatedly. When the sparks clear, Jenny and Pepper both scream as a long, burly, white-tailed rat falls from the ceiling and bounces off Jenny's chair and darts across the floor in circles. "Get it!" screams Carmine.

"Get it OUT OF HERE!" screams Jenny.

Pepper can't look.

"Dirty rat. You dirty rat," Carmine yells over and over again, chasing it around the office, attempting to crush it with a paperweight.

"Get it OUT!" Jenny screams.

Carmine succeeds in striking a partial blow to the rat's head, before it burrows through broken glass and into a vent. "Dammit!" Carmine pants as he watches the rat disappear. "You couldn't kill her with an axe!"

Just then the telephone rings. "Good morning, Speaker-elect Richmond's office," Pepper offers in her best happy voice.

"It's good *afternoon,* not good *morning,*" Carmine corrects her, reaching across her breasts to cup the receiver. "Unless you're living in California with all the other fruits and nuts."

The voice on the other end of the line is tired, raspy. "Cuh, Cuh, Carmine Rossi, puh, puh, puh, please," it coughs.

"Sure," Pepper says, handing the receiver to Carmine. "It's Larry Sweeny," she tells him.

Carmine's brow crinkles. "How do you know?" he asks.

Pepper shakes her head. "I recognize that stutter anywhere," she answers.

"Give me that phone!"

She hands it to him.

"Fuck this," Jenny shouts, storming out of the office.

"No, fuck YOU, Jenny!" Carmine screams after her. Placing his right hand on his chest, he takes a deep breath with his eyes closed. "Apple pie, apple pie," he mutters. "Ah, the sweet scents of apple pie." He uncovers the receiver. "Hello, Larry. What's the news?" He listens silently for a moment, his lips quivering in and out as if they are on kiss autopilot. "Okay," he finally says. Another pause, then: "Black, Spanish, whatever. It doesn't matter now, those little fuck-ups! You're a stupid fuck-up, Larry!"

Slam! The receiver shatters against its carriage.

"What was that all about?" Pepper asks.

"Let me show you something," Carmine says, beckoning Pepper into the back room. He brings her to a large oak wardrobe. Swinging its double doors apart, he pulls open a five-foot drawer, revealing a long, black snake. Shiny and moist, the snake pulses and hisses, its thin, rose-colored tongue shooting out between the interwoven wires of its cage. The snake's body, thick with scales, coils and uncoils as it slithers about, its eyes wide and fixed.

"Watch *this*," says Carmine, plucking a brown sack from the top of the wardrobe. In the sack is a Chinese food carton, from which he drops a shivering black rat into the cage. "Eat it, Johnson!" he shouts as the snake cocks itself. In one strike it hits, snapping its mouth over the rat. Pepper winces as the snake struggles to swallow its prey whole, the rat's tail twitching wildly before falling limp as it is consumed by expanding lips.

"That was absolutely charming," says Pepper, sighing with disgust. Her stomach churns with revulsion and she finds herself a bit dizzy, not just from the sickening display, but also, rather inexplicably, from overwhelming desire. Acute lust for Carmine flows through her spine, tingling wet between her thighs. She feels so heavy that it is difficult for her to stand.

"Ah, if only Johnson would have been ready for that damn Leslie Thompson—the one that got away!" Carmine closes up the wardrobe and looks at her suspiciously. "All of this is part of a scheme, you know. If only I could concentrate!" His gloved hands clap with a bang before he opens his arms wide. "Jenny has betrayed me in her thoughts," he says. "She is toxic. I can't trust her. It's now to the point where there are only a few moments a day during which she isn't scheming to crucify me. And as time progresses, these moments might become fewer and fewer."

"I understand," Pepper murmurs in a soft, sensual manner. "Let me help you." She caresses his shoulder.

"No!" Carmine squeals. He drops to one knee and begs Pepper to resist his unbridled sexuality. "Please," he asks, tears rolling down his cheeks and dripping to the floor, where they mix with nose fluid into a small, mint-colored puddle. "Resist this charisma, my wicked birth curse."

Pepper backs off and nods a tacit promise. Carmine decides he will reward her discipline with a handsome raise.

Neither of them tells Jenny.

Gloria wants to take a break, get herself a sandwich or something juicy. But with the Capitol building hotter than a sauna, she loses her appetite. The welded wall thermometer in her office reads eighty-two degrees and is rising. Menstrual cramps set in, shredding her concentration. Longing for a cigarette, she dismisses her staff for the day.

It's too fucking hot in the office to enjoy a smoke, so she seeks refuge in the basement latrine—a quiet little dungeon tucked inside a dark corner down the hall from the mailroom.

For years, the toilet had served as Gloria's favorite temple of thought. Cigarette in hand and nicotine rushing through her brain, she had brainstormed many political quests there, dating back to the beginning of her public career.

Sitting on a public toilet decades ago as a Macomb County activist, Gloria dreamt up the Doublewide Housewives' Revolution of 1980. True to her vision, she, along with a posse of lathered-up urban locals, rioted in protest of a neighbor's foreign car, smashing it to bits with boots, clubs, and hammers. The notoriety and news coverage spurred by the event catapulted Gloria into the state legislature, where she earned the moniker *The Darling of the Doublewides.*

The public toilet—a temple of dreams.

The dank john is empty, dark except for the minimalist light of failing fluorescents—and quiet but for the intermittent dripping of water from a sweaty wall pipe. Gloria twists open the cold water faucet and leaves it running as she nests her ass in the last of four stalls. The sound of rushing water is soothing. Gloria sighs, lifts her wooden leg up with two hands, resting it over the rust-speckled toilet paper dispenser. Thumb to knob, she slides open its ashtray before flicking her lighter. Sparks mature into flame, illuminating the rotted gray walls of the stall. She raises the match to her lips, scorches the tip of a Marlboro. Her pink forehead is speckled with tiny beads of perspiration as she inhales deeply on the drag, releases her bladder, and ashes into the stainless steel compartment carved into her leg.

Christ, it has been some week. Slade Pickens: dead. The radio show: dead. Her gender equity bill: just about dead. A sense of urgency grips Gloria; her lips tense, pressing a small impression into moist cigarette paper. Chip Richmond's words ring through her ears: *'You could just take it up with Jizzy LeDoux.'* Take it up with LeDoux? What the fuck was Richmond thinking? LeDoux is small potatoes. LeDoux is nothing. Take it up with him?

Richmond had to be kidding. *I'll take it right to the source,* Gloria thinks. *I'll take it right to that fuckhead Wayne Van Anders.* After all, Van Anders owed her, owed her big time, and not just because of the reasons those esoteric Capitol insiders might expect.

They had no idea.

Five years ago, in the private woods of *Rod & Rifle*, shots dropped Gloria to the mud, the tattered and torn flesh of her leg sifting through frantic hands like boneless spaghetti. Just in front of her, an attractive young man writhed against the stump of a maple, a bullet lodged in the bone of his hip. Confused, betrayed, he raised his rifle and attempted to fire back as two, three, four bullets whizzed by, kicking bark off trees. The fourth bullet buried itself in his shoulder and armpit, causing him to slump in a contorted crouch. The fifth shot whistled through his neck, spraying blood over Gloria's face.

The boy died. Gloria lost her leg.

Cancer my fucking ass, she thinks, dropping her cigarette into the toilet, where it plops into water with a hiss.

Only two people knew the truth. Gloria was one of them and Wayne Van Anders was the other.

He owes me, big-time.

The Capitol furnace is going berserk, blowing out hot air like it's Slade Pickens in hell. Chinita chuckles at the thought of pasty Slade wasting away in the underworld. It is hot: the temperature in Sonny Boy's office pushes its way past ninety degrees. Sonny Boy is back in the district, raising money like an elected official should. It's a good thing, too, considering that any climate over 65 degrees causes him to sweat like a bag of ice in the summer sun. In Sonny Boy's absence, Chinita is in charge, so she orders the office closed, telling all the administrative bitches to take a hike for the day. She even grants Tonja, the lone white employee, an afternoon's clearance. The girl is so grateful that Chinita almost feels guilty for biting her hand during last week's squabble.

The closed office is a blessing for Chinita; she decides to run some long-neglected errands. She gathers her bills, heads downstairs. But the House post office is closed. *The lazy bastards,* she thinks. *What gives them the right to close down?* The basement isn't nearly as hot and sticky as it is upstairs, where the paint is practically peeling off the walls. Chinita is without stamps, so she can't just drop her letters in their proper slots. *Those lazy fucking postal employees.* Most of them are Vietnam veterans, and Chinita hates Vietnam veterans, especially those working at the post office. They have their nerve, taking holidays on Martin Luther King Day, Veterans Day, and even Columbus Day. Those were *legislative* holidays NOT to be shared! Besides, the postal veterans were always fucking around, lacking both concentration and discipline. Chinita contemplates teaching them a simple lesson: she'd use a handful of blank envelopes for toilet paper, then drop them into the outgoing mail slots. That would teach the lazy bastards not to close early. And it would be easy, given the proximity of the women's bathroom.

As if on cue, Chinita's bladder flinches for attention.

The bathroom is dark and wonderful, just like Chinita remembers it. Under the mirrors, one of the sink faucets is running, a tiny waterfall filling its rusted basin at a pace soon to capsize. She stares into the bubbling pool, imagines a miniature Slade Pickens with his foot caught in the drain. The image reminds her of Tyrone Jackson's *White Man Drowning,* her favorite feature from the Detroit Independent African-American Film Festival. She chuckles again.

Chinita stands in front of the mirror, smiling. Her left cheek had been tingling all morning with an awkward tightness, and just as she suspected, its surface is ripe with a zit just begging to be popped. On a normal day, the zit would have annoyed Chinita to the point where she would have fondled it with her fingers, pressing and pulling until it burst open. But today is different, special. She dips her hands into the sink and cackles, flicking water onto the dirty mirror, where it makes streaks like tears muddied with mascara. Chinita can't stop giggling, she is flying high from the Slade Pickens' assassination, high as a Texas Republican on the day JFK's brains spilled all over the Dallas pavement.

Slade Pickens, the pasty old bastard—surely, his death has been heaven-sent! Shot down in cold blood by his crazed wife—it was storybook! And to think, the crazy bitch was friends with the wacked-out Gloria Manson! Word on the street is that Manson was her gun tutor, teaching her how to shoot, maybe even giving her the very gun used in Pickens' murder. Too bad the association wouldn't hurt Manson politically. Her constituents, a legion of Macomb County white trash, would no doubt laud her role in the violence, real or perceived. Chinita knows them as illiterate trail dwellers who hate taxes, blacks, and government, in that order. Holding an unbridled thirst for violence, they invest their time in guns, white rap 'artists,' and Jerry Springer. Gloria Manson, firmly entrenched in the trailer park aristocracy, is their schlock leader.

But Manson isn't going to be a problem; she is but a gadfly in the works of Chinita's master plan.

Chinita has bigger fish to fry . . .

Leslie Fucking Thompson.

Charismatic and popular, the incoming Attorney General would be riding her overwhelming defeat of Carmine Rossi to a do-good mandate, sticking her nose into every semi-questionable government contract and hire. That sort of activism would not bode well for Chinita and Sonny Boy's soon-to-emerge regime.

Chinita sighs. Fate had taken care of Slade Pickens, but, sadly, it had failed to wipe out Leslie Thompson, at least thus far. Chinita still holds hope, buoyed by the attorney general's current critical condition.

Chinita takes the first toilet stall for nostalgic reasons. *The Sanctuary,* as she once called it. She latches the lock on the door, squatting over the bowl as her black Vanderbilt pants crumple down over size twelve stilettos. Faint smells of cigarettes trickle into her nostrils. *Marlboro Lights? Was someone smoking in here? Oh well. Better to smell smoke than shit.*

Sitting in the old stall is comfortable, nostalgic. She recalls the numerous money drops made for Lamar Wilkens, the crooked little janitor who'd do just about anything for a buck. *"You would have made a good legislator,"* Chinita used to tell him. Indeed, they had a great system: she'd leave the cash rolled up inside the toilet paper dispenser (this was back in the days before they put locks on the clamps to prevent homeless people and college students from stealing rolls of tissue). Then, two days later, she'd receive copies of documents ripped off from Slade Pickens' office. They were just copies . . . paper reproductions that Lamar would produce during his midnight rounds. Pickens never suspected a thing. Lamar (*"Soft Hands,"* as Chinita would call him) was good—maybe too good. Once Chinita's favorite Capitol employee, his stock plummeted when whispers of his alleged illegal involvement with Manson surfaced. Apparently, Manson was paying Lamar to "soft hand" documents from the Black Caucus. There was talk on the House floor of suspending her, but nothing could be proven. In a churlishly wicked floor speech, Gloria openly challenged Speaker Hyde to *"act on these allegations or forever shove them up your ass."* Aware of Chinita's corrupt association with Lamar, Morris had no choice but to completely sidestep an investigation.

"Manson Sticks it up Detroit's Hyde," screamed the headline in the *Macomb County Caucasian* as Manson got off clean. Of course, her constituents loved it.

Chinita shakes her head. Even after all these years, Lamar's betrayal stings her. The fucking janitor was a discredit to his race: working for Manson's white trash crowd, he had set the Black Caucus back thirty years. What an Uncle Tom! *If I see him again, I might kill him,* Chinita thinks. *I'd drive an ice pick right through his neck, the fucking traitor.* Chinita shifts her weight, and whistles a tune as her urine bounces off the water. "I'm a survivor!" she sings out loud, tapping her heels, oblivious to the thickening smoke crawling over the bathroom from the far stall. She fantasizes about killing someone. She would love to do it under the right circumstances: someone she hated, caught in a workable situation in which Chinita wouldn't get caught. She'd love to strap one on and rape a white girl— just to see the look on her face when she stuck it in and started thrusting. She'd kill Lamar if she could find him, and Slade, if he were still alive. Hell, she'd especially love to kill Leslie Thompson, but the stakes were too high now, with the Pickens assassination fresh in everyone's mind. Law enforcement's usually myopic eyes were wide open. And this was no time for risks.

Sonny Boy is sure to ascend to the Democratic throne, and that meant center stage for Chinita. Ah, the joy! The circus—that was the first step to greatness. Clowns, animals, cotton candy, *and lots of money*! The excitement grips Chinita. $350,000 had already been raised! That fuckhead Wayne Van Anders—Chinita laughs at how easy it had been to use him. Kidney dialysis? Chinita has no intention of keeping her end of the deal. Once Sonny Boy is in charge, they'd flush Van Anders and his monopoly dreams right down the fucking toilet. As much as Chinita hates Leslie Thompson, she hates Van Anders even more.

Oh, if only I could only kill them both . . .

Chinita paints the air with her finger, singing "I'm a Survivor." She hears the creaky door swing open, quiets herself. She is annoyed that her sanctuary is being violated.

Jenny walks through the twisted basement corridor a solitary figure, her elongated shadow floating against the wall like a ghost ship fading into oblivion. High heels click against old marble, echoing through the hallway just as the day's frustrations echo through her head. The floor is hard and slick as brown ice; steam rises from it as folds of heat creep down from the air above.

Jenny's hairline is damp with frustration. Once again, overwhelming hate for Carmine Rossi has infiltrated her cognitive system, throwing her world out of balance. She truly hates Carmine. Really hates him. Her hate is loud, burning. It's embossed on her forehead for the rest of the world to read. It's all she can think about. Jenny hates Carmine so much that she wishes he would drop dead of a cancerous puss infection.

Her day would have been fine if it hadn't been for his interference. The morning had been enjoyable, highlighted by Gloria Manson's stormy exit from the office. It was funny, Jenny yelling, "Come again!" as the peg-legged brat hobbled away in an exasperated huff. Even Speaker-elect Richmond seemed amused, which was totally cool, since Jenny had the hots for him more than any other boy since the dimple-faced boy-next-door in high school. She called him Ten-inch Thomas, and he was oh-so-cute except for his uncircumcised penis, which was so fat, discolored and so unshapely that Jenny couldn't put it between her lips without choking.

Speaker-elect Richmond is boyish and radiant; Jenny bets that hidden in his pants is a nice, smooth, *cut* cock. She imagines taking it in her mouth, working it with her lips, hands and tongue until his cum is squirting off her tonsils like Republican custard cream.

This morning, Smooth-cock Richmond had left the office at about ten o'clock. Soon after, the morning went to hell in a handbag. Carmine returned from an appointment, barking out supply orders like a tyrant. Pepper, fresh from her third coffee break, repeated his instructions over and over again like a retarded drunk.

It took the two of them forty-five minutes to complete a pen order before Carmine changed his mind and instructed Pepper to re-order the "snappy red, white and blue beauties that I like so much," referring to a pen style he had flirted with a week ago before sending them all back to the manufacturer.

Carmine and Pepper: theirs was a comedy routine both unintentional and monotonous. The pen ordering fiasco was continuous and predictable. Pepper had fallen in love with Carmine! Thought he was *sexy*. What on earth did she see in him?

"I don't know, I just find him sexy. Maybe it's his look."

His *look*. The green knit sweater with JESUS DIED FOR YOUR SINS stitched across the chest. His thick, foggy glasses and the twitching, waxed moustache that rose from his lip in a single line. *Sexy?* Maybe it was his fake hair that made Pepper tingle: shiny, black, it floated on his head like a piece of sod in the ocean.

"I can't explain it. I'm just drawn to him. He has charisma."

Charisma? As if! Carmine Rossi spoke in large, exaggerated enunciations. *"I swear to mother-fucking-god,"* he'd moan, stressing each syllable as if he was painting it with his tongue. "I don't care how the other offices operate. This is how *we* do it. Speaker of the House Richmond is my boss and I'm your boss—it's that simple." Impatient and forgetful, he would pay overnight shipping for Sanford Uni-balls. "You don't understand. I can't write without them. My hand cramps and I sweat. These pens are essential!" he'd yell over the phone, only to send them back to the supplier immediately upon arrival. "I never ordered this shit," he'd explain with a shrug of his bony shoulders, big blue mug in hand. "Makes my handwriting look like Nigger scribble." His infatuation for ordering pens was limitless, just like his fondness for drinking coffee and wasting soda. He lapped his Starbucks quickly, like a dog, often while talking. Occasionally, he'd gulp it down while sucking on a Camel and fall into a coughing fit, misdirected coffee leaking out from his nose onto his sleeve.

Charisma.

Jenny wanted no part of it. Slipping into the kitchen, she *had* siphoned a bit of diet Pepsi into a foam cup. What was the big deal? There were dozens and dozens of soda cans in the fridge, most of them opened and flat. Carmine would pop the tab, take a sip, then put it back on the shelf amongst Lonna's mossy leftovers. There it would sit for days, sometimes weeks, its fizz but an evaporated memory. The next day, he would do it again. Eventually, the fridge would be overwhelmed with flat pop. Inevitably, Carmine would scream for the girls to dump it all out, accuse *them* of wasting "valuable soda."

Today, Jenny *did* take a soda: it was the one and only occasion. As luck would have it, she got caught. Predictably, Carmine threw a tantrum. And just when Jenny thought she had seen it all, he threw a new wrinkle into his Rumpelstiltskin routine: a snap-happy bullwhip. It was bullshit, that bullwhip, but at least the outrageousness of it gave her an excuse to leave the office, which was one hundred degrees and covered with a million splinters of whip-shattered glass.

Jenny stops by the empty House post office and drops her Marshall Field's bill into the *OUT OF TOWN* mail slot. The basement is deserted, quiet, everybody sent home for the day. Jenny's gait stiffens; a river of diet Pepsi fills her tensing bladder. Relief is across the hall in the women's bathroom.

The place reeks of cigarettes; smoke creeps along the ceiling in psuedo-mystic swirls. Water pours out from a faucet, tumbling over a full sink and crashing to the floor in waves. "Fucking animals," Jenny moans, twisting the water off. She steps over to a dry sink, takes off her bluebonnet ring and splashes her face with water. She reaches for a paper towel, but the plastic dispenser is cracked and empty. "Goddamn it!" she cries, dabbing wet cheeks with her blouse sleeve.

From the corner of her eye, Jenny notices movement from under one of the stalls. She turns, looks, sees two bundles of big black toes tucked into a pair of red stilettos.

The toilet flushes with a roar, the door from the first stall swings open, and Chinita McCloud Clapton-King Hyde emerges from the echoes, her arms stretching toward the sink like the long, twisted branches of a dying tree. She chuckles, moans. Her face contracts from an elongated grin to a contorted grimace. "You're in my way," she says.

Jenny is livid. "Excuse me?" she asks, although she heard Chinita plain and clear.

"You heard me," Chinita snarls. "You're in my way."

Jenny rolls her eyes. "In your way?" she asks. "Oh, I'm so sorry. Maybe I could turn the water back on for you? Perhaps light you another cigarette?"

Chinita takes the next sink, planting her bulbous hips uncomfortably close to Jenny. A grin ripples through her lips as she nestles the zit on her cheek between two fingers, applying just enough pressure to burst it. Pussy blood squirts all over the mirror.

Some of it hits Jenny hot and wet over the brow. She cringes, screams, flicks water on Chinita.

Chinita's pupils shrink to the size of tiny dots. She lashes back at the girl with razor-sharp fingernails, narrowly missing Jenny's face.

Jenny steps back, recedes into the doorway. Her heart pounds with excitement. "Yeah, try to hit me," she says. "That's soooooooo Detroit. So fucking Detroit."

"EAST SIDE! You show some respect!"

Jenny flips her the bird. "Here's your respect," she says. "Fuck you and your stupid city. Fucking Detroit—if the Arabs blew it up tomorrow, nobody would know the difference. It wouldn't even make the national headlines. The fucking place looks like a battle zone as it is."

"You don't know what you are talking about or who you are talking to."

"Of course I do."

Chinita lunges again, slaps her with an open hand.

Jenny immediately slaps her back.

Chinita grabs the bluebonnet ring from the sink. "Ah!" she exclaims with wide-eyed amusement. "A leaf, a stone, a bluebonnet ring!"

Jenny's face crumples like a leaky balloon. "Give me that," she begs. "Please!"

Chinita laughs, drops it into the sink. It falls down the drain with a muffled plop.

Jenny rushes Chinita, screaming. They swing, grab, flail, rolling off the sink and into the wall. Chinita unleashes her nails, tearing a piece of flesh from Jenny's forehead. Jenny clutches a patch of Chinita's hair. Blood and hair fall to the floor in dotted clumps.

A man is yelling. "Hey, hey, HEY!" The door swings open and janitor Lamar Wilkens rushes in, wedging his large frame between the wailing adversaries. "What on earth is going on in here? Chinita?"

Chinita's eyes glisten in the darkness; the light's dim reflection makes them seem yellow.

Jenny wipes blood from her lip. The skin on her chin is split in two wedges. "Holy cow!" says Lamar Wilkens. "Looks like you're gonna need stitches, champ."

"Looks like I'm gonna need a lawyer," Jenny says, growling at Chinita. "Because I'm gonna sue your black ass."

Chinita lingers in the doorway, hunched over with broken nails. "Two pigs in a poke," she hisses, shaking her hair like a wet dog. "I should kill you both." She kicks the door open and leaves.

"You okay?" Lamar asks Jenny.

"Yeah, I should be," she says. Lamar grabs a wad of toilet paper from the stall and hands it to her.

"Here, this should help slow the bleeding," he says.

"Thanks, but no thanks," Jenny says, letting it drop to the floor as she exits.

Lamar shrugs before heading upstairs to grab a mop.

Gloria, undetected in the last stall, shakes in quiet laughter, holding her one good leg with both arms until Chinita and company leave. "Un-fucking believable," she mutters, laughing. She lifts her wood prosthetic from the toilet paper dispenser and plants it on the ground. "Un-fucking believable."

At that point, the latrine has not only provided unbelievable entertainment; rather, it has again served as a great temple of thought.

Gloria, her bladder empty and mind buzzed, decided right then and there to make a personal visit to Chuck Hriniak.

Adam watches Chuck Hriniak slide past the Persian Shiraz and over the wooden floor to the wall-unit bar, where he pours them each a whiskey. Hriniak is calm, assuring. Sans toupee, his crown is trimmed tight and neat. He wears a pair of tightly creased khakis and a fresh, black, long-sleeve cotton shirt.

Hriniak's family room is brightly lit, yet darkly rustic with copper plated glass tables and heavy mahogany furniture.

Adam bites his nails, scratches the back of his neck. "Okay, enough with the suspense already," he says. "Why don't you just tell me what's going on?"

Hriniak's eyes blaze with excitement. "You already know," he says. "Now it's only a matter of the details." He hands Adam a square glass, thick ice cubes cracking inside a brown pool of Jack Daniel's. "I know how you like details."

"No foolin." Adam's voice is tinged with sarcasm. He shakes his glass like a tiny tambourine so that the ice spins in quick circles. "Why don't you just spill the beans, for crying out loud?"

"I don't want to have to repeat myself, so let's just wait until Josh gets here."

Josh?

Adam gulps his drink, winces. *Josh.* The name sparks a yearning. "Who is Josh?" he asks without considering a connection between Friday night's Josh and today's Josh.

Hriniak sits down, taps his feet. "Josh Brisco," he says, "a cop friend of Slade's. He ran for the House in the 75th."

"Oh yeah. I know who he is, just never met him."

"Nice young guy. Attractive, blonde, maybe your type." Hriniak smiles, goes back to the bar.

"Is he gay?" Adam laughs, kidding.

"He had a fiancé. You know Pepper Robinson from Richmond's office?"

"No, should I?"

"Yeah, she worked for Democratic staff. You know: mousy little broad, black hair. Looks like Lucy from the Peanuts."

"Nope. Don't know her."

"Well, you're better off. She broke up with Josh when he lost the election. Now she works for Chip Richmond. Rumor has it that she's dating that rodent Carmine Rossi. Imagine that." Hriniak uses a long, thin knife to slice a piece of lime, which he drops into his drink. "How are your dating exploits going, by the way?"

"Don't even ask."

"Why?"

"I don't want to talk about it."

"Adam, you need to put yourself out there. Believe it or not, it is possible to meet someone special. You just need to create opportunities."

"Come on, Chuck. Give me a break."

"Dating is like anything else. The more you do it, the better you become. You learn things about yourself, take note of your behavioral weaknesses, and adapt accordingly."

"Wasn't that the Slade Pickens philosophy? Flail, flail, flail, until you get it right or die trying to? I don't know what world you're living it, Chuck, but this part of Michigan isn't exactly Chicago or San Francisco. It's not that easy to meet boys."

"Boys?"

"Boys, guys, men . . . whatever."

"You have to try."

"Who says I'm not trying?"

"Well, goddamn it, try a little harder. Stir it up a bit. Be a little more pro-active."

"I don't exactly sit at home every weekend sulking, you know."

"You need to get a piece of the action. Get a little, you know—action."

Adam shakes his head. "Jesus Christ."

"My niece has a friend she wants to set you up with. His name is Howard, and he's an electrician from Atlanta."

"An electrician?"

"Yeah."

"How old is he?"

"Why does that matter?"

"Because it does, Chuck."

"Why?"

"Just tell me how old he is."

"Thirty-nine."

"Nope."

"What do you mean, 'nope?'"

"No dice. No thanks."

"Why?"

"I like guys my own age. You know that."

"This Howard's real young-acting, likes extreme sports. He even likes to skydive!"

"Wow, sounds like a real jesse."

"A real what?"

"A real jesse. Nevermind."

The doorbell rings.

Hriniak twirls, disappears down the corridor. Adam hears voices and rises as the footsteps falling across the foyer approach the family room, totally unprepared for what he is about to see.

Josh Brisco, blonde, sturdy, and looking only slightly more relaxed that he did Friday night, follows Hriniak into the family room.

Adam's jaw drops and his heart races a thousand miles a minute. "You're Josh *Brisco?*" he manages, voice squeaking slightly. "I thought you were Josh *The Salesman.*"

Hriniak's mouth contorts. "You guys know each other?" he asks.

"Sort of," Adam says.

Hriniak offers Josh a drink. He declines. "I've hit my quota for the week," he explains with heavy eyes, offering Adam a weak smile.

"Very well," says Hriniak, refilling his own glass.

They all sit down as Hriniak continues. "Boys, let's cut the crap with a chainsaw. I'm switching parties."

"Why would you do that?" Josh asks, a trace of alarm in his voice.

"Simple: it's the right thing to do."

Josh scratches his head. "In an ideal world, maybe."

"There's no such thing as an ideal world," Hriniak says. "You sure I can't get you that drink?"

"Positive. I'm not saying that there's an *ideal* world. What I'm saying is that there's no practical reason for you to switch parties. In fact, you'd be committing political suicide. Political suicide, maybe worse."

Adam leans forward. "What do you mean, *'maybe worse?'*"

"If Chuck switches parties, the Republican army is gonna come after him with all their soldiers, legitimate and otherwise."

"I've been fighting this war for years, son," Hriniak says.

Josh raises a finger with caution. "Yeah, but it's more dangerous than you think."

Adam is uneasy. "What are you talking about?" he asks.

The bullets. Josh wants to tell them, *the bullets don't match.* He wants to blurt out, *Darla Sue didn't kill Slade Pickens.* But he doesn't. Rather, he pauses, collects himself, says, "I don't know," his heart racing. "Maybe I don't know what I'm talking about."

"Wayne Van Anders doesn't scare Chuck," Adam says.

"Wayne Van Anders has been on my ass for years," says Hriniak.

"That's because you're not a good Republican," says Adam.

"Well, imagine what he's gonna do to your ass when you're no longer *any* kind of Republican," says Josh.

"Bring it on," chirps Hriniak. "We can go at Van Anders if we snuff out some of his connections. Think about

256

it. He has control of the governor's office, he has control of the Senate, and he has control of City Hall. We can't make a difference there. *However,* we *can* get to him by taking back the House. And there's Leslie Thompson. You know he's worried about Thompson. It's only a matter of time before she pulls the plug out of this little dialysis monopoly he has going. He knows it. He's watching her. But the House? He won't see that coming."

"Leslie Thompson is on her death bed," Josh points out. "Besides, how can you flip control of the House? Dems would still be in the minority by one seat, so it wouldn't make a difference. You changing parties isn't enough."

"I didn't say it was."

"What *did* you say?" Adam asks.

Hriniak smiles. "Nothing, at least not yet."

Adam shifts nervously. "Then for crissakes, Chuck, say it."

"I've cut a deal."

"With whom?" Adam wants to know.

"That I'm not saying. If you want your enemies to know your secrets, tell it to a friend first."

Adam frowns. "Thanks a lot. That's an overgeneralization if I ever heard one."

"Point is, the House went 56-54 after the election. I made a deal two weeks ago with Slade, was gonna switch parties. That made it 55-55. Shared power. Now Slade's out of the picture. But consider me a Democrat already. The Republicans are back up 55-54, until the governor calls a special election for Slade's seat. Or, at least that's what they think. That's when my wild card comes into play. I've got a friend, a partner so-to-speak, who's ready to cross the line with me. We pull the big switch, make it 55-54 in favor of the Dems, who vote me in as Speaker. A shocking scenario for the GOP and a crippling blow to Van Anders."

"The Dems would never pass over their own loyalists to elect you leader," Josh says. "You'd be considered an outsider."

Adam agrees. "How would you muster the caucus votes for speaker?" he asks. "What about Kalumba King and his mom?"

"Let me worry about the Africans."

"Then there's Slade's seat," Josh adds. "If the Republicans win the special election, then it's back to 55-55 shared power."

"They won't." Hriniak's tone is confident, assuring.

Josh laughs. "What makes you so sure?"

"Because, Josh, you are going to get your shit together and run for that seat. You are Slade's protégé, his pride, and you need to do it."

Josh shakes his head. "I can't get into that again. I can't fight a good battle. Besides, I don't live in the district."

"Your mom does, and that's where you've been living since the election, right? So you're all set . . . You *can* win. And you will. Look at it from the point of view of what you *ought* to do, not what you want to do."

"Come on, Chuck."

"No, you come on, Josh." Hriniak waxes Slade-like: "It's the saddest thing in political life when a decent person like you runs for office, only to suffer ignominious defeat at the hands of people like Wayne Van Anders and his disgraceful tactics."

"I was humiliated."

Hriniak shakes his head in agreement. "You were beaten down and pissed on in public. This is your chance to get even."

A rush of nervous excitement rushes through Josh like an electrical current.

Hriniak continues: "I want you to spit on your hands, hoist the black flag, and start slitting throats. The only thing the voters like less than a dirty fighter is a pussy who doesn't fight back. It's time for you to fight back. This is your shot at redemption, revenge. How many people get a second chance like this?" Hriniak pauses for a deep swig of his whiskey. "This state is fucked up, let me tell you. If somebody from far away asked me what '*Michigan*' stands for, I wouldn't know what to say. Cuz right now, it stands for nothing, and we have a great chance to lend it some definition. You show me some courage, some conviction and some creativity, and I'll show you a winner."

"What if I screw up again?"

"You didn't screw up. And besides a just cause isn't ruined by a few mistakes. We can derail Van Anders in a few swift strokes. Then we take on the Hydes. Sure, they're each dangerous adversaries—diabolical, but not unstoppable. The only way they can triumph is if we do nothing."

What a day, Pepper thinks. She unlocks her apartment door and tosses her tan and white purse onto the couch. The phone rings. It's Carmine. "Jesus fucking Christ," he says in a chipper tone betraying his harsh choice of words. "What takes you so long to answer the phone?"

"I just walked in the door," she explains.

"Oh, that makes sense." Carmine pauses. "Listen, these lacerations, while a bit of a hassle, are nothing to set me back. I've been making some big plans, and it's high time to get a move on."

Pepper squeezes the receiver with excitement. "Lacerations? What are you talking about?" she asks.

"I never said *lacerations*, missy. I said *latest developments*. Come over, I'll explain. Yes, come to my house, I'll tell you everything."

"You want me to come to your house?"

"That's what I said, didn't I?"

"I was just making sure."

"Clean out your fuckin ears! We need to get a move on, you and me. It's up to us. Do you have plans this evening?"

"Uh, I guess not," Pepper fibs. Anxiety fills her insides like creeping, black tar. Was he going to pop *the* question? She didn't want to think about it, although thoughts of love—and the financial security that would accompany it—flutter with a giddy lightness. This is so much more than she ever felt for Josh.

So much more.

She takes a deep breath, calms herself.

"This evening, then," Carmine says. "Come at sundown, as I don't keep conventional clocks in my home. Plan to spend the night."

Pepper has no problem locating Carmine's mansion. This is surprising, given that his directions were little more than, "Green house on the river: North Hooker off West Division. You can't miss it." A crisp southern breeze ruffles her hair; she arrives just as the sun is retiring to its western bunk.

The house is at the end of a dusty, barbaric drive more common to rural outskirts. Squeezed into a typically small city lot, its patch of grass is speckled with all kinds of posted bird houses and feeders. From behind this clutter of feathered shanties is the cavernous, emerald domain of Carmine Rossi: a ripe lime rising out of the dreary landscape as if its surroundings are grainy black and white film stills.

With overnight bag and purse slung over her left shoulder, Pepper scuffles to the front porch and rings the bell. The outside lights flicker on, and through the narrow twin windows adjacent to the front door, she watches Carmine float towards her through a bright flickering hallway.

"Welcome to my humble dwelling," he says, swinging open the door. Bright orange light floods Pepper's eyes, temporarily blinding her. "Please come in: enter freely and of your own will." From behind blue tinted sunglasses, his eyes are puffed and blackened. His manner is unusually calm, yet his appearance is small and pale, as if being away from the Capitol has neutered him. His wrinkled lip is shaved bare, his hair slicked back wet and greasy. He is very still and makes no gesture of greeting Pepper, as if the house has fixed him into stone. The instant, however, that her shoes click onto the dark foyer tile, he moves impulsively forward and shakes her hand as if she is a stranger. The feel of his skin is clammy cold—the feel of dead fish meat.

He beckons Pepper to a wide-open kitchen dominated by wood floors and enormous walls. Three of these walls are of white stucco, cluttered with gray and blue water colors of old people and tired-eyed dogs. The remaining side boasts a spectacular view overlooking the downside of a large hill that rolls flat into the muddy bed of the Cedar River.

Pepper sits herself at an oak table angling sharply across the stretched, hollow room. "Would you care for coffee?" Carmine asks her.

"Uh, do you have anything diet?"

"Diet Coke," he says, pausing. "As you know, I do not drink . . . Pepsi."

"Then why do you have all that—"

"Don't say it!"

"I just thought—"

"Don't worry about semantics."

He brings Pepper a tall glass of diet soda and takes a seat directly across from her at the table's end.

He talks about the house. "My parents lived here once," he explains, gesturing with his hand. "That was before the bank took it away from them and sold it to some low-life California hustler. That was way back in '75. It wasn't until '84 that I finally mustered up enough money to get the place back. And by then, it was almost too late, as the scumbag occupant had let the place degenerate into a rat infested, watery hell-nest. To this day, I'm still fighting to reconcile this manor's image, and believe me, I'll do it, since this place is all I have left of my parents. This and my cherished existence."

"Did you buy it back for your parents, then?" Pepper asks.

"Yes, figuratively. They passed away back in 1981. Health food poisoning, if you can believe it." He chuckles bitterly. "Here they were, vegetarians . . . health food fanatics . . . infatuated with each new university study offering healthy living advice . . . and they died as a direct result of what they ate. Turns out that the crazed daughter of a beef and pesticide magnate poisoned the peas at an organic food stand in Vermontville. Seven people, including my parents, died anthrax-like deaths."

"Vermontville? Jesus," Pepper whispers. She imagines the blue people from the wall paintings screaming, spitting gray vomit, their skin bursting with carbuncles and lungs filling with water.

Carmine stares at the wall as if reading her mind. "No Jesus could save those people," he says. "Nor could Louis Pasteur, a man with many a more practical group of followers."

Pepper is confused. "I thought you were into the Jesus movement?" she asks.

Carmine sighs. "Again, semantics," he says. "I want to run for public office again, you know. Voters like that religion crap. They NEED it. Especially Republican primary voters—they eat that shit up. So I feed it to 'em. It's a charade, really. You do things to please people. Yeah, you sell out." He forms a fist and presses it to his chest. "Here, on the inside, I don't believe a fucking stitch of it. How can you? It's all nonsense, lies. Jesus is a bigger myth than Zeus, Hercules, and Reagan combined. Deep down inside, *everyone* knows it. But the fear and uncertainty of death is a tough sell. Feel-good lies are much better sellers, especially when they guarantee some sort of afterlife franchise. Christianity sells, baby." He reaches into his breast pocket and lights a cigarette.

"Oh, do you mind if I do?" he asks.

"No," Pepper says. "But thanks for asking."

Carmine's lungs pump smoke into the air like a steam-spitting humidifier. "They say this causes death," he says. "Cancer sticks, red meat, drunk drivers, plane crashes . . . people love to worry about these external killers, as if physical death is absolutely avoidable and not the least bit random." He pauses to puff. "We are the ones killing ourselves, and we do it internally. Not so much by smoking and drinking as by suffering through the cognitive torments of our own creations. Those are the untruths that kill our souls: media, government, and, of course, religion . . . isn't it amusing how the three of them all influence, control, and fight each other at the same time, like a three-headed monster spitting and chewing at itself?"

Something outside the window distracts Carmine. He whirls to his feet, cocks his head toward the hill. "Did you hear that?" he asks Pepper. "Tell me you heard that," he begs.

As much as she wants to say *"yes,"* she shakes her head *"no."* The night is quiet.

"What about the foul stench? Smells like worms, don't it?"

She doesn't smell anything, but helps him close all the windows just the same. Carmine excuses himself, momentarily leaving the room to flick on the air conditioning. At this point, Pepper's thighs moisten as she begins to wonder if they will sleep together.

"I know what you're thinking," Carmine snaps, sitting down again. "We'll get to that stuff in due time, my pretty."

"What?" Pepper asks. The veins in her legs pulse with anticipation.

"I know that's why you came—the intrigue," Carmine continues. "Don't worry, in due time." He finishes his smoke, asks Pepper to follow him out back. "I have some interesting sights to show you," he offers.

They go through twin doors to a sprawling deck closely overlooking the property's hill. Immediately, the unmistakable stink of nightcrawlers brushes the membrane of Pepper's nose, making her gag.

"See, I told you," says Carmine, his blue glasses reflecting the bloated moon. He points to a bird feeder post standing naked in the flat land of the riverbank below. "Definite pecking order there—that's why I had to move the birdhouses up front. Initially, it was quite a scene: only a reference book could properly identify all the marvelous creatures that once ate out of that feeder. Then the goddamn pigeons came, knocking most of the seed to the ground. It was a fucking mess of a food spill: that's when the rats first started coming. They get that smell of food and their red eyes glaze over. I read somewhere that they'll come from near and far once they get that scent. I didn't wholeheartedly believe it, but sure enough, when all that seed spilled, legions of them started swimming down the river to my property like the Mark Spitz Army. Quite honestly, I blamed the pigeons for the whole thing. One day I killed one with a stone and threw it into the river. This only served to worsen the situation: like cartoon termites gnawing through wood, the rats devoured the carcass before it could get 100 feet downstream. Man, the yard really smelled bad that night—*like Auschwitz.* It was the first time I had to close the windows and put the air on." He pauses for another light. "You try to make a positive contribution to this world, and look what happens. At first, everything is great—all bliss. Then the vultures come in—in this case, the pigeons—and proceed to shamelessly knock your seeds all over the place and then the next thing you know is that you got rats all over your livelihood. Rats, broads, the IRS, Health Department, Friend of the Court, you name it. Even when there's no more seed, they won't stop coming at you. More, more, more!

"I remember in '84 when we were looking at the house to buy it back. A dead rat was floating down the river. The real estate agent made a joke of it, even bounced a rock off the carcass with a heavy thud. 'Not to worry,' he said. Kind of like they now say about the degeneration of America. 'Not to worry.' Jesus.

"Anyway, that night I killed the pigeon, the rats were slithering into the house. At the time, Yvonne was pregnant with Hector."

Pepper is stunned. "You have a wife?"

"Technically, since the lawyers aren't through with me yet. She's gone, though, and all of her barristers and all her boyfriends could never put Yvonne back together again."

"Did she take the kid?" Pepper asks.

Carmine lowers his glasses and stares blankly at the sky. "No," he says, scratching his chin stubble. "The rats did." Pepper's gaze travels the perimeter of the house as something slithers under the boards beneath her feet. "Not to worry," Carmine says. "No rats in the house tonight. I

265

have systems in place to keep them out. I know how to do it well. Come, let me show you."

He takes her around the stairs to the bottom of the deck, where she is awestruck by a wide trench dug in a "C" pattern into the hilltop and around the house. Wide and rapid, it is filled with glistening green liquid. The hairy beasts floating in it are dead and bloated. "It's chemically treated to expand their lungs until they explode inside them," Carmine explains, smiling with stained teeth. He points beyond the moat to a side of the hill presumed unfit for digging. There, the creatures run full speed up a steep incline, charging into a five-foot tall wooden fence. "I'm going to stick some spikes in that barrier soon, let the little bastards impale themselves." He looks at Pepper and laughs, perhaps at her degree of horrific fascination. "I'd like to drain the river, be rid of them forever, but that would be like sucking up all the waters of the world for sake of destroying the mosquitoes. Let us not forget that all creations have their dirty externalities. Yvonne, for example, was a beautiful, yet myopic creature. You've heard of people creating their own private traps—digging holes so deep that they can't ever crawl out of them? Attention deficit, money spending, vanity: those were the traps Yvonne was caught in. Especially vanity. She'd gnaw her own leg off, would it render her more beautiful to strangers. So immersed in hobbies was Yvonne that she ignored the needs of our son. "She was busy painting French landscapes when Hector wandered into the river to meet his death." Carmine pauses, waving a hand. "Oh how I'd like to drop a bomb on those French."

Carmine shows Pepper to the guesthouse, which is just off the front driveway. A plain, garage-like building, it stands in the most protected area of the yard. "This," he says, "is where my odyssey shall begin."

They enter his facility, which is an impressively equipped indoor shooting range. Pepper is able to breath easier, as the air inside smells of lemon Pledge, a refreshing change from the odorous outdoors.

"Let me tell you about guns," Carmine says, waving his arms. "They are the only sanity that I have ever had." Slipping on a camouflage World War II army helmet, he pulls out a .22 from his pants pocket. "Guns, they are my true savior. Especially when the three-headed monster seems determined to push me out of the political business. Should the fucking heads succeed in doing so, at least I have my guns, and with them, I'll go firing away noisily into the sunset." Carmine twists a switch and a carnival-like contraption churns, flipping up cardboard targets one at a time. A dragon with three heads pops up, painted fire shooting from its snout. Carmine squeezes three shots, missing with each effort.

"That's not to say that I'm prepared to fade away from the political landscape. Far from it. Not long ago, though, I wasn't strong enough to fight back." He looks at Pepper with blazing eyes. "But now, with you, my loyal, strong assistant—powerful enough to rise above fleshy temptations—I am a warrior poised for the most wicked of all battles." The machine whirls a chorus line of images and Carmine shoots while talking, distracted, as if looking for rats out of the corner of his eye. "I'm working real hard," he says convincingly as sweat squirts softly off his hands and onto the floor. He *is* working hard, laboring as if his body cannot keep pace with the demands of his brain and heart. Perspiration glistens over his naked lip. "Even so, the pundits think I'm not big league material, not for an office like attorney general. At least that's what they *think*. Yeah, that's what they think, all right. He fires at a series of Democratic presidents, missing JFK and Bill Clinton by six inches. "I'm a big-time player, don't let my election performance fool you. But at 56, I'm running out of time. I can't wait another four years." Pepper doesn't doubt him. "That's why I've decided to take out Leslie Thompson. *Now.*"

Pepper stops breathing. "What did you say?"

"I said that I've decided to take out Leslie Thompson—and I don't mean on a date." He opens his hands and holds them up like a preacher. "There's a little known clause in Michigan's constitution that states '*should an individual elected to office expire before having been sworn in, then the vacant position shall be appointed by the governor.*" And we all know that Governor Bungle is a good, good, damn good friend of mine. That's why I've decided that I'm gonna take on the three-headed monster once and for all." As if on cue, the machine spits out a cardboard cut-out of Leslie Thompson. The black and white image of her face is distorted, a curly mustache and devil horns added courtesy of a felt tip marker. "If she shows up to Kalumba King's charity circus, well," Carmine aims, fires, rips one right through her forehead. "She'll be as good as dead."

"But she's on her death bed now," Pepper reminds him.

Carmine grunts, shuts down the machine and ushers Pepper back into the house to the third floor sleeping quarters, where he leaves her to ponder the situation. The room is plush tangerine, complete with a heated whirlpool in which she soaks briefly before falling fast asleep in a plumb and fluffy bed.

Pepper's slumbering mind drifts back into the whirlpool, hot raspberry water swirling around her. Her fair wrists dangle over the side of the tub as the scent of sour, ripe blood folds the steam. At once, Pepper realizes it to be cyclical, the blood, and she spots Lonna so grotesquely squatting over the side of the tub behind her.

Auschwitz.

A trickle of Lonna's blood rolls off Pepper's shoulder, dripping off her nipple into the tub. "The best kind of blood is that which drips off a nipple, dewy virgin or not," Lonna explains.

"What?" Pepper asks calmly.

"The best kind of blood." Lonna reaches toward her with a sharp, foreign instrument. "The best sample drips from the nipple. Here, let me prick you."

Lonna leans toward Pepper's breast, panting. The blue people and tired-eyed dogs from the kitchen mural *dance around them. Pepper recognizes one: Chinita McCloud Clapton King-Hyde.*

She's holding Jenny's head, which is dripping blood from its fleshy, severed neck tissue.

Startled and sweaty, Pepper wakes to echoes of loud cracking. There is no clock, but she knows it must be sometime in the early morning, the time between light and dark, night and day. She wonders if Carmine, in a manic burst of insomniac energy, has returned to the shooting range. She looks out the window to the river below. Carmine, distant under the foggy glare of the house lights, is in the middle of the river, snug in a bobbing raft. The raft, tied by rope to a post, dangles over black, rippling water. In it sits Carmine, on his knees and swaying intermittently to each side of the water, frantically bludgeoning invader rats with a nail-spiked bat.

When it is completely light outside, Pepper wakes again, this time to the songs of many birds frolicking in the front yard. Carmine, however, is nowhere to be found. Pepper searches the house. On the kitchen table she finds a note. It says:

I've left for some muther-fucking business. See you at the office.

Even though she concluded her workout with a shower at the athletic club (where perfectly pressured water sprouted from sockets in sparkling blue streaks), Jenny's pink forehead is again salty with tiny beads of perspiration as she searches her cluttered purse for the key to her fourth floor apartment door. After a brief struggle, she fingers the bizarre, triangular shaped key on her chain, slides it into the hole, and turns the lock. Just like almost every night since graduation, she slips through the doorway, dropping her purse, work bag and attaché case onto the floor as she pushes the door shut with her hips. *I'm gonna smoke a joint tonight,* she thinks. *I deserve it.* Leaning to her left, she turns on the light switch with a nudge of her shoulder.

But the lights don't flicker on.

Through a mist of twilight shadows there is a figure, a woman, with arms and fingers like tree branches, extending out of the darkness.

A familiar image.

"Mom?" Jenny asks in a dumbfounded reflex. Goosebumps prickle the side of her shoulders like tiny thorns as half-breaths sting her lungs with a chill. The stranger lurches closer. "Who are you?" Jenny asks.

Then she realizes: *Chinita Clapton McCloud King-Hyde.*

The cell phone. Where is it? "What do you want?" Jenny asks. She strains to think. *Keep cool, keep cool,* she reassures herself.

Silence as the figure approaches in slow, frozen movements.

The cell phone, it's in the gym bag. Keep cool, be smart. "I've got money. This bag here, it's in the bag, the money" *Good. That was it, keep cool.* "Here, I'll show you." *Forget the cell. Grab the door and run like hell.*

Jenny turns, half-crouched, caught under a flurry of spidery movements. There is a pop—of a switchblade opening with a click—and the knife slashes under the lobe of her ear, slicing through her cheek like cheese. "Oh my God, stop. Please stop!" Chinita claws at Jenny with quick grasps, knocking her to the floor with spastic, hurried stabs. The pain is scalding, vague and omnipresent. Scalp numb and eyes wet with blood, Jenny runs from her attacker. She falls to the floor. Chinita, her face caked in white powder and red lipstick lurches over her. The room is dancing in a blurred joining of walls and ceiling.

"*Ah, sweet Jenny,*" Chinita cackles. "*Sweet, sweet Jenny.*" Chinita's body is squeezed into a smelly rubber suit that creaks and whistles as she moves, her left eye twitching wildly.

Jenny's mind is a screen of shadow puppets as the stiff blade filets her abdomen. *A dominatrix.* Jenny squirms over the wood floor, coated with plastic: layers and layers of thick plastic Chinita put down for easy cleaning.

Bags—blood spilling all over them. It was like filling the kiddie pool.

Jenny can't scream. Air and blood escapes through chest punctures that are bursting with tiny red bubbles. She flails at Chinita, managing to land a half-clamped bite on her wrist. The knife sticks Jenny again, shoveling into her wet, concrete ribs in a savage, rhythmic scraping of steel against bone.

Stale dental scents fill Jenny's nostrils as the mortar between the bricks in the south wall seems to melt into ruins of small villages pummeled by the ravages of war. She imagines people screaming as giant spiders tear at their limbs with savage vigor. Books, tucked into shelves opposite the bricks, seem to fly open, their pages crumbling like dried cakes.

So this is death.

Jenny's lung clogs and she is able to scream, just for a fraction of a second, until, after several harsh tugs,

Chinita pulls the knife out of her chest and buries it into her gargling throat.

There is a musical rush of bold, harsh strings. Chinita, her black eyes glistening and twitching, tips Jenny's head back by pulling her hair. She cups her curled red lips over the black, pulsing neck wound as Jenny's eyes go wide in amazement with the realization that *This Is It*. There are poetic spasms and scores of pints of blood: red and purple, swirling, dancing in colored snowflakes and spider webs, and although Jenny is engulfed by their morbid beauty, she is now but a spectator to this event and her thoughts begin to fade as she wishes that, in her moment of death, at least she could be naïve enough to accept some sort of Christian myth.

Close-up and viewed through sober eyes, Adam has the dewy look of a little boy, and a buffet of nervous habits that include toe tapping and the scratching of his hair, even while he is driving. "I wanted to take you out for breakfast the other day," he says in a tone deep with frankness and vulnerability. "But you were gone before I could even blink the sleep out of my eyes."

Josh smiles with benign confidence. His hair, tossed with gel, reflects some of the light falling through the window and across the dashboard, rendering his bangs slightly sandier than his eyebrows. He's even more beautiful than Adam remembers.

Adam is surprised, almost shocked at how quickly things with Josh are progressing.

"So you got me out a couple days later," Josh says. "It didn't kill you to wait, did it?" he laughs.

"No, but only because I got lucky with the circumstances. Who would have thought you were Josh *Brisco*? Amazing. Anyway, I got a lucky second chance. Is your hoop stuff in your bag?"

"Yeah, I just bought some new shoes last weekend, as a matter-of-fact."

"Sounds good. The circus thing doesn't start until seven, so that pretty much gives us the whole afternoon to shoot around."

"That's cool. But listen, you didn't have to come all the way out to GR to pick me up. I have a car, you know? I would have driven out to see you. I drive to Lansing all the time."

"Yeah, I know, but I had to do some stuff in the district anyway. Besides, it's no fun driving alone."

"It's only like an hour away."

"Exactly, that's why I don't mind picking you up. And I won't mind giving you a ride back tonight. Or tomorrow, if you decide to stay over."

Josh grins again, making brief eye contact before quickly averting his glance down to his seatbelt in embarrassment. He jostles with the buckle, fastens it. "I used to pull people over for this shit," he explains. "No sense in being a hypocrite."

"I wouldn't worry about that," Adam says. "Besides, cops are stupid." He grins, glancing at Josh, who doesn't smile back. "I'm kidding," he explains. "Don't you remember when I said that Friday night?"

Josh breaks into a delayed smile, laughs. "Oh yeah! I forgot. I thought you were ragging on cops. Believe me, just about everyone does these days."

"You told me you were in sales. I had no idea you were a cop."

"Yeah, it's coming back to me . . . slowly. Honestly, I don't remember too much about the ride home. I'm definitely not in sales, though. I'm not so sure that I'm much of a cop, either. I haven't worked in the squad in months. I've been out of sorts, you know."

"Do you miss it?"

"Huh?"

"Being a cop." The words seem to chop their way into Josh's ear.

"Oh, the Job. No. I mean, not really. Okay, some things about it, yeah. But not most of it. I doubt if I'll go back."

"What are you gonna do with yourself?"

Josh shakes his head. "I don't know."

"What about the politics thing? Think you might run again? I mean, Chuck really thinks you can do it."

"I don't know." Josh sighs, rubs his forehead. "I was thinking about Slade's funeral before you picked me up today. Carmine Rossi was there, laughing like the twisted fuck that he is. My ex was with him, clinging to his side like some kind of groupie. She pretended that she didn't even see me. It made me sick. It made me think about running again . . . I'd like to win just so I could shove it right in their goddamn faces and say 'see, told ya I could do it.'" Josh's forehead crumples slightly and he pauses, examining his spent words before offering a recant: "I didn't mean that, not exactly anyhow. I mean, spite is no reason to run for public office. If that's all I have in me for inspiration, then forget it. I might as well crawl under a log and die. Hate is the wrong kind of energy to run on. If I do run again, it'll be for the *right* reasons, inspired by more than just negative energy. It'll be because I want to do something good, because I want to make a difference. People don't think about that anymore. Everybody is so caught up in the details of their everyday lives that they don't think about their capacity to do good. No one feels like they can make a difference, so they stop trying. They stop learning. They stop reading. They stop following the news, even go out of their way to ignore it. It's too complicated and they're too fucking tired and lazy to deal with it. They withdraw into their own little fiefdoms and let the bad people, the bastards, take over. When all the good people lie down, all it does is make it that much easier for the shit to rise to the top."

"That's pretty much what Chuck was saying when we were at his house."

"Yeah, I think he was paraphrasing Slade. Slade used to say that shit all the time. So did my grandpa. I didn't even realize until now how similar their roles were in my life— Grandpa and Slade, that is. I've been lazy since I lost the election. I really need to get my shit together. I think about how much I've disappointed people and how disappointed my grandpa would be if he saw what I've been doing with my life."

"What do you mean by that?"

"I've been a waste of a person." Josh reaches in his pocket, pulls out a pack of gum. "You want some?"

"Yeah."

He unwraps two pieces, gives one to Adam, pops the other into his mouth. "That's the thing about politics," he continues. "You get so sucked into it that you forget who you are and where you came from, always listening to people like campaign managers, advisors, media consultants. Pretty soon, you don't even pay attention to what you are saying and thinking. You're like a doll with a voice box full of punch lines and sound bytes, and everyone else is pulling the string. You forget what you're saying. You lose count of your instincts. You forget who you are. You're programmed not to be yourself and you grow to resent it. Before long, you're all full of spite and hatred."

Adam nods his head. "That's what it was like for me—growing up gay," he says. "I was programmed not to be myself."

"Jesus. Who wants to live their life like that? That's not me. My grandpa always told me just to be myself and encouraged me to do what I knew in my heart was right. And look what I've done. My life is all screwed up because I forgot who I am. Has politics done that to me?"

"I don't think it's just politics," Adam says. "For me, politics has been the opposite. Politics has been good for me, given me an identity. Really, there have been times when politics has been my only thing to hold on to during the high winds. Your political experience was a sour one, but I bet it's more than that. You're dealing with all kinds of issues. You're dealing with adulthood, with your sexuality. You watched your friends grow up, get married, have kids. You tried to emulate them, to be like them, to fit in. But in the end it didn't work because it wasn't real for you. And the real world can be pretty crippling, especially when you don't have a place to fit in. Some people can ignore themselves, settle for lies, but you're bigger than that, even if it took you awhile to accept it."

"I'm still adapting."

"Oh, I know. You'll be adapting for a while. My advice, if you want it, is to keep adapting, keep moving towards that honest place in your heart, and then give politics another chance. Then you'll see that it's not so evil. At the very least, you have your grandfather's example to follow. And Slade's, too. You're lucky to have that, to have them inside of you. You can use that feeling as an inspiration to run again. Besides, everybody loves a happy ending. Do you believe in them? Happy endings, I mean?"

"No," Josh answers. "Since I can remember, life has always been complicated, difficult, and mean. There aren't happy endings because all good things are ephemeral. You make the best of them and appreciate them while they're here, then do what you have to do to roll with the punches when they're gone. That's all you can do."

"Hmmn. Well, I do believe in happy endings. Sometimes it's the only thing that keeps me going."

"I wish I was as well-off as you."

Adam is startled. "What do you mean?" he asks.

"You're on your feet, you've got a good job that you're good at. Seems to me like you've got your shit together. What's the downside?"

"Well, you only know me from my job—and from one night at the bar. I'm a lot more complicated than that."

Josh laughs. "Yeah, but I like what I see. You're much farther along in being yourself than I am, that's for sure."

"Two months ago, you had a fiancé. You're not out yet, and you're still trying to figure it all out. It's happening pretty fast for you."

"Well, yeah. I don't know about *anything* right now. It's unsettling sometimes. Did you go through this? Have you been where I am right now?"

"I never liked girls, nor did I pretend to. I fell in love with another guy when I was in middle school. We were together for a long time."

"You're kidding me?"

"Hell no. I loved him very much. Still do."

Josh remembers the Carolina shorts photo. "How long did you guys date?" he asks.

"Through college. Thought I would be with him for the rest of my life. There was no doubt we were meant for each other, even with my parents trying to make us miserable."

"What happened?"

"He died."

Thunder ripples through the center of Josh's skull and he is engulfed by his new friend's loss. "How did he die?"

"It was a hunting accident."

"Jesus." Josh's eyelids flutter. He turns away from Adam, pretending to look out the window.

It was a hunting accident.

Josh makes a concerted effort not to grab his head as a flurry of asteroid information bangs against the side of his brain.

A young boy, shot dead at some private range. An accident: cursory investigation. An accident: they shelved the case. It was an accident, they said. Only a rookie could have accepted that explanation. Only a rookie—or, perhaps, someone on the take.

Someone like Norm. Lazy-ass Norm.

Josh snaps out of it. "Norm has to know something," he says unwittingly.

"What?" Adam asks.

"Nothing."

Adam gives him a funny look. "Hmnn," he murmurs. "I do believe in happy endings, though. Hope dies last."

Hope dies last. The words echo through the car like a prolonged whisper.

Adam's cell phone rings. He looks at the caller ID: it's Nick . . . he ignores the call, decides not to answer it.

The basketball game is as evenly matched as the air of affection and attraction emanating from each of them. Adam, muscle-toned in white shorts and blue tank top, mixes his slightly superior size and shooting touch to alternate back and forth between posting-up Josh in the paint and drilling jump shots from behind the three-point circle. Josh, in black shorts and a gray t-shirt, uses his agility to beat Adam to the hole in quick, driving bursts. Their bodies rub off each other as they fight for loose balls and rebounds. Adam hand-checks Josh on the edge of the paint. Josh uses his forearm to push on Adam's back as he posts up. They bump and grind. Adam's sweat, dripping from his conditioned hair, smells like wet body mint. Josh's is like sour apple flavored candy.

Josh wins the first two contests before Adam takes the next two, coming from behind in both. Josh, a playmaker in the full court game with a full repertoire of crisp passes, backdoor cuts, fancy dribbles and scissor picks off the high-post, finds himself limited in the one-on-one game. He manages to keep the fifth and final game close, figuring that Adam's jumper will fade as his legs tire. Adam, a scrappy, but determined scorer, considers his game doggerel as compared to Josh's poetic, fluid moves. At any rate, he hopes that he can win by pounding the ball inside, wearing Josh down to the point that he'll lose a step on his drive as his legs fatigue.

Adam's strategy proves right.

He waits patiently at the top of the circle, checking the ball in a poised stance, palms up, toes forward. With a chance to clinch the final game, Josh jukes, dips, and pedals through the paint with an athletic twist, but Adam is able to recover, stripping the ball before shuffling it behind the three-point line and stroking it in for a winner.

"Not bad for a smoker," Josh jabs as they shake hands. "Nice game."

"Not bad for a binge-drinker," Adam shoots back.

They laugh together, arms hunched over knees, sweat dripping onto the polished wood floor. "I'm glad we were able to do that," says Adam, exasperated. "This place will start filling up in a couple hours and there'll be an hour wait to run full court."

"That would suck."

"Yeah, it would." Adam dangles his locker key. "Do you want to shower here or at my place?" he asks.

Josh doesn't want his first glimpse of Adam's naked body to take place in a locker room. "Your place," he says after quick deliberation.

Josh has already dried off and is half-dressed when Adam comes out of the shower and walks into the bedroom with just a towel around his waist. His skin is smooth and pink from the hot water. They kiss; Josh is overwhelmed. He falls backward onto the bed. Adam hesitates, a drop of water running down his smooth chest and over his belly button. Josh wants to press his finger over it, dab it against the soft flesh, but he is afraid. Adam leans over, kisses him again, quickly, like the soft, playful bite of a small dog. Adam drops to his knees, wraps his arms around Josh's bare legs. Josh looks down on Adam's wet hair, which smells of mint. *Everything about him is like mint,* he thinks, running his fingers through watery soft locks. Adam moans, looks up, lets go. "I hope this isn't too much, but I want to date you," he says. "Do you feel that way, too? Do you want to date me? Do you want to be my boyfriend?"

Josh wants to say yes, but something stubborn in him, a fear both cheap and conservative, refuses to let go. He wants to grab the back of Adam's neck, pull him closer, but he is afraid and his arms won't move. He can't break away from his primitive anxiety, even as Adam's eyes remain glued to his face and slowly fill with tears.

"Oh my God," Josh whispers, his heart overflowing with warmth and longing. The tears are too much: he wants to protect Adam, love him. He wants to let go, and he does, for the moment. The feeling is like falling from the sky into a safe, plush landing. The sensation is overwhelming and liberating, if only ephemeral. Josh knows that fear waits around the corner, biding time for its return. He wants to avoid a kiss, a risk, an embrace that may open him so raw and make him so vulnerable that it will impend his emotional doom.

But he can't.

The boys' lips meet, forming a bridge to their tongues. They kiss deep and passionately for minutes, until Josh pulls away dizzy, his heart racing at a frantic rate. "I've never made love with a man before," he says.

"I'm a boy, really," Adam says. Their eyes lock. "So are you."

"Then how does a boy like me make love to a boy like you?" Josh asks.

Adam drops his towel, pulls Josh closer. "It's easier than playing basketball," he says in a mint-wrapped whisper. "I promise."

Kalumba is startled awake from the vibration of his own farts. Melted remnants of a peanut-butter chocolate chip ice cream drip down his neck, over his pillow and onto scattered bed sheets. "Ancient damnation!" he yells, snapping upward. His face is blushed red, except for his lips, which are smeared with chocolate drool. His t-shirt is stained sticky sweet and needs to be replaced, but the shirt, tie, and suit coat Mother had laid out this morning are still hanging safely over the doorknob. Kalumba breaths a sigh of relief, thankful that the day's outfit is still intact. That would have been the kind of disaster Mother warned about. *"This is our big day, Sonny Boy,"* she had said with a lick of her lips. *"Let's be responsible about it."*

Kalumba knows just how important punctuality is to mother—especially today. *Better get a move on,* he thinks. He glances at a yellow sheet of paper tucked into the breast pocket of his caramel sport coat. *The itinerary. Mustn't forget the itinerary!*

The cell phone is ringing. He grabs it with a gooey hand. "Who is this?" he asks.

"It's Nick. I'm in trouble."

Kalumba's heart warms. "Oh, hi Nick," he gushes. Nick only called when he was late for one of their appointments. *He must think we have an appointment today,* Kalumba thinks.

"Serious trouble, Big Daddy. I'm in serious trouble."

"Come on Nick, it can't be that bad." Kalumba comforts him, figures that he is late on the rent again.

"It is that bad."

"Things have a way of working out."

"I need money. I need enough to buy a plane ticket out of town. I've gotta get out of here. I'm in serious trouble, Big Daddy."

"I'll tell you what: wait a couple days until after the leadership vote and we can go away anywhere you want. We'll go together, all by ourselves—it'll be so much fun! Anywhere you want, I promise."

"*You don't get it. This isn't about stress management, this is about my fucking life. I have to get out of here now.*"

"Who—"

"*Please don't ask about details. Please, Big Daddy. Just help me. I need money. I'll make up for it later, I swear. I'll let you do anything, I promise. I'll make up for it.*"

Kalumba flips open his wallet. "I have $600 on me. That's it. And I don't have time to go to an ATM. I need to get to the Lansing Civic Center by seven o'clock and I haven't even left Detroit yet. Meet me at McCoy's at half past six and the money is yours, okay?"

"*Can't we meet somewhere else?*"

Mother's voice in Kalumba's head: "*This is our big day, Sonny Boy.*"

"No!" Kalumba yells into the phone. "I have a circus to tend to, and there's no time for these sort of distractions. I'm already running late. McCoy's is just off the highway on my way downtown. It's the only option."

"*What about that liquor store down the street? That's even closer.*"

"Only bums and winos hang out there."

"*So what? Say yes. Please say yes, I'm begging you!*"

"Fine. Half-past six."

He totally falls into her fucking lap. Well, not literally, for if that was the case—Kalumba King literally falling into her lap—Gloria Manson's hip would be shattered into more shards than a clay pot dropped from the top of the Sears Tower. Just the same, there he is, crossing Washington Avenue in that sloth-like, slow moping gait of his, wading through the wind like a white-suited whale through the ocean.

Gloria slams on the breaks of her El Dorado with a spontaneous squeal of excitement. Joan Jett's version of *Crimson and Clover* is pounding through her stereo speakers. Gloria pulls to the curb and into the parking lot of Big Al's Liquors. She twists down the volume, flicks open the glove compartment, draws her .22. She revs up the gas, cutting off Kalumba as he is about to waddle past. "Get in here, you big marshmallow," she yells, directing him with her gun. He doesn't move, so she fires a wild shot in his direction, causing him to scamper into the backseat of the car. "Not back there! Get up front," she yells. The car wobbles and shakes as he negotiates his way into the front seat, clutching a yellow piece of paper. His eyes are wide and child-like.

"What's that piece of paper?" Gloria asks.

"This?"

"Yes, that."

"It's my itinerary for the circus."

"Sweet Jesus! Gimme that!"

Kalumba wets his pants.

"I think the itinerary has changed!" Gloria screams in delight, car tires squealing as she high-tails it to the Civic Center.

For more than a week, Lansing is convulsing with a high state of excitement over the impending circus, as if this one event can pull the depressed town away from the drain it has been circling for almost two decades. Carnies—short, tall, and of all sizes in-between—bustle to and from their downtown camp to the Civic Center. Dressed in all colors of the rainbow, they speckle the gray, snow-less streets and drab storefronts with an exuberant light. Curious families who would otherwise stay home embark upon downtown to dine, holding hopes of encountering an exotic character. Lansing's enthusiasm echoes across the state all the way to Detroit, where newly reinstated radio host Albert Dawson predicts a Kalumba circus crowd in excess of 25,000. Even the *Macomb County Caucasian* gets in on the act, its editorial board adopting the event as a war engine in their campaign against Morris Hyde and his *"debauchery-laden Negro successors."* Criticizing the motive behind the event, as well as the source of financial backing, the *Caucasian* calls for an investigation *"should the attorney general-elect live to do so."* Various funding theories are floated by the publication, including one involving the *Nation of Islam* as a financial source, and another involving the *New Age Black Panthers*. However, neither the *Caucasian* nor any other Michigan news source manages to expose the connection between the blacks and Wayne Van Anders.

The brutal slaying of Republican House staff member Jennifer Love also receives press coverage, albeit barely. *An inconsequential death,* whisper members of the press corps. *Especially on the heels of assassination!*

Carmine Rossi is also convulsing with excitement. Not necessarily over the circus, but more so at the reports out of Grand Rapids detailing the rapidly failing health of Attorney General-elect Leslie Thompson.

Carmine is not pleased, however, at the prospects of having to enter the Civic Center with Chinita Clapton McCloud King-Hyde and her stuttering assistant Larry.

"What the Christ?" he grumbles. "This is the assignment that Richmond and Van Anders give me? What the fucking Christ!"

"I used to work for Larry Sweeny and her," says Pepper, sweating under the heat of the Lar-dog's wanting stare. "How do you think I feel?"

"Irrelevant," snaps Carmine.

"What?"

"You heard what I said. You're just a staffer, dammit."

"Oh really? Then what exactly are you?"

"I'm the next attorney general."

"Excuse me," Chinita clucks, feeling fantastic in her peach-colored Whitney Houston gown. "Won't you two stop bickering for a moment and show me to my seat? I was promised easy access to the stage."

"Goddamn it," Carmine mumbles under his breath.

"Your seats are over in section six," Pepper says, pointing to the north end of the concourse with her ring finger, nearly grazing Chinita's chin with her blue bonnet ring.

The ring sounds a chime in Chinita. "I'm so sorry about your friend," she says with dramatic sincerity. "I suppose she was quite dear to you."

Pepper thinks about that for a moment, then answers: "Yes, at times she was."

"Nevermore," Chinita whispers. Smiling with warmth as they approach the gate, her eyes are stoned with nostalgia. Four years ago, at the very same Civic Center, she and Morris had brought Michigan Democrats to their knees with rousing back-to-back speeches. They were on top of the political world and the thrill of accomplishment was fresh. It was only months later when their politics became stagnant and ceased moving forward. Stuck in a perpetual status quo, Morris and Chinita turned to corruption for the purpose of keeping things interesting. They committed careless personal blunders (she had been suspected of stealing vials of blood from the abortion clinic she had fought so voraciously to fund; he was caught using campaign funds to finance a vacation to Jamaica), but witnesses and members of the press were always paid off. Except for the Ross Perot supporters, the public was more detached than restless, and the general attitude was one of 'who cares?' After one year in control, Morris was more confident in his incumbency than ever, publicly proclaiming that he could beat anyone, even Jesus Christ, in a Detroit election. "Unless Jesus comes back as a black man," cautioned Chinita. "And in that case, we'll just run commercials associating him with that Jew, Pickens, and it'll be all over before it even started."

Chinita laughs out loud at her remembrance.

"Jesus mother-fucking Christ," Carmine grumbles under his breath as they penetrate Gate 6 and enter the concourse. "Smells like somebody tossed their cookies in here!"

Pepper sighs. "You're very loquatous for a man with such a foul scented automobile," she hisses.

"*Loquatous?*" Carmine snaps around as if he's going to bite her. "What kind of word is that? What do you think this is, *Match Game*?"

"What the hell does that mean?"

Carmine lunges at Pepper, but before he can hit her, the Lar-dog steps between them.

"Suh, s-s-suh, stop it!" he orders.

A little girl with bouncy pigtails comes running out of the women's toilet.

"Mommy, look, it's the Mayor!" screams the little girl, pointing at Carmine. The mother, a dainty brunette in a navy business suit and heels, hustles after her daughter in a hurry, sliding herself between the little girl and Larry.

"I'm sorry, Mr. Rossi," says the woman. "My daughter mistook you for Mayor Roscoe." The woman smiles, offers Carmine her well-manicured hand in a gingerly fashion betraying her attempt to project confidence.

Carmine's face illuminates; he shakes the woman's hand with a firm grip. "Yes, indeed," he says, beaming—first at the woman, then at her little girl. His brain clicks, matching snapshot memories from every meeting, fundraiser, and speech of his career. He has a talent, a knack for remembering faces and gestures, a specialized ability that plays very well into his profession. In seconds, he places the mother and daughter at a rally two years ago. The girl had grown since then, as had her thick locks. The mother looked the same and was easily remembered by her reluctant professional manner. "Miss Iris Durham and her beautiful daughter Molly," Carmine says with a bow and a wave of his hand. "How pleasant it is to see you again." It was magic, his combination of mellifluous expressions and gestures. Chinita observes with jealousy; Larry absorbs it with appreciation. As Carmine and his group make way to their seats, a series of Joe and Jane Publics approach him. Many he recognizes, their names jump from his lips. And for all those that advance upon him, Carmine conveys a bold, reassuring charisma that leaves them feeling the sort of satisfaction one feels after visiting a long estranged friend or relative. Carmine knows what to say, and he knows how to say it. He has all the right moves: eye movements, nods, gestures . . . his is the stuff of legend, the stuff that seduced women and men alike, the stuff that made rivals jealous, the stuff that was capable of relaxing the most jaded of observers. The stuff that made Carmine so confident of his inevitable ascension to statewide office, no matter how high his poll negatives were flowing. The right stuff.

Yet, there was also the wrong stuff.

An old woman wearing a stained purple dress and crumpled fedora with a broken feather poked into it like an afterthought confronts Carmine just as he crosses under the curtained entrance to his box seat section. "I gave five dollars to your attorney general campaign, you goddamn loser!" she shrieks, waving her bony hand in his face. "Whatcha doing about it, besides romping around here like you're some kind of movie star?"

Carmine is disturbed by the oddly tall woman's choppy, hyper mannerisms. "Settle down, Grandma. I did my best," he assures her with a nod, placing his hand upon her sloped shoulder.

The old woman springs backward. "Don't you patronize me, *man*!" she screams, ripping the feather from her hat and poking Carmine in the eye with it.

"GODDAMN WHAT WAS THAT?" Carmine screams, clutching his eye with both hands. There is no blood, but Carmine feels like his iris has been punctured. His knees buckle as he imagines it oozing like jelly out of the socket and into his hand.

The woman lunges at Carmine again, but Larry, with his stiff and brazen arms, wrestles the feather away from her, snapping in two.

Chinita is startled by the old woman's choice in perfume—it is tremendously cheap smelling, and thus recognizable. "Why, you're Martha Lewbie, aren't you?" she asks.

"Indeed I am." The old woman's voice cracks with pride. "Lieutenant Governor of Michigan from '70 til '90. Twenty years of public service. They don't make 'em like that no more."

"Certainly not," Chinita says. She pretends to rub her brow in order to hide the mad twitching of her eye. "Won't you come with us to our seats?" Grinning, she grabs the old girl's wrist and digs her fingernails into the downy, loose skin just hard enough to cut through the flesh and into the purple vein beneath it. The woman elicits a hoarse grunt, but nobody around them notices, as the condition of Carmine's eye commands a monopoly of attention. A shot of blood, a single thin line, squirts from the swiftly punctured vein casing, sailing over Chinita's shoulder, landing in a bright red question mark on the gold curtain separating the concourse from the arena seating. Chinita squeezes hard, clamping the blood flow with a cold vice grip. "Walk this way," she commands. The old woman, rendered white with fear, hopelessly follows Chinita, whose grasp is unrelenting: she clutches the former lieutenant governor's bloodline with the vigor of a swelling cobra.

They duck under the curtain and an usher, a swarthy little black-haired teen, directs them to their seats. Smells of cotton candy, peanuts, and beer dance above the rising hum of the crowd, which Larry estimates at, "At least fuf-f-f-fif, fifteen thousand. Muh, muh, maybe more."

Once seated, Larry fetches Chinita a large soda that she quickly and covertly empties under the red plastic seat in front of her. Setting the empty plastic cup onto the concrete ground, Chinita holds the old broad's leaking wrist over the cup and firmly presses the blood into it. It takes only seconds for the swirling pool of cherry red liquid to fill the cup, yet Chinita feels unsatisfied, displeased: something about the blood is wrong. A stench, rotten and feral, rises from the crimson cocktail and vaporizes under Chinita's nostrils.

"Please stop," the old woman begs.

"Why should I?" asks Chinita, suppressing a cough. A shriveled, sallow little bald man sitting in front of them half turns around. "You mind your own business," Chinita tells him. Snatching up the cup, she re-establishes her grip on Martha Lewbie and leads her through the aisles and concourse to the women's bathroom, where they quickly slice through a chatty crowd to an open toilet in a closed stall. The sight of the old woman in the bright light of the bathroom propels Chinita into a wave of blue, piercing nausea. The twitch in her eyes spreads to the rest of her face. She feels cold, hard coolness oozing out of her every pore. *Sonny Boy, the power . . . mustn't do anything to jeopardize it.* Yet, her control is ebbing away. She shudders, recalling the days of her childhood, back near the old Harper Theatre in Detroit.

Chinita had never known her mother. When her father, a hard working man who peddled fur coats for a shrewd, greedy Turk, passed away, she was just entering her teenage years. Janicia, her twenty year-old half-sister, took her under her wing, raised her, tutored her, devoting every last drop of attention to the detail of Chinita's intellectual and emotional development. Janicia: oh, how Chinita adored her. It didn't matter that they were just half-sisters. Janicia was more than that: she was like a sister and a mother. And so what if Janicia's father had been a white man? Janicia's soft cherry lips, large green eyes, and fair hair that dropped strand-by-strand over quiet porcelain skin was exotic, almost foriegn. Yet, she was beautiful, and at any rate, it didn't matter to Chinita if Janicia was half-white, half-Indian, or half-Jew.

That was until Thomas thrust himself into the picture.

First there were the casual dates: the dinners, the movies, the nights out on the town. Then came the small little gifts: the paperback books, the jazz albums, the semi-cheap rings—they were all preludes to the canary.

Oh, that blessed yellow bird! Like a cat staring out from behind a screened porch, Chinita watched it for days, following it's every flutter, twitch, and contort. She had to fight the urge to grab it in her hands and squeeze the life out of it with her fist. She could have pulled the heart out of it with her sharp, crimson polished nails. Or simply snap its head off with her teeth. But she didn't. Instead, at night, when Janicia would cover the bird's cage with a light blanket, Chinita would sneak out her bedroom window and set the squirrel traps for the next day. By the end of the summer, she had enough pelts to make a coat for her late father.

A double wave of nausea buckles Chinita to her knees, dirtying her Whitney gown. Her last conquests had been a gem, a healthy young woman in her buxom prime. This shriveled, expired beast is nothing of the quality and moniker of youth. Just the idea of draining her blood into the layered belt pouch disgusts Chinita. But why waste it? The blood of a strong dog would provide for more suitable, youthful bathing, but Chinita is far past the chrysalis of bleeding canines, except when under the maddening influence of alcohol. Suppressing the urge to vomit, Chinita gags as she dumps the soda cup of blood between Martha Lewbie's knees and into the toilet beneath them. Then she grabs the old beast's floppy hat and scissors her nails through it, tearing it to bits like it is paper.

"Why are you doing this to me?" the woman asks.

Chinita snarls, gnashing her teeth like a vicious wolf. "Does the *Macomb County Caucasian* mean anything to you?" she asks.

An orgasm of nostalgia comes over the old beast, seducing her into hypnotic recollection. "Why yes! '*The Macomb County Caucasian*: all the news and then some.' I wrote a column in the *Caucasian* for over eight years! They don't write like that no more."

Chinita is panting. She wipes a drool bubble from the corner of her mouth. "You referred to my son as a '*babbling heir to the gulag.*' You called him '*a big black Baby Huey.*'"

The lieutenant governor laughs. "It seemed funny at the time." She looks at Chinita with a sly grin before drawing her lips together in a pursed kiss. "Freedom of the press, man. Freedom of the press," she says, spitting in Chinita's face with a degree of force that is extraordinary, coming from a poor, weak creature wilting away in a filthy public restroom.

"There are consequences for what you wrote," Chinita snaps.

"As there are for killing people," the old woman murmurs, clutching a tiny golden crucifix affixed to a chain around her neck.

"He can't hurt me," Chinita laughs, suppressing an urge to rip the ornament free and cast it into the bloody toilet bowl. "And he can't help you. *People*. It's all people. Don't you understand that by now? People make the rules.

People help you. People hurt you. And at the core of it, people are animals. We are swine. And we do what the fuck we want—especially when our animal rages take over. And even when they don't—when you think you have control of yourself—the rage lingers underneath our each and every fiber, pushing us, driving us to savagery. A white lie, a petty theft, a cold-blooded murder: if the gains outweigh the risks, then we strike. The rules, real and imagined, can only provide so much attention."

The old woman sighs, looks away from Chinita.

"Look away, sure," Chinita says. "Look away and close your eyes as it all dwindles."

"Oh, these are some kind of seats!" exclaims Carmine with a big smile as they settle into their box. He makes sure to enunciate loud and clear so that all the people sitting around him catch a glimpse of what a happy, fun-loving, grateful guy he is: the kind of man who would make a perfect attorney general.

"No sense in working *this* crowd," Pepper gripes, acknowledging the collection of rumpled ruffians populating their section. "These people are all relatives of the circus carnies."

Carmine lowers his voice. "Why do you have to be so cryptic? Just shut up, will you?"

A wrinkled little man with sallow skin turns around to face them. White hair, coarse and frazzled, sprouts from a single pore located at the top of his round, lampshade head. He leans over, his tea-leaf breath sifting into Carmine's nose as he speaks. "My daughter trains the elephants, you know?"

"Oh, the elephant trainer! Wow, that really is something special." Carmine tries to sound enthusiastic, forcing his hands together in robotic claps of approval. The strange man continues to utter nonsense about his daughter, speaking with wild hand gestures. In a ploy for silence, Carmine slips him a five-dollar bill and turns his attention to the chirpy sounds and cotton candy scents that please him. *Oh, if only Hector could be here to share in this,* he thinks, tears refilling his pink and swollen eye.

Pepper tries to avoid making eye contact with two cone-headed lesbians sitting in the second row. Sharing close-cropped, platinum blonde hairdos, they hold hands and chew gum voraciously, snapping their lips with cracks and pops until the stouter of the two decides that a cigarette is more to her liking.

"Hey, no smoking, sir," yells a tan usher with cracked skin.

Where the fuck is Chinita? Carmine wonders. One section over to the left, a leopard man, spotted discolorations in his skin bursting about like peach fireworks, sucks on the bottom tip of an unpeeled banana. "When are they gonna start?" he asks no one in particular. "Why is this taking so long?" He pauses, taking a bite out of the banana. "All this waiting is really taking a toll on me. I wish they would start already."

Carmine cringes as the peel crunches loudly under the man's brown, pointed teeth. *Where the fuck is Chinita? Shit, they should just fucking start without her!*

As if on cue, the lights fade and a large, collective, excited gasp escapes from the thrilled standing room only crowd. "*Ladies and gentlemen, children of all ages!*" a voice roars, the crowd cheering wildly. Spotlights crisscross though the seats, merging together on the ringmaster in the center of the floor. Explosions ring to rap music as two pillars of fire shoot up several stories in height. Lithe trapeze artists and bright, exotic animals dart in and out of sight under the flashes of light. "*Welcome to the Kalumba King Charity Circus!*"

Cheers and applause from the enthusiastic crowd shake the stadium foundation.

If only I was on that podium, thinks Carmine as Wayne Van Anders strolls up to the microphone, flanked by Cobb and Chip Richmond, whom he introduces as "Michigan's First Great Speaker of the House." Van Anders, erect in a crisp suit and fully in control, then offers a prayer to awkward murmurs and sparse applause. "And now, please welcome your host, Kalumba King," he concludes before surrendering the stage.

Doesn't he know that Fat Ass ain't here yet? Carmine wonders.

Suddenly, feedback pierces the air and the music screams to a brutal halt. A woman's voice, shrill and amplified, rips through the resulting silence with piercing authority. "Hello, everybody!" the voice booms. Van Anders and Richmond crane their heads toward the stage, where they are greeted by a beaming Gloria Manson.

"I said *'Hello, everybody!'*" she says again, eliciting a muffled response from the confused crowd.

Gloria is remarkably confident, joyful and radiant. "I said *'hello, everybody!'*"

The crowd finally murmurs back. "*Hello.*"

"Well, ain't this a honey? Here we are, gathered together today in celebration of Kalumba King, who once said 'I have no ambitions beyond my current stepping stone.'"

Uncomfortable laughter rises as the cold demeanor of the crowd begins to thaw into a genuine enthusiasm raw for exploiting.

Gloria continues: "Ah, Kalumba King. He is the Hyde Legacy, next generation. You know what that means: indictments, scandals, petty theft. No doubt you've read about the Hydes in the papers. Stolen televisions, fax machines, VCRs, Capitol ornaments . . . ah, theirs is a legacy indeed. Perhaps that's why this circus is so fitting a celebration. Their leadership reign was the greatest circus ever to set camp in Michigan.

"My family has had the distinguished honor of serving side-by-side with the Hydes as they systematically raped the taxpayers of this state. My father, Rudolph Bosco Manson, was the Otto Van Bismarck of the Michigan legislature. And yes, he was a Democrat. A proud, Mussolini Democrat. I'm sure some of you recall that."

A smattering of applause ensues, as do a few hoots of appreciation.

"It was during the first great budget scandal when he uttered the famous words, *'He who has his thumb on the purse has all the power.'* Well, Daddy died in that House Appropriations committee room. He died working to bleed corruption from a 400-page bill that was nothing but a pure hustle job from Morris Hyde. The three-day effort to protect taxpayers ended up bleeding Daddy, who finally slumped over at four in the morning of that last night, dead from a massive aneurysm.

"See, the King-Hyde dynasty has always been about bloating the state payroll. They appoint their unqualified family members to high paying jobs. They appoint their unqualified friends. On the Republican side, it's a little different. Rather than giving out jobs to friends and family, we simply hand them government contracts. Big, fat, juicy contracts. Hand-outs. That way, they can continue to champion the successes of slimmer government at those thought-provoking Chamber of Commerce luncheons. Bemoaning the expansion of payroll, the GOP gods call for privatization—as if they're looking to save the taxpayers' dollar. They tout the efficiency of privatization, laud its desirability. But let's call it what it is: a sham, a loophole for spoils. Anything that the public sector can do, the private sector can do worse, especially without oversight. What a sham.

"Speaking of which, the state of the legislature is a sham. A charade. Wayne Van Anders showing up and offering a prayer at a Hyde-King event? That takes the cake. Surely, it amounts to something sinister. I keep waiting for David Copperfield or Doug Henning to step out from behind a massive curtain of mirrors and declare it all an illusion. Wayne Van Anders: *The Wizard of Oz.* Or, rather, *The Reverend of Oz.* Such a proud Christian, that Van Anders, hiding behind his religion while ruthlessly exploiting people for his every possible political and capital gain. He's one of those guys who advocates lower taxes and fewer government services. He doesn't want the government to spend anything, unless it's spent on one of his borderline illegal projects. It's his business to keep government out of business, unless his business interests need money or protection. Why, look, there he is below! Pushing, stomping, and swearing like Rumpelstiltskin in a mosh pit."

I've had enough, thinks Wayne Van Anders, his suit coat seemingly shrinking into a sweaty, skin-tight straight jacket. He wishes he could kill Gloria Manson right there and then, and a wave of maddening regret flushes his cheeks as he recalls his opportunity to do away with her at *Rod & Rifle* five years ago. *Damn it all, what a cowardly failure!* Now he would suffer for it, for as much as he wanted to strangle the bitch, or have Cobb shoot a bullet through her neck, there was no way he could get away with it. Not here, and not now. Rather, he would have to use his political clout, summoning all of its brutality, and kick her out of the Republican Party to the streets, where she'd never be heard from again. But was that possible? He had been unsuccessful in his efforts to do the very same to Chuck Hriniak, and that was in his very own backyard. What then? A surge of anger chokes his throat, cutting off oxygen to his head for a moment. At that very instant, as he turns to Cobb with the intention of ordering him to remove Manson from the stage, Wayne Van Anders is thunderstruck at the sight of his son, Adam, who is standing side by side with Josh Brisco ten paces behind Cobb.

Having abandoned themselves and all awareness of time in a prolonged fit of lovemaking passion, Adam and Josh are late to the circus, missing the opening minutes. Unaware of his father's introduction and prayer, Adam has no reason to anticipate his presence at a charity event—especially one honoring a black Democrat from Detroit. All things being even, Father would never be caught dead attending such a fiasco. Adam doesn't notice him hovering close to the stage until Gloria Manson's wildly entertaining monologue targets the old man, eliciting his angered reaction. Van Anders is in the front section of the floor, about seven feet below the elevated stage. He yells something vile, pointing violently at Gloria, who flippantly taps her wooden leg in defiance.

Gloria taps her lumber with a long walking stick. "See this—my dead leg? You people read that I lost it to cancer, right? Well, cancer my ass. This prosthetic has Wayne Van Anders' name written all over it, as does a young man's death some five years ago. Hunting accident my ass."

Van Anders turns to his son with wide, trembling lips. "Shot down like a pheasant, that boy!" he boasts. Indeed, the little faggot had no business coming to the Rod & Rifle, whether he was someone's guest or not. Rod & Rifle was a *private* club. 6,000 acres of exclusive woodland and meadow, reserved for a better class of hunter, a better class of men. Schwartzkopf, Westmoreland and Eisenhower—they were amongst the great men who had graced the Rod & Riffle, as were Wayne Van Anders himself and various other captains of industry. They were a better class of men, Van Anders and his fraternal hunters. Rod & Rifle was a tribute to nature, to the great outdoors. It was a place for men— men's men, and was certainly no place for homosexuals, especially the one fucking his son. "Shot down like a pheasant, that Jimmy," Van Anders repeats with great satisfaction. "He didn't belong."

Adam looks at his father, realization striking him like a lightening bolt. He tries to shake it off, the idea of his own father killing his lover—an act that seems too insidious even for Wayne Van Anders. But he would be idiotic to step around what he knows is the truth.

Josh wedges himself between father and son, a vision of the boy in Carolina blue shorts rips through him as well. Indeed, it is true: Jimmy Dillon, murdered by Wayne Van Anders at that hunting lodge of the privileged. Crumpled in the forest like cheese on a salad of greens.

A hideous wave of nausea passes over Adam, his knees lock, and all strength is whisked from him like straw buffeted by a storm. He wants to hear no more.

Gloria, unaware of the specific nature of the exchange unfolding below, continues. "Enough about the sad hypocrisy of Wayne Van Anders. Let's talk about the state of our state. We know in our heart of hearts that our budget is real, that the money we spend is real money, is your money, the taxpayers' money, yet we are still attacking twenty-year problems with five-year plans staffed by two-year personnel working with one-year appropriations.

"The Hydes, Kings, and Van Anders: they're always using the taxpayers' money to build something for themselves, or for their friends. It has to stop. Meaningful legislation? Forget about it. Accomplishments for the people? None to speak of. Their performance at the top would convince us, by comparison, that Rip Van Winkle was on amphetamines. Such is the legacy of these fat cats.

"Before Sine Die—which is what we policy wonks call the session's last day—each party will elect a new leader for the next two-year term. Kalumba King and Chip Richmond think that they have each respective leadership race in the bag. Well, in the words of the immortal Harry Truman, *'It isn't important who is ahead at one time or another in either an election or a horse race. It's the horse that comes in first at the finish that counts.'* Those words ring so true of the Democrats caucus leadership post, especially since Slade Pickens was assassinated.

"The times are ripe for bold, new leadership. Not from Chip Richmond, the spoiled heir of a liquor magnate— he isn't worth the salt in his booze. And certainly not from Kalumba King, the man-child hiding behind his wicked mother's dress. Neither of those two characters represents a break from Michigan's corrupt past. In fact, they embrace it. That much is clear from the open-door policy each has with Michigan's number one tyrant, the born-again Christian frolicking below me."

"You piece of trailer trash," Van Anders puffs, stepping in front of a stunned Chip Richmond.

Gloria continues, unabated. "Ladies and gentlemen, I'm switching parties. Today is my official announcement to you, the people of Michigan. It *is* time to make a difference. The Republican party is corrupt beyond reconciliation. The Democratic party, on the other hand, has a chance to redeem itself—by separating itself from the King-Hydes. As Chuck Hriniak and I cross the aisle together, we join a galvanized coalition poised to overthrow the Hyde-Kings and their Detroit ways. Then we can take on Van Anders and his moral minority, sweep them into the gutter where they belong. Today, I stand before you as a newly incarnated, proud Mussolini Democrat in the vein of my late father.

"It's time to clean up, people."

"I'll clean YOU up, traitor," Van Anders yells.

Gloria responds with terse bravado: "I'd like to see you do that. You crazy psycho. You overstuffed lunatic. You sick, elderly child."

"How dare you?" Van Anders is furious. He repeats himself, swinging fists in the air as if to punctuate his angry words. "How dare you?"

Adam is slumped and wilted, buoyed only by Josh's embrace. Their lips touch, briefly. The sight of this pushes the old man over the edge.

"You are a disgrace!" Van Anders screams, pointing at his son. "In fact, I know that this whole round of developments is your fault. You're behind it! You and that fucking pimp Hriniak." Infuriated, he throws himself over Josh, clawing at the air in an attempt to strike Adam. Van Anders tussles and scuffles, but he can't push Josh aside. He growls at his son, teeth gnashing. "Shot one down like a pheasant, that homosexual Jimmy. And I'll shoot down this one, too!" Van Anders glares at Josh and screams like a woman, advancing towards Adam with clenched fists. "Like a pheasant!" Adam backs away, still astonished at his father's revelation. With a quick three-step, Cobb swiftly clears Josh from Van Anders, who grabs Adam by the shoulders and shakes him violently. "Did you get the fun you wanted, you little homosexual?" he asks.

Adam's eyes are lifeless, his lips astonished into silence. He is still as Van Anders strikes him in the face with the brute force of a retarded giant.

"Cast-off! Whore! Sinner!" Van Anders' screams choke into whistles, his voice folding into wheezing gasps for breath. He knocks Adam backwards, attacking him with both fists at random. Full, vile visions of his son fucking men in cum-stained bath houses and public restrooms fill Van Anders' head, haunting him, driving him to blind madness. It is personal: his son's debauchery defies everything: his work as a father, his standing in the community, his relationship with God. And what decency, what moral worth does Adam have left to save?

None. Van Anders would rather see him die than succeed, the fool homosexual. Sure, his wife held conflicted sympathies, but damn the excuses she makes for the boy. For Wayne Van Anders, it is cut and dry: Adam is a goddamn sinner. Wayne Van Anders didn't raise any boy to become an earring-wearing, tattoo-sporting, lifestyle-flaunting homosexual. It was simply unacceptable—in the eyes of the Lord and in the eyes of Wayne Van Anders. Adam will pay for his sins, the sooner the better. The boy will suffer. Van Anders hopes he lives to see it.

Adam, his milk white cheeks wet with silent tears, falls to the floor, his panting father kicking him with sharp dress shoes that thud against his forehead like a hammer against splintering wood. A hollow crack rings out like a breaking egg, and blood squirts out of Adam's fractured nose.

Josh grabs a chair and hurls it past Cobb at the old man, who manages to duck without missing a kick.

Gloria, not to be upstaged, pulls out her .22 and fires it at the ceiling. "I'm not finished and I WILL Be HEARD!" she proclaims. Three shots ring out. A light fixture explodes, sparks cascading like fiery rain. The workers in the sound booth, startled, inadvertently kick on the house music.

Just offstage, behind a large purple curtain, Delhi the elephant, having expressed symptoms of extreme nervousness all afternoon, is sent into a blind panic by the gunshots. Frustration from years of limited food, cramped conditions and incessant abuse rises to a crescendo and explodes. In a show of adrenalized brute strength, Delhi kicks upward, breaking loose from her chains and flies past her whip-bearing trainer. Tearing through the curtains like a fist through paper, she tramples over the fence separating the first row of spectators from the circus rings. Several people are rolled under the chain-link wire, dragged along, and crushed. Their cries fly into the air, appeals for help dissolving into the high-pitched, pulsating techno music. Screams from the rest of the crowd cascade upward as mass panic ensues. Terrified throngs of spectators rush to the higher seats and out the exits, stumbling as far away from danger as possible.

"Oh, Christ," mutters Larry Sweeny without a sign of stutter.

Carmine Rossi is white with his growing disdain for all animals. "Ah, Christ," he says, shooting Sweeny a sour, insolent scowl. "You've got that *'I fucked up again'* look written all over your fucking face. What'd you do this time?"

Larry offers him a rude hand wave and looks the other way.

"Don't you sass me," Carmine snaps.

"I didn't."

"Yes, you did. You sassed me, and I take offense."

Pepper gawks in wide-eyed horror as Delhi romps out from the trampled row of stands, stomping, whipping, kicking a small red and white mass tangled under its massive legs. "Look at that big old sock!" a ruddy fat-faced man says to his daughter.

"That's not a sock!" screams the Leopard Man. "It's a human being! A human being for crissakes—a little girl, just like your daughter!" Indeed, upon closer examination, the cotton glob is a small child, its bloody body contorted and twisted like chewed taffy.

Carmine continues to needle Larry, expressing complete disinterest in the horrors taking place around him. "You're no stranger to fucking things up," he says, clicking his tongue. When Larry again turns away, Carmine snaps a finger off the soft flesh of his cheek.

"Ouch!" Larry grumbles, trying to grab Carmine's hand.

"Did you hear what I said?" Carmine flicks his finger again, this time harder.

"Knock it off already! Yes, I heard what you said."

"You and your Negro friends were supposed to take care of that cunt Leslie Thompson. Look what fucking

303

happened! And this—are you responsible for this? What a disaster."

"Shush!" Larry holds a finger to his chubby lips. "I did what I could with Leslie Thompson. Why don't you just broadcast it to the world?"

"I would, but nobody's fucking listening. Besides, it looks like she's gonna die after all. I just don't like being made to wait."

"Well, someday you'll thank me, because there's no way they'll trace it back to us."

"Only because you got lucky. You and your fucking Negros."

"They were Spanish."

"Whatever. At least they got blown to bits before I had to pay them anything."

"I paid them my share up-front."

"That's your fucking problem, isn't it?"

The two lesbians light menthols, watching in awe as a muscle-bound, horse-faced woman emerges from behind the wreckage. Dressed in a sequined orange suit and matching microphone head set, she runs after the elephant, striking a whip against the floor with every step. "That's my daughter," yells the Leopard Man. "Like I told you, she's *the trainer*. That's my daughter, Loreli. Oh, glory be! Save the day, Loreli. Save the day and make the papers!"

Loreli catches up to the elephant, poses in mid-stance and cracks her whip against its ass with the gusto of a superhero. "Man, that chick is just plain stupid," says one of the lesbians. "I mean, she's really asking for it."

The Leopard Man is silent. His daughter whips the elephant as it snaps and kicks the tangled child from its large, powerful feet and stomps it into a flat mass of crushed flesh and bone. "Oh, man," he sighs. "This is taking a major toll on me."

Screaming spectators cover their children's eyes as the elephant, her rage fueled by chaos, kicks the flattened carcass across the floor and lumbers after the trainer with surprising agility. Delhi catches Loreli in mid-stride, crushing her under a flurry of merciless, 8,000 pound stomps. Her headset microphone, twisted but not broken, amplifies the snapping of bone, making it audible to the sickened crowd. Cries echo through the arena. In the concourse, displeased parents make angry accusations to ushers as others plead for an authority to take action.

Wayne Van Anders looks around at the swollen, red, contorted, frightened faces in the stands with horrid contempt. "Do something, do something!" he implores of Cobb, who is in no mood for orders.

Cobb Nelson, rather, is on edge, having been sent into a shower of nerves brought on by a band of midgets scattered into the audience by the elephant. Although their tiny, muscular bodies scamper past at a fair distance, Cobb shakes in dreadful fear.

Father, no!

Cobb's father, an angry, alcoholic dwarf, subjected his young son to afternoon beatings with a metal rod. The abuse lasted for years, until the harried son was old enough to drive, which he did—crushing the tiny, inebriated bones of his father all over the driveway.

Van Anders' thoughts are a blur. He hits Cobb with open hands and closed fists. "Do something, dammit!" he screams. "Grab the microphone, make an announcement, for crissakes. This is not my event. These stupid people need to know that! The last thing I need is some goddamn lawsuit on my hands!"

Cobb's black eyes are glistening nervously as he watches the circus dwarfs with grave concern.

"Do something, mother-fucker!" Van Anders is screaming now. Everyone is screaming. The trainer is nearly dead, a snapped artery from her carcass spraying a fountain of blood into the air. Delhi pauses for a moment to trumpet her victory with a wail, then heads directly at Van Anders and his assistant.

Gerald Van Anders, for the first time in his life, feels helplessly exposed. Fear rushes over him in a series of sharp, quick bolts that rip through his flesh and shred his innards like cooked pasta. The sounds of screams, cries and pulsing rap music . . . the smells of cotton candy, peanuts and fried snacks . . . they all dance in front of Van Anders as his sensory impulses cave under the sockets of his eyes. Nothing fits: his shoes feel tight, pinching his toes. His bowels fail. The arena seems smaller; it closes in on him. There isn't enough room. All the people are right on top of each other. The air is thin, poison. Wayne Van Anders is dizzy, sweaty, weak, and nauseated. Pressure, aches and burning sensations rupture his chest in waves. His knees buckle and he drops face-first over a fence barrier, clutching his heart with both hands.

He is unconscious before his front teeth shatter against hard metal and scatter like broken china over the concrete floor.

Unaware that his boss has collapsed behind him, Cobb pulls out his .38 and squeezes off three shots at the charging elephant before it rams him off his feet and into the stands. One of Cobb's bullets lands in the coarse flesh of the beast's neck, but the other two sail errantly into the crowd, one ricocheting off an empty seat, one slicing through the eye of a Phi Delta Theta fraternity president.

Josh slips past to Adam, embracing his battered lover in both arms like a baby. "I'm sorry, I'm so sorry," he cries.

Adam moans, wiping a piece of caked blood from his brow. "His blows aren't what hurt," he says.

Josh closes his eyes with regret, pulling Adam close. They rest heads on each other's shoulders.

Chinita flees the john upon hearing Gloria's voice booming over the P.A. system. Mad with betrayal, the corners of her mouth quiver with the dire taste for Wayne Van Anders' blood. Gloria Manson on the podium? Chinita has no doubt that Van Anders had orchestrated it. She blames Van Anders and Richmond. *This is my event,* she thinks, her chin tensely pinched. *My event. Gloria Manson on the podium? How dare they!* Her thoughts fall to Sonny Boy. *Where is he?* Paranoia stains her thought process with a myopic, red blindness. *Is my irresponsible Sonny Boy typically late, or is he part of this conspiracy?* If so, she would destroy him. *I brought him into this world; I can take him out.*

Gunshots ring out; Chinita ducks for cover. Chip Richmond, wide-eyed and pale, scuttles past her and out an exit door. *That pussy. Forget about him.*

Chinita enters the arena, looking for Van Anders. Her brain rocked by continuous flashes of bright blue fire, she pulls out her knife with the grand desire to rip him open from neck to bladder and watch him wallow in his own Christian Reformed fluids.

She finds him crumpled in a heap on the floor amongst discarded hot dog wrappers and crunched-up candy morsels. The scent of blood fills the air. The ground shakes and Chinita is surrounded by heavy tremors. An elephant, savagely riled, rushes by her in a cloud of dirt, dragging a sequin-uniformed woman behind it. The woman, beautifully sculpted with veined muscles and leathered skin, is caught in the long chord of a whip tangled in the animal's tree trunk leg. She twitches wildly, her bloody hips bouncing of the floor, winding her into a spool of knots as the rampaging animal attempts to shake her off.

Chinita, knife propped as the elephant rumbles past, cuts the girl loose with a deft swing of her wrist. The girl's limp body, caught in the force of inertia, rolls over with violent turbulence, a mass of disheveled muscles tossed from a speeding train.

Commotion surrounds Delhi, who runs into the first row of the south stands, knocking over the barrier, trapping seven people under its bent metal.

No one notices as Chinita grabs the gurgling young trainer, pulling her up into a sitting position, all the while hoping that it's not too late . . .

Oh, do pray!

Convulsing under the shower of her own blood, the taut woman is beautiful but without hope, like a butterfly with crushed wings. Chinita cuts the remaining chord from under the poor creature's neck and armpit. Careful not to cut herself on its serrated edge, she wraps it into a fifteen-foot coil and tucks it around her belt. Gripping the woman's wrist, Chinita feels a faint, slowing pulse. Blood rhythmically squirts in streaming spurts from her ruptured neck with each beat. Yet, she is alive, and that's all that matters to Chinita, who squeezes the blue flesh in the creature's neck, just above a piece of broken shoulder. Deftly working her fingers, she slides a tube under the punctured skin and into the savaged artery. Blood flows generously through hollow plastic, filling a pouch tucked into Chinita's belt in only minutes.

Ecstasy and passion grip Chinita as she imagines returning home to a hot bath. *Oh, if only I'd packed another pouch, but who would have guessed there'd be an opportunity like this?* Indeed, this was a sweet surprise, especially coming so soon after the horrible episode involving the former lieutenant governor and her pungent, rancid old fluids.

Chinita twists the pouch closed. Just as her thoughts refocus, she sees Van Anders stir out of the corner of her eye.

He's alive!

She wants to kill him.

Cobb, blinded by tears, is bent over the old man, mistaking him for dead. Palms up and open, the faithful assistant appeals to the sky.

With the quick, silent two-step of a cat, Chinita seizes Cobb's unsuspecting head and buries her knife deep into the top of his throat, yanking the blade all the way down to the top of his collarbone. He kicks and flops like a fish, an enormous pool of blood expanding in a perfect circle on the ground beneath him.

Chinita chuckles as Van Anders, wide-eyed and soaked with carnage, clutches at the air with rigid fingers that won't quite bend. "Ah," Chinita says, pressing her face close to his. "The rigor mortis setting in . . . and you're not even dead yet."

Delhi, fueled by the horrors of her past, rambles through the arena into the concourse, scattering terrified spectators in all directions. She runs from fear, fear of being confined in a cage so small that she can't turn around; fear of being whipped; fear of being poked in the eye with a metal rod . . . it is a blind fear, manifested in a white panic that smothers her healthy instincts like a wet, heavy blanket. There is no controlling her, no consolation. Chased by thousands of beatings and other tortures, she bursts through the hallway towards the first sign of natural light. Barreling through a tight exit, she sends buckled doors flying off their hinges into the twilight landscape. She storms out into the streets, splintering a street vendors' booth and crushing a family sedan as if it is cart full of bugs. Gloria Manson and her .22 give chase, as do the police, their peashooter bullets burying themselves in Delhi's rugged flesh with little consequence. She rambles through traffic, knocking over a mini-van. Vehicles swerve into each other, skidding across the pavement with screeching tires. Alert drivers whip through the median, turning around to avoid the wilding. Less savvy motorists continue onward into the collision course. Crossing Martin Luther King Drive into the ghetto, Delhi charges a group of young black men wearing bandanas and drinking alcohol on a warped porch. The porch cracks like a hollow eggshell under her stride, and the men are sent scrambling over a weed-infested, brown and yellow lawn. Delhi rolls over a shack house, crushing it like a paper bag. The bandana-clad young men return to the yard to uphold their ghetto manhood, letting loose a generous helping of profanity and semi-automatic artillery. Delhi remains on her feet, shaking for a full two minutes, absorbing the impact before finally buckling down in the storm of cop-killer bullets. Flopped on her side, puffing thunderously, the dying giant lets out one deep, human-sounding cry of agony spurred by the terrible pain of her life and death, and then falls silent.

Chinita grabs Van Anders' arm so hard that he fears it will tear out of the socket. With brute strength, she flings him over her shoulder, carries him off the floor, and tosses him into a feed cart. "Get your hands off me, you dirty ape," Van Anders growls. His lips, heavy with numbness, barely move when he speaks. His eyelids flutter in brief spasms.

Chinita stabs him several times in the shoulder, driving her blade just deep enough under his suit coat to draw blood. "Don't mouth off to me while you're in this cart. Do you hear me?" She gives him another stab just to make sure. Van Anders winces, letting out a squeaky cry that almost sounds like a silly laugh. His bloody suit no longer crisp, he is but a shriveled, sallow little man with sagging shoulders.

Following the path carved out by the Elephant-Run-Wild, Chinita wheels Van Anders through the broken-down double doors and over the sidewalk to the Capitol. Chord strapped to belt, her left hand grips the cart handle tightly. She kicks off her heels for better mobility and balance. The knife, tucked in her right palm, is poised for attack should trouble arise. She's soaked in blood, as is Van Anders; they leave behind them a series of red footprints and smooth crimson lines laid down by the cart's rubber wheels.

Lansing is frantic from the escaped elephant; no one notices as Chinita scales the handicapped ramp with her cart, up to the Capitol, the sun dropping behind her like a sinking orange.

Amongst the circus ashes of candy wrapper ruins and broken bodies, Josh holds Adam, who is crumpled in his lap. His ear pressed tight against Adam's back, Josh listens as a normal breathing pattern slowly returns, displacing scattered gasps and hiccups. Josh is red with frustration; frustration with his inability to shield his new lover from physical and emotional pain. *Van Anders: what a wicked bastard*, Josh thinks. More than anything, Josh is troubled by his own failure to piece together Jimmy Dillon's murder. *I should have known, dammit.* In days gone by, Josh could sniff out a murder from only the faintest of clues. But not this one, despite bold clues that were right in front of his nose.

And clues from my dreams.

Rather, Josh had grasped only a vague sense of connection until it was almost too late. There was too much confusion, uncertainty.

Damn that Norm Washington!

If Norm knew about the assassination conspiracy, then surely he knew about the *Rod & Rifle* cover-up. Hell, Norm might even have been in the middle of it, taking payoffs to keep quiet.

That double-crossing bastard fuck.

Josh sighs, running his fingers through Adam's hair.

Adam's weary eyes blink to adjust as he wipes blood from his dripping brow. Paramedics hustle in the opposite corner, devoting one hundred percent of their time and attention to the slightly bruised families pinned under the divider fence. "It's like we're not even here," Adam says.

"They aren't interested in us," Josh says, attempting to rise. "Come on, let's get you to the hospital."

Adam offers an exasperated protest. "No. I've got a few lacerations and bruises, that's all."

"You're bleeding all over the place. Christ, look at your pants! Can you even walk?"

"I can walk fine. Chuck's got a first aid kit in his office. Let's go get it, get cleaned up. I can walk fine."

"I really think you should let me take you to the hospital."

"No. Not now. I don't feel like sitting around in a waiting room for eight hours. I just want to get cleaned up and go home. If I need to, I'll go tomorrow."

"For sure?"

"Yes, I promise."

As they make their way towards the exit, Carmine Rossi erects his presence in the concourse, holding court with the press. "I denounce the carelessness of the authorities involved in this event," he pontificates, cameras clicking and video machines recording. "Safety is not an extravagance-it is a necessity!" His arms gyrate and eyes blaze with manufactured intensity as waxen-faced reporters anxiously record his every word with nervous scribbles looped over the pages of frayed notepads. "If I was elected to office—any office—you would see my philosophy written in big, bold letters over my title: SAFETY IS PARAMOUNT!"

A woman wearing tight black jeans and a straw hat steps to the front of the circle, thrusting her tape recorder at arms' length. "Will you ever run for attorney general again, Carmine?" she asks.

Rossi smiles like a cat who just ate the canary. "I'm glad you asked!" He raises a fist, thumb facing upward and gently dabbing the air as if to punctuate his enthusiasm. "We all know the very, very unfortunate situation surrounding our attorney general-elect. Quite simply, it is only matter of time before she passes." There is a pause, a shared moment acknowledging the expectation of communal grieving. "Given her current condition, I feel it important to enlighten you with a little known section of Michigan's constitution. Allow me to paraphrase, please. You see, should an elected officer pass away before having been sworn into office, the constitution states that the governor shall appoint a replacement to serve until the next election is held. It is my hope, at least for the family's sake, and the state's sake, that Leslie Thompson pass quickly, at least before the year is out. That way, I can ascend to office before Sine Die."

Rossi's bold commentary is met with a collective gasp. "Simply put, all of the attorney general's horses and all the attorney general's men could never put Leslie Thompson back together again."

"So you have an agreement with the governor?' asks a horse-toothed journalist tucked away in the back of the crowd.

"You could say we have an understanding, yes. An understanding to benefit the good of all."

Lamar Wilkens greets Chinita at the entrance of the Capitol, warns her not to go inside. Van Anders can feel the heat, but she is oblivious to it. Lamar is eating cheese and crackers.

"I know what I'm doing," Chinita says, glancing at the chord on her belt.

"So do I," says Lamar.

"Where are the sergeants?"

"Gone. It's hot inside like an oven. It's not safe, but help is on the way."

"Help? No sergeants?"

"No sergeants."

With the deliberate motion of a robot, Chinita buries her blade in Lenny's left breast, half amazed that he doesn't react in time to deflect her tired thrust. "Oh?" is all he offers, phrasing it like a question as he slumps to the ground, his cheese and crackers tumbling down three short concrete steps.

In one motion, Chinita snatches the plastic snack box and wheels Van Anders around the fallen janitor.

"Just where the hell do you think you're taking me?" Van Anders demands. His head is light, dizzy. Sweat gathers in tiny dots on his forehead, dripping down his face and soaking into the white cotton of his shirt collar.

Chinita doesn't answer, simply pushing Van Anders around the rotunda and into the elevator. Rising with the heat, they exit on the fourth floor, Chinita's raw feet pumping against marble with dogged determination as folds of boiling air ripple in front of them. "Where are you going?" Van Anders asks her in exasperation, expending great effort not to faint.

She offers no answer, moving in trance-like strides to a locked door leading to the top of the Capitol's cast iron dome. With a determined grip, Chinita is able to twist the copper handle from its rusted screws, swinging the door free on its hinges. A staircase, dusty and narrow, awaits them.

I've gone too far to turn back now, Chinita thinks, ripping Van Anders from the cart and tossing him over her shoulder like a sack of fertilizer. The corridor is like an oven, transparent air flickering as if all the oxygen is combusting into invisible flame. Rough, concrete steps rub off the raw bottoms of Chinita's soles as she hoists Van Anders skyward, the two of them twisting to the top of Michigan like two wounded dogs searching for a solitary place to die.

As they reach the top of the Capitol and embark on the dome's open-air observation tower, the landscape below reveals itself like an unfolding expanse. "This area is forbidden," Van Anders gasps as Chinita tosses him against the stone façade. He is short of breath, his body and clothes soaked with salty blood and perspiration.

But Chinita is cold as stone. She thrusts the half-eaten case of cheese and crackers into the old man's face. "Eat this," she says, her lips pulling into a tight frown.

"I'm lactose intolerant," Van Anders offers tiredly.

"Your intolerance no longer matters," Chinita snaps, gnashing her teeth. "Eat them." She slips the knife out from her belt and snaps off a two-inch section of chord. "I said *eat them.*"

Van Anders does his best to oblige. He munches in pain, closing jagged teeth over the stale pieces of snack. Bits of tiny, bloody cracker roll off his lips into his lap. "I think I suffered a heart attack this evening," he says, the words spitting with food off his tongue like water from a plugged spigot.

"People will hardly believe it," Chinita laughs, fixing the chord around his neck. "Rather, I'd wager on a stroke. Under stress, a person's true character reveals itself. Look at you. You're a wicked beast."

"What about you?" Van Anders asks.

"I am as cool as ice. Why, I'm not even breaking a sweat. Look at me."

Van Anders still has some spunk left. "Why, of course not," he sasses. "You people sweat through the mouth, spit dropping from your panting tongues like the drool of an animal."

Chinita bristles. "Nevermore," she whispers. Unraveling the other end of chord and looping it around a marble column, she ties it into a knot with three hard, two-armed tugs. "The people hate you," she growls. "The air, the land, the trees . . . they all hate you, too. You have no meaningful purpose."

Van Anders corrects her. "The Lord is my shepherd," he says.

Chinita chuckles at Van Anders' naïve ineptitude.

The Capitol building moans, as if unable to suppress its own drunken laughter. Even from the very top of the neoclassical structure, the cacophony kicking around the furnace bowels rings loud, emanating through layers of brick walls and ceilings, marble floors and Roman arches.

Chinita's eyes glass over, her pupils shrink to tiny dots. "Well, let's see if your religious convictions hold true," she says. "On some level, I'm sure you've always wanted to know if your devout efforts were, well, a waste of time more than anything else. I'm going to give you the opportunity to find out, cowboy."

"Cowboy? What is this, a 'B' western?"

"No. Rather, it's a good ole fashioned horror picture. Goodbye, Dr. Frankenstein."

With a languid thrust prettier than a Ginger Rogers pirouette, Chinita lifts the chord-collared Van Anders from his slumped position and tosses him over the balcony.

"From many . . . one," she screams from the ledge as he tumbles through the air, the slack on his serrated neck-chord barely long enough to last a small fraction of the 267 foot drop.

As Van Anders falls, the furnace emits a howl so horrific that it cuts through Chinita's short-lived joy with a savage finality: her hair floats upward in dancing strands, as if suspended in space and time. Silence drapes the Capitol— a silence that Chinita instinctively recognizes as the supernatural stillness preceding impending doom.

The silence breaks as the furnace gasps for air, sucking, wheezing, screaming. Finally it belches, releasing a gaseous fury of breath that bellows outward, exploding viciously just as the chord around Van Anders reaches its limit, jerking his head skyward in a wicked angle as bone and cartilage snap like brittle taffy.

Summoned to City Hall, Norm Washington conveys modesty, gratefulness and respect as he presents himself to Mayor Kuipers and Lieutenant Tesanovich. Tesanovich, chewing on a mint, stands in the middle of the mayor's austere office as if it is his own. The mayor, appearing distracted and anxious, twiddles a silver fountain pen between his fingers, repeatedly dropping it onto the blotter pad stretched across his desk. "Oh, excuse me, I'm sorry," he mumbles each time the pen drops.

So this is it, the big moment of truth, Norm thinks. He envisions himself as Grand Rapids' first black deputy police commissioner. For weeks, he had debated with himself just what to do. Tesanovich had made it very clear that the Pickens murder case was closed, with all questions dropped and forgotten—and it would stay closed, even if Leslie Thompson dies. This is where Norm is torn. Should he go over Tesanovich's head? The ballistic facts presented concrete, pervasive evidence of a conspiracy. If Kuipers was willing and able to hunt down corruption, Tesanovich would go down in flames with Carmine Rossi and Larry Sweeny, putting Norm in a position to reap great rewards. But what if the mayor isn't willing and able? Rather, what if he is part of the conspiracy? Norm would be screwed blue in the ass.

It isn't worth the risk. Besides, Rossi and Sweeny had been paying him off nicely, and their pockets would be a source of profitable shakedowns in the future. And then there was Tesanovich. Was he sincere in his promise of a promotion? It was difficult to tell. Norm studies him closely, but the wrinkles and liver spots on the lieutenant's forehead distract from the cocksure glimmer of his steel blue eyes, making it exceedingly difficult to pick up any sort of read.

Please be sincere, you old bastard!

A promotion is so close that Norm can practically taste it. An undeserved promotion? Maybe so. Even still, he'd take it in a snap. Hell, so what if he had been a shitty cop? He'd paid his dues to society, that was for sure. Besides, any cry for honesty at this point would be superstitious. And what did the truth matter? It certainly wouldn't bring back the dead. Rather, it would only serve to further soil the images of Grand Rapids and the Michigan Legislature.

Still, the discrepancy in bullets made for a startling case. Surely, someone, somewhere, must know the real story. What if that someone started talking?

Norm grinds his teeth. What if that someone was Josh Brisco? If only he hadn't opened his big mouth in front of him. If only Rossi and Sweeny had started paying him off sooner, Norm would have kept his mouth shut from the beginning.

It was their fault.

"I hope Chuck's office is in here next term," Adam says as he and Josh trudge across the Capitol lawn. "That would be huge." The sun is setting behind them, a streaking ball of orange fire sinking into a sleepy sea of blues and blacks.

Downtown Lansing is far from quiet as the sirens of police hurdle their way into the Martin Luther King neighborhood, where a full riot has broken out. The cause, initially, was proud celebration: the circus beast that bested authorities had met its match in the ghetto! But as the celebration spread, the cause diluted until there was no reason known or remembered, just drug-induced fighting, burning, looting and random shooting.

"Don't you like having your office in the Olds building?" Josh asks.

"Nah, it's just a bunch of sterile cubicles."

"Well, if all holds up, Chuck's office should end up in the Capitol. The speaker's office is *always* in the capitol, at least that's what Willie Mudville told me."

Adam laughs, wincing slightly as they descend down the eastern sidewalk. "It's just across the street," he quips before Josh can yet again question his ability to walk.

"You're probably dying for a cigarette," Josh says.

"Nope."

"Really?"

"You bet. I don't wanna be perceived as one of those angry-bitch chain smokers. Plus, I plan on making it past 30, you know."

A scream rips through the air, startling them both.

"Run! Run!" calls a shrill voice from behind. The boys whirl around. Josh's first instinct is to reach for his gun, which he doesn't have on his person. Adam simply stares in bewilderment as Lamar Wilkens comes running at them, stumbling down the capitol steps like a drunken clown.

"Goddamn!" he screams with womanly terror. "The place is going to blow!" The janitor raises a bloody arm before falling into the grass.

Amidst an eerie calm, the boys' attention is diverted upwards at the capitol dome, where the ghastly Chinita McCloud Clapton King-Hyde stands expressionless, her palms raised to the sky as Wayne Van Anders drops below her, his arms held out to each side like a free-falling Christ.

Hundreds of feet above the ground, a chord affixed to Van Anders' neck jerks him into mid-air oblivion, where he dangles and twitches for a brief second before his head severs and the capitol erupts with great power, exploding under the pressure of its mistreated heart. Pieces of stone, marble, glass and the like scatter in various directions as waves of detonation blast into the air, casting debris over a rising ocean of orange fire. Adam and Josh gasp, backing across the street as the inferno crawls up to the clouds, a million tongues of bright flame rising to voice the loudest extemporaneous speech in Michigan's history.

Epilogue: five years later

CAPITOL BEAT: *News for Capitol Insiders*
REPORT NO. 240 –FRIDAY, NOV. 21

CAPITOL REWIND:
WBCG's ALBERT DAWSON
INTERVIEWS FORMER DEMOCRATIC
CANDIDATE JOSH BRISCO

AD: Josh, your campaign for state representative five years ago is still remembered in Democratic circles as one of the most heartbreaking of all time.

JB: (laughing) Yeah, I guess that's true. But I think we made up for it with my mom's campaign two years later.

AD: Yes, Hazel Brisco's first run, considered to be the campaign that changed everything in this state.

JB: For the good, I hope.

AD: Most people would say so.

JB: Actually, all those changes were set into motion when I lost my campaign. The circumstances and tactics turned out way worse than I ever would have thought. The way I was portrayed by my opponent, you know, kind of showed people that Michigan wasn't a very nice place anymore—if it ever had been, that is.

AD: Unless you were white, rich and male.

JB: Unless you were white, rich, male, AND straight AND Christian—but that all came crashing down with the Capitol in December of that same year.

AD: You were there when it happened.

JB: Yes, I was there with Adam Van Anders, who had been pummeled by his old man at the Kalumba King Charity Circus. This all went down as that elephant went wild. Adam and I had just met a few days earlier.

AD: And you're still together?

JB: Yes, we're still together. Married, partnered . . . whatever you want to call it. We're very happy.

AD: Neither one of you were out of the closet when you met, were you?

JB: He was, I wasn't. I was very unhappy, channeling all my sexual energy into booze and drugs.

AD: Were you hooked?

JB: Not exactly, but I had manifestations of addiction with booze, especially after a couple nights of binging. It was like I could feel my blood sugar drop and my mind would spin into overdrive, running overboard from stress. The phantoms of odd dreams and horrific nightmares haunted me each and every night.

AD: What saved you from the phantoms?

JB: Adam. It all changed when I met Adam.

AD: What do the two of you do for a living now?

JB: Well, after Mom won her first election, winning back Slade's old seat in Grand Rapids, we went into the consulting business. Things were fun at the new Capitol, especially while Chuck Hriniak was speaker. When term limits forced him to retire, however, Adam and I realized it was time for us also to move on. It was sad to see some of those characters, the old-time legislators, pack it up and hit the road out of Lansing for good.

AD: Characters like Chip Richmond and Gloria Manson?

JB: (laughing) Well, I never cared much for Richmond. Sometimes people who have lots of family money get into politics for a nice ego trip. That was Richmond. Gloria, however, she was genuine. Maybe a bit unorthodox, but at least she was genuine.

AD: Is it true that she shot an animal rights activist the night that elephant went on a rampage through the streets of Lansing?

JB: I don't know anything about that. I did hear that she's running for Congress next time around. Is that true?

AD: So far, no one seems to know for sure, but redistricting presents an interesting scenario where she could be pitted against Attorney General Carmine Rossi, who wants a shot at going to Washington. There's also been speculation that State Senator Larry Sweeny may throw his hat in the ring.

Getting back to you and Adam, what happened after you went into consulting?

JB: Well, we opened our business in Grand Rapids, mostly because of Mom's campaign—and because it was our hometown.

AD: *Was* your hometown. You put extra emphasis on the *was.*

JB: Yes, because, well . . . after Mom won the election—

AD: —in rather triumphant fashion, I must say.

JB: Yes. Well, that opened quite a few doors for us, including an opportunity to do some policy and community liaison work for the mayor in Chicago. An opportunity that we jumped at.

AD: And why did you jump at it?

JB: Well, I love Adam. He loves me. Ours is a love that Grand Rapids, with its simple-minded church culture, isn't ready to embrace. Chicago is different. Adam and I are able to share domestic partner benefits. We are protected by the law. When we have kids, we don't have to worry about an angry mob of ill-informed Christian yahoos trying to take them away. We want to raise our kids in a warm, multicultural environment, not in a hostile land full of naïve social beliefs and people who need a religion to tell them what and how to think. That's not good for anybody.

AD: I can see I touched a bit of a nerve there.

JB: Perhaps, but truth be told, Grand Rapids has made great strides just in the past five years. It's really grown up, so-to-speak.

AD: Well, when Wayne Van Anders died, so did many of his policies and ideals. It all came crashing down with the old Capitol building. Grand Rapids, once a Republican stranglehold, has become much more politically competitive, as illustrated by your mother holding one of the Furniture City's two Democratic seats.

JB: I think she'll make a great speaker of the house. She'd be the first woman speaker, you know.

AD: Yes indeed.

JB: I have no doubt she'll be successful.

AD: Indeed, Michigan politics has come a long way in the past five years. As I mentioned earlier, the fall of Wayne Van Anders lifted a spell, as did the demise of the King-Hyde Dynasty. Kalumba King, the last surviving heir, hasn't been seen in Michigan since the settling of his circus lawsuits. It's as if all the old politics buried itself within the ruins of the old Capitol.

JB: Yeah, it all came crashing down like the old castle at the end of one of those classic Universal monster movies.

AD: That was arguably the lowest point in Michigan political history. What, in your opinion, are the lessons to be learned from that debacle?

JB: Well, it's easy for the bad to rise to the top in politics, because the average person doesn't make an effort to pay close attention. As a result, Michigan is disproportionately influenced by the rich, the single-issue fanatics, and the entitlement panhandlers. Until folks in the middle stand up and take notice of what's really going on, politics will remain easily corruptible—that's what happens when a majority of the people obtain most of their knowledge from gossip and 30-second soundbytes.

AD: Interesting point. Any last thoughts

before I let you go?

JB: How many days before Sine Die?

AD: Around 40. Why?

JB: I just don't want to blink and miss it—Slade Pickens would say that.

AD: Thank you for sharing your time, and your thoughts. Indeed, you have proven to be of the most compelling personalities in Michigan political history.

JB: Must be a pretty thin history, then.

SINE DIE

ISBN 1553955536-6

9 781553 955368